Pride Publishing books by K. Evan Coles and Brigham Vaughn

Single Books
Wake
Calm

The Speakeasy
With a Twist
Extra Dirty
Behind the Stick

By Brigham Vaughn

Anthologies
Right Here, Right Now: The Soldier Next Door

By K. Evan Coles

Boston Seasons
Third Time's the Charm

The Speakeasy

BEHIND THE STICK

K. EVAN COLES AND
BRIGHAM VAUGHN

Behind the Stick
ISBN # 978-1-913186-06-7
©Copyright K. Evan Coles and Brigham Vaughn 2019
Cover Art by Cherith Vaughan ©Copyright August 2019
Interior text design by Claire Siemaszkiewicz
Pride Publishing

BEHIND THE STICK

Dedication

For my husband, who is patient with my endless scribbling.

For my son, who makes me laugh every single day.

For the people in and around my life who inspire me and make me feel brave.

And for Brigham Vaughn, who puts up with my thousands of questions, listens to my rants and is ready to put pen to paper when our stars align.

— K. Evan Coles

This book is for my friends who were patient when I was too busy writing or editing to spend time with them. For the people who cheered me on and had faith in my writing long before I did. For my parents who are the best patrons of the arts a writer could ask for.

And mostly, for K. Evan Coles, who got me into reading and writing gay romance in the first place. I wouldn't be here without you! It's been a wonderful — and occasionally frustrating — journey. There's no one I would rather have done it with.

— Brigham Vaughn

K. and Brigham would also like to thank their patient beta readers, Shell Taylor, Rebecca Spence and Allison Hickman. We couldn't have made The Speakeasy what it is without you.

Chapter One

September 2015

Kyle McKee set down his gym bag and yoga mat and pulled up a seat at his gym's juice bar. The class he'd taken had warmed his skin and stretched his muscles and joints to their limits. He felt like the world's most relaxed slab of single New York man, which was good for Kyle's state of mind. He'd been stressed lately, about his love life in particular. Because damn if every guy he'd been out with in the last two months hadn't turned out to be a shitheel of epic proportions. So much so, Kyle had decided to stop dating entirely.

Eyes closed, Kyle forced away thoughts of dating catastrophes. He rolled his neck from side to side but peeled his lids open again when the chair on his left slid back and his friend Malcolm Elliot dropped into the seat. Malcolm gave Kyle a lazy grin. At six-three, he stood a few inches taller than Kyle, and he looked rosy-cheeked and loose limbed, his blue-gray eyes shining.

"I am a man-sized untwisted pretzel," Malcolm said. "I'm not sure what that means, so don't ask."

"You're yoga-stoned, dude." Kyle smiled at Malcolm's laugh.

"Is that a thing?"

"Totally a thing."

Malcolm narrowed his eyes at Kyle. "You're the one with the bloodshot eyes — what did you do after class?"

"Ugh, nothing but itch from allergies. Ragweed is my kryptonite." Kyle pinched the bridge of his nose between his fingers, then nodded at the menu on the wall behind the counter. "What are you drinking?"

"I'll do a Kale Storm with protein," Malcolm said.

Kyle held up a hand when Malcolm reached for his wallet. "I'll grab these — you paid last week." He smiled at the barista who'd stepped up to take their order. "A Kale Storm with a protein powder shot and a Peanut Butter Baby with chia, please. You headed home after this?" he asked Malcolm.

Malcolm shook his head. "I've got errands to run. My kitchen has mysteriously emptied itself of food since my brother and his girlfriend came back to town. What about you?"

"I'm opening tonight, so I'll just head to the bar. I have extra clothes at the office I can change into." Kyle co-owned a speakeasy called Under with his friend Jesse Murtagh and, while he loved his job, the commute uptown from Chelsea to Morningside Heights could be a pain in the ass. He welcomed the option to skip extra stops when he could.

Malcolm ran his gaze over Kyle's gray Henley and dark jeans. "You could always serve in what you're wearing, you know. You'd blow Jesse's mind."

Kyle covered a theatrical gasp with one hand. "I would never!" His preference for black or dark gray clothing while working was a source of gentle teasing among his friends. "Seriously, I don't feel like I'm working unless I've got my blacks on. I've done it for so long it's just part of how I do my job."

A thoughtful expression fell over Malcolm's face. "I think I get it," he said. "The black clothes are your uniform. I've got one too, though it's a lot less hipster bartender." He grinned at Kyle's snicker. "When I worked in advertising, I wore a suit or a good jacket with dress trousers. It took me a while after I started at Corp Equality to feel okay about not dressing formally." Malcolm waved at his hoodie and joggers. "I wouldn't go into the office dressed like this unless I was working on a weekend even now."

Kyle nodded. Malcolm worked as a social organizer at the headquarters of Corporate Equality Campaign, an organization dedicated to defending the rights of LGBTQ people in the workplace. While a non-profit, the CEC maintained a business-casual culture, and Malcolm always dressed with understated chic.

"Did you start wearing black at work on purpose?" Malcolm asked him. "Definitely seems like a smart idea given you mix drinks all night and could get splashed with booze."

"I only get splashed when Jesse is mixing drinks," Kyle replied, his tone dry. "But it was more an accidental habit. I got a job at a nightclub right after I moved to New York, and everyone on staff wore black," he explained. "Not like that's out of the ordinary—unless a club has a gimmick, staff usually wear black so they don't stand out. Can't have the clientele feeling like they're not as pretty as the guy schlepping booze behind the bar."

The barista appeared with their smoothies, and Malcolm quirked an eyebrow at Kyle.

"I get what you're saying, but that doesn't work, does it? I mean…it's not like anyone forgets you're a good-looking guy whether you're wearing black or not."

Kyle shrugged. "It's more about fading into the background than anything else. Staff in any bar or club are supposed to keep the customers happy without their noticing the hard work going on."

He sipped his smoothie and let out a satisfied sigh. He'd need something more substantial to eat before he started his shift at Under, but for now, his taste buds and stomach were happy with the combination of banana, peanut butter and chocolate almond milk.

Kyle ran a thumb over the moisture on his cup. He'd given Malcolm a pat answer, and though he could leave it at that, he didn't want to. Compared with other friends in their shared circle, Malcolm was reserved to the point of appearing introverted. He'd become very close with another of their mutual friends, Carter Hamilton, who also worked at the CEC, and he'd also formed a connection with Kyle in the last several months.

Initially, being single among so many coupled-up friends had brought Kyle and Malcolm together, but Kyle had found he liked hanging out with Malcolm. Malcolm had introduced him to Sunday afternoon yoga classes, and Kyle had ushered Malcolm into the world of Fallout, an event Malcolm sometimes rued, particularly after an all-nighter of playing hard. Malcolm had listened while Kyle grumbled about men, and Kyle had taught him to mix killer drinks and cook fish tacos, and now, as the weather turned autumnal, Malcolm shared the occasional personal detail. Kyle knew those overtures were a sign of Malcolm's trust, and he wanted Malcolm to know he trusted him in return.

"The real reason I stuck with the black clothes at work is because I was broke," he said. "I moved here with fifteen hundred dollars total and a bus ticket back to Vermont, and I kept the ticket and most of the money in a safe deposit box at a bank in Midtown. Jesse jokes that I had more interest in buying food than clothes back then but he's not wrong. Even if I'd spent my cash on clothes, I didn't have a place to store them." Kyle gave his friend an easy smile, but Malcolm's expression sobered.

"You stayed with friends, right?" he asked.

"Friends and acquaintances, yeah. Guys I dated if they were okay with it. I'd kick in with extra food and I'd cook to help out, and people were cool about it. Sometimes, I'd take over a room if someone left, and if that wasn't an option, I moved every couple of weeks to keep from wearing out my welcome."

Kyle ran a hand over his dark hair. "Couch surfing meant keeping my stuff in one duffel bag so I could pick up and move at a moment's notice. I bought three changes of blacks for work, and I'd do laundry every couple of days to make sure I had something clean. The pattern worked for what I needed at the time, but the habit stuck even after I got my own place and unpacked my duffel bag."

Malcolm smiled. "Did you burn the bag?"

"No way, babe. I kept it! What do you think I used the last time we went to Southampton and stayed with Carter and Riley?"

Malcolm furrowed his eyebrows as he considered Kyle's words, then his eyes went wide. "Your big green bag is the bag? Where the frock did you even buy that thing?"

"It belonged to my dad," Kyle replied. "He served in the army and the sea bag is standard issue." He wrinkled his nose. "Topic change, dude, because what is up with the 'frocks' and the 'darns' and the 'back that truck ups'? Why are you talking like a summer camp counselor all of a sudden?"

A flush crept up Malcolm's neck. "I might have let loose a bunch of f-bombs in front of Carter's kids." He held his hands up when Kyle's jaw dropped. "Before you give me crap, I didn't know Sadie and Dylan were within earshot. Carter's ex brought them by on her way out of town with her boyfriend, and the kids set up a fort in the closet in Car's office. They were supposed to be in the employee lounge, though, so Astrid and I didn't check when we ducked into the office to talk about an event that started going pear-shaped."

Too late, Kyle tried to smother his laugh and failed. It bubbled up out of him even as Malcolm's expression shifted from contrite to aggrieved.

"It's not funny, Kyle."

"Oh, yes, it is."

Malcolm scrubbed his forehead with one hand. "I swear a lot when I'm stressed."

"You know, I'd never have guessed that about you."

"That's because I don't usually do it out loud in front of people!" Malcolm exclaimed. "I was in the middle of a full-on rant when the kids started laughing, and of course, Carter walked in at that moment. Sadie told him I have an 'even bigger potty mouth than Jesse,'" he grumbled, and the air quotes he drew with his fingers made Kyle laugh harder.

"Oh, man," Kyle got out. "Car wasn't mad, right?"

"I don't think so. He told the kids they weren't allowed to use the grown-up words, but I could tell he was having trouble keeping a straight face. I didn't dare ask about it because I want him to forget it ever happened."

Kyle leaned over and ruffled Malcolm's light brown hair, still damp from the shower. Malcolm normally wore it cropped short, but he'd been growing it out, and his hair spiked up in soft peaks under the playful touch.

"No offense, but I'm pretty sure Carter won't forget if you keep up with the soft swearing. He knows you didn't mean it, and he'd have told you by now if he had a problem with it. Just be yourself and don't worry about it." Kyle sipped his smoothie. "Maybe keep the 'what the frock,' though. That shit is funny."

Malcolm's lips twitched up into a smile. "Okay."

* * * *

After making plans to meet Malcolm for dinner later in the week, Kyle walked to 23rd Street and caught a train uptown. He read a book on his phone during the ride and had finished several chapters by the time he reached his station near Columbia University.

Pleasure stole through Kyle as he walked through an ordinary pub called Lock & Key. He waved at the bartenders, then made his way through the blank doors, secret hallway and hidden staircase to the speakeasy located in the basement. He unlocked the door and hit the overhead lights.

Kyle loved everything about Under. The place was his baby, and every time he walked through its doors, he felt at home.

After locking the door behind him again, Kyle headed through the space. His watch read four-thirty and Under wouldn't open for another three hours, which gave him plenty of time to ready stations and straighten furniture, not to mention restock bottles and supplies that had run dry over Saturday night.

Kyle walked past the long bar that ran the length of the room. Open shelves of rare and high-end liquors lined the wall. The lights behind the shelves were still dark, and the place seemed preternaturally silent without the buzz of voices and the pulse of house music.

A melancholy feeling reared up in Kyle as he opened the office door. Six months ago, Jesse might have been seated at the desk, his handsome face drawn in concentration over financial statements or the marketing strategies he cooked up to keep Under's name on people's lips. Not that the bar needed much help—it thrived almost without Jesse or Kyle doing anything. And not that Jesse didn't still work hard at growing the business, either, despite the time he also spent helping run his family's growing media conglomerate. He just did it from home more often these days. Not surprising considering Jesse had a partner who made working from home extra fun.

Walking to the closet, Kyle left his bag and yoga mat on the floor. He pulled the hanger holding his black dress shirt and trousers from the rack and tried to shake off his blue thoughts.

During their years as friends, Jesse had been adamantly anti-relationship. A notorious playboy and flirt, he'd kept a wide number of sexual partners of both genders, many of whom, like Kyle, had become Jesse's friends. Jesse was Kyle's playmate in bed and his partner in crime as well as business, and they loved each other fiercely.

Things between them had changed after Jesse's partner, Cam, came on the scene however. While Jesse and Cam had an open relationship, Jesse's solo overtures toward Kyle had stopped. He and Cam still arranged threesomes with Kyle, and Kyle found those evenings immensely fun and very, very hot. They also reminded him of his third wheel status.

Kyle understood why his friendship with Jesse had changed, and he was truly happy Jesse had found love and a relationship that worked for him. Still, he missed his friend more than he'd ever have guessed.

Kyle dressed in his blacks and re-laced his brogues. He rolled up his shirtsleeves and cast a hard look at himself, making sure his dark hair was neat. Nothing he could do about his utter lack of tan though—working inside all summer had left him even paler than usual. Kyle grimaced at the bloodshot cast to his eyes. The dose of Claritin he'd taken that morning hardly registered now, and he'd need to stock up on eyedrops or people really would think he'd started smoking weed on his breaks.

By six-fifteen, Kyle deemed Under ready by his standards. His servers and barback were on site doing their own prep, so he shrugged on his jacket and headed out for a bite.

"Hey, Jim," he called out to Under's head of security, who stood at his usual place by the bar's entrance.

Jim Taylor stood the same height as Kyle and shared his fair skin and dark hair, but he was built like a tank.

A Boston native and unfailingly pleasant, Jim somehow managed to be polite even on the rare occasions he escorted people out of the bar. He gave Kyle a sunny smile.

"What's up, boss?"

"Just going to grab some dinner. I know I could order down from the pub, but I feel the need for some Burger Barn goodness. Can I bring something back for you?"

Jim's brown eyes lit up. "Dude, that would be fantastic. You sure you don't mind?"

"Not at all. Just text me what you want, and I'll bring it back with my order."

Once outside, Kyle crossed Broadway to a small, nondescript storefront on 111th Street that served some of the tastiest burgers he'd found on the West Side. Once inside, he called out a hello to Maya, who worked in front taking orders and payments while her husband, Nestor, managed the kitchen.

"Kyle!" Maya gave him a big smile "Where have you been? We thought maybe you'd gone vegetarian!"

"Oh, I'm not sure I'm capable of going meat free, Maya, at least not while I know you guys are over here making all this amazing food." He beamed at Maya's tinkling laughter.

Maya flapped a hand at him. "What kind of amazing food can we cook for you today?"

"I need two applewood smoked bacon cheeseburgers, one with fries and a side of the three-bean salad. Please and thank you."

Maya jotted the orders on a pad then raised an eyebrow at Kyle. "What about dessert? Nestor made carrot cake this morning."

Kyle's mouth watered. Nestor's desserts were outstanding. "Oh, man. I can't. I'll fall asleep on my feet if I eat even a small slice of that cake. But thank you anyway."

Maya nodded. "I'll wrap up a couple of slices for you to eat after you finish your shift."

"Oh-h-h...okay." Kyle snorted with laughter at the triumphant gleam in Maya's eyes.

A trio of young women walked through the door as Kyle made his way down a long hallway to the left of the counter to the men's room. He washed his hands and wet some paper towels, folding them into a compress for his itchy eyes. He had it pressed against his face when a loud banging nose caught his attention. Puzzled, Kyle lowered the damp wad. Another loud bang startled him, followed by yelling, and he tossed the toweling into the trash as the shriek of a smoke detector rent the air.

Kyle hauled open the door and made it most of the way back down the hall before he stopped dead in his tracks. Burger Barn was on fire. Thick black smoke poured out of the open kitchen door on the left side of the hallway, followed by flames that were already large enough to block the path to the dining area and front door. Kyle saw a girl with long dark hair pressed up against the wall a short distance from where he stood. She rose up onto her toes and coughed into her fist, craning her neck in a clear attempt to see past the fire.

"Hey!" Kyle shouted over the alarms. The girl whirled around and her eyes went wide. "Where'd everyone go?"

"Out the front, I think!" she called back, her voice shrill and fearful. "I saw my friends near the door when I came out of the bathroom, but I couldn't get through! I don't see them anymore!"

"What about Maya and the kitchen staff?" Kyle inhaled smoke and coughed.

"I don't know!" the girl cried. "I didn't see where they went!"

Kyle nodded. "We have to use the fire exit out back!"

He held out a hand, and the girl grabbed hold. Kyle turned around, squinting against the smog, and led her away from the kitchen door and toward the back of the building.

Fuck, this is bad.

Heat from the flames already filled the hallway, and Kyle could barely see its end through the thick air. He raised his arm and covered his nose and mouth as he coughed but couldn't get enough air. Abruptly, the hallway seemed to shrink inward. The space went even hotter and darker, and Kyle swore it narrowed, as if it was squeezing down around him.

"Get down low!" he choked out and bent at the waist in an attempt to avoid the smoke.

An eternity seemed to pass before Kyle's elbow met something solid. Instinct told him maybe twenty seconds had elapsed, but it was difficult to judge. He put out his hand, patting the door's surface with his palm and searching by touch for a way to open it. He found the push bar and shoved hard, but the door didn't budge. Kyle's heart sank.

Oh, no.

"It's jammed!" he shouted over his shoulder. "Help me figure out where!" Kyle stood straight and let go of the girl's hand, and together they felt blindly around the doorframe, both coughing. Kyle continued shoving at the push bar, trying to get past whatever kept the door from opening, to no avail.

"It's no use!" the girl cried out, and they hunkered down again, searching for clean air. Sweat and soot smudged her face. "What about the bathrooms?"

"No window in the men's!" Kyle yelled, but the effort of speaking made him choke. A coughing fit rolled through him and he doubled over, and the girl grabbed his hand and squeezed hard.

"Fire Department, call out!"

The shout from behind them cut through the noise of the alarms. Figures appeared around Kyle and the girl, huge and hulking in the gloom. Kyle heard voices but they were muffled, as if they came from behind glass. Hands landed on his shoulders. They moved Kyle away from the door then pushed him down and even closer to the floor with startling ease.

"Stay down! We're gonna get you out of here!"

Firefighters, thank God!

Kyle squinted up at the shadowy figures bending over him. His head spun and his heart thrummed so hard he could feel it beating in his throat. He leaned back against the wall, one arm still wrapped around the bottom half of his face, and clutched the girl's fingers again with his free hand.

Two firefighters turned toward the fire exit. Ten seconds passed. Then twenty, and thirty and a series of loud slamming noises sounded before the fire exit flew open. Light flooded into the hallway, and relief surged through Kyle, so intense he thought he'd throw up. He turned to the girl, but the firefighters were back. They helped Kyle and the girl stand, their gloved hands surprisingly gentle.

"Okay to walk?" A male voice came from the firefighter on Kyle's left, and he nodded, his throat too rough and dry to answer.

Kyle and the girl were ushered outside. Clean, wonderfully cold air washed over Kyle in a sweet rush. His knees wobbled and he drank it down in great gulps that made him cough even harder, but he couldn't get enough. His eyes stung, and the tears that leaked onto his cheeks cast a weird haze over the scene around him. The firefighters were leading him away from the building, and he saw moving bodies and flashing lights and the long red shapes of fire trucks.

"C'mon over here, Kyle, and we'll get you checked out."

Kyle blinked at the use of his name, uttered by a deep voice he couldn't place. He rubbed at his eyes, trying to clear his vision, and struggled to focus on the man beside him.

"Don't do that," the voice scolded gently. "You'll irritate your eyes even more."

Kyle glimpsed strong brows and blue eyes beneath the black fire helmet and golden dark skin. The firefighter sat Kyle down on a stretcher beside the back end of an ambulance and quickly strapped an oxygen mask over his nose and mouth. He held a hand to the back of Kyle's head and encouraged him to breathe while another set of hands placed a wet pad over his face. Kyle sucked at the air blowing through the mask and tried to stay quiet as the cool gauze soothed his eyes and face. He knew he'd failed when the firefighter rubbed his fingers over the nape of Kyle's neck.

"Take it easy. We'll keep the mask on as long as you need it."

Kyle forced himself to relax as much as he could, and soon his frantic gasps eased. He listened to voices around him reel off details about his condition and the girl's. Kyle heard the girl speaking, her voice muffled by what must have been her own mask, and relief pulsed through him.

Finally, the gauze pad lifted and Kyle blinked at the change in light. He peered at the firefighter kneeling in front of him, sooty smudges on his face but his eyes bright, and Kyle's muddled brain put the pieces together. He'd met this guy before. Inside Burger Barn, actually, and how weird was that considering what had just happened?

"I know you," Kyle rasped through his mask.

He paid for the words with another explosion of coughing. This time, the firefighter let go of Kyle's neck and pressed a drink pouch into his hand. Once the fit had passed, he helped Kyle move the mask enough to sip water through the straw and coached him to go slow and breathe.

Kyle lowered the pouch, and the firefighter slipped the mask back in place. He forced himself to speak again, though his voice was wrecked.

"It's Luka, right?"

"That's right." A gentle smile lit up Luka's face and made the corners of his eyes crinkle. "I wondered if you'd remember me."

Chapter Two

Luka Clarke jumped down from Engine 47, his brain still filled with images of a handsome face and soot-streaked fair skin. He'd seen that face for the first time at Burger Barn several weeks ago, and he'd been very interested then. Luka and the guy named Kyle had talked and flirted for a bit while they waited for their orders, but a call had interrupted their conversation before Luka could ask Kyle for his number. He'd been hoping to run into him since.

"Looks like we won't be going to Burger Barn any time in the near future," Tom Munson groused. He shut the door of the rig and the sound pushed Kyle from Luka's thoughts. "Fucking grease fires."

"What I don't get is why they had the damned fire door deadbolted shut." Luka shook his head. "I know they passed the last fire inspection and that's not like Maya and Nestor at all."

Munson shrugged, a contemplative look crossing his face. "There's a new kid working as a line cook. Maybe he did it?"

"Maybe." Luka shrugged off his turnout coat. "But they could be fucked for insurance because of that. Guess it depends on what the inspector finds."

"True," Munson said. "Damn. We really won't be getting burgers if they've been negligent."

"Not to mention Maya and Nestor losing their business."

"Sure, that too." Munson grinned. Luka had known him long enough to know that overall, he was a decent guy. He made the occasional asshole comment, but Luka trusted him with his life.

"How long have you been going to Burger Barn anyway?" Luka asked. "You were the one who introduced me to the place."

"Shit, a long time," Munson said. "You've been here how long? Seven? Eight years?"

"Almost nine."

"So, maybe eleven years? Eating at that place is a time-honored tradition at this house." Munson bumped fists with Luka. "Hell, Nestor had hair when I started going there."

Luka shook his head, laughing. "Damn, that's forever ago." The man was balder than a cue ball now.

Munson slapped him on the shoulder. "Come on. Let's get this gear taken care of and hit the showers. Shift is almost up and I'm ready to get the fuck out of here."

"You and me both, man."

Half an hour later, Luka stood under the streaming water, soaking up the heat and pressure that loosened his shoulders. It didn't matter how many emergency calls he went on, the tension was always an underlying factor. The reminder that any call, he could lose someone. Any call could be his last.

Every firefighter was aware of the possibility of death, of course. The first death of a civilian always hit hard. Like Luka, whose firefighter father had been killed in the line of duty, many of them had lost family or friends.

Luka didn't dwell on his fears during calls. He couldn't or he'd be too paralyzed to do his job. He'd seen that happen too, with new recruits and even veterans after a particularly bad call. But while Luka kept his worries under control, he prepared for the come-down after the adrenaline wore off and reality crept in.

Luka rotated his shoulders, pushing away the dreary thoughts. Despite his concerns about Maya and Nestor, today had been good. Other than some smoke inhalation, no one had been injured. And, hey, he'd met Kyle again.

With his eyes closed, Luka could feel the soft prickle of the dark hair at the nape of Kyle's neck under his palm and see his deep brown eyes, rimmed in red, against his pale skin. From the first time he'd seen Kyle at Burger Barn, he'd been struck by the confident way Kyle carried his broad-shouldered frame.

While Luka had hoped he'd run into Kyle at the restaurant again, or even visit the bar Kyle had mentioned working in—Luka had planned to do that during his time off—he'd never expected to see Kyle on an emergency call.

Today, he hadn't even recognized Kyle until he'd gotten him outside the smoke-filled building. The wave of relief that had followed had taken him by surprise, too. He and Kyle had hardly exchanged more than a few dozen sentences when they'd met last month, but Luka had liked the way Kyle's lips curled up on one side when he smiled and the lean strength of his forearms.

He'd also liked the way Kyle had joked with Maya. The fact that she'd treated Kyle like she treated Luka and the guys at the firehouse told him plenty about what kind of man Kyle seemed to be—polite, friendly and open-minded.

The brief interaction had been enough to intrigue Luka, and the eye contact and subtle flirtation in their conversation had tipped the scales in favor of Kyle being attracted to men. Luka had fully intended to follow up on that, but he'd been on duty and the call had come and, well, that was a firefighter's life, wasn't it?

That life hadn't led to many great relationships for Luka. Sure, people were all about the uniform, but once they realized it came along with a crazy work schedule, the risk of death and a hell of a lot of stress, their interest often cooled. Luka hoped Kyle wasn't the type who chased uniforms, then bolted once the reality set in. Because Luka now felt doubly determined to visit the bar where Kyle worked and ask him out. He heard the rattle of the shower curtain rings.

"Dude, are you in there jerking off or what? Shift is up. Let's go."

"You can come in and check," Luka called back.

Munson made a sound of disgust. "No thanks."

"Give me a sec and I'll meet you out front," Luka said. He rinsed the soap from his body, shut off the water, then dried and dressed quickly. Fatigue had settled in and he looked forward to crashing when he got home.

Exiting the firehouse, Luka found Munson talking with Lane Hawkins, one of the paramedics. Munson glanced up with a wide grin at Luka's approach.

"Looks like our little rescue today paid off. We just got an invitation to the club down the street."

"Which club?"

"Underneath, I think," Hawkins said, her tone doubtful. "No, Under. The bouncer gave me a card. He said the guy you rescued sent him over with them to say thank you. I guess the club is a hipster speakeasy thing. But who cares? Free drinks, my man."

"You in?" Munson asked.

"Hell, yes."

Hawkins snorted. "Yeah, I saw the way you were flirting with the guy you pulled out of the fire. Went above and beyond there, didn't you?"

"Hardly. We'd talked at Burger Barn one time a while back."

Munson rolled his eyes. He'd been standoffish with Luka when he'd first joined the firehouse. Based on the way Munson treated the other men of color at the station, Luka had figured his being mixed-race and looking like a black man wasn't the issue.

"Hawkins got the number of the chick she treated."

Hawkins gave him a sly look. "Hey, she offered. It would have been rude to refuse."

Luka laughed. "You don't get to give either of us shit, Munson. You met your wife, Elly, on a call."

"True, true," Munson replied. "And Hawkins' chick was bomb, I'll give her that."

"Hotter than any woman you could get, you bonehead, your wife aside." Although medium height and slim, Lane Hawkins had a huge personality, was fearless and every bit as tough as the firefighters in the house. Her short dark hair and numerous tattoos gave her an edgier appearance than most of the female paramedics, and her looks often drew attention. She and Luka hung out sometimes outside of work, as much because they had similar senses of humor as that they were both members of the LGBTQ community.

"I'm gonna tell Elly you said that," Munson teased.

Hawkins blanched. "Fuck, no. Don't do that. Your wife will kick my ass."

Luka held up a hand. "Okay, cut it out, you two. I thought you wanted to get out of here, Tom?"

"I do, I do."

"Then how about we agree to meet at Under tomorrow night and get our free drinks?"

"Works for me."

"You in, Lane?"

"Obviously, I'm in. I'm the one with the passphrase to get past the bouncer," she called as they turned away. "See you bozos tomorrow!"

Luka hefted his bag on his shoulder, then strode toward the nearby subway station with Munson on his heels.

The shit they all gave each other was one of the things Luka loved about working at the firehouse the most. The tight-knit sense of family and camaraderie was rare to find anywhere else.

It took nearly thirty minutes on the train for Luka to get from the station house in Morningside Heights to his two-bedroom apartment in Sugar Hill, located in the Hamilton Heights of Harlem.

Sugar Hill had gotten its name during the Harlem Renaissance when it had been a popular choice of neighborhood for wealthy African Americans like W. E. B. Du Bois, Thurgood Marshall and Duke Ellington.

Luka loved the architecture, rich cultural history and sense of community. The affordable rent—at least by Manhattan standards—didn't hurt either. The neighborhood had declined during the 1950s, but its demographics were always shifting and bringing change and renewed interest in the area. As far as Luka was concerned, it was the perfect place to live.

He felt bone-tired by the time he reached the second-floor apartment, and he unlocked the door with a relieved sigh. He dropped his bag on the bench to his left and was greeted by a soft chittering noise, then tiny feet padding toward him on the wood floors.

"Hey there, gorgeous," Luka crooned. He reached down and picked up the wriggling tube of excitement winding around his ankles, better known as Robbie the ferret. Robbie had a cream-colored undercoat with longer blackish-brown guard hairs, a white mask and ear tips, and inquisitive black eyes and nose.

"Sure, say hi to the ferret before me," Luka's human roommate teased.

Matías was equally gorgeous and at least as nosy as his pet ferret. His body a good deal more compact than Luka's big frame, Matías radiated personality. Right now, he was dressed in all black with his dark hair perfectly styled, and he wore a face full of makeup, which meant he was either on his way to or from work.

"I didn't forget you," Luka said.

"Like you ever could." The tilt of Matías' chin made Luka laugh.

"True enough," Luka said. While stunning to look at, Matías was also the best roommate Luka'd ever had. He gave Robbie one last pat before he set him down. "How was your day?"

Matías sighed. "Lots of high-maintenance customers wanting makeovers."

"So, a great day."

Matías' second sigh was even more dramatic. It made Luka smile. "Totally great." Matías worked at a MAC store in Harlem, not far from Morningside Heights. He complained a lot, but Luka knew Matías thrived in the store's glamorous atmosphere. If all the stories Matías' co-workers told were any indication, he was well loved, too.

"How was your shift?" Matías bent and scooped Robbie up and out of the way. The ferret was adorable but always underfoot and technically illegal, as ferrets were banned in New York City.

"Not bad. Rescued a hot guy from a restaurant fire. I told you about him maybe a month ago."

"The one you described as yummy?"

Luka opened his mouth to retort that he'd never called anyone that, then remembered he had described Kyle as such to Matías. In his defense, he'd had a couple of beers after working a twenty-four-hour shift. He was lucky he hadn't said anything worse. "Yes."

"Do tell."

Luka gave Matías a quick rundown of the fire that day. "He invited the whole squad to the place where he bartends. I am definitely doing that tomorrow night."

"Any plans tonight?"

Luka stretched. "Fuck, no. I'm going to bed. What about you?"

"Going out with some friends later. I'm about to hop in the shower then decide if I want to put my face back on." Living with Matías meant Luka knew way more about makeup than he'd ever expected to, despite having two sisters. Most days, Matías wore more makeup than both combined.

"Cool. I'll grab some food before I crash."

"If you want, there's *pernil* and *arroz con gandules* in the refrigerator," Matías said.

"If I want? Dude, yes. Your mother makes the best food. Thank her for me." Luka's mouth watered at the thought of slow-cooked pork shoulder and rice and beans.

"I will."

Luka leaned against the kitchen counter and waited for the food to reheat. He was a decent cook himself, and Matías wasn't bad either, but few things beat Mrs. Acosta's Puerto Rican food.

She didn't seem to know what to make of her son stepping outside of gender norms or him calling himself Matías rather than his given name of Ernesto, but she loved him anyway. Once she'd decided Luka was all right, she'd doted on him too. The microwave beeped and Luka pulled the plate out, wincing as it scorched his fingers.

"Just so you know, the brownies on the counter are special," Matías called out from across the apartment.

"Thanks for the warning!" Luka had smoked weed a few times while growing up, but the FDNY's zero-tolerance policy against drugs made indulging too risky, even during his time off. Matías didn't make pot brownies all that often, but Luka knew never to eat his baked goods without asking first.

A jaw-splitting yawn crept up on Luka, and he mentally willed his food to cool faster. Once it had, Luka wolfed it down, making appreciative noises that drew Robbie's attention. The inquisitive ferret stretched himself to full length, his sharp-clawed front paws resting against Luka's thigh.

"Oh, no," Luka murmured. "I don't care how pathetic you look, you little weasel. You are not getting even one bite. You don't need any encouragement to be naughty."

Robbie made a soft chirping sound.

"Nope, not gonna work on me." Luka scraped up the last tasty bites and put them in his own mouth. Too good to share. He washed the few dishes, chugged a glass of water and scooped up the ferret. "You can take a nap with me if you want though."

He draped Robbie over his arm, carried him through the apartment and paused in Matías' bedroom doorway. Matías sat at a vanity table in boxers, applying foundation. Like Matías' mom, Luka hadn't quite known what to do with Matías' love of makeup when they'd first met. But Luka had liked his roommate from the start and grown to appreciate him over the years. Now, as far as Luka was concerned, Matías' makeup was as much a part of him as his Puerto Rican background and just as essential to his persona.

"Have fun tonight."

"Oh, I always do." Matías glanced at him in the mirror. "Stealing my ferret, huh?"

Luka shrugged. "It's not my fault Robbie likes me better. He has good taste."

"You're an asshole."

"Yeah, but you knew that." They grinned at each other. "Night, Ernie."

Matías flipped him off. Luka only called him that to annoy him. It had backfired, though, because Luka's sister Regina sometimes referred to Luka and his roommate as Bert and Ernie.

Once in his bedroom, Luka tossed Robbie on the bed and watched him scamper, leaping and cavorting as though he had springs on his legs. Luka went to the bathroom to brush his teeth.

Luka also washed his face and took a moment to moisturize his skin. Matías had been horrified to discover Luka's skincare routine had consisted of slapping some generic drugstore-brand moisturizer onto his face when he remembered and had promptly set out to fix that. Sweat, soot and the dry, hot air of a fire didn't do anyone's skin any favors, and Luka was man enough to admit Matías' advice had made a world of difference.

Luka dabbed toner over his face and spread on the rich moisturizer, then finally ready to crash, padded back down the hall to his bedroom. He turned out the light but left the door open a crack. Robbie might sleep with him for a bit, but he'd need his litter box in the living room eventually. Luka knew from experience that being woken up by a ferret hell bent on escaping a room sucked.

Luka wrapped his hair in a durag to keep it from drying out, stripped down to his boxers and crawled into bed. Robbie curled into a ball near Luka's chest and made a few soft sounds as he got comfortable. Luka petted him for a few minutes before his hand slowed, his eyelids grew heavy and he slipped into sleep.

Chapter Three

"Hey, Kyle? I checked the egress routes for both bars and everything looks good — clear paths, no obstacles." Jim set the checklist Kyle had given him on the bar. "I tested the emergency lighting and checked the fire doors too, which you know since they buzz when they're opened."

Kyle chuckled, his voice still raspy. "Yeah, we heard them." He scanned the list, then looked back to Jim. "Does Matt think I'm going totally overboard?" Matt, the general manager at the pub upstairs, had been in his car en route to work when Kyle has called him, dead set on organizing an in-house fire inspection for both Under and Lock & Key.

"Nah," Jim said. "He gets it. Everyone does after yesterday."

Jim's lopsided smile pricked at Kyle's conscience. He'd asked Jim to complete some unusual tasks in the last twenty-four hours — including tracking down another bartender to take Kyle's place and hunting down the paramedics who'd transported him to the hospital following the fire—and the stress showed.

Kyle reached out and patted his shoulder. "Thanks, man. I know things got weird last night, and I appreciate you helping me out."

The worry on Jim's face smoothed out. "No problem, boss. I'm happy to do it." He paused and checked his phone then glanced back up. "How do you feel? Mostly okay?"

"Sure—I had an unplanned night off and slept at least ten hours. Outside of my voice being wrecked, I feel great."

Kyle smiled at Jim's laugh. Yes, his voice was a mess, and he had a plastic inhaler in his pocket and alarms on his phone to remind him to use it. However, he felt one thousand percent better than he had after being pulled out of Burger Barn last night. He'd thanked the firefighters as the paramedics loaded him into the ambulance and made a point of shaking Luka's hand. He'd been out of it, though, partly from the smoke inhalation but more because he'd experienced the mother of all adrenaline crashes.

Kyle had dozed on the ride to Mount Sinai Hospital and slept through most of his time under observation in the Emergency Department. He'd napped in Carter and Riley's car after they'd picked him up too and fought to keep his eyes open while they steered him into the guest room of their Murray Hill townhouse. But Kyle had managed a croaky laugh after Carter joked about seeing him in his underwear, and that had made all three of them feel better.

Kyle watched with interest as Jim crossed the room to open Under's door, and he blinked when Carter and Riley stepped inside with Malcolm right behind them.

"Hey!" Kyle exclaimed. "What are you guys doing here?"

"We're here celebrating you not being dead, duh," Riley replied. He beamed at Kyle, but tension lurked in his handsome face, as though he was forcing himself to act carefree.

A burst of affection stopped Kyle from rolling his eyes. Carter and Riley had looked shell-shocked over breakfast that morning, and he knew they worried about his decision to work tonight.

"I'm fine, as you can see," he said. "Surprised to see you on a Monday night, of course, but happy you made the trip."

"We left work early and called Jim on our way here, so he'd let us in," Carter said. He clapped Jim on the shoulder then walked to the bar with a quick kiss for Kyle. "You sound super sexy with that frog in your throat, by the way."

Kyle wrinkled his nose. "I sound like I ate cigarettes wrapped in sandpaper."

"That's a disgusting image." Carter laughed. "Is it okay we came by? I know you invited the crew from the firehouse tonight…"

"Of course. There's always room for you guys." Kyle gestured at the room around them. "I decided to limit attendance tonight to fifteen max, and Jim sent out a text blast to the guest list with the heads-up. They'll need to be here early if they want in."

Malcolm hummed and settled into a seat. "Could you maybe add another six or eight to that number?"

Kyle nodded at once. "Totally cool, just give Jim the new names. Your friends have the passphrase, right?"

"Yep, but they're not just my friends," Malcolm replied. "They're yours, too. Will and David are coming, and Jarrod and Gale, Astrid, Audrey,

Max...you get the picture. Jesse and Cam, of course, though I suppose they don't need to be on the guest list at all."

Kyle stopped in his tracks. "Say what now?" he asked. He saw most of the people Malcolm had named at Under's monthly private party, not on a random day in the middle of the month. Will and David lived out on Long Island, for heaven's sake, where Will taught legal history at a university and David worked as a state senator.

Riley scoffed. "Everyone else is glad you didn't die too, Kyle. And since you're here tonight like the fucking workaholic we all know you are, we came to you to celebrate."

A trembly feeling made its way through Kyle's insides. "You didn't have to do that," he said, his voice gone quiet. "I'm okay, guys, really."

"Yeah, well, maybe we're not." Carter shrugged. "So, indulge us and feed us booze, and we'll try to behave around your new firefighter friends. What time are they getting here?"

"Um. I don't know," Kyle said, his face burning. He focused on the ingredients he'd already laid out on the counter. "Jim told the paramedics on the ambulance to spread the word to anyone who could make it. I guess we'll see."

Kyle muddled strawberries in a shaker. He hated that his friends were making a big deal over him, but he loved them for caring, too. He especially loved that none of them were calling him out for blushing and acting extra awkward.

"I looked up a couple of recipes for tonight," he said and filled the shaker with ice. Masen Jones, Under's second in command behind the bar, walked over to observe.

"Of course, you did," Riley replied. "I trust they're somehow fire-related but without literal flames?"

"You are correct." Kyle added peppered vodka, lemonade, aloe vera juice and simple syrup to the shaker, the act of mixing smoothing his ruffled feathers. He sealed the container and rattled the contents until it grew chill in his hand, then strained the mix into rocks glasses.

"This is called a Hot Firefighter. I like the contrast of spicy and sweet, and I figure they're fun even for someone who's not into craft cocktails."

"You're just looking forward to orders for 'Hot Firefighters,'" Malcolm teased, and the others broke up laughing.

Kyle garnished the glasses with lemon wedges and basil leaves and set the first down in front of Carter. Carter raised his drink and sipped, and the delight that registered on his face was instant.

"Yeah?" Kyle smiled at the way Carter's big, hazel eyes shone.

"Mmm. Oh, yeah, babe." Carter licked his lips. "My mouth is on fire in the best way."

Malcolm peered at his own glass. "Should I be scared?"

"Nope," Kyle said. "The aloe vera juice in the mix cancels out the pepper sting."

Malcolm raised his brows. "Really?"

"No, doofus, I made that up." Kyle reached over the bar and ruffled Malcolm's hair.

At six on the dot, Jim flipped the switch on Under's passphrase phone, marking the speakeasy open for business. The phone rang immediately, but before Jim could answer, the door swung open and Jesse and Cam stuck their heads around the frame.

"Hey, party people." Jesse's blue eyes gleamed with mischief. "There's a line of hipster booze nerds in the hallway upstairs, so I hope everyone's ready for some brisk business."

Kyle laughed over the others' catcalls. "Get your big head out of the doorway, Jes, and let the paying customers by."

Jesse and Cam had Will and David with them, and the rest of the group Carter and Malcolm had invited turned up moments later. While Masen served the patrons from the guest list, Kyle attended to his friends. He also found himself retelling the story of the fire and fending off well-meaning questions about his health.

Such a bunch of busybodies, Kyle thought with a fond smile. At this rate, his voice would be gone before midnight. He actually felt relieved when his phone reminded him to use his inhaler.

Kyle let Masen know he'd be stepping away, then slipped out from behind the bar and into the office where he went to the bathroom and washed his hands. He wasn't surprised to hear the office door snick open and closed. He'd expected Jesse would seek him out at some point, even if only to bitch him out for working. Still, Kyle was glad he'd shut the bathroom door — he didn't want anyone watching him huff and puff like a wheezy dragon.

Quickly, he used the inhaler, taking care to hold the medicine in his lungs for the prescribed ten seconds before he exhaled. A shaky sensation ran through Kyle as he rinsed his mouth, and he pressed his hands together, his eyes on his reflection to ensure he looked human before he faced his friend.

Kyle found Jesse leaning against the desk they shared, arms crossed over his chest. He surprised Kyle by saying nothing and going instead to the mini-fridge they kept near the bar cart. He retrieved a mineral water, then came back and handed it to Kyle, his face troubled above his fine brown tweed suit.

"Are you all right?" Jesse asked, his voice somber.

Kyle cracked open the water. "Yes. I feel fine."

"And why is Masen here early?"

"In case I need to take more breaks than usual. I haven't. I had a follow-up with primary care today and got the green light to do almost everything I'd normally do."

Jesse nodded. "Almost?"

"No heavy aerobic activity for the rest of the week," Kyle replied. "I certainly won't be smoking cigarettes anytime soon. Lucky for me that I quit a couple of years ago."

"Your voice is shredded."

"It should pass."

"And the inhaler?" Jesse asked.

"I have to use it a couple of times a day for the rest of the week as a precaution," Kyle said. "My airways are irritated, and that may be as much from allergies as the smoke. The stuff makes me jittery, but it wears off after an hour or so." He sipped from the water bottle while Jesse focused on his shoes, and the seconds ticked by.

"Why didn't you call me last night?" Jesse finally asked. "I mean…I know you're an independent guy, but text messages from a hospital are beyond the pale. Not that I knew you were in the hospital because all your message said was 'Got a sec?'"

Kyle moved to the leather sofa and sat down. "My throat was jacked up a lot worse last night, Jes, and I messaged instead of talking. You wrote back that Cam's family were at your place for dinner, so I tried Carter and Riley next."

"Kyle, come on." Hurt marked Jesse's face. "Yeah, we had people over, but I would have left and come to get you if I'd known what happened."

Kyle took a turn staring at his shoes. "I know," he said.

But did he really? Hadn't he tried Carter and Riley because he'd felt unsure what Jesse would say if he knew the truth?

Kyle licked his lips. No way could he say that without denting Jesse's feelings in a big way. Not to mention the thought was completely unfair. Jesse would have come if Kyle had told him the truth, and Kyle knew that. He drew in a deep breath and fixed Jesse with a steady stare.

"Honestly, I wasn't thinking straight last night. By the time the doctor released me, I was so wiped out I had trouble texting at all. I just wanted out of there. The second Carter said he and Ri were home without the kids, I asked him to come get me."

Jesse's expression shifted from hurt to contrite. "Fuck," he muttered. He straightened up, then crossed the room and sat beside Kyle. "I'm not trying to give you a hard time. I'm...so fucking relieved you're okay. I'm sorry."

"Jes—"

Jesse shook his head and raised a hand to Kyle's cheek. "I wasn't there when you needed my help. If I could do it over again, I would call you right back and ask what you needed." He searched Kyle's face, a range of emotions flickering in his eyes—worry and affection chief among them—and Kyle's throat ached for a whole different reason.

"Jesus, Kyle." Jesse knit his eyebrows. "You could have died."

"I know."

"Are you really okay? Carter sounded pretty freaked when he called last night."

"I am," Kyle replied. "He and Riley took good care of me. They didn't even make me shower before they tucked me into bed. Which is too bad because I'm sure I ruined the sheets in their guest room. Everything about me smelled like Satan's sulfuric butthole by the time I passed out."

Jesse swept him into a sudden hug, and Kyle's laugh turned into a groan under his friend's crushing grip. "Dude. I really am gonna die if you keep doing that."

"Oh, shut up," Jesse huffed. His voice sounded strained, but Kyle heard a thread of laughter, too. Kyle couldn't say anything himself, though, because then Jesse's mouth was on his.

Kyle closed his eyes. Jesse kissed him deep, just the way Kyle liked, and Kyle pulled Jesse in tighter. Jesse pushed him back against the couch and heat coiled in Kyle's groin.

"Mmm, baby," Jesse whispered against Kyle's lips. He teased his fingers under the collar of Kyle's black shirt and cupped the side of his neck.

Kyle nipped at Jesse's upper lip and relished the rasp of stubble against his skin, but he forced himself to break away when a low noise rolled through Jesse's chest.

"Your timing is shit," Kyle groused. He rubbed Jesse's back to lessen the sting of his words. "There's a room full of people out there and more on the way. I can't do this right now."

Jesse pressed his forehead to Kyle's "I know. Not sorry, though." He sat back and stroked Kyle's shoulders, his touch possessive and rough. The intensity in Jesse's gaze spoke volumes to Kyle, as did the tight set of his jaw. He looked stressed, so much so it read like anger, and Kyle's gut tightened in understanding. Jesse was scared.

Before Kyle could wrap his head around that extraordinary fact, a knock sounded at the door. He raised his hands so he could grasp Jesse's forearms. "We'll talk more later, okay?"

"We'll talk tonight," Jesse said, his tone firm. He visibly reined himself in before he let Kyle go. "I've got my car and I'll take you home after work. Cam's going to hitch a ride with Carter and Ri. He knows not to wait up."

"Okay." Kyle frowned. He had no idea what to make of Jesse's mercurial mood, but now was not the time for figuring his friend out.

He stood and crossed the room to open the office door and found Masen leaning against the frame. Masen's bright green eyes flashed with good humor.

"Sorry to bother, boss," he said. "Jim says the paramedic he talked with yesterday just called. She and some of the squad from the firehouse are on their way down. You okay to come back out?"

Energy fluttered in Kyle's gut. His nerves were shot now that the time to thank his rescuers had arrived. Comping their drinks in exchange for saving his life seemed ridiculous a day later. *Ugh.*

"Absolutely," he said to Masen. Kyle glanced back at Jesse, who gave him a small smile. "C'mon, babe. We've got guests to entertain."

Masen headed back into the speakeasy while Kyle and Jesse followed close behind. Kyle saw people filing in past Jim at Under's door, but before he could get to his station, a beautiful young woman with long dark hair bounced into his line of vision and made a beeline toward him. Kyle's jaw dropped.

"Oh, my God, it's you!" he blurted, and the girl he'd been trapped with during the fire at Burger Barn threw her arms around his neck.

Kyle wrapped her up in a gentle hug, not at all surprised when she trembled against him. Seeing her—safe and seemingly healthy—sent Kyle's emotions into overdrive, too. His eyes stung and his breath got caught somewhere between a laugh and sob as they held each other close.

"Are you okay?" Kyle and the girl asked each other at almost the same time, and they broke apart laughing, still connected in a loose embrace.

"Holy crap, I'm a mess," she said, her voice raspy in the way Kyle's had been since the fire. She smiled wide and her big dark eyes shimmered with unshed tears. "I'm so glad to see you again!"

Kyle chuckled. "Me too. The nurse who took care of me said you were okay when I asked. I meant to come over and check on you once we were at the hospital, but I was zonked."

"Dude, same!" the girl replied. "My friends practically poured me into their car yesterday. Oh! My name is Charita, by the way. Charita Singh."

"Kyle McKee," he said with a laugh.

Charita nodded approvingly. "Now I can call you something other than 'the cute guy in black!' Well, you're still in black, hah, but you look a lot better than the last time I saw you."

"He looks less like death, that's for sure," someone drawled in a dry tone.

Kyle glanced to his right and met the gaze of a slim woman with short dark hair styled in a glossy pompadour. She was watching him and Charita, along with several other people, including Luka, who appeared both curious and amused. The woman who'd spoken, however, stared at Kyle with clear challenge in her expression.

"Shit, the two of you together are like a live-action romcom," she said and raised an eyebrow when Kyle shook his head.

Charita turned a frown on her. "Lane, don't be weird."

"That's…yeah, that's not what's happening here," Kyle said. He let Charita go. Great. This Lane person was probably a friend of Charita's, and now she and Luka and everyone they'd come with would think Kyle had been looking for a hook-up.

Ugh.

Quickly, Kyle cleared his throat and stepped forward with his hand outstretched. "I'm Kyle," he said and offered a tight smile to Charita's friend. "This is my place, and I'm happy you all could make it tonight so I could thank you in person."

"Ah, don't mind Hawkins," Luka said, his eyes kind. "She's just mad because your hair looks cooler than hers." He poked the woman—Lane? Hawkins?—with his finger.

Laughter rolled through the squad, and Kyle smiled, the knot in his belly loosening when the woman grasped his hand in hers. She had the grace to look abashed.

"Sorry, man. First day with the new sense of humor." She gave Kyle an impish wink. "Your hair looks fly though."

"I'll give you my guy's number if you want it," Kyle promised and chuckled as she bumped his fist.

"Okay, you know Charita, and I'm Lane Hawkins," she said. "I'm a paramedic and I ride with Engine 47. This is my partner, Michaela—you might remember her from the ride because she sat in back with you while I drove."

Kyle exchanged a grin with Michaela, a cute redhead who did look familiar now that he thought about it.

"Back there are Felipe and Marco," Lane continued. "They're from another house, but they took Charita in their rig. That's Munson next to Mike—we call him Mikey Bag of Donuts, by the way—and Ricky, Stephan and Luis. And Luka, of course, who says you guys met a while back."

Kyle shared a smile with Luka then nodded at the faces around him. He found them all friendly, Luka in particular. Goddamn, he was tall and broad and that smile of his was about a hundred times more attractive than Kyle had even remembered.

Jesse made a low noise in his throat then, and Kyle's cheeks flooded with heat. His friend had been standing there watching everything the entire time, and Kyle had been so flustered he'd fucking forgotten all about him.

"This is my business partner, Jesse Murtagh," Kyle said. He turned to include Jesse in the circle. "He's the brains behind this operation."

Jesse snorted. "An operation that wouldn't exist without you, babe." He cast a glance at the squad from the firehouse who were looking on with amusement. "Kyle had the idea to open a bar in the first place, and he's one of the best bartenders in the city."

"Way to put the pressure on," Kyle grumbled.

Jesse just smiled. He knew it was all for show—Jesse and Kyle filled specific roles within Under's confines, and Jesse enjoyed playing consummate charmer while Kyle worked his own magic with his bottles of spirits.

Kyle waved a hand at the bar. "Please, folks, step up and I'll get behind the stick," he called. He made a point of reaching out to Charita again as people started moving.

"I'm glad you're okay," he said. "Truly." Charita nodded, her expression somber this time.

"Me too. I don't know what I would have done if you hadn't been there, Kyle."

"I feel the same. We're damned lucky those guys were looking out for us." Kyle squeezed her hand and led her toward the bar where Jesse was introducing everyone to, well, everyone.

Over the next hour, Kyle got his groove on. He filled orders for his friends and the firehouse squad and made a point of stopping to chat whenever he had the opportunity. He learned that Charita and Hawkins had come together, and while neither could say they were dating, it seemed clear from their mutual flirting that they would be soon. Kyle also learned that Munson, Marco and Mike were big into fishing while Luis and Ricky played in a range of recreational sports leagues. They, along with Stephan, were the party guys of the group, and all of them were familiar with Ember, the nightclub where Cam worked part-time as a DJ.

Then there was Luka, a lieutenant in Engine Company 47, 'The Pride of Morningside.' Luka was friendly with everyone in the firehouse squad but close with both Hawkins and Munson. Kyle also discovered Luka shared an apartment in Morningside Heights with a couple of guys named Matías and Robbie. Younger than some of his comrades and congenial, Luka hit it off with Malcolm and Cam almost immediately. Kyle found him more serious and thoughtful than the others and suspected — hoped — Luka seemed more than a little interested in Kyle, too.

"This place is beautiful," Luka said to Kyle. "When you mentioned a speakeasy, I imagined something out of a noir movie, but Under is sleek."

"Exactly what we aimed for," Kyle replied. "We want it to feel welcoming, too. Warm and inviting."

"You've got that. I'm comfortable, even though your furniture is a hundred times nicer than mine." Luka appeared amused. "What did you mean by 'get behind the stick'? Is that code?"

Kyle set a highball glass down in front of Luka and admired the way his light brown shirt set off the gold in his skin and made his blue eyes pop. "Mmm, no. Behind the stick is bartender nerd slang. It just means going behind the bar to do my work."

"Well, hey. I learned new stuff today." Luka picked up the fresh drink. "What's in these margaritas, by the way? They are delicious."

"It's called a Smoke & Ember. Don Julio Blanco Tequila, lime juice, smoked agave nectar and fresh raspberries, with some lava-smoked salt around the rim. I'm glad you like them," Kyle added.

"I do." Luka sipped. "Pretty cool you looked up a bunch of recipes for us, too." He gestured around the room. "A lot of your friends are here and there's us firehouse guys, but the rest are paying customers, right?"

Kyle nodded. "Yes. People sign up for our nightly guest list through our website. There are a certain number of slots — usually thirty — and people on the list get a password each day to let them in the door. Friends of Jesse's and mine don't need to be on the list though. They can just call ahead to say 'Hey, I'm coming tonight' and they're greenlit to come in. Our friends also tip the staff, even though their drinks are on the house."

"Got it. Even when you guys have private parties like tonight?"

"Yes, though tonight was kind of spur of the moment." Kyle cleared his throat, which had grown more ragged as the night progressed. "We cut the regular guest list in half and turned away the rest so there'd be room for your squad. If we're having a true private party, the bar is closed for the night except to friends of Jesse's and mine. We do that once a month." He paused again and coughed, and when he looked up, he caught Luka watching him with a frown.

"Are you feeling okay?" Luka asked.

"Yeah, I'm good. A bit hoarse, but eh." Kyle grabbed another water from under the bar and cracked it. "My emotions are kind of all over the map. I got sort of weirded out this morning in the hallways, but I've been back and forth a couple of times since then and felt fine. I made everybody in the building review the fire safety rules and set up an inspection for Under and the pub upstairs, too." He sipped from the bottle and grimaced. "But other than the voice and having to use the inhaler, I feel decent."

"Glad to hear it," Luka replied. "I'm just sorry that fire exit was blocked, and you guys got stuck in the first place."

Kyle frowned. "I stopped by the Burger Barn and checked on Maya and Nestor. They're upset for a variety of reasons. They've been in that space a long time and never had anything like this happen."

"I know. They always pass their inspections, too," Luka said. "There's no telling how long that door has been blocked, so I think it'll take a while for them to straighten everything out."

Kyle nodded, then glanced across the bar when Masen called his name. "Excuse me a sec," he said to Luka just as Malcolm and Cam turned up.

"We'll keep an eye on him for you," Cam said. His teasing smile made Kyle roll his eyes.

Hopefully, he'd get back in time to prevent Cam from talking Luka into a group scene with Jesse and himself. Then again, that didn't sound half bad if the group included Kyle. He hadn't yet sussed out whether Luka liked men but had no doubt Cam would manage before the night's end.

Cam and Malcolm appeared to have done that very thing when Kyle rejoined them ten minutes later because Luka was relating a story that sounded like it involved both of his roommates and very few clothes. Well, that figured. If he hadn't been so disappointed at learning Luka was already involved with at least one man, Kyle would have been intrigued.

"Yeah, well, Robbie has no regard for anyone's privacy, of course," Luka said. "He just barges into the bathroom like we're not even there. He got in the shower with me yesterday."

Malcolm laughed. "No shit? Where was Matías?"

"At the sink, shaving. He either didn't notice Robbie sneaking in or purposely let him scare the ever-living hell out of me when I realized I wasn't alone." Luka glanced from Malcolm to Kyle. "They were both laughing at me by the time I finished screaming, that much I know."

Cam's bright brown eyes gleamed. "What did you do?"

Luka shrugged. "I shampooed Robbie's lazy ass and gave him a massage because he's a spoiled brat with no boundaries."

Kyle put on a smile while the others joked and laughed, then excused himself after a moment. He moved around the bar, filling orders and checking in with his guests, and though he thought he sensed Luka's eyes on him, he kept away a while longer. As much as Kyle enjoyed talking with Luka, he didn't feel much in the mood to listen to more shower and massage stories.

He waited until Malcolm and Cam had moved over to one of the seating areas with some of the others before he approached Luka again. Kyle found him chatting with Munson, and they looked at Kyle with interest as he stepped up in front of them.

"More of the same?" Kyle asked.

Munson jerked a thumb at Luka's drink. "I like the Fireman's Sours you've been making me, but Luka says I'll regret not trying a margarita. So, I'll take a Smoke & Ember, please." He slid his empty rocks glass across the bar toward Kyle. "Hopefully, mixing rum and tequila at this hour doesn't render me comatose tomorrow."

"Be quiet, you big baby." Luka knocked his shoulder with Munson's. "Why don't you ask Kyle about the thing we were talking about?"

Munson aimed an exasperated look at Luka. "I'm not asking him out for you, dude," he said. "Hell, Kyle invited us here and comped us a whole night — I think it's your turn to step up."

Kyle froze in the act of measuring liquors and watched Luka's eyebrows rise high.

Munson frowned, clearly aware his words were unexpected. "What? That's not what you wanted me to ask him?"

"Err. No." Luka scrubbed his forehead with the fingers of one hand. "You wanted to know how Kyle and these guys all knew each other, remember?" His gaze flicked to Kyle's then, and suddenly, both of them were snickering.

Munson grimaced. "Okay, my bad. I did want to know though," he said to Kyle. "I mean, you've got a state senator and some teachers, two business guys and some non-profit nuts, including one who looks like a swimsuit model — how does that happen?"

"The short answer is I met everyone one way or another through Jesse, one of the business guys, and Carter, one of the non-profit nuts," Kyle said over another chuckle. "And don't worry about the other thing — I won't turn down a laugh, even if it's at my own expense."

"What other thing? You mean Luka asking you out? How is that at your expense?" Munson asked. He stared at Kyle, his eyebrows furrowed. "He does want to ask you out. He told me so when we met up to come over here."

Luka sighed. "Dude, why?"

"Well, you do, right? So, what's the big deal? Ask the guy out already!"

Kyle rattled the contents of the shaker as much to drown out the tiff brewing in front of him as to mix the cocktails. He poured out the new drinks and served them up while Luka and Munson fell quiet again. Luka looked adorably flustered when Kyle caught his eye.

"Munson's not wrong," he said with a helpless-looking smile. "I've been trying to figure out how to ask you out all night. If he'd go away" — Luka cut his eyes at his friend — "I might work up the nerve."

"I'm not going anywhere," Munson said. "You clearly have no fucking idea what you're doing and need my help." He sipped his margarita and stared at it. "Okay, hold up because, damn, you were right. This is one of the best things I've ever tasted."

Kyle laughed. This night had turned out all sorts of weird, and he was enjoying himself. "I might say yes, if you actually asked me out," he said to Luka, then worried his bottom lip with his teeth. "But how do the roommates fit in? Do you guys have an open-ended kind of thing going?" Kyle was cool with flexible relationship boundaries, but he liked knowing what he might be getting into.

Luka frowned at him. "Roommates? You mean Matías? He is legitimately just a roommate. Great guy and a decent person to share space with, but not my type."

"Okay, what about Robbie?" Kyle asked.

"What about him?"

"Well, from what you were saying, you two sound close. You sure he won't mind?"

"Wait." Munson held up a hand and smiled broadly. "Kyle, you do know Robbie isn't human, right?

Now Kyle frowned. "He's not?"

"No." Munson cackled. "He's a ferret! A ferret with a dude's name," he added and poked Luka's shoulder with his finger. "I fucking told you guys not to give your pet a human name. People think he's your boyfriend!"

Luka shook his head at Munson's laughter. "What? No, they don't."

"Yes, they do!" Munson insisted. "You talk about 'showering with Robbie,' and 'massaging Robbie,' and fucking 'sharing a pillow with Robbie' — of course, it sounds like you're talking about a guy. You should have just named the damned thing Shadow and you wouldn't have this problem!"

Several moments passed before any of them could stop laughing, and Kyle's eyes were watering by the time he pulled himself together.

"Okay, so now that we've cleared up that mystery, I have a question for you, Kyle." The sparkle in Luka's eye made Kyle's insides go flip-flop. "Would you like to go out sometime? Just me—no roommate, no ferret and definitely no Munson."

Kyle grinned at Munson's scoff. "That sounds great," he said to Luka. "I'd love to go out with just you."

Chapter Four

Luka pulled to a stop at the curb in front of Lock & Key and put the borrowed car into park, the first flutters of nervous anticipation building in his stomach. He hopped out onto the sidewalk, but seeing Kyle step out of the bar stopped him in his tracks.

Luka would swear Kyle got better looking every time he saw him. He'd dressed casually tonight in jeans, scuffed boots, leather jacket and a dark gray V-neck T-shirt. Casual, but very, very sexy. *Hello, handsome,* Luka thought.

He and Kyle had been texting since Monday night, but Luka's schedule had proved difficult as usual, and it had taken a few days for them to figure out a time to meet up. *It's going to be worth the wait though,* Luka thought as he strode toward Kyle.

Kyle's face lit up as he spotted Luka. "Hey there."

They met each other halfway, and Luka slid a hand along Kyle's waist as he leaned in and pressed a kiss to his cheek. Even though this was their first date, the gesture felt easy and natural. The scent of Kyle's leather jacket, soft under Luka's palm, mingled with Kyle's cologne or aftershave. Much nicer than the acrid smoke from the fire.

"Good to see you, Luka."

"You too. Your voice sounds better," Luka said as he pulled away. Kyle's voice still held a hint of raspiness, but it had improved since the last time they'd seen each other. Luka quelled the urge to reach out and stroke the pale skin of Kyle's throat.

"It feels better, too. Just a few more days of the inhaler and I should be back to normal. Whatever that is."

"Glad to hear it." Luka jiggled the keys in his hand. "You ready to head out?"

"I am. And very intrigued by the idea of mini golf," Kyle said as he rounded the front of the car.

"I thought something active sounded more fun than the typical coffee-drinks-dinner bit."

"Oh, trust me, I'm not complaining," Kyle said when they were settled in the car. "But Randall's Island? That's a hike from Harlem."

"Yeah, thanks for being a good sport about it and meeting me here, too," Luka said.

Between their work schedules and the facts that their neighborhoods were at least half an hour apart on public transit and neither of them owned vehicles, the date had been complicated to plan. Luka snuck another glance at Kyle. *Worth it though.*

"Oh, it's fine. I needed to come in anyway."

"Am I keeping you from working?" Luka asked as he buckled his seat belt.

"Yes and no."

Luka quirked an eyebrow at Kyle. "How's that?"

"Well, left to my own devices, I usually work a stupid number of hours. Jesse is always on me to take time off.

Is there more I could be doing? Sure. Am I sorry I took the afternoon off to spend it with you? Not at all."

"Glad to hear it." Luka started the car and pulled away from the curb. "My schedule isn't exactly dating friendly, I'm afraid."

"Mine isn't always a picnic for guys either. I have more flexibility though. There are some nights I absolutely have to be at Under, but for the most part, I can make my own schedule. Jesse and I work hard to make sure the speakeasy is a well-oiled machine." Along with some pride, Kyle's voice held a shy note that Luka found rather endearing. "Jesse and I were friends before we had the idea for Under. We created the business plan together."

"How long has it been open?"

"Since 2014, so we're coming up on a year and a half and doing well. We're operating in the black and have been for a while now."

"That's impressive." Luka's cousin Daniela had opened a bakery called Sugar Street almost five years ago, and he knew from her how hard starting a small business could be. The bakery was flourishing now, and she'd recently opened Sugar Street Coffee and Sweets, a street cart that offered coffee and baked goods to busy commuters.

"What about you? How long have you been a firefighter?"

"Eleven years. I applied to the FDNY the minute I graduated high school and went right into the fire academy. I'm thinking about going back to school for fire sciences though. Maybe emergency management. I love what I do, but a degree will give me more options for future advancement and career possibilities after active duty."

"That seems like a smart plan."

"What about you? Did you always want to be a bar owner and mix up phenomenal cocktails?"

"No, not quite. I got my Bachelor's in English literature, which isn't good for much in the real world." Luka snorted. "I planned on going to grad school, maybe get into writing or teaching, but that didn't work out. So, I bounced around from job to job and discovered I was good at bartending. I moved to New York, eventually met Jesse and the rest is history."

"Seems like you did well for yourself, and I don't mean the money. You seem to enjoy what you do."

"I do. I feel very fortunate."

Traffic thickened as they approached the Robert F. Kennedy Bridge, and they fell silent as Luka navigated through the tangle of vehicles.

"How'd you discover this place?" Kyle asked as they finally approached the golf and entertainment center.

"Most of Randall and Ward Islands are parks, but the fire academy is here too. During training, we checked out the batting cages and mini golf. We were usually too wiped out to play, but some of us went after graduation to celebrate. We kept coming back because it's fun as hell."

"Very cool." Kyle drummed his fingers on his knees. "I can't remember the last time I went mini golfing. High school, maybe?"

"It's been at least four or five years for me." Luka eased the car into a parking spot near the clubhouse. "I don't even know why. Just got busy, I guess."

"Well, that's better than fifteen years! Promise you'll go easy on me?"

"Not on your life!" Luka looked over at Kyle and grinned. "I play to win."

"Competitive, huh?" Kyle's eyes gleamed.

"Oh, you have no idea."

"Sounds like I'm about to find out."

Tension charged the air between them, and Luka resisted the urge to lean in and press his lips to Kyle's. *No, better to let it build. Like a fire. In a controlled burn, you have to gently fan the sparks to allow them to catch flame. Good conversation, some friendly competition…it won't take much.* Luka looked forward to it. Kyle's lips curled up as if he'd caught a glimpse of Luka's thoughts.

"You ready?" Luka asked, reaching for the door handle.

"Oh, yeah."

The air outside the car was pleasantly cool. The balmy nights and pleasant sunny days of September had continued into October, but there was an undeniably autumnal scent in the air.

Luka stole another glance at Kyle as they walked to the clubhouse. It had been quite a while since he'd gone on a first date he'd looked forward to so much. The stress of work melted away, replaced with anticipation.

"Whose car did you borrow anyway?" Kyle asked. "I contemplated asking Jes if I could use his Range Rover but that thing's a beast."

"That's my sister Ruby's car. She loaned it to me on the condition that I wash and wax it. I figured I'd take it to the station house and get some of the rookies to do it."

Kyle chuckled. "Smart thinking. How many siblings do you have?"

"Three. Two older sisters — Regina and Ruby. After my dad died, my mom remarried. She and my stepfather had my younger brother, Marcus."

An expression Luka couldn't quite identify crossed Kyle's face, but he reached for the door of the clubhouse and held it open before Luka could ask what he was thinking.

"Can I get this?" Kyle reached for his wallet as they approached the counter. "Since you drove?"

"Sure."

After Kyle bought their passes, Luka used the excuse of helping him select the right length golf club to get close, and they headed onto the course.

"You can start," Kyle said and gestured at Luka.

"Want me to show you how it's done?"

"Oh. Trash talking already, I see," Kyle teased. "Go on then. Wow me."

Luka set his ball down, surveyed the putting green then lined up his shot. The ball rolled around the obstacles before dropping into the hole with a satisfying clatter.

"Nicely done!" Kyle cheered. "I see I need to be on my game tonight."

"Are you wowed?"

"Not yet. But I could be." The heat in Kyle's gaze made Luka's smile widen.

"Your turn."

Kyle went through the same routine of lining up his shot, but he hit the ball too hard and it sailed past the hole and rolled partway back toward them.

"Damn it," Kyle muttered, but he was still smiling. "I'm as rusty as I expected."

"I can show you some moves," Luka said. "If you need help."

"I'm sure you can." Kyle's gaze flicked up and down Luka's body. "But hold that thought. I'll be back on my game in no time."

"Go ahead then. This hole is a par two. Think you can get it in one more shot?"

"Yeah. How about you keep score?"

"Sure," Luka said. "I promise I won't even cheat."

Kyle dug in his pocket, then slapped the scorecard and small pencil into Luka's outstretched hand. He was deliberate about his next shot and it worked. The ball rattled in the hole, and Kyle let out a whoop.

"On par."

"Nice. Maybe I'll have some competition," Luka said. "I used to beat the guys from the academy all the time."

"Clearly, it made you cocky."

"Cocky? I don't know about that," Luka said. "Just confident."

They played their way around the course. Luka maintained his narrow margin over Kyle, and their conversation was light and fluid. The difficulty of the game increased, and the sparks Luka had detected earlier crackled in kind.

"We'll be tied if you get a hole-in-one," Luka pointed out as Kyle lined up his shot for the final hole.

"No pressure, right?"

"None whatsoever. The outcome of our entire date is just resting on whether you beat me or not." Luka made sure the sarcasm was clear in his tone.

Kyle snickered. "Now he tells me." He tapped the ball with the club, and they both watched it swing wide and roll along the edge of the hole before it stopped a few inches away.

"That's a win for Luka Clarke!" Luka crowed.

Kyle laughed and clapped him on the back. "Congratulations!"

Luka pulled him into a side hug, once again fighting the urge to kiss Kyle. He thought once he did he wouldn't want to stop, and the middle of a public mini golf course wasn't the place for them to lose control.

Oh, but this was good. He couldn't remember the last time he'd had such a fun date. And the more he learned about Kyle, the more he liked him.

"How about another round? We have unlimited games with the pass, and the night is still young," Kyle offered.

"I'm in." The sun hung low in the sky, but the weather was still gorgeous. Luka had no desire to quit now.

The second game went faster and, to Luka's pleasure, Kyle proved an even fiercer competitor. They were neck and neck the entire time, and by the time Kyle sank the last shot on the eighteenth hole, Luka knew he'd been beaten.

"Well done, McKee!" Luka hugged Kyle again, his touch lingering this time. "Hell of a game. What do you think about taking a quick break? We could walk along the river," Luka said. He reluctantly let Kyle go, but Kyle's hand lingered on Luka for a moment, warm where he tucked it between Luka's jacket and T-shirt.

"Sounds great."

They wandered away from the golf course and down to the paths that ran along the shore. Randall Island lay between the Harlem and East Rivers and offered spectacular views of the boroughs of Manhattan, Queens and the Bronx. Now, the sun was setting behind the skyline of East Harlem.

"That's gorgeous," Kyle said, his voice quiet. "I don't see a view like that too often."

"Sometimes, it takes leaving the heart of the city for me to remember how incredible a place it is." Luka snapped a few pictures with his phone before he tucked it back into his pocket.

"Yeah, agreed. I need to drag the guys out here sometime," Kyle murmured.

"Jesse and Carter and Riley and all of them?" Luka had been slightly taken aback by Kyle's easy friendships with some prominent public figures, but he'd found them all friendly and likeable, and nothing like he would have expected.

"Yes. Sometimes referred to as 'The Speakeasy Crew.' I believe the illustrious senator started that one."

"Got it. I got the gist of how you all met the other night," Luka said, "but can I ask what your relationship with Jesse is? I met Cam and I know he and Jesse live together, but you and Jesse seem...close. That's one reason I hesitated to ask you out. I didn't know quite how to read that situation."

Kyle gave him a lopsided smirk. "I'll be a total cliché here and say that it's complicated. The simple version is that Jesse and Cam have an open relationship. Jesse and I hooked up a lot before they met, and while their relationship changed some things, I hook up with them both on occasion."

Luka's brain whirled with images of Kyle in bed with both men. They were all incredibly attractive, so it was quite a nice picture. "Have you ever hooked up with Cam? I mean, without Jesse?"

"No. I'd be happy doing that with Cam at some point though, if he wanted. He's a lot of fun."

"Interesting."

Kyle shot him a sidelong glance. "Are you comfortable with that?"

"Open relationships or what you have going on with your friends?"

"Both? I'm not steadfast in needing something open the way Jesse is, but I enjoy it. I don't know that total monogamy is my thing. A little...wiggle room is nice." Kyle offered him a small smile.

"Sure, I get you," Luka said easily. "I don't have any experience with groups of men, but I did have a couple of threesomes with women back in my probie days that were very fun."

"You're bi then?"

Luka went very still. "Yep. That a problem?" He tried to keep his tone neutral, but his bisexuality had become an issue too many times with people he'd dated, and it had never been fun. Luka would be really fucking disappointed to find Kyle as closed-minded.

Kyle's eyes widened. "Shit, no. I'm not attracted to women, but I have zero issue with you being bi."

"Glad to hear it." Relief washed over him, and it must have shown because Kyle reached out and touched his upper arm.

"That been a problem for you?"

Luka grimaced. "Ugh, yes. On more than one occasion."

"How is it at the firehouse?"

"Generally, a non-issue there, to be honest. Munson wigged out a bit at first, but he got over it."

"He did help you ask me out," Kyle said drily. "So yeah, I'd say so."

"A few of the older guys scoff when my dating dudes comes up, but by now, everyone knows I'm a damn good firefighter, no matter who I'm attracted to. They know it doesn't impact my ability to do my job."

"That's great. Beyond not being sure you were into dudes when we met at Burger Barn, I had no idea if you were out at work either. That's why I didn't hand you my card then. I didn't want to complicate the life of a guy who relies on his co-workers the way you do."

"I appreciate that you recognized that." Luka was touched by Kyle's concern. "It worked out anyway. It took a fire for us to meet again but…"

"Here we are."

Kyle smiled and the heat inside Luka kindled again. He looked away and noticed their loop along the river's edge had brought them back to the path to the golf center.

"How about a bite to eat?" Luka asked. "There's a place with decent food just over there."

"Sounds perfect."

In a short time, they were seated in an open-air beer garden with drinks and an appetizer to share.

"I still can't believe you ordered an energy drink slushy," Luka said. "I know it's a fancy version and it didn't taste bad, but…" He shuddered.

Kyle laughed. "Chalk it up to being a bartender. I felt compelled to try it."

"I'm gonna enjoy my IPA here." Luka clinked his glass against Kyle's.

"I bet I could make a version you'd like."

"That I believe. You threw together some damn good drinks the other night, and I'm not much of a mixed-booze guy."

"Now that's the kind of compliment I like." Kyle's expression was confident.

"You love what you do, don't you?"

"I do." Kyle sat back in his chair. "I'm not changing the world like David and Carter — or hell, like you — but I enjoy that rush of pleasure someone gets when I've made a drink that suits their tastes."

"Hey, I'm not putting down what you do," Luka said. "You give people a place to unwind and recharge from work and life. That's not small."

Kyle shrugged. "It's a good feeling."

"Is it true that people unload their problems on you?" Luka asked.

"A sympathetic ear and some alcohol can loosen almost anyone's tongue. I've heard some wild stories over the years. The regulars at Under are more like family though, and I'm closer with the speakeasy guys than with most of my own actual relatives." A frown crossed Kyle's face. "Are you close with your family?"

"Yeah," Luka said. He sipped his drink. "It hasn't all been a picnic, but we get along well. We have moments where we drive each other nuts, but my dad's death brought home how easy it is to lose someone. I think we keep that in mind when we get frustrated with each other."

"I'm sorry to hear you lost your dad." Kyle paused as though he wanted to speak further but remained silent. Luka could guess what was on the tip of his tongue.

"He was a firefighter," Luka said softly. "His company responded to a five-alarm fire at an apartment building in Harlem. He got separated from his crew and the roof collapsed. By the time they found him, it was too late. Several other firefighters were injured along with some of the residents."

Kyle learned forward and rested his hand on Luka's arm. He gave it a reassuring squeeze. The gesture said as much as any words, and Luka appreciated it. "How old were you when you lost him?"

"Way too young. I had just turned eight."

"Oh, man, that's rough."

"What's your family like?"

"I lost my dad, too, actually," Kyle said. "He had a heart attack — very unexpected. I was older though and had already graduated from college."

"Doesn't make it any easier though, does it?"

"No, it doesn't."

"What about your mom? Do you see her much?" Luka reached for a fried pickle and dunked it in the spicy mayo. The long pause that followed made him glance up at Kyle.

Kyle offered Luka a half-hearted smile. "No. Our relationship is pretty fraught. Spending time around her makes me feel shitty, so I avoid it, then feel guilty about it." This time, Luka reached out and give Kyle a reassuring squeeze.

"My brother Oliver and I are close though. He moved to Boston recently, and that makes it easier to see each other. He visited over the summer, and that was nice."

"That's good." They were both silent for a few minutes as they sampled the food. Kyle stirred his melting slushy with a contemplative look on his face.

"So, if your dad was FDNY, you grew up here then?" Kyle asked.

"Yeah. You?"

"I was born and raised in Vermont. I go back occasionally but haven't seen my hometown since I moved here."

"When was that?"

"Five years ago. I brought everything I owned in a duffel bag and couch surfed until I got my feet under me."

"That's both tough and impressive."

"I had some great friends who helped me out," Kyle said. "Gave me a place to sleep and didn't complain when I overstayed my welcome."

Luka couldn't imagine going it alone. Sometimes between the firehouse, his parents, and siblings, he had more help than he wanted, but he counted himself lucky.

"I think one of the things I like most about the firehouse is that we're a tight-knit bunch," he said. "Most of the people there would drop everything to help out if I needed it."

The waiter arrived with their food and they dug in. Kyle took a bite of his buffalo chicken sandwich and made a low sound of pleasure. "Holy shit, this is good."

Luka grinned and set down his turkey burger. "Yeah, I've had it and it's killer. It's worth making the trip out here for the food."

"I agree." Kyle wiped his mouth. "Nowhere as convenient as Burger Barn."

"Tell me about it. I hope they can get the insurance crap resolved. I'm worried about Maya and Nestor." Luka grimaced.

"Maybe I can talk with the people I know and see if we can get them some legal representation."

"You'd do that?" Kyle's generosity surprised Luka. "After what happened to you?"

"Of course. They're good people and it would be a shame if they lost their business. Charita and I made it out safely, and I don't hold any ill will toward them."

As they ate, Luka told Kyle about Sugar Hill. Kyle sounded genuinely enthusiastic and curious about the history of the area, and by the time they'd wrapped up, Luka had promised to take him on a walking tour.

"What do you think about one more round of golf?" Luka asked.

"I'd be up for a tie-breaker. But what does the winner get?"

"Well." Luka leaned closer. "We could always make some kind of wager."

Kyle raised an eyebrow. "A wager for what?"

"Is it too soon to suggest sexual favors?"

Kyle's smirk was downright devilish. "I'm open to suggestions."

* * * *

Half an hour later, Luka let out an excited whoop. "Good game, McKee, but not good enough."

"Looks like you're the winner." In the bright lights of the eighteenth hole, Kyle's teeth gleamed. "You know what that means."

"Time for me to collect my prize."

"Mmhmm. What are you waiting for?"

Luka tugged Kyle off the green. The place was nearly deserted, and it had grown dark enough that one of the shadowed sections of the course would work for what he had in mind.

"We need someplace more private than this for me to collect on what we discussed earlier," he said, his voice husky. "But I can do this."

Luka stepped forward, bringing their bodies close together. Kyle stood a few inches shorter, so all Luka had to do was tilt his head for their lips to meet. Kyle let out a soft sound and met him eagerly. Luka splayed his hands across the back of Kyle's leather jacket, holding him close as they explored each other's mouths. The smoldering heat that had built all afternoon kindled into a flame and Luka's skin heated. Kyle slid his hands under Luka's jacket, kneading the muscles of his back as they kissed. Every part of Luka wanted to continue, but he was conscious of where they were. Equal parts relief and disappointment went through him when Kyle slowed the kiss.

"Mmm." Kyle pulled back with a contented expression. "I've wanted to do that all night."

"Me too." Luka licked his lips. They still tingled from the touch of Kyle's.

Kyle slid his hands lower and pulled Luka's hips tight against his own. Neither of them was fully hard, but there was no denying the fact the kiss had turned them both on.

"What do you say we head back before we continue this?" Kyle asked.

"My place or yours?"

"We've established you have both human and ferret roommates. I live alone. My place?"

"Done." Luka forced himself to step back. "I'll need directions."

They returned their golf clubs and balls to the clubhouse and made a beeline for the parking lot. Neither talked much as Luka started the car and Kyle called up some directions on his phone. Luka drove with single-minded focus, intent on getting to Chelsea, but Kyle threatened to undo that by laying a hand on Luka's thigh.

His touch was warm through the denim of Luka's jeans. At first, Kyle kept his hand still, which was distraction enough, but when he started rubbing slow circles with his thumb, Luka's cock stirred with interest. Luka groaned and shifted in the seat.

"Careful there." His voice held a rough edge.

Kyle's answering laugh was low and teasing as he slid his hand higher. Sweat broke out on Luka's forehead.

"How much longer?" he asked.

"Thirteen minutes." Kyle sounded infuriatingly calm. "But parking can be a nightmare."

"Now he tells me." Luka resisted the urge to press his foot harder on the accelerator. Traffic was light, all things considered, but he didn't want to be pulled over for driving while black in a vehicle he didn't own.

Kyle squeezed his thigh. "Want me to stop?"

"No." Luka spread his knees wider. "Just don't do anything that'll make me wreck the car."

Luka had never been more grateful when at last Kyle directed him to a parking spot half a block from his building. Luka was out of the car as soon as he'd parked, with Kyle just ahead of him. Luka barely noticed the building number or the lobby as they jogged up several flights of stairs.

Kyle stopped in front of a door and reached for his keys, and Luka pressed close, fitting their bodies together. He pressed a kiss against Kyle's neck, just above the collar of his jacket. "You do know there's gonna be payback for the teasing you did in the car, right?"

"I certainly hope so."

Kyle sounded smug, but the keys rattled in his hand when Luka slid a hand under his jacket and teased his nipple through his shirt. Luka was hard now, anticipation fueling the erection he pushed against Kyle's ass.

"If you don't want this to happen in the hallway, I suggest you get that door unlocked," Luka breathed against his ear. He slid his hand across Kyle's groin and found him hard and ready too. A needy sound left Kyle's throat as Luka stroked him through his jeans.

"I'll never get this door open if you keep that up," Kyle said, voice gruff. "And there's a bed and lube and condoms on the other side of it. Your choice."

They were both on the edge, threatening to explode into an inferno. Flashover conditions, Luka thought. A fire spreading very rapidly across a gap because of intense heat. Intense. Uncontrollable.

He stepped back.

Chapter Five

Kyle silently cursed the locks on his damned door. He was so hard he almost hurt, and he let out a noisy exhalation when the final lock gave. He shoved the door open then reached back with one hand and grasped Luka's black bomber jacket to tug him over the threshold. The teasing words he'd planned to say faded the moment he met Luka's heated gaze however. Kyle's mouth went dry.

Fuck, he is gorgeous.

Luka pounced as soon as the door closed behind them. He swept Kyle up in a rib-creaking hold that forced Kyle up on his toes and covered Kyle's mouth in a kiss, the curve of his bottom lip warm and soft and oh so fucking good. Kyle groaned under the onslaught.

"The alarm," he ground out the next time they came up for air. Kyle made a grab for the keypad, but Luka ignored him and buried his face against Kyle's neck instead. Kyle's knees wobbled. "Jesus," he muttered. "I gotta disable the alarm, Luka."

"Disable it then," Luka replied, his voice low. He continued kissing and teasing but loosened his hold so Kyle could reach the keypad. The second Kyle's hand fell away from the pad, Luka mashed him up against the door.

Kyle's head spun. Damn, Luka was strong. He wasn't shy about using his big body to his advantage either, and he manhandled Kyle with startling ease. The side of Kyle that liked rough play pulsed white hot, but he'd always liked giving as good as he got. He pulled back, away from Luka's wicked mouth and tongue, and tightened his hold on Luka's shoulders until Luka stilled. They stared one another down, the air around them crackling.

"Want you," Kyle said, his voice so rough he hardly recognized it as his own. He couldn't blame smoke this time either.

Luka smirked. "Want you, too," he said. He dropped his hands to the clasp on Kyle's belt and kissed Kyle some more, slower this time but with no less intensity.

Fire built in Kyle's belly. His head fell back slightly as Luka unzipped his fly and slid a big, warm hand over Kyle's cock. It would be so easy for Kyle to take his pleasure here. He could go to his knees and suck Luka, loving every second while they rode the buzz they'd generated during their date.

Kyle wanted more than quick and dirty tonight though. He'd been thinking about a moment like this with Luka since that night at the speakeasy. He wanted to feel Luka for days, inside and out.

Reaching down, Kyle grabbed Luka's ass with both hands and kissed him harder and deeper. Desire curled inside him at Luka's hum. Kyle pushed off the door and got Luka moving, and somehow, they made it across the little apartment to the bedroom.

They peeled off each other's clothes in silence and dropped them on the floor then fell onto the bed. Kyle basked in miles of warm, silky skin.

Luka rolled on top of him and sealed their mouths together. He sighed as Kyle spread his legs, then reached down and wrapped a hand around Kyle's cock. Kyle's bones turned liquid.

"Fuck, yeah," he whispered and smiled at Luka's throaty chuckle.

"Damn, you're hot."

"Says the smoking-hot guy."

Luka pulled back and peered down at him, his amusement clear. He gave Kyle's cock a lazy stroke. "That's a terrible pun, McKee."

"Plenty more where that came from, I'm afraid." Kyle's voice faltered when Luka pumped him again. "O-h-h, man. Keep doing that. It's true, you know. You're gorgeous."

"And you're good for my ego," Luka said before Kyle cut him off with a dirty kiss that went on and on until Kyle thought he'd lose his mind. Luka finally tore his mouth away and dragged his tongue up the side of Kyle's face.

"Fuck. Need you to tell me what you want, Kyle."

"Need you in me," Kyle whispered.

Luka flared his nostrils. He pressed his face into Kyle's throat again, nipping and sucking hard enough to mark the skin. Kyle couldn't bring himself to care. He rested his hands on Luka's head and slid his fingers against the soft, short twists of his hair. Luka worked his way lower, his grip on Kyle's body unrelenting, and

Kyle swallowed back a yell when Luka ran his teeth over a nipple.

"Need lube," Luka murmured against Kyle's skin.

"Nightstand," Kyle said. He couldn't resist cupping Luka's cheek with one hand, and when Luka turned his face and dropped a kiss on Kyle's palm, Kyle swallowed against a swoop of giddy pleasure. "Condoms, too. I'm negative," he added.

Luka nodded. "Same."

Arousal thrummed through Kyle as Luka pushed up onto his knees. He had a beautiful body with long, graceful limbs, and every inch of him radiated power. He reached toward the nightstand drawer, the hard planes of muscle in his broad shoulders flexing, and the warmth in his gaze when he turned back made Kyle's heart thump.

I'm in trouble, Kyle thought.

Luka dropped a condom on the mattress but shook his head when Kyle shifted to roll onto his stomach. "Not so fast."

Kyle laughed. "I'm not going anywhere."

"Oh, I know," Luka said in a teasing tone. "You're not ready for me to fuck you yet either."

He wet his fingers with lube and moved his gaze over Kyle's body, admiration and lust clear in his face. Kyle's cock twitched against his abdomen.

"So sexy," Luka murmured. He reached down and wrapped a slick hand around Kyle, then used the other to tease Kyle's balls.

Kyle hissed. He was almost too aroused for teasing. He grabbed the sheets with both hands, sure he'd blow any second, and locked his gaze on Luka's. Luka sank down between Kyle's legs, and his wanton expression sent Kyle's desire into overdrive.

Luka took Kyle deep. He slid the hand on Kyle's balls lower, rubbing small circles into his skin. That pressure combined with the wet heat around Kyle's cock dragged a moan out of him, and he clenched his eyes closed when Luka fingered his rim. He raised his hands to Luka's head again and fought the urge to thrust but lost the battle when Luka worked a finger inside him. Kyle bucked up hard, and Luka's hum made stars explode behind his eyelids.

Time lost all meaning for Kyle. His skin felt hot and tight as his body edged toward orgasm, his breaths harsh to his own ears. He shuddered as Luka slipped another finger inside him, and he gasped when Luka curled it just right.

Kyle forced his eyes open. His breath hitched at the sight Luka made—lips stretched wide and his eyes watering from exertion. Then Luka groaned again and Kyle's toes curled.

"Gonna come," he gasped out a second before the orgasm roared through him.

Every muscle in Kyle's body strung tight. The moment stretched and stretched until a low shout built in Kyle's throat, and when it broke, he lay boneless on the mattress, panting and sex-stoned. Luka pulled off.

"Christ," Luka muttered. "Need to fuck you." He crawled up over Kyle, eyes flashing with blue fire while Kyle tried to pull himself together.

"Mmkay," Kyle murmured, voice broken and brain too blitzed to say much else, and he managed a goofy grin at Luka's laugh. Luka's cock pressed hard as iron against Kyle's hip.

Luka pushed up enough so Kyle could roll onto his stomach, and Kyle closed his eyes, coasting on endorphins while the lube bottle clicked again and a foil packet rustled. He hummed low as a pair of big hands spread his thighs.

Luka nudged Kyle's rim with his cock, teasing for a bare moment before he split Kyle open with one smooth motion. Kyle clenched his teeth through the stretch and burn. He shook, his prostate almost too sensitive to go again so soon, but he didn't care. He wanted this with Luka and more, if he could have it.

Luka bottomed out. "So tight," he said, and the wonder in his voice crushed Kyle flat.

Luka got an arm under Kyle and held him close, then nosed at the nape of Kyle's neck. Goosebumps broke out over Kyle's skin. He grasped Luka's arm and pulled Luka into him, each movement shifting the ache in Kyle's body to hunger. Kyle reveled in the weight that pinned him to the sheets and Luka's murmured words, and the way their ragged breaths mixed. His cock began to fill.

Blindly, Kyle reached out. He found Luka's hand where it was braced on the mattress by his head and curled their fingers together while Luka drove into him, his pace punishing. Luka pushed especially deep, the motion lighting up every nerve in Kyle's body and tearing a shout from his throat. He shook as Luka dragged his cock over Kyle's gland, a storm of brutal thrusts that left Kyle lost.

Luka's gasp cut the air. His rhythm stuttered and slowed, then grew languid, and he curled into Kyle as he came back down, forehead pressed into the space between Kyle's shoulders and breath gusting over his damp skin. Kyle turned his face into the pillow, his skin prickling, and bit back a complaint when Luka slid out.

Luka fell beside him. He urged Kyle onto his side, his touch grounding on Kyle's unsteady limbs. Luka kissed him hard, then took Kyle's cock in hand. Kyle's entire body jolted.

"Nuhhh." Kyle bit his lip. He hung on as Luka worked him, unseated by the intensity of the ache inside him. "Oh, God, Luka. You—I can't."

"Yeah, you can." Luka kissed him again, and the slide of his tongue sent Kyle soaring high. Luka pulled back, his gaze rapt. "Give it to me, Kyle."

Kyle broke apart at the seams. He gasped and closed his eyes, and the world around him receded and left nothing but the bright pulse of bliss, a strong arm around him and a low voice in his ear.

Slowly, Kyle came back to himself. Luka let him go and got out of bed, and Kyle listened to him pad out of the room. He heard running water next, followed by more footfalls, and Kyle opened his eyes again as the mattress dipped under Luka's weight. Luka wiped Kyle down with a warm, wet washcloth, then set it on the floor and stretched back out on the bed before Kyle gathered wits enough to speak.

"Damn. I think you broke me."

Luka looked smug. "I'd apologize, but that would make me a liar."

They both went still when Luka's stomach rumbled loudly, and Kyle bit his lip against a snicker. "Dude."

Luka put one hand over his eyes and laughed. "Man, talk about humiliating. I guess it's to be expected after all that exercise," he said and moved his fingers enough to share a smile with Kyle.

"Uh-huh, I see." Kyle rolled up on one elbow. "Don't feel bad. I'm feeling peckish myself."

Luka dropped the hand completely. "Only English nerds say 'peckish.' Oh, wait."

"Hah." Kyle poked Luka's ribs and made him squirm. "There's food and booze in my fridge, waiting to be raided if you're hungry."

"My car should be fine, right?" Luka shifted and pillowed his head in his hands.

"Yep. You're parked on the right side of the street for a Friday, and the parking meters are free until tomorrow morning just like the rest of the city. You're good."

"Cool."

Kyle's insides curled a little at the idea of Luka heading out, but he shoved the feeling aside and winked. "C'mon. I'll make you a stack of pancakes the size of your head."

They climbed out of bed and picked up the mess of clothing they'd left strewn over the floor, and both of them dragged their jeans back on. Luka insisted on helping Kyle with the cooking, so while he fried up a package of bacon, Kyle mixed a round of breakfast-themed cocktails.

"I like your place." Luka glanced around. "It's small but doesn't really feel like it."

"Yes, it does. Jesse calls it my shoebox," Kyle said. "It works for me. I'm not one for clutter, which is fortunate seeing as there's no space for it. I've had roommates in the past and the messier ones were challenging."

"Roommates? As in more than two of you here? Must have been cozy."

Kyle shrugged. "Everyone made do, and only a fool complains about a break in rent. It's a good place to sleep, and the neighborhood's decent. I'm very cool with living alone now though."

Luka nodded. "I'm okay with sharing space, but my place is bigger." His eyes went round as Kyle presented him with a glass filled with a foamy garnet-red concoction. "Damn, what is this?"

"It's a take on the Clover Club Cocktail," Kyle replied. He sipped from his glass before he set it down and started mixing dry ingredients for the pancakes in a bowl. "Gin, vermouth and lemon juice, with egg white and a touch of cherry jam. I'm not a huge breakfast-for-dinner kind of guy, but they taste great with almost any kind of pancake or waffle."

"Mmm, it's delicious." Luka licked his lips as he set down his Clover Club. "You do a lot of late-night entertaining in your line of work?"

"Not really." Kyle's mood dipped a bit, though he knew Luka didn't mean anything by the remark. He didn't want Luka thinking this date was just run of the mill for him though. Because it wasn't.

I'm in so much trouble.

"I'll go out after a shift now and again, but more often than not, I'm beat by the time I get home," he said. "Especially if I'm the one closing. I've crashed at the bar on occasion."

Luka grimaced. "Ugh."

"It's not often I do that, but yeah. There's a comfy couch back in the office, and I keep a go bag there to make it easier." Kyle pulled another bowl from the cabinet. "I don't hook up with customers because that's bad for business. You don't count, by the way, because I met you outside the bar."

"I was going to give you shit about that." Luka laughed.

"Uh-huh. I saw it on your face." Kyle smiled. "Anyway, it's been a while since I've been out with anyone besides the speakeasy guys."

"Yeah?" Luka raised a brow at him. "That's hard to believe given you're, you know—you."

Kyle couldn't help preening a bit. "Well, it's true. I took a break from dating." He went to the refrigerator. "Okay if I use almond milk? There's orange juice if you're allergic to nuts."

"Almond milk's fine," Luka said. He furrowed his brow. "What made you take a break?"

"Eh. I haven't had much luck finding a guy I can just hang with and not worry he's hiding something." Kyle poured the milk into the empty bowl and added oil and vanilla. "Like he's married or has a gambling problem or thinks I should make over my life."

Kyle stirred the dry ingredients into the wet. "Chris— the last guy I went out with—seemed okay. Then I caught him using my phone to stalk my Instagram posts. He told me it was for my own good because I am, and I quote, 'too wrapped up in my friends.' At the time, he said he meant Jesse and Cam, but then he accused me of fooling around with Carter behind Riley's back, too. Like either of us would ever do that to Ri." Kyle sniffed. Chris' words still rankled.

Luka blinked, clearly mystified. "What the fuck? Why would he think that at all?"

"Carter and I dated for a while back before he got together with Ri. Jesse and Carter dated back then, too." Kyle flapped a hand in the air. "It's a long story and I'll tell you sometime, if you want to know. But Carter and I were always more friends with benefits than boyfriends. When he and Riley decided they'd make a go of it, I was more than happy being just a friend."

"Sounds complicated."

"Only at first glance," Kyle said. "Anyway, I needed a break after the Instagram guy."

Luka set down the tongs he'd been using to turn over the bacon strips. "I feel lucky you agreed to go out with me at all."

"Well, I figured it'd be stupid not to make an exception for someone I literally trusted with my life." Kyle savored the pride that filtered over Luka's face. "Again, it's not like I never go out — I just put the dating on hold. I still see my friends and have them over."

Luka nodded. "Like Jesse and Cam, you mean?"

"Oh, sure. Jesse came over the night you met him, and we caught up, so to speak." A hot flush splashed across Kyle's cheeks, and Luka gave him a sly smile. Still, Kyle wasn't about to deny he and Jesse had fucked each other silly after they'd left the bar. "It had been a while since we did that, and we did a lot of talking, too.

"I see more of Malcolm, Carter and Riley than Jesse and Cam these days. My friends Jarrod and Gale live a block over from here, too, but I'm not sure you met them the other night." He stepped up beside Luka at the stove and poured batter into the pan he'd put on to heat. "Cam and I do some gaming, but that almost always happens online because of our schedules."

"Oh, yeah? What do you play?"

"Fallout, mostly. We have plans to go dark for a couple of days together in November when 4 comes out. Cam likes StarCraft, too. Do you play?"

"No, but some of the guys at the firehouse are into it. What about Jesse? Does he play?"

Kyle smirked. "No. He's uniformly terrible at anything that involves a screen and controller. Jesse needs physical stimulation to stay focused on most things entertainment-based. I got Malcolm playing over the summer and he's pretty good."

They kept up the back and forth as they finished cooking, and Kyle mixed up another round of drinks before they took the plates of food to his small dining table. Luka's expression grew thoughtful as he worked through his pancakes, and Kyle's insides knotted a little as he tried to parse out why. He thought they'd had a fantastic afternoon, and this evening was turning out even better. Luckily, Luka didn't hold back for long.

"You mind if I ask you a question?" he asked.

Kyle set down his fork. "Not at all."

"It really doesn't bother you that I'm bi?"

"No." Kyle frowned. "Why would it?"

"It's rare I meet someone who doesn't have an opinion about it." Luka forked up pancakes and dragged them through the syrup on his plate. "You haven't said a word since I told you, even though you've been open about a lot of other things."

"Well, I'm not usually like this." Kyle nodded when Luka looked askance at him over his mouthful of food. "I grew up in a family that's not big on sharing."

"So why are you sharing with me? I mean, you don't know me very well."

"I'm not sure." Kyle licked his lips as he considered the question. "Maybe because you've been open with me. Do you tell everyone you're bi on a first date?"

"Actually, yes." Luka shrugged. "I've found it's better getting it out in the open from the start than wait and risk a misunderstanding. Even then, lots of people who say they're okay with bisexuality in concept can't deal with it in real life. You truly seem like you don't care."

"I don't."

"That's atypical." Luka wiped his lips with his napkin, his face somber. "I've had relationships go bad because my partner couldn't get their head around the idea I could also be attracted to someone of the opposite sex. One of my sisters makes comments any time I'm with a man, too." A gentle scowl crossed Luka's face. "She means well, and I know she's not a bigot, but it still sucks she can't just be supportive."

"I'm sorry," Kyle said. "Some of my best friends are bi or pan, and I suppose that's the reason I don't think much about it from anyone other than 'that's what this person likes.'" He nodded at Luka's raised eyebrows. "Carter and Riley were both married to women before they got together, and Jesse...well, Jesse's attracted to everybody. And I mean *everybody*. He'd screw a space being with tentacles if the mood struck him." He grinned at Luka's obvious amusement.

"My brother's fairly sure he's either bi or pan. Oliver's only dated women up to now, but he finds both genders attractive. I figure he'd date a guy if the right one came along." Kyle picked up his glass and sipped, then swallowed the mouthful. "I don't know, Luka. We both know nothing in life is guaranteed. Why not be open to the opportunities for love that we're given?"

Ugh, I'm such a cheeseball.

Kyle set his glass down and ignored the heat in his face. But then Luka's hand was on his shoulder and he pulled Kyle close. He traced his fingers over Kyle's cheek and kissed him, his lips sweet with maple syrup. The kiss spread warmth in Kyle's belly and made his insides all melty. He felt dazed when Luka pulled away.

"What was that for?" Kyle's heart thudded a touch harder when Luka simply smiled and turned back to his plate.

"Just because. All right with you if I stay tonight?" he asked. "I'm off again tomorrow, and I'd like to buy you breakfast. Though I guess we'll have to find a place that serves steak and eggs considering we just killed a week's supply of pancakes."

Kyle laughed. "I love steak and eggs," he said, and went back to polishing off his stack.

Chapter Six

Luka spent a portion of the train ride from Sugar Hill to Riverdale in the Bronx thumbing through the photos on his phone. More specifically, the photos he'd taken on the dates he had with Kyle. Mini golfing. Kyle's midnight pancakes. A dinner they'd shared at a pub near Kyle's apartment. The walking tour of Sugar Hill.

Luka paused on a selfie Kyle had taken. In it, he lay sprawled on the couch, half-dressed in the neat black clothes he wore while tending bar. His shirt was open, exposing a section of his pale, toned chest and abs. He'd unbuckled his belt and his hand rested on the solid length under the dark fabric.

Goddamn.

Luka flipped to the next and licked his lips at the image of Kyle shirtless. There was a whole series showing Kyle undressing and stroking himself. In the final photo, he lay back with a lazy smirk on his face, and his hand rested on his spent dick. Cum dotted his torso. Luka shifted in his seat as his cock hardened.

He tapped out a message to Kyle.

Looking at the photos you sent the other day. On the train though. This could get awkward.

Thankfully, the car wasn't full, and he sat toward the back where no one could see over his shoulder. But still. Luka's phone buzzed in his hand.

Ha! Careful. Don't want to get arrested.

I do not. You're a bad influence.

Me? You started it.

Luka had started it. Sure, the teasing messages had flown both ways, but Luka had escalated the flirting by sending a photo of himself shirtless in his turnout pants with suspenders, boots and hat. It was a cheesy firefighter calendar pose, but Kyle had enjoyed it enough to reciprocate with a photo of his own hard cock straining at the fly of his jeans. The pictures had gotten progressively lewder as the week went on, but Luka wasn't complaining. Particularly as he'd gotten the impression Kyle didn't sext with just anyone.

The announcement of the train's approach to Riverdale Avenue prompted Luka to send a hasty goodbye.

Nearly at my stop. Catch you later tonight?

Working but I've got my phone. Have fun with your family.

Thanks. Have a good shift.

Luka stood and pocketed his phone as the train slowed and stopped. The cool air was crisp when he exited the station, but the sun made for a pleasant walk through the tree-lined streets. Luka approached the house with a smile. Due to his schedule and preoccupation with Kyle, it had been over a month since he'd been in the Bronx. It always felt good to come home.

Losing his father had been hard for Luka, and he'd struggled after his mother began dating Tomas Padilla, a handsome and soft-spoken man who co-owned a small accounting firm. Luka had grown fond of Tomas with the passage of time. After Tomas and Luka's mother married, they'd moved the family from an apartment in working-class Kingsbridge to the more affluent Riverdale, and Luka had fallen in love with the three-story brick house. Its fenced-in yard and basketball hoop had sealed the deal for a pre-adolescent boy.

Luka had always suspected Tomas had installed the hoop himself. They'd bonded over basketball, shooting hoops in the yard during the evenings and weekends after Luka's homework and chores were done. Tomas hadn't said much during those sessions and neither had Luka, but the game gave them a shared language. In time, Luka had come to love Tomas even more than the home he'd created for the family.

Now, Luka jogged up the front steps and let himself in. "Mom?" he called out as he strode through the living room.

"In here!" she replied from the kitchen. Her face lit up as she spied Luka. Standing nearly a foot shorter than Luka, Lydia Clarke appeared much more youthful looking than her sixty-five years. Her medium-brown skin bore few wrinkles and only some gray lightened the tight corkscrew curls she wore gathered at the crown of her head. Her dark brown eyes sparkled.

"Hey, baby." She tilted her cheek toward Luka for a quick kiss, then resumed seasoning a whole chicken. "Let me finish this up here, then I'll wash my hands and give you a hug."

"Need help with anything?" he asked.

"You can set the table."

"Okay. Who all is going to be here?" Luka called out as he left the kitchen.

"Regina and James, and Marcus and Ruby."

Luka nodded and gathered plates for seven, which included his siblings and brother-in-law. "Is Daniela at the bakery today?" he asked. His cousin and her family joined them for family dinners when they could, too.

"Yes, and James and the kids are doing a sports thing. Daniela's sending a couple of pies however. Apple crumb and blackberry, I think."

"I knew she was my favorite." Luka heard a laugh from the kitchen. "Where's Pop?"

"He and Marcus ran to the store and to the bakery for the pies. They'll be back soon."

Luka set the plates out and moved on to napkins and flatware, working his way around the large wooden table. "How's work been for you?"

"Oh, not bad. They're cutting staff again, and I keep reminding them that the best damn money they can spend in the hospital is on nursing." Lydia worked as the director of nursing for Bronx Presbyterian Hospital. She'd been a floor nurse for years and had gradually moved up into management. "They cut staffing, patient satisfaction scores go down, lawsuits go up, then they're scrambling to fix the issue they caused in the first place."

"They never learn, do they?" Luka asked.

"They don't seem to," Lydia agreed. "Once I'm done with the chicken, we can catch up."

With the table set, Luka wandered toward the living room. Framed family photos lined the mantel, and he smiled at himself as a toddler in one. Luka wore his father's boots and hat, dwarfed by the massive turnout gear but still grinning proudly.

On a whim, he snapped a photo of it with his phone and sent it to Kyle.

Me, aged 4.

Kyle replied almost immediately.

Adorable. Not sure I've got any, but I'll check.

Luka frowned. He couldn't imagine having grown up in Kyle's world.

I look forward to it.

Luka slipped his phone back in his pocket and picked up a photo of himself with his father. Luka was older in the photo, maybe six, and his father was pushing him on a swing at the park.

His mother approached and rested her head against Luka's upper arm.

"He was a handsome man, your daddy. You look just like him."

Luka resembled Ian Clarke in many ways, including his broad shoulders and blue eyes. Not to mention his career path. It had been hard on his mother to watch Luka enter the fire academy. She'd hated his choice to follow in his father's footsteps, and she'd cried for days after he'd told her. She'd begged him to do something else. Anything else. It had been difficult for him to stand firm, but with time, she'd come around and she'd clapped the loudest of anyone at his graduation.

"Think he'd be proud of what I've done?" Luka asked.

Lydia placed a hand on his cheek. "He'd be bursting with pride. You're a good man and a credit to his legacy."

Luka pulled his mom close. They stood silent for a few minutes before Lydia stepped back.

"I put some coffee on," she said. "Would you like some?"

Luka cleared his throat. "That would be nice. Are you sure there isn't anything you need help with?"

"Not at all. The chicken is in the oven and everything else is on hold until Tomas and Marcus come back. Your sisters won't be here for a bit yet. Come have a seat in the kitchen. I have some questions for you."

Luka followed behind her, eyes narrowed. Someone had blabbed that Luka was dating someone. Ruby, he assumed. If so, she was in serious trouble.

He sat at the table, and a few minutes later, Lydia brought over mugs of coffee and a plate of Oreo cookies, a favorite indulgence. Luka had inherited his mother's fondness for them and knew if she was sweetening him up before dinner, he was in for it.

"Your sister said you borrowed her car for a date," Lydia said.

Subtle, the Clarke women were not.

"Ruby talks a lot." Luka filched a cookie off the plate and twisted it open. "But, yes, I took him to play mini golf on Randall Island."

"What's his name?"

"Kyle McKee."

"Is he as Irish as his name makes him sound?"

Luka nodded. "Born in Vermont, but, yes."

Lydia pressed her lips together tightly. "You know I don't want to interfere, but are you sure you're making a smart choice? What if he's like Matthew? Happy to be with you until it comes time to bring you home to the family?"

Luka sighed at the mention of his ex. "Kyle is nothing like Matthew." *At all.*

"I hope not," she muttered.

Luka's mother had taken a dim view of him dating white people after Luka discovered his ex, Matthew, had been hiding Luka's race from his family. Matthew'd claimed that he'd done it to spare Luka from a nasty encounter with his bigoted parents, but Luka'd harbored doubts. He'd suspected Matthew had been ashamed of Luka and his race, and it had soured the relationship.

Luka had been young then, though, and had learned a lot since. "I'm not a kid anymore, Mom," he said gently. "I need you to trust me on this."

"I do trust you. But you have such a good heart, baby. You want to believe the best of everyone and not all of them deserve it."

"So that's it? You're just writing Kyle off before you know anything about him?" A stab of disappointment went through Luka. He loved his mom — he truly did — and knew she was just looking out for him. Her dismissal hurt however. He was a grown man. Why didn't she trust his judgment?

"I'm just saying be cautious," she said. "Don't go jumping into something until you're sure what the bottom looks like."

"I'm not jumping into anything," Luka protested. "I'm not moving in with Kyle or running off to the courthouse to get married. We're dating. I like him. It's going well so far. That's all I'm saying."

The rattle of the doorknob interrupted their tiff. "Well, it sounds like we got back just in time," a familiar voice said. "Do I need to referee?"

Luka chuckled and some of the frustration leaked out of him when he turned and saw his stepfather's wide smile.

"Hey, son," Tomas said. Like Lydia, he looked younger than his years, though silver now touched the black hair at his temples.

"Hey, Pop." Luka stood and engulfed Tomas in a hug. "I'm afraid you were right about needing a referee."

Tomas was nearly a decade younger than Lydia. Regina hadn't taken kindly to the idea of her mother dating a younger man at first, but he'd won them all over, even Regina. After the chaos of Ian Clarke's death, Tomas had been an oasis of calm to the family. The security of his safe, stable job had been a relief to all of them, and not a day went by that Luka didn't feel grateful Tomas had become a part of their lives.

It couldn't have been easy for Tomas to become a stepfather to three kids ranging in age from eleven to twenty-two, especially since they'd still been coping with their father's death. But Tomas had done it with grace and strength. He'd become a supportive male figure in Luka's life without trying to take his father's place and listened avidly when Luka and his sisters talked about Ian Clarke. Rather than pushing them to move on, Tomas'd encouraged the reminiscing. He'd never pushed them to call him Dad either. Eventually, Luka had started referring to him as Pop or Pops, and Ruby had followed suit. Regina, already in her early twenties, had simply called Tomas by name, though with great affection.

The door banged open now and Luka grabbed for it and held it open as his half-brother, Marcus, shouldered his way into the room, carrying three reusable grocery sacks. At twenty-two, Marcus was built much like Luka. Marcus had inherited the big, sturdy frames of Lydia's family as well as his father's blinding smile and quiet sense of humor.

Marcus set the bags on the kitchen table with a thump. "Why'd you leave me to get all of this out of the car, Pop?"

Tomas grinned at his younger son. "Because you're younger than me."

Marcus scowled back at him, but his eyes brightened behind his black-rimmed glasses when he turned to Luka. "I didn't know you were coming tonight."

"Surprise." Luka pulled him in for a hard hug. "Good to see you."

"You too." Marcus thumped him on the back.

"What's all this?" Lydia said as she surveyed the grocery bags. "Aside from the pies, there were only three things on the list I gave you."

"Marcus needed to do some shopping," Tomas explained.

"Are your roommates eating you out of house and home again?" Lydia asked. She shook her head. "I'm going to give those boys a talking to."

Marcus groaned. "Please don't. I'm an adult. I can deal with it."

"Why do my boys keep reminding me of how adult they are?" Lydia said with a sniff.

"Because you keep forgetting!" Luka and Marcus said, nearly in unison. They bumped fists.

Lydia threw up her hands. "Fine, fine. You're grown men," she muttered under her breath. "I'm just the woman who brought you into this world."

Marcus draped an arm over her shoulder and kissed her cheek. "I haven't forgotten. I promise."

Luka hadn't either. He respected his mom's opinion. She was a smart, capable woman, and he had no problem turning to her for advice when he needed it. But Luka hadn't asked for her opinion of Kyle, not to mention she was wrong about him. Nothing about Kyle had struck Luka as bigoted, and it irked him that his mother didn't trust her own son to make good decisions.

"Dare I ask what you two were disagreeing about?" Tomas asked. He reached into one of the bags of groceries and started withdrawing produce, which he handed to Lydia.

"Luka is dating a white boy." Lydia carried the vegetables to the counter.

Tomas raised an eyebrow. "What's the concern?"

"There isn't any on my part," Luka said. "Kyle is a great guy. His friends seem like nice people, and he's kind to every single person we encounter every time we go out. Hell, he offered to figure out legal help for a couple whose restaurant just burned up and Kyle was trapped in the fire. What more do you want from him?"

"I just think Luka should be cautious." Lydia waved a paring knife for emphasis, and Marcus stepped back with his hands up. She scowled at him, but there was humor in her eyes. "Given what happened with Matthew, it's worth Luka being wary."

"Your husband and my brother are Latino," Luka reminded her, his annoyance continuing to grow. "Since when is race an issue in this family?"

Lydia tutted. "It's different for people of color. You know that, Luka."

"Okay, so my grandmother was white," Luka pointed out. "Which means Dad was part white. Therefore, Regina and Ruby are part white, as am I. Until Kyle proves otherwise, I'm giving him the benefit of the doubt that he's not a racist asshole. I'm disappointed you won't."

He walked out of the kitchen and into the living room. He paced for a few minutes, needing the physical outlet to clear his head before he flopped onto the couch. He looked up as soft footsteps approached, unsurprised when Tomas appeared. He'd played the role as peacekeeper many times throughout Luka's life. He was good at listening and smoothing ruffled feathers so people could sit down and really discuss whatever had caused the unrest.

"Your mother didn't mean to upset you."

Luka looked up at Tomas. "I know that, but some of the things she said bother me."

"I can understand that." Tomas' tone was soothing.

"Am I being unreasonable here?" Luka asked.

"No. But I think you're being hot-headed." Tomas sat in a nearby chair.

"Wouldn't be the first time," Luka admitted.

Tomas cracked a smile. "No, it wouldn't. You got that from your mother. That's why you argue like this sometimes. But she wants what's best for you."

"I know." Luka sighed. Maybe he was being hard on his mom. Lydia had been unconditionally accepting when he'd come out as bisexual and never once treated the men or women he'd dated any differently. That's why this race thing had taken him by surprise. "I like this guy, Pop. If it gets to a point where I bring Kyle here for dinner, I don't want him to feel unwelcome."

"Give her some time. I'm sure she'll come around."

"Do I have a choice?" Luka asked.

"Not unless you're planning on ditching family dinners. And that won't work. The Clarke-Padillas are a tenacious bunch."

"Don't I know it?" Luka laughed. "You'd all show up at the firehouse with food and make me have dinner with you there."

"That sounds about right." They were both silent a moment. "C'mon. You don't have to agree with your mother, but it would be nice if you joined us while we finish getting dinner ready."

They stood and Luka walked over to lay a hand on Tomas' shoulder. "Thanks for listening."

"Any time."

In the kitchen, the scent of roasting chicken made Luka's stomach growl. "Man, that smells good."

"Dinner should be on the table in half an hour. If you're hungry, there are some vegetables and hummus in the refrigerator," Lydia offered. Her smile seemed a little forced.

"Thanks, Mom." Luka gave her a small side hug as he passed by her. His mother's comments still irritated him, but he knew they'd work through it in time.

Luka rummaged in the refrigerator for the snacks, and he'd just put together a small plate when the front door opened.

"Mom?"

"In the kitchen, Regina."

The clack of high heels on the wood floors announced Regina Owens' arrival. She stood tall, nearly five-ten, and carried herself with impeccable posture and confidence. Over the years, Luka had watched many men stop in their tracks at the sight of his sister, dazzled by her long, dramatic ringlets and beautiful smile. As the director of development for a non-profit, Regina was one of the most driven people he knew, but she was also still Luka's big sister.

"Queenie!" Luka grabbed her in a hug. He'd discovered the name Regina meant 'queen' as a young boy, and he'd used the name against her when she got bossy. Over the years, it had morphed into 'Queenie,' a nickname Regina claimed to loathe. Luka was certain she secretly loved it however.

"I didn't know you'd be here, Luka." Regina extricated herself from his hug and smoothed down her tailored dress. "And I've told you not to call me that!"

"Yeah, well, I never learn."

Regina rolled her eyes at him. "Hi, Mom." She greeted her mother with a hug and kiss. "How are you?"

"Good, baby. I'm glad you and Wade could make it." Luka could hear Regina's husband, Wade, in the living room talking with Marcus.

"How are you, Tomas?" Regina greeted her stepfather with another hug. "How's work?"

"Good," Tomas replied. "The new accountant we hired has helped make the workload more manageable. What about you?"

Wade joined them in the kitchen while Tomas and Regina chatted. He kissed Lydia's cheek. Wade's deeply toned skin, goatee and tight fade haircut gave him a strong, elegant appearance, but his dark eyes danced with light.

"Hey, Mom."

"Hey, Wade. Good to see you." The meat thermometer beeped, and Lydia patted his shoulder. "Excuse me a minute while I get that."

"What can we do to help?" Regina asked.

Lydia issued instructions with the practiced ease of a drill sergeant, and everyone sprang into action to get dinner on the table. Luka grabbed a beer for himself when he was done and held one up for Wade.

Wade took it with a nod. "Thanks, Luka."

Luka liked Wade. Despite Regina's claims that she'd never date a cop or a fireman, the Harlem police officer had won her over, and they had a happy marriage and a beautiful home. Luka knew the one thing they were missing was children. Regina didn't talk about it much, but she and Wade had been trying for years.

"How's things at the firehouse?" Wade asked.

"Good. Nothing too wild. Thankfully."

"Right?" Wade laughed. "Always a good day when it's quiet, huh?"

"For sure. How's work been for you?"

"Not bad. A detective at the 28th just put in for his retirement, and my sergeant's been pressuring me to take the exam." Wade worked in the bank robbery division of his precinct. "I know the people in the community, and we have a good relationship, so I'm definitely thinking about it. I'm just not completely sure it's the right move. It would change what I do, and I don't know that's what I want."

"Sure, I get that." Luka held out his beer bottle and tapped it on Wade's. "Here's to working a job you love, whatever it is."

"Amen to that."

"Dinner's ready, everyone!" Lydia called. "I got a text from Ruby saying she's running late so we should start without her or it'll all get cold."

Once everyone was seated and Tomas had said grace, they all dug in. Luka had just asked Marcus for the salad dressing when they heard the front door open yet again.

"Ugh. Sorry I'm late." Ruby hurried into the dining room and paused in front of the empty chair beside Luka, her hands on her hips. "You couldn't wait ten minutes?"

"If we waited for you every time you were late, we'd never eat," Luka teased.

Ruby's lateness was legendary in the family, although Luka assumed she managed to arrive on time for work and her musical gigs. She worked in the garment district with a well-known design house, and even in a creative field, he knew chronic tardiness wasn't tolerated.

Ruby thwacked Luka on the shoulder and the bangles on her wrist clacked together. "Don't be mean."

Luka pushed back from the table. "How about I get you some wine? Will you forgive me then?"

"That's an offer I'll take." Ruby kissed Luka's cheek, the tight coils of her hair brushing his skin. Always fashion-forward, she'd taken to wearing her hair in a sizeable afro lately, and Luka loved it.

"You would not believe the day I had," she said, and the babble of voices greeting her followed Luka into the kitchen.

"Anyone else want anything while I'm up?" he called out.

"I'll take another beer," Wade shouted back.

When Luka returned to the dining room with the beers and Ruby's wine, she'd taken the empty seat beside his and was talking with Regina. If Regina was the queen, Ruby was the diva. She'd always been larger than life, putting on shows for the family, creating ever more elaborate costumes and performances for them all. Even now she loved performing. She had a gorgeous voice and commanding stage presence, and she performed at various clubs around the city in her spare time.

I should take Kyle to one of her shows, Luka thought. He hadn't been in a while.

Dinner passed in a blur of good food and catching up. It was rare everyone made it, especially with Luka's and Wade's work schedules, but they came together as often as they could.

Tomas stood when everyone had eaten their fill. "Dishes, Marcus."

Marcus grumbled but he stood too and followed Tomas into the kitchen while everyone else broke off into smaller groups. Regina took the seat on Luka's other side.

"Ruby said you're dating someone."

Luka stifled a sigh. Never a moment of peace in this family. "I am. His name is Kyle. I rescued him from a fire."

Regina wrinkled her nose delicately. "A guy? Nothing serious then?"

"I never said that," Luka said, trying to keep his voice pleasant. He'd had enough with family arguments today and Regina knew how to work his last nerve. "I like Kyle a lot. He's a great guy."

She waved Luka off. "I should set you up with Shawna from the office. She's a lawyer. Very smart and attractive."

"And a woman."

"You like women."

"I do," Luka said. "I like men, too. And why is it you act like the men I date are only temporary? You never take the time to get to know them. Never offer to set me up with any of the men you work with either."

Regina straightened her shoulders. "I'm just thinking about your future in the long-term. You want a family and that's a whole lot easier with a woman, Luka. I want what's best for my brother, that's all."

"What if a white boy is what's best for me?" Luka shot back, unable to hold back any longer. Regina's eyes went wide at his tone. "Kyle is the first decent person I've met in a damn long time — male or female. I'm not throwing it away just because he happens to be a man and too white for Mom."

"Luka —" Regina protested. Their conversation had caught the attention of the others.

"No, I'm tired of this. I'm happy. Is it so much to ask for my family to be happy about it?"

Luka stood and pushed back from the table. Marcus and Tomas gave him a startled look as he strode through the kitchen and yanked open the side door. If he didn't get out of there, he'd say something he regretted. And in a situation like this, it would be like tossing an accelerant on a fire.

God, his sister drove him up the wall sometimes. Bossy and opinionated, she treated him like a son rather than a brother. Then again, Regina had been a high school senior when their father had died. With Lydia working night shifts, Regina had dealt with Luka's nightmares of being burned alive. He'd crawled into his sister's bed, sobbing, and she'd soothed him by singing him to sleep and promising she wouldn't let the fire get him.

Luka loved his sister. He loved her like crazy. But sometimes, he wanted to strangle her, too.

He heard the scuff of sneakers on the concrete, then a ball being dribbled.

"Want some company?" Marcus sounded hesitant, as if afraid Luka might take his head off. Luka couldn't blame him.

"Sure. Toss it here." Marcus passed the ball and Luka grabbed it and made an easy bank shot off the backboard. "You know, I swear, it's like Mom and Regina still think I'm a kid."

Marcus snorted. "Dude, I'm the baby of the family. They drive me nuts, too."

Luka grimaced and caught the rebounding ball. "Yeah. But I really like this guy and I think they'd like him too, if they'd just give him half a chance." He sank a jump shot next, and Marcus let out a low whistle.

"They need time," Marcus said.

"You sound like Pop."

"Well, he's usually right when he says stuff like that."

"Yeah, good point," Luka conceded. Some of his tension faded as he passed Marcus the ball. Marcus sent it swishing through the net.

"How are things with you?" Luka asked. "Classes going well?"

"Busy, but good," he said. "I should be studying right now but I needed a break." Marcus had started a master's program in biochemistry at Columbia University, and Luka knew he'd been stressed.

"Nothing wrong with giving your brain a rest from time to time," Luka replied. "Are you still seeing that girl, Kyra?"

"Nope." Marcus dribbled the ball a few times then held it against his chest. "We broke it off."

Luka walked over and clapped his brother on the shoulder. "Sorry." This was a good reminder that other people in the family were dealing with stuff too.

"Nah. It's for the best." Marcus stepped back and dribbled some more. "We've gone back and forth a few times but there were things we couldn't get past."

"You want to talk about it?"

"Nope. Thanks though."

Figuring he'd pried enough, Luka held up his hands. "Pass it back," he called, but the side door opened as he caught the ball.

"If you want dessert, you'd better come in!" Ruby called out.

Luka threw the ball back to Marcus. "Well, this was fun, but I'm out. I'm not missing out on Daniela's pies."

Marcus laughed. "Save me a piece, will ya? I'll put the ball away."

Some of the tension in the room had dissipated by the time Luka rejoined his family, and talk had turned to politics and current events as they chatted over dessert and coffee.

Luka took pieces of both blackberry and apple crumb pies and went for the blackberry first, making sure to get vanilla ice cream on his fork too. He closed his eyes with pleasure at the first bite.

I need to swing by Sugar Street soon and pick up something sweet to share with Kyle.

Luka smiled to himself. Funny how his thoughts kept coming back to Kyle. He couldn't remember the last person he'd dated who'd grabbed his attention so thoroughly.

"There's more pie left if you want it, Luka — you don't have to eat the plate," Ruby said drily after he'd scraped his dish clean.

"Ha, ha. Very funny." He sat back in his chair. "Don't tempt me. I want more, but I don't need it."

"You and me both. I don't know how Daniela stays so skinny running a bakery."

"One of life's great mysteries," Luka agreed. He stood with a groan. "I'm going to head out though. Long day tomorrow."

"Hang on a minute, will you? I'll walk to the station with you," Ruby said.

Luka said his round of goodbyes to everyone, making sure he hugged Regina and his mom, though his heart wasn't fully in it. Lydia gave him a worried look after he'd pulled back.

"I love you, baby. You be safe." She said that every time she told him goodbye, and he always answered the same way.

"I love you too, Mom." Luka kissed the top of her head. "I will."

Luka waited as patiently as he could for Ruby to wrap up her conversations, but he was at last forced to herd her out the door. Ruby's vibrant yellow heels clacked over the pavement as they walked.

"How do you manage those damn things?" he asked.

Ruby shrugged. "Practice."

"Better you than me."

"Can I see a picture of this white boy you're dating?" Ruby asked after they'd reached the train station and were waiting on the platform.

Luka eyed her warily. "I suppose." He thumbed through his photos until he found a G-rated shot he'd taken of Kyle. Ruby studied it in silence then flashed a sly grin.

"He's very good looking."

"Why do you sound so surprised?" Luka elbowed her. "He's also smart and funny, and a successful business owner. What more do they want?"

"To be sure he's treating you well. And doesn't hurt you. You were crushed after Matthew, Luka."

"I know." Luka exhaled. "But it's like Mom and Regina have already made up their minds."

"Give them a little time. They'll come around," Ruby said quietly.

"That's what everyone keeps telling me!"

"Well, maybe we know what we're talking about."

"Ugh." Luka shook himself internally. "How about you? Seeing anyone?"

"I've met a few interesting people of late." Ruby grinned again. "Broken some hearts." Ruby was in no hurry to settle down. When Lydia pestered her about being single, she'd reply she was living her best life and didn't need a man to do it. Their mother would roll her eyes, but it stopped her asking if any of the men Ruby dated were serious.

"You're a menace to humankind," Luka said.

She hooked her arm into the crook of his elbow. "I try."

Loud clicks on the tracks signaled the arrival of their train, and a minute later, Luka followed his sister aboard. He settled into the seat beside her, and when Ruby pulled out her phone, Luka followed suit, unable to resist reaching out to Kyle.

Hey. How's your night?

It only took a few minutes to get a response.

Good so far. How was your afternoon?

Not the best.

Want to come here? Unload your troubles on the bartender and enjoy a drink?

Luka smiled.

You don't have to ask me twice.

Chapter Seven

Despite being elbows-deep in an order, Kyle knew the moment Luka walked through Under's door. The speakeasy had reached capacity within an hour of opening that night and its customers were a lively bunch who filled the space with conversation and laughter. Even so, the air around Kyle buzzed as Luka crossed the room toward him.

Kyle set a deep purple cocktail on a tray of orders and flashed Luka a smile. Pleasure curled in his belly at Luka's wink. He looked stupid handsome in black jeans and a thick gray knit pullover under a denim jacket, but his big, beaming Luka-style grin was absent, replaced by tense shoulders and a tight jaw. Worse, Luka's eyes lacked some of their usual spark.

Well, that just won't do, Kyle thought.

"Can I pour you a drink, Lieutenant?" he asked once Luka had settled into a seat.

The corners of Luka's mouth quirked up at the use of his rank. "I'd love one. What are you mixing up there?"

Kyle pointed at the purple concoction. "This is Fall to Pieces," he said. "The rocks glass is a Concord Grape Transfusion, and in the martini glass we have Autumn Apple Cocktail."

"Do I sense a theme?"

"You do. We launched a new menu at the beginning of the month featuring drinks suited to harvest time." Kyle nodded at Jenna, one of Under's servers who'd come back to collect the tray of orders.

"Thanks, Kyle," she said.

"You're welcome."

Luka exchanged a quick smile with Jenna before his focus returned to Kyle. "So, the menu is seasonal?"

"Loosely, yes." Kyle leaned his elbows on the bar. Luka mirrored the gesture, bringing them closer. "We make changes based on the season, but the inspiration can come from anywhere. Colors, flavors, woods, the media. Even people. Anything goes as long as the ingredients are quality and the taste is up to standards."

Kyle cocked his head and studied Luka, pondering what he could mix up to put the shine back in his eyes. "Now for you...yeah, I've got something in mind that isn't on the menu. I've been playing with the recipe, but I think you'll like it."

He brushed the knuckles of his right hand against Luka's forearm and straightened. He measured Tincup whiskey and fresh lemon juice into a shaker, then added an egg white and measures of two syrups he'd cooked up over the weekend. He filled the shaker with ice and topped it with the metal tin, then rattled the contents with a flourish that brought Luka's good humor out of hiding.

"You're so extra."

Kyle batted his eyelashes. "You like it."

"No question." Luka laughed.

Kyle poured the mix into a coupe and garnished it with a cherry-speared lemon wedge. Luka raised his eyebrows as Kyle set it down in front of him.

"This is gorgeous." He fingered the glass's base. "What's it called?"

"Smokey Sour," Kyle replied.

Luka's eyes twinkled. "You still mixing firefighter drinks, Kyle?"

"Hah, no—the name is a coincidence. Still mixing drinks for firefighters though. Stefan and Luis were here on their nights off this week."

"Yeah? They didn't mention it. Guess they signed up for the guest list."

Kyle moved to the sink and started washing the equipment he'd used. "They came on separate nights. Stefan brought a couple of friends, and Luis had a date with him."

"Trying to impress her," Luka said, his tone approving. "Go, Luis."

"He tried," Kyle replied. "His girl ordered the Hot Firefighter and Luis practically melted."

"Oh, jeez. That boy is a fucking nerd." Luka's laughter set Kyle chuckling, too.

"We've had lots of requests for the firefighter cocktails since the party, so I expect I'll keep mixing them." He watched with interest as Luka lifted his glass to his lips and sipped.

"Whoa." Luka held it away from himself and examined its contents. "Sweet and spicy. Cinnamon, right? And something smoky down low."

Kyle nodded. "There's cinnamon bark for spice and the smoke is from lapsang souchong tea. I made the syrups myself. What do you think?"

"I think it's delicious. And that you're an even bigger nerd than Luis with your syrup making. Totally worth the effort though. My sister, Ruby, would be all over this."

Right — the family. Kyle figured one of them had put that wistful expression in Luka's gaze. He had a sinking suspicion he knew the root of the problem, too. Kyle dried his hands and settled his elbows on the bar again.

"You told me Ruby works in design, right?" he asked.

"Yep. Kind of marches to the beat of her own drum, if you know what I mean." Luka sipped his cocktail again.

"Sure, I get that. Is she your favorite sister?"

Luka looked as though he was biting back a grin. "We-l-l... I always say my cousin Daniela is my favorite sister. She's the baker and buys my affection with food. She couldn't make dinner tonight, so she sent over dessert and it was phenomenal, as usual. The blackberry pie about killed me."

Kyle grumbled. "Dude, you're killing me here. No fair."

"Sorry," Luka said with a soft laugh. "I thought you'd enjoy trying it yourself sometime actually."

He laid a big hand over Kyle's forearm where it rested on the bar. "To answer your original question, Ruby's the sister I talk with the most. We're closest in age, and we probably understand each other best among the siblings. She's open-minded and doesn't judge. I can't always say the same about the rest of the family unfortunately."

Yeah, that's not good.

Kyle could guess what Luka would say next. He just hoped this wouldn't be the end of things. He really liked this big, handsome firefighter. Far more than he should, given he already knew at least some of Luka's family didn't dig the fact Luka was into both men and women.

Kyle moved his hand to cover Luka's and kept his tone gentle. "Did your other sister give you shit again?"

"Regina is the one who disapproves of my being bi. She won't come out and say it, of course, so she talks around it but everything implies disapproval." Luka sighed. "It's tiring."

"I'm sure she just wants what's best for you," Kyle offered, but his words made Luka's expression darken.

"Yeah, that's what she says, but she can't truly mean it, Kyle. Not when she dismisses people from my life based on their gender. What if the best thing for me is a man and not some lady lawyer named Shawna?"

"This is off topic, but if you dated the lawyer, you'd have one hell of a cutesy couple name," Kyle said, his tone dry. "I mean, it's hard to beat a portmanteau like 'Shawka.'"

Luka gaped for a silent second then burst out laughing. The sound warmed Kyle down to his toes.

"You're a weird dude, but I like it," Luka said, the affection in his voice unmistakable.

"I come from a long line of weirdos," Kyle replied. "But I've got just the one brother, so at least it's semi-contained." A thought struck him, and he patted Luka's hand. "C'mon. Keep me company on my break."

Kyle waved at Jeff, the second bartender, to signal he'd be stepping away, then walked around the bar. He led Luka to the office, and Luka's eyes brightened as Kyle unlocked the door.

"Damn, I get to see the inner sanctum? I thought you guys didn't let people in here." He laughed at Kyle's snort.

"Jes and I don't let everyone in here, that's true," Kyle said. "But friends and family are welcome on occasion."

Inside the office, Kyle left Luka to look around and went to the mini-fridge for a mineral water. He settled himself on the big leather sofa and noted Luka's unabashed admiration of the liquors on the bar cart.

"You guys don't fool around. I don't even recognize half of these names, but I can tell it's premium shit."

"Jesse's the Scotch drinker," Kyle said. "I'm more of a bourbon man, but I'm also a tequila lover. A really good, simple margarita is a thing of beauty. Rocks, salt, lime juice and booze — perfect. Please, help yourself if you're not feeling that cocktail."

"No need. I'm enjoying this," Luka replied. He raised his glass once more and sipped. "I meant it when I said Ruby would like it, too."

"She's welcome anytime, with or without you."

Luka raised a brow. "You mean that, don't you? You're not just being polite?" he asked, his tone teasing. "Because she will show up, and she might drag one or more of my siblings with her."

"Of course, I mean it." Kyle laughed. "The more the merrier." He waited for Luka's smile before he spoke again.

"My brother's coming in from Boston next week, and we'll drive up to Vermont together on the weekend for a thing. What do you think about grabbing some dinner with Ollie before he and I head out? It's cool if you can't or don't want to," he added quickly as Luka's expression sobered. "I know we haven't been seeing each other very long, so I get it if you think — "

"I think you wanting me to meet your brother is great," Luka said, his voice soft.

Despite his words, some of the light had drained out of Luka again, and Kyle's stomach twisted.

"Hey," he said. "Luka, come here." He waited until Luka sat beside him on the couch before he gripped Luka's shoulder. "What's wrong? I mean it — you don't have to meet Oliver. You will get zero pressure from me to do things you don't want."

Luka set his glass on the low table in front of them and laid a hand on Kyle's thigh. "It's not that. I'm happy to meet him. I'm...blown away that you'd ask. But at the same time, I'm not surprised at all because it fits with the guy I've been getting to know." He leaned in and covered Kyle's mouth with a kiss so tender Kyle's throat ached.

Kyle forced a smile after Luka leaned back again. "You've already met my closest friends," he said and kept his voice light. "My dad's gone, and my mother doesn't give a shit — Ollie's the most important person in my life. Why wouldn't I introduce you?"

"Not everyone's like you, McKee. The more time I spend with you, the more I realize that." Luka gave him a small smile. "I haven't dated as many men as I have women and...well, I've only ever dated one other white person. And Matthew did a real number on my head."

Kyle hid his surprise and frowned. "What happened?"

"It's not so much what he did as what he didn't do. Matthew was great. We had a lot of fun together, and I liked him a lot. I'd started to think we had something, you know? Something long term. He worked in tech at one of the big financial firms downtown and coming uptown drove him nuts because he was constantly on-call. We spent all our time together at his place in the West Village." Luka rubbed his chin with his hand.

"One Saturday, we were walking around the flea market in Chelsea, and I heard someone call his name. And Matthew just went pale. I didn't even realize that could happen because his ass was at least as white as yours — I thought maybe he felt sick, for Christ's sake." Luka shot Kyle a smirk to soften his words. "Turned out his sister had spotted him in the crowd and wanted to say hi."

Kyle stayed silent. He knew from Luka's grim expression he had more to say, and that it wouldn't be pleasant. He gave Luka's shoulder a gentle squeeze.

"I figured out from the get-go his sister had no idea Matthew and I were together. I mean, no wonder when Matthew introduced me as a friend, right? 'Oh, hey, Claire, this is my friend, Luka. We play in the same softball league.' I just stood there like a fool because I didn't know what to say." Luka blew a noisy breath out through his nose.

"Matthew was out to his family, so I knew his sister wouldn't be surprised to see him with a guy. She seemed tense while they talked though. She kept looking between Matthew and me like she could tell we were hiding something from her. I knew from her expression she wouldn't like it."

"What happened?" Kyle asked again. He couldn't bear the tight set of Luka's jaw or the way his lips pursed, like he'd tasted something bitter.

"Nothing. They said goodbye and promised to see each other for dinner at their parents' house the following week. I waited until Matthew and I were away from the crowd before I confronted him about the 'friends' thing. He admitted he hadn't told his family about us. He wouldn't give me a real answer as to why, but I'm not stupid." Luka picked up his drink. "I asked him straight out if it was because I'm black. Matthew didn't have an answer for that either, but he sure as hell didn't say 'no.'"

"Fuck." Kyle swallowed against the outrage and hurt stirring inside him on Luka's behalf. The idea anyone could be so cruel and petty over the shade of a person's skin or who they loved, or which fucking sky spirit they worshiped... Goddamn, people were exhausting.

"Anyway. We never made it back from that," Luka said. "Matthew finally explained his parents wouldn't have approved. He said he'd wanted to spare my feelings, but I didn't know if I could believe him. I did know he'd decided it was better to hide me from his family than tell them the truth. And, really, where could we go from there?

"As you can imagine, my mother was pissed after she found out what happened. She never forgave Matthew for the way he acted. I found out yesterday that she hasn't forgotten either."

Oh.

A chill passed over Kyle. "She thinks I might do that to you?" he asked. He fixed his eyes on the drink in Luka's hand but sensed Luka's regret in his long pause.

"She doesn't know you, Kyle," Luka said at last. "But she's worried about me being hurt."

Kyle hauled in a deep breath. This...was not good. Two strikes against him, both with Luka's family for fuck's sake, and over things Kyle absolutely couldn't control. A smart man would walk away now before he got in any deeper and save himself some pain. Kyle couldn't do it though, not with Luka already hurting. He could ease some of that. And, frankly, he just liked Luka too fucking much.

"I can't fix what happened with Matthew," he said. He wove his fingers with Luka's. "Or make your sister or your mom trust that you know what's best for you. But I can tell you that I'm excited for my brother to meet you, Luka, whenever you're ready for that. I know Ollie's going to like you because he's one of the best people I know."

Luka's raspy chuckle made it possible for Kyle to lift his gaze, and Luka kissed him, his hands warm and strong.

Lust bolted straight through Kyle. Without a second thought, he climbed into Luka's lap, sliding his knees over Luka's powerful thighs to hug his hips. Kyle's head spun as the kiss lengthened. His cock hardened at Luka's low groan.

Heat flooded Kyle's veins. God, he wanted to crawl inside this man. He ground down slowly, making sure their bodies touched wherever possible. Luka ran his hands over Kyle's back, his motions rough and hungry, and dropped one to squeeze Kyle's ass. Kyle wrenched his lips free with a grunt.

"Damn, you are killing me, Clarke." He pressed his forehead against Luka's, and they shared a breathless laugh.

"No chance there's another door out of here, huh?" Luka rubbed circles of warmth into Kyle's lower back.

"There's the fire door," Kyle muttered. "But I can't leave Jeff alone. Ditching him would be a shitty thing to do."

"Such a good guy." Luka grinned at Kyle's raised eyebrow.

"Says the man who runs into fires and not away from them." He dropped a lingering kiss against Luka's lips and sat back onto Luka's knees. "I should get out there actually. Any chance you feel like hanging around tonight until I can leave?"

"What time is last call?"

"Two a.m. on Sundays, but I'll leave around midnight. Jeff's scheduled to close." Kyle watched Luka's smile broaden.

"I can do that. You gonna comp me all night again?"

"Duh, of course. In fact, you can help me taste test a couple more things I've been working on."

Kyle'd started clambering off Luka's lap when the office door opened, flooding the room with noise and surprising them both.

"Hey, babe—oh, fuck. Sorry, my bad."

The familiar voice that rung through the space almost knocked Kyle off balance.

"Jes?" He shot a glance back over his shoulder, and sure enough, Jesse stood in the open doorway, his eyes big. "What are you doing here?" Kyle asked. "Just— well, come in and shut the door, for starters."

The door swung shut and muted the music and bar sounds again, and Luka held on to Kyle's waist, steadying him as he got to his feet. Kyle gave Luka a hand up, then turned back to Jesse, who still stood by the door. Jesse was smiling now, but a tightness lingered around his eyes that Kyle didn't like.

"Jes, you remember Luka."

Kyle's words got Jesse moving and he stepped forward with his hand outstretched.

"Of course. It's good to see you at Under again, Luka."

Jesse's tone held a practiced smoothness Kyle had heard a multitude of times over the last two years. This was Jesse the businessman and charmer, the man who could sweet talk his way in and out of just about anything. For the first time ever, that tone struck the wrong note in Kyle's head. He worried his bottom lip with his teeth as his friend chatted with Luka and waited for a pause in the conversation.

"Do you need something, Jes?"

Jesse put his hands on his hips. "Just a quick word. And I apologize for busting in on you like this. Jeff didn't mention you had company when Cam and I got here."

Ah. With Cam in tow, Kyle knew what Jesse wanted from him. Kyle had other plans tonight however, and they did not involve Jesse, Cam or anyone other than the big man standing at his side.

"No worries. Luka and I were just on our way back out to the bar anyway." Kyle turned to Luka, whose blue eyes were practically dancing with amusement. He looked like a kid who'd been caught with his hand in the cookie jar and didn't give a damn what kind of trouble he might be in.

Kyle smirked. This man was going to kill him.

"I'll meet you out there," he said. "I'm sure you and Cam can find some kind of trouble to get up to while Jesse asks me his burning questions."

"Sure." Luka gave Kyle's waist a squeeze then headed for the door.

Kyle turned and picked up the empty glass Luka had left behind. "What's up, babe?" He moved past Jesse to the bar cart.

"Cam's got the day off from school tomorrow, and we came by to see if you'd like to come by after you'd finished." Luka closed the door behind him, and Jesse cleared his throat. "I had no idea you'd be entertaining someone mid-shift though. Especially in here."

Kyle faced Jesse. "I took a break. Luka and I were talking."

"Talking to each other's tonsils, you mean." Jesse frowned. "We agreed we wouldn't fuck around in here with anyone but each other."

Kyle frowned right back. "We weren't fucking around. Yeah, I kissed Luka, but I'm sure you've done the same in here and more with Cam and God knows who else."

Jesse's cheeks flushed pink. "Kissing yes, but no, nothing else. I've never brought any hook-up in here besides Cam." His eyes snapped with fire. "I'm slutty, Kyle, but I can respect a rule that's in place for good reason. You ought to know that, considering I'm the one who made the rule, in partnership with one of my best friends."

Kyle swallowed. Fuck. Too many conversations between Jesse and himself seemed to go wrong lately.

"You're not slutty," he said, his voice low. He stepped forward and took hold of one of Jesse's hands. "You're...you. I know you respect the rule. I do, too. Luka and I were not fucking around in here. I wouldn't do that to you or him."

Some of the tension in Jesse's frame faded. He nodded, his mouth still pressed flat. "So, this thing you have with him is more than fucking around?"

"Feels like it. We've been out a few times." Kyle licked his lips. "Our schedules make connecting tricky, so we're still figuring that part out. It's been good though."

"That's great." Jesse gave him a crooked smile. "Good to hear the ban on men has been lifted. How long has this been going on?"

"A few weeks. He asked me out after the fire at Burger Barn."

"The night the squad from the firehouse came in?" Jesse's smile faded at Kyle's nod. "How come I'm just hearing about this now? Do the rest of the guys know?"

"Malcolm does. We go to yoga every Sunday and it came up. I told Carter, too, and Ri," Kyle said. "I haven't talked to David, but I messaged with Will last week and I mentioned it. You haven't been around, Jes. You've been in London every other week the past month, and you're busy when you're back in New York with a brand-new niece to spoil. How is Caroline, by the way?" Jesse's brother and sister-in-law had welcomed a baby girl at the beginning of the month, and one of Jesse's favorite things was singing Neil Diamond's *Sweet Caroline* to his niece.

"She's fucking adorable, of course, and Eric and Sara are sappier over each other than ever before. Don't change the subject." Jesse shook his head, his heavy eyebrows drawn. "You and I talk at least once a week whether I'm out of town or not."

"About business, yeah. Luka and me…that's my life, not business. I don't want to squeeze in talk about life between financial reports and hiring decisions."

Jesse sighed. "What do you want from me, Kyle? I know I've been a shitty friend, but I'm trying to be better. Fuck a duck."

"Hey, come on." Jesse swearing about waterfowl was rarely a good thing. Kyle leaned against the desk and dragged Jesse with him. "I don't want anything from you that you're not willing to give. I get that you're still figuring out how your schedule works now that things have picked up in London and with Cam in the picture. I'm happy you're happy, babe, and that you've got so much good stuff going on. Just…keep in mind that the world doesn't stand still because you're busy, okay?"

Jesse made a face. "Meaning what?"

"That I'm dating someone new. That Malcolm's been wrapped up with his mom's house on Staten Island. Will and David are talking about adopting another dog. Carter's doc tweaked his anxiety meds and he's having trouble adjusting. He even said the other day he wasn't sure you'd be able to run the marathon with him." Kyle licked his lips as Jesse's face fell. "Stuff happens, Jes, and not just to you. I know you're trying to be more plugged in —"

"But I need to try harder," Jesse finished.

"If that's what you want, yeah. A couple of calls around to people that aren't about work will do it."

"Of course, that's what I want." Hurt filtered across Jesse's face. "I'll do better with you and the other guys. In fact, Cam and I came here tonight to see you and spend time catching up. I figured you guys could game, too."

Kyle allowed himself a slow smile. "What would you be doing while this gaming occurred?"

"Catching up on some work. It's true I'm too busy to even breathe right now." Jesse cut his eyes at Kyle. "But after I'd finished, I could distract you both." His leer made Kyle laugh.

"Any other night and I'd be happy to be distracted, but I've already got plans with a handsome man tonight."

Jesse's eyes gleamed. "Dude, bring Luka along. I am all over getting up in that big guy's business, if you know what I mean. I could climb him like a tree."

"Nope." Kyle put a hand over Jesse's mouth. "Not happening. You put that thought out of your filthy brain right the fuck now."

Jesse leaned back and away from Kyle's hand. "Ugh, you're no fun. You need to learn to share your nice things with others."

"Luka is mine." Kyle pinched Jesse's side and made him squawk. "Now quit whining and come help me mix drinks so he and Cam don't think we've forgotten about them."

* * * *

"Did you want to head over to Jesse's tonight? Because we could have." Luka ran his nose over the nape of Kyle's neck. They lay boneless and content in Kyle's bed, the sheets tangled around them, and Kyle smiled.

"You sayin' you'd rather be there with them than here with me, Clarke?" He put a hand over the arm Luka had slung around his waist.

"Definitely not." Luka kissed Kyle's shoulder. "Just curious, that's all. I don't mind spending time with your friends when we're together."

"I'll keep that in mind." Kyle rolled over and faced him. He scanned Luka's sleepy expression and felt smug—no signs of stress in his face now. "I turned them down because I'm more interested in hanging out with you. But in the interest of full disclosure, I should mention that Jesse and Cam had more on the agenda planned than gaming." He saw the penny drop in the way Luka's eyes widened fractionally.

"I see. So-o-o Fallout is, what—foreplay for you and Cam?"

Kyle laughed so hard tears leaked from his eyes. "Oh, man, I'm telling Cam you said that. He will love it. But, no, we don't game before we start fooling around."

"What would have been different about tonight?"

"Jes is feeling guilty about going MIA for so long. Cam too, I think. I guess they figured they'd sweeten the pot and mix in more than just sex. That's my preference anyway, and they know it." Kyle brushed his knuckles against the scant hair on Luka's sternum. "I like dinner and a show, if you know what I mean."

Luka chuckled. "I do, yeah. Your...evenings with them go for a while, huh?"

"If we plan them out beforehand, sure. We usually make food and drinks at Jesse and Cam's and hang out for a while before anything else. Maybe watch a movie or go out dancing. But other times, they'll show up at Under the way they did tonight, and we skip the rest and just fuck like minks."

"Wow." Luka let out his own belly laugh. "You think Jesse and Cam wanted that?"

"I know they did. Jesse told me as much while we were talking in the office. He also made sure to mention that you were more than welcome to join in."

"How very generous of him." Luka shook his head. "How does it work when the three of you are together?"

"You mean, who's on top and when? You're such an alpha male," Kyle snarked, and Luka broke up laughing again.

"Hey, the engineer in me wants to understand the mechanics!"

"Yeah, okay. The answer is we're all flexible."

"Thanks to the yoga."

"Hah, you goof." Kyle stroked Luka's ribs with his fingers. "I meant that we do what feels good in the moment. All three of us are vers, which makes it easy to go with the flow."

"Fuck." Luka hummed. "I told you I've never hooked up with more than one guy before."

"But you're thinking about it now, right?"

"Maybe?" Luka rolled up on his elbow and snugged in closer to Kyle. "I guess I'm curious. About you more than anything else. I mean...you're so hot." He slid his knee between Kyle's. "I feel like watching you with another man would be mind-blowing."

Kyle's body responded to the idea. "I like the idea of you watching," he murmured.

Luka moved his hand from Kyle's waist and palmed his hardening cock. "Yeah, you do. A lot." Another hum rumbled through Luka's chest, and Kyle's shaft twitched under his touch. "You like being watched?"

"I don't know, maybe." Kyle closed his eyes. Heat spread through him in a slow wave. "When I'm with Jes and Cam, sometimes Cam pulls back while Jes and I keep going. All of us like that, especially Cam. With you there—" Kyle broke off and bucked his hips as Luka took him in hand. "Mmm, Luka."

Luka bent down and pressed his mouth close to Kyle's ear. "With me there, what?" he asked, his tone teasing. His deep voice prickled Kyle's nerves and raised goosebumps on his skin.

"It'd be even more intense." Kyle slid his arms around Luka's neck. "You could just watch if you wanted," he got out between kisses. "Don't have to join in if you don't want. Just watch us like porn."

Luka hauled him closer. "The more you talk, the more I like this idea. Tell me what they'd do to you," he demanded.

Luka rolled on top of Kyle and kissed him until he could barely string two words together. Kyle liked that just fine.

Chapter Eight

"I can't remember the last time we had a night that slow, can you?" Lane tossed a pair of shorts into her bag.

Out of habit, Luka glanced at the clock on the wall of the locker room to be sure she hadn't jinxed them. Nothing guaranteed a call coming in like talking out loud about a slow night, but nah, they were safe. Luka could hear the next shift filtering in, and he and Lane were off duty as of now.

"Same, actually." Luka closed his locker. "I got a solid amount of sleep for the first time in forever."

"I know. I don't know what to do with myself!"

"You could always visit that girl of yours."

"Yeah, I dunno. I think maybe stuff with Charita is fizzling out," Lane said as they left the locker room. "She's not on board with my schedule, and she freaked out over the thing that happened last week when that dude took a baseball bat to the rig."

"Ugh. I've been there. Way too many times to count."

Lane nudged Luka with her elbow. "How about you? How are things with the sexy bartender?"

A wide grin split Luka's face before he could stop it. "They're going really, really well."

He was half-afraid to say that for fear of jinxing it too — firefighters were a superstitious lot when it came right down to it — but things with Kyle just felt right.

"Damn." Lane sounded envious. "They must be for you to look like that."

Aside from the bullshit with Luka's family, everything with Kyle had been great. "It's...seamless, you know? None of the usual games or bullshit where we're holding back or trying to pretend like we don't want to be together. It's a refreshing change of pace."

"I'm happy for you," Lane said. She waved goodbye to her work partner, Michaela, and Munson. "A part of me wants to punch that stupid look off your face, but I'm happy for you."

"Thanks, asshole," Luka said with a laugh. "Thanks a lot."

"Yeah, anytime," she said. "You off to see your man then?"

Luka considered the idea. Thanks to both his and Kyle's work schedules, they'd had little time together lately. And if Kyle would be gone for a few days, why not sneak in some alone time before Oliver showed up?

"We had plans to meet up later today so he could introduce me to his brother — they're going on a road trip this weekend. Now that I think about it, maybe I'll go straight there. Kyle said he'd be doing laundry and stuff around his apartment today. I was planning to crash at home, but now that I don't need to..." Luka nodded. "Yup. I'm heading to Kyle's."

"Go get 'em, tiger," Lane said.

"If I never heard those words come out of your mouth again, I'd die a happy man."

* * * *

It took nearly an hour to get from the station house to Chelsea. Luka jogged up the stairs to Kyle's door with high spirits. A decent night's sleep and the prospect of a few extra hours with his man had him in a good mood nothing could shake.

Luka restrained himself from pounding on the door. He'd systematically cleared apartment buildings countless times with a good heavy knock and "Fire Department! Open up!" However, Luka suspected neither Kyle nor his neighbors would appreciate that approach and gently rapped his knuckles on the door instead.

Luka shifted his duffel bag higher on his shoulder as he waited, anticipation building in his stomach. When the door opened to a shocked-looking Kyle, Luka grinned at him. "Surprise!"

"Hey! What are you doing here?"

Kyle raked a hand through his wet hair, his expression puzzled. Unease stirred in Luka's gut. This was far from the enthusiastic welcome he'd expected.

"I had a great shift and actually slept last night, so I decided to come here straight from work rather than go home for a few hours first. Hopefully, it's a good surprise?"

"Yeah, sure, definitely."

Luka nodded toward the doorway. "Uh, are you gonna let me in?"

Kyle grimaced. "Oh, man, I'm sorry. Of course. I just want to talk to you first."

Luka heard a door open inside the apartment, then a tall guy wearing nothing but a white towel stepped into his field of vision. The guy scrubbed another towel across his hair as he walked across the room, and despite Luka's better instincts, his gaze was drawn to the water dripping down the pale skin of the guy's chest and across the abdomen, both muscular and lean.

"Kyle, I used up the last of the shampoo..." Half-naked guy stopped dead in his tracks as he met Luka's gaze. "Oh, hi there."

Luka's stomach gave an odd lurch. It was one thing to talk with Kyle about watching him with Jesse and Cam, but meeting a random hook-up was another thing entirely. Luka stifled a sigh. Beyond a passing comment or two, he and Kyle hadn't discussed where their relationship was headed or what the parameters were. It looked like they'd be having it sooner rather than later now though.

Luka glanced back at Kyle. "Is this what you wanted to talk to me about?"

"Yeah." Kyle rubbed the back of his neck with one hand. "Oliver got here early."

Luka's gazed flicked back and forth between the two men. *Oliver? But isn't that...?*

The anxious feeling in the pit of his stomach melted. He hadn't even considered the idea Kyle's brother could be in his apartment.

Luka laughed. "Right. Your brother."

Kyle went even paler than usual. "Oh, no, Luka. Did you think...?"

Luka shrugged. "Well, it's still early in the morning, your hair is wet, this guy walks out of the bathroom half-naked, and...yeah. Without context, my brain went places."

Oliver's eyes got comically large. "Oh, shit! You're Luka. Um, it's great to meet the guy my brother is so smitten with and all, but I'd rather do it with pants on. So, I'm gonna go take care of that and give you two a moment to talk." He reached for a backpack on the couch and fled into the bathroom.

Luka sagged against the doorframe. "Surprise?"

Kyle let out a chuckle and opened the door wider. "Let's start from scratch. Please, come in, Luka. I'm glad to see you."

Once inside the apartment and the door shut behind him, Luka dropped his bag on the floor and held his arms out. Kyle stepped into them willingly, and Luka captured his mouth for a quick but heartfelt kiss.

"That was awkward," Luka said when he drew back.

Kyle gave him a squeeze. "To say the least."

"Oliver got here early?" Luka prompted.

Kyle straightened, but he didn't let Luka go. "He made good time last night and decided to drive straight through. He got in at about two a.m. and crashed." Kyle jerked his thumb to indicate the rumpled blankets and pillow on the couch.

"Well, I thought I'd come over so we could have some alone time together before he arrived, and we all went out to dinner. You know what they say about good intentions and all."

Kyle grimaced. "The timing couldn't have been worse."

"No harm done," Luka assured him. "I feel like a complete asshole though."

"Why?"

Luka bit his lip. "I kinda checked out your brother."

Kyle snorted. "Well, don't tell him. His ego doesn't need it. But under the circumstances, I think I can forgive you."

"We're good then?" Luka pulled him closer.

"Yeah, we're good." Kyle smiled. "Thanks for not flying off the handle when all the signs pointed to something else going on."

"Frankly, I was still trying to process," Luka said. "Enjoying checking out the hot half-naked guy on one hand and feeling conflicted over meeting a hook-up on the other."

Kyle rubbed Luka's back. "Let's talk more about that soon. I know we discussed the thing with Jesse and Cam, but I haven't hooked up with anyone since you and I started seeing each other, and —"

The door to the bathroom swung open, stopping Kyle mid-sentence. Oliver poked his head out. "Is it safe to come out?"

"If you have pants on, yes." Kyle aimed a glance at his brother.

"I am fully dressed."

Luka looked at Oliver as he emerged from the bathroom. With the pieces in place, Luka could see the resemblance between the brothers. Equally dark-haired and fair-skinned, Oliver was tall and rangy like Kyle, though his shoulders weren't as broad. Something about his dark brown eyes seemed very familiar, and under other circumstances, Luka might have picked up on it.

"It's great to meet you." Oliver reached out and shook Luka's hand. "Kyle tells me you saved his life."

"Just doing my job."

"And he's modest, too." Oliver smiled at his brother. "Where do you find these guys, Kyle?"

"In burning restaurants," Kyle said in a deadpan tone. "I wouldn't recommend it."

Luka snickered.

"I know we talked about doing dinner, but since we're all here now, why don't we grab breakfast?" Kyle suggested. "Unless you've already eaten, Luka?"

"I had a smoothie at the station earlier, but I could go for more," Luka said.

"Well, I'm starving so I'm in. Can we go to that hipster diner place?" Oliver asked.

Kyle frowned. "This is Chelsea. Hipster diners are on every block, so you're going to have to be more specific."

"Well, the one we went to last time," Oliver replied. "Where I had the cheddar grits I liked so much?"

"Oh! The one around the corner on 10th? Sure," Kyle said.

"I've been thinking about those grits since the last time I visited," Oliver said in a wistful tone.

Kyle glanced at Luka. "Sound good to you?"

"Sounds great. Mind if I leave my bag here?"

"Not at all." Kyle glanced over at his brother. "You ready to go?"

"Yep. Just let me grab my wallet and phone."

"How'd you discover this place?" Luka asked as they headed for the door.

"Oh, just wandering around the neighborhood," Kyle replied. "It's less than a ten-minute walk. Their breakfasts are fantastic."

Luka raised an eyebrow. "Why haven't you taken me there yet?"

"I made you pancakes."

"Yeah, you did." Luka smirked at him. "They were damned good, too."

Oliver clapped them both on the back. "Less talking about food, guys, and more going to get some. I am starved. Kyle didn't feed me last night."

"I'm going, I'm going," Kyle said. "And I made a damn potful of spaghetti for you at two o'clock in the morning, Ollie. What are you talking about?"

"So, what do you do?" Luka asked Oliver when they'd reached the street and fell into step.

"As little as possible," Oliver said with a smug look.

Kyle aimed a glare at his brother. "Ollie has a BA in linguistics and an ESL certification."

"English as a second language?" Luka asked.

"Yeah," Oliver replied. "I float from school to school along the Eastern Seaboard as needed, so I'm kind of nomadic."

"Interesting. You enjoy it?"

"I love it. Teaching students who are so eager to learn is hugely fulfilling, and I enjoy not being tied down anywhere. What about you? Are you happy with the FDNY?"

"Oh, I love my job," Luka said. "It veers between tedious and exhilarating, depending on the day, but there's nothing I'd rather do."

On a Thursday morning, the Old Amsterdam Diner was busy but not packed, and they were seated without delay. The place was upscale — a swanky version of an Art Deco diner — and the smells were mouth-watering.

Kyle ordered a pitcher of Bloody Mary and a basket of buttermilk biscuits. Oliver flashed a grin at the waitress.

"I want a vat of your cheddar grits, too," he said.

She blinked at him. "A vat, huh?"

"He means the largest order you have," Kyle said with a laugh.

Oliver nodded. "Yes, that. With two sunny-side-up eggs and a side of sausage. Please and thank you."

Luka ordered a scrambled egg breakfast sandwich and Kyle the smoked salmon pastrami and poached eggs, and Luka teased him about the lack of pancakes.

"I saw they had Vermont maple syrup, Kyle."

"Which I'll get my fill of this weekend," Kyle replied. "Plus bring some bottles home."

"Now you're talking," Luka said with relish. "You know I'll expect you to make pancakes for me again as soon as you get back, right?"

Kyle's grin was slow. "I think that can be arranged."

"If you guys weren't so grossly cute together, I'd say it's a shame you snatched Luka up before I could meet him, Kyle," Oliver said from across the table. Luka remembered then that Kyle had told him Oliver identified as bi or pan.

"You might have more luck meeting someone if you stayed in one place instead of moving around all the time," Kyle said. "It's a bit harder when you're a nomad."

"Where would you suggest I live? New York?" Oliver shot back.

"You love it here when you visit."

"Yet I have no desire to settle down in one place."

Luka smothered a laugh at the squabbling.

"Sorry." Kyle glanced over at him as he spread butter on a biscuit. "When we get on a roll..."

"I get it," Luka said. "You should see me with my sisters."

"How many sisters do you have?" Oliver asked.

"Two."

Oliver looked intrigued. "Either of them hot and single?"

Kyle snorted, which turned into a coughing fit, and Luka glanced over at him to be sure he wasn't actually choking on biscuit before answering Oliver.

"Ruby is single. She works for a fashion house here in Chelsea, and she's a hell of a singer."

"If she's half as pretty as you, I'm in," Oliver said with a wink.

"She got the blue eyes from our dad like I did," Luka said. "More style and vocal talent though."

Oliver nodded. "She sounds gorgeous. You'll have to make introductions."

"Uuuuuuh." Kyle buried his head in his hands. "Please, no."

Luka chuckled. "I can just imagine my mom's head exploding. 'Two white boys? Why, God?'"

Oliver looked back and forth between them. "Your mom's not okay with the race thing?"

"Not particularly." Luka sighed. "There's some history there with an ex of mine. She'll come around eventually. It just sucks right now."

"Ah, got it." Oliver shared a look with Kyle. "It sounds like it's coming from a good place at least," he said, his voice sober. "Good to know your mom cares. Our mom didn't want kids. She cared for Kyle and me, but she wasn't particularly loving or nurturing."

"Oh, man, I can't imagine that," Luka said, shaking his head. He'd never doubted how much his mother loved him for a second in his life. "My mom may occasionally go too far in the other direction but..."

Kyle shrugged, his tight expression broadcasting discomfort. "Oliver and I have each other, even if we don't get together as much as we'd like."

"True enough."

The conversation moved on to other topics, and Luka enjoyed getting to know Oliver more. He seemed comfortable with Luka and Kyle's relationship and any reservations Luka might have had melted away.

After breakfast, Oliver paused on the sidewalk outside the diner. "Okay, here's the plan. I'm going to clear out for the day." Kyle opened his mouth, but Oliver made a slashing motion with his hand. "Look, we're not planning to leave until tomorrow anyway. I've got some stuff I want to do while I'm here in New York, and I'm sure you guys want time together. It's a win-win."

Kyle shook his head. "By stuff to do, I assume you mean someone you want to hook up with?"

"It's possible." Oliver's grin was sly. "Don't you worry your pretty head about it. I'll be back in time to get plenty of sleep tonight. But just to be on the safe side, I'll call on my way back to your place. I think there's been enough awkward pants-less moments for the three of us today."

"You're right about that," Kyle said with a laugh. "Go do your thing and I'll see you when you get back."

Luka stuck a hand out. "If I don't see you later, it was great meeting you, Oliver."

Oliver shook Luka's hand, then pulled him in for a half-hug. "You too, Luka. I'm sure I'll see you again."

Luka's chest warmed. Oliver seemed sure Luka and Kyle would be together in the future, and that was a good thought. After the stress from the Clarke-Padilla family, an open and welcoming attitude from the McKee side was a relief.

* * * *

Luka flipped onto his side and propped himself up on one elbow. Kyle gave him a lazy, sated smile. The moment they'd gotten back to the apartment, they'd been all over each other. They'd made it inside, but barely, and only gone into the bedroom because they needed condoms and lube. Luka had even contemplated always carrying some with him. Not that he was complaining. Kyle had pushed him down onto the bed and ridden him hard.

No, he had no complaints at all.

Luka leaned down and pressed his lips to Kyle's in a slow, thorough kiss. "That was nice of your brother to clear out," he said when he drew back. Luka skimmed his nose along Kyle's throat before nipping at the soft skin there.

"Mmm, I'll have to thank him." Kyle sounded a little breathless.

Kyle dragged his blunt nails down Luka's back, making him shudder. He'd catch shit at the station if Kyle left marks, but Luka couldn't be bothered to care.

He wanted to keep going, and he didn't think Kyle would argue either, but a thought had been nagging at him since before breakfast. Luka drew back with a reluctant sigh.

"We should have that talk now. About whether or not we're seeing anyone else."

Kyle sighed, too, but he shifted on the bed and met Luka's eye. "Yeah, I agree. Jesse and Cam had a hell of a time with things because they didn't talk, and I don't want it to become an issue for us."

"Same," Luka agreed. "I know we haven't been dating for long, but it seems good to lay it all out. Plus, we've already talked about how things work for you with Jesse and Cam."

"Well, like I started to say earlier, I haven't gone out with anyone else."

Luka nodded. "Neither have I."

"And, to be frank, I'm not looking to."

A pulse of relief went through Luka. "Same here. I don't want to put any pressure on you about your expectations for the future, but I feel good about where things are heading with you."

"Me, too," Kyle said. "This thing between us feels like it has potential. I want to explore that."

His expression was so open and honest, and affection washed over Luka in a warm rush. *How is it so damn easy with Kyle?* What could have been a difficult conversation just wasn't.

"Me too. With my previous partners, I've always been monogamous once things started to get serious," Luka said. "I know you've said you like wiggle room however. And the idea of watching you with Jesse and Cam, and potentially joining in…well, it's a huge turn-on for me."

"It seemed so when we talked about it the other day."

Luka's cock stirred with interest again at the thought. "I'm not ruling it out."

"I'm glad to hear that," Kyle said. "I could live without the hook-ups, but it's nice to know I don't have to."

Luka hesitated. That thought nagged him. "Could you? I mean, you and Jesse seem so close, and it sounds like you've really missed him since he and Cam got together."

"I have missed him," Kyle said. "He's one of my best friends and I love him. Not in a romantic way."

"I understand."

"There have been some huge adjustments to our friendship, but Jes and I talked about it. I realized I was missing my best friend more than anything. Don't get me wrong, hooking up with him is a lot of fun. So is hooking up with him and Cam. But I can live without both of those things. I don't want to live without Jesse's friendship though. After he and I talked, we agreed to reach out to each other more often. Prioritize the friendship."

"I understand that," Luka said. "So you're up for the two of us being monogamous except for the occasional group thing with your friends?"

"Yes. I am definitely up for that."

"That's good to hear."

Kyle leaned in and kissed Luka hard, but there was a thoughtful expression on his face when he drew back. "Luka, I'm sorry if this doesn't come out right, but would you ever miss being with a woman?"

Luka thought about it for a moment before he shook his head. "No. As long as I'm happy with my partner, I don't feel like I'm missing out on anything, no matter who I'm with."

Kyle let out a small hum as if considering Luka's comment. "Okay," he said. "But do you want to keep that door open a tiny crack? If you ever changed your mind, you should feel free to bring it up so we can discuss it."

"Well, I think it's always good if the door is open for discussion in a relationship," Luka said. "Just to be clear, if I ever did say I wanted to be with a woman, would you take part, too? I got the impression you had no interest in that direction."

"I don't," Kyle said.

"Have you ever had sex with a woman?"

"Yes. My hometown was small, and I didn't know any other gay guys while growing up. I dated a few girls. But I slept with my high-school girlfriend and it didn't do much for me, and that was kind of the light-bulb moment, you know?"

"Sure."

"I don't have any real desire to have sex with a woman. But if that mattered to you, we could figure out how to make it work. Even if it just involved me watching."

"It seems to me we each have a bit of voyeur and exhibitionist in us."

"Yup." Kyle slid a hand over Luka's hip and pulled their bodies flush. "One that I think could be very, very fun to explore."

Luka made a small sound of pleasure and pushed Kyle onto his back again. "How about we start now?" He pressed a kiss to Kyle's chest, then one a bit lower. And another lower yet. "You lay back and watch while I suck that gorgeous cock of yours. No closing your eyes. I want you to see me take. Every. Last. Inch."

Kyle raised his arms and rested his head on his joined hands. "Challenge accepted."

* * * *

"What are you guys planning on doing in Vermont this weekend anyway?" Luka asked later that afternoon.

He and Kyle were seated on the bed, eating *gang gai* and *pad see ew* from a takeout Thai place down the street. They'd flipped a coin to see who would put on pants and leave the bed long enough to collect the bags and pay the delivery guy.

"We're going to visit our dad's grave," Kyle said, his voice quieter than usual. "It's his birthday this weekend, and Ollie and I make the trip up to Barre every year. That's where Dad was born and where he's buried."

Luka nudged him with his knee, his hands too full with the takeout container and chopsticks to reach out and touch Kyle like he wanted. "That's a nice tradition. It's been a while since I've gone to visit my dad's grave. I should do that soon."

"Well, if you ever want company…"

"Thanks." Luka offered him a small but sincere smile. "I appreciate that. I wish he could have met you."

Kyle licked his lips. "Do you think he'd be okay with you dating a white boy?"

"Yeah, I do," Luka said. "He had a big heart. And he just wanted us kids to be safe and happy. I think he'd be annoyed by my mom's attitude right now."

"No luck there yet, huh?"

"I'm afraid not," Luka said. "Maybe it'll be better once she meets you." His mood brightened at the thought. Surely, once Lydia and Regina met Kyle and saw him with Luka, they'd feel differently. "Do you feel up for meeting some of the Clarke-Padilla clan?"

An uncertain expression passed over Kyle's face. "Yes?"

"You don't sound too sure about that."

"I'm nervous," Kyle admitted. "I already know two of them aren't thrilled with who I am. It's hard starting with a handicap."

"I understand." Luka leaned in and brushed his lips across Kyle's. "But I know who you are. They'd be fools not to like you."

Chapter Nine

Ignoring the knot in his stomach, Kyle walked east on Bleeker Street with Luka at his side. Three weeks had passed between Luka inviting him to meet the Clarke-Padillas and an actual date being set, and now that the time had come, Kyle wanted to back out in the worst way. As in take hold of the hem of Luka's navy wool peacoat and turn him right back around so they could find someplace else — someplace friendly — to spend their evening.

Kyle stifled a grumble. Outside of his makeshift band of friends and Oliver, Kyle didn't do big families. He didn't do biphobic siblings. And he really, really didn't do mothers who disliked him sight unseen. Kyle had handled enough maternal bullshit of his own growing up, thanks. He didn't want anyone else's. Fuck, he'd spent almost an hour deciding what to wear tonight, and how stupid was that?

Except...Luka had been looking forward to this evening. He'd talked about it often as the date approached, his excitement obvious and sweet in the most endearing way. He grinned at Kyle now, his face alight, and Kyle smiled back.

Tonight isn't just about you.

Right. This night was about Luka sharing the people he loved most in the world with Kyle. About him letting Kyle deeper into his life because Luka thought their relationship could be built upon. That knowledge amazed and humbled Kyle and made him willing to put up with a little bullshit in return. He'd said as much to Oliver when his brother had asked how Kyle planned to work around Luka's mom.

Kyle gave himself a hard, internal shake. He could do this.

"The band's name is Lune Rouge, right?" he asked.

"That's right." Luka turned their tickets over to the bouncer at the entrance of the art cabaret where Ruby's band would perform that evening. "Otherwise known as Red Moon to those of us who chose Spanish class over French in high school."

They stepped inside and Kyle smirked. "Something tells me having a bilingual family member might have had a lot to do with your choice."

"Busted." Luka rested his palm on Kyle's lower back as they moved to the coat check. "Tomas helped us all out with language classes. Well, most of us anyway. He tried to help Ruby, but girlfriend just had to take Italian to be different."

"I heard that, you brat."

Kyle blinked in surprise at the voice that spoke directly behind them, but Luka laughed and turned to embrace a woman clad in black with a headful of glossy platinum-blonde hair. Aside from a long-sleeved leotard, she wore what Kyle thought was a long skirt made of leather-like material, cut from waist to ankle into long narrow strips. The skirt showed off a whole lot of leg when she moved, the deep, toned skin flawless and smooth from hip to impossibly high heel.

Wow.

Luka's sister was a total knockout, all long limbs and ripe curves, and Kyle was totally staring at her. That had to be a first.

"What are you doing out here?" Luka asked her. "You tryin' to peep my man before everyone else?"

"Of course." Smiling eyes peered over Luka's massive biceps at Kyle. "I'm Ruby," she said, "and if this big oaf ever lets me go, he can introduce us."

Luka turned his sister loose, and she stepped forward to extend a hand to Kyle. Ruby's clear blue eyes were beautiful like her brother's, and her smile could have powered a jet engine. If Kyle had ever found women desirable, Ruby would be at the top of his list.

"I'm Kyle." He shook Ruby's hand while Luka handed their coats to the woman behind the counter. "I'm sure you guessed as much."

"I could tell from Luka's smile when you walked in together that he was in the company of someone who makes him happy." Ruby winked. "Since he talks about you all-l-l-l the time, I figured you couldn't be anyone but Kyle."

Kyle's cheeks went hot. "That's —"

"A sign my sister's wig is too tight," Luka cut in. "You need to take that thing off your head and let some blood flow back to your brain." His voice held a teasing note despite his narrowed eyes, and Kyle thought he looked outrageously appealing in his button-down and black cargos.

Ruby flipped yellow curls over her shoulder with a practiced hand. "Don't you talk about my wig, Luka

Clarke," she said, her tone haughty. "If Kyle doesn't already know you like him, that's on you." She cocked her head at Kyle. "My brother means well, but he can be a bit emotionally constipated when it comes to expressing his feelings."

"Oh, no." Luka offered an arm to Ruby, his expression a mix of pained and amused. "I need a drink and for you to stop talking before Kyle gets spooked and takes off running."

Kyle belted out a laugh. "I'm fine. A little overwhelmed, maybe, but okay."

Ruby linked her free arm around his. "That's the spirit. Now you just have to get through meeting the rest of the family. What can I get you boys at the bar?"

"Kyle's a tequila guy," Luka replied, "and he likes a margarita." He met Kyle's gaze over Ruby's head. "You think you can stomach another man's cocktails?"

"Of course." Kyle waved Luka off. "I've worked in nightclubs. I learned more about mixing drinks inside them than I ever would have back in the tavern in my hometown."

"Hey, Luka!" a voice called from a knot of people gathered by the bar, and several faces turned their way.

Kyle quelled a sigh. So much for getting a margarita down before meeting everyone. He summoned up a smile.

Ruby turned him and Luka loose, then flagged down a bartender while Luka made introductions. He kept a hand on Kyle's shoulder the whole time, and Kyle welcomed that touch because he felt dangerously over his head within seconds. Two parents, three siblings, and a brother-in-law...what the fuck had he gotten himself into? At least, the bakery cousin and her husband had stayed home with their kids.

The next five minutes passed in a blur of handshakes, greetings and smiles — some wider than others — while Kyle assigned names to faces. The Clarke-Padillas were an attractive bunch for sure, though none so flamboyant as Ruby. Enormous energy radiated from all of them, and Kyle sensed the affection underlying their often-teasing exchanges. Unfortunately, they were all curious about Kyle, too, and the weight of that attention twisted his insides so tight he couldn't even enjoy the margarita Ruby passed his way.

"I've got to get backstage," she said over the chatter building around them. "Everybody be nice to Kyle and try not to scare him too much." She flashed a grin Kyle's way, then pushed through the crowd.

"I'm surprised Luka's stories haven't scared you off already, Kyle," Tomas said. His dark eyes twinkled, and he settled an arm around Lydia's waist. "I'm sure he's told you some."

"A few here and there, yes," Kyle replied. The group moved toward a seating area near the stage, and he tried not to falter under Lydia's intense gaze. "All complimentary though, and nothing at all scary."

"Yeah, I don't believe that for a second." Luka's younger brother sat beside Kyle. "Wade ran the gauntlet once." Marcus cocked a finger gun at Regina's husband. "He made it through in one piece."

Wade tipped his glass Kyle's way. "Barely. Luka was seventeen and already as big as a house the first time Regina took me to dinner in Riverdale. I thought for sure he'd pound me into lunch meat if I even looked at his sister the wrong way."

"I'm a lover, not a fighter, Wade. You know that." Luka settled an arm over the back of Kyle's chair. "Besides, I wasn't the one you had to worry about."

"Oh, no question." Wade raised both hands in surrender. "I knew I had to impress Miss Lydia before anyone else."

Luka's mother smiled, her expression smug, but Tomas made an offended noise. "Did you even bother trying to impress me?"

"Everyone knows you're a soft touch, Tomas." Wade clapped him on the shoulder. "Besides, you were too busy keeping the peace among everybody else to get all up in my face."

Laughter rolled over the table and nerves jangled under Kyle's skin.

"This is why none of the other kids bring anyone over for dinner," Tomas said to him. "They learned lessons from Wade and Regina's tribulations."

Regina waved Tomas off. "Ruby and Marco are holdouts, yes, but Luka's brought a few girlfriends to dinner. A couple of them even stuck around long enough for us to get to know them."

Kyle thought Regina meant to make a point by mentioning only Luka's ex-girlfriends, but Luka had already geared up for a counter attack.

"That was back in high school, Queenie," he said, "before I knew better than to expect any of you to behave yourselves. That's the primary reason I set up this night in public."

Regina huffed. "That's funny. I figured we met here to give you and your friend an easy out if you found something better to do."

Kyle's own peacekeeping instincts kicked in the second Luka's lips tightened. He laid a hand on Luka's thigh under the table, but Lydia's delicate throat clearing silenced everyone.

"We're here to listen to your sister sing, not watch you two spar like roosters," she said. Lydia aimed a mild smile around the table, and Kyle's stomach tumbled when it lingered on him. "Luka mentioned you have a brother, Kyle."

"Yes, ma'am."

"Are the two of you as argumentative as this lot during family gatherings?"

"No, ma'am. But there's just the two of us, so our arguments are short-lived." Kyle chuckled, and Luka's hand closed over his. "Oliver lives in Boston right now anyway, so I don't see him as often as I'd like."

Lydia nodded. "That's too bad. I sometimes wonder if some distance might give Luka and Regina some much-needed perspective." She raised a brow at Luka. "Then again, you haven't been out to the house for dinner much, baby."

Kyle swallowed a groan. If Luka wasn't working, he'd taken to meeting Kyle after his Sunday yoga class. They usually ate a late lunch and engaged in acts far too risqué to discuss with family.

Fantastic.

Luka didn't seem at all fazed however. "We talked about this already, Mom. I'll be there tomorrow," he said.

Kyle would sure as fuck make sure it happened, too. He gave Luka a small smile. "I'm going to grab some water at the bar," he said. "Can I get anyone anything while I'm up?" He checked Lydia's glass and found it half empty. "Mrs. Padilla, would you like another?"

Lydia's dark eyes were inscrutable, but she nodded. "Yes, thank you. This is a Manhattan, and Tomas is drinking gin and tonic."

"Yes, ma'am." Kyle turned to Luka again. "You mind meeting me at the bar? I'll need help schlepping everything back."

"Sure. I'll be right there."

Once safely away, Kyle hailed a bartender to start the order, then stood with his hands pressed flat on the bar's surface and pretended he wasn't sweating under his black cashmere sweater. He sensed more than saw a figure step up beside him and fought hard to hide his disappointment when he met Marcus' gaze and not Luka's.

"My mom sent me up here, and I know better than to argue," Marcus said. "Once she gets an idea in her head, it's hell talking her out of it."

Kyle smiled. Marcus' sunny disposition and confidence reminded him of Oliver. "Luka's mentioned that tenacity runs in your family."

Marcus laughed. "Oh, he's not wrong. They're all hard-headed in their own way."

"And you're not?"

"Meh, I suppose I am. I just don't need to talk about everything the way the rest of them do." Marcus leaned his elbows on the bar. "None of them wants or knows how to keep anything private."

"I have some friends like that. Meddlesome, but they mean well."

"These would be the guys in the paparazzi photos, right?"

Kyle winced. "You saw those, huh?"

"Oh, we all saw them," Marcus replied. "Tomas googled your speakeasy and it kind of mushroomed from there. My mom thinks you're one of the best-looking bunch of white guys she's ever seen, by the way."

"Oh, God."

Marcus laughed. "Hey, I'm just teasing. Don't sweat it, Kyle—everyone you hang with is gainfully employed and *that* she noticed. You've even got some flavor mixed in there, what with the Japanese senator and that girl who looks like a beauty queen."

Now Kyle wanted to order a shot for himself. "David is Japanese-American, and Astrid is, in fact, a former beauty queen. They're both stupidly smart, too, each with more degrees than you and I combined. My friends are great people, even when they're meddling."

"My family could give them a run for their money." Marcus exhaled noisily. "Take you and Luka, for example, and the fact everyone knew Luka was on a date before he even picked you up to go mini golfing."

"Uh. Say what now?"

"Yup. I mean, they didn't know who you were, of course, but they knew he was taking someone out. Ruby called Regina the second Luka drove away in her car, then Regina called Mom and Pop."

Kyle raised his eyebrows high. "Then someone called you?"

"No." Marcus chuckled. "I had lunch with Luka earlier that week and he told me himself. I figure that doesn't count since I got it straight from the source. Plus, I kept that intel to myself."

"Got it." Kyle shook his head. "Is it true you've never brought anyone to your parents' house for dinner?"

"Hell, yes, it's true," Marcus said, his tone fervent. "If I ever meet a woman I feel serious about, I'll do what Luka did and make everyone come out to a public place so there are plenty of witnesses. At least, for the first meeting." He sniffed. "It's not like I have anything to worry about anyway."

"Yeah? Luka told me you're studying biochem at Columbia. There aren't women interested in your big brain?"

"Oh, there's interest, but with school keeping me so busy, it's a bit one-sided right now." Marcus nodded at the bartender, who set a Manhattan and a gin and tonic down in front of them. "I was dating someone, but it got super complicated and didn't work out. To tell you the truth, I'm still processing some of how that went down."

Kyle frowned at the light scowl that marked Marcus' handsome features. The breakup had clearly affected him. "Did you get too much feedback from the family on top of everything?"

"No. I didn't tell them about it." Marcus winced. "Sometimes, I'd rather not deal with the fussing, you know?"

"Sure, I get that."

Kyle watched the bartender set a Scotch and soda and a glass of red wine with the order, then cast a glance over his shoulder at Luka and his family. They were immersed in talk, their faces and hand gestures animated and their enjoyment in one another's company clear. Something pulled at the space behind Kyle's heart.

"This is going to make me sound like a patronizing ass, and I'm sorry for that," he said to Marcus. "But the next time they drive you up a wall, just tell yourself there are worse things in the world than people caring about what happens to you."

Marcus knitted his brows together. "I never thought about it that way."

"I'm glad you haven't had to." Kyle handed the bartender his credit card and started a tab.

* * * *

As the evening went on, Kyle thought he hid his nerves from the Clarke-Padillas well. While Tomas, Wade and Marcus were easy to hang with, Regina's and Lydia's attitudes remained frosty. Kyle dreaded the moments their gazes landed on him, but even more so when they skipped over him instead. Which Lydia's often did. Outside of a few brief interactions with Kyle, she ignored his presence much of the time, and though Kyle should have been relieved at being out of the line of fire, her behavior pinged his buttons in all the wrong ways instead.

Kyle had spent years dealing with his own mother's cold-shoulder routine, first as a kid, then as a teen through to the present, and he remembered now that he'd always hated it. Being cut out left him feeling both anxious and helpless, and he knew the tension showed on his face after he caught Luka's eyes on him. A little line worked its way between Luka's eyebrows as his gaze moved between Kyle and Lydia, and oh boy, Kyle was glad to know he was even more fucked up than he'd ever realized.

Thankfully, things got easier after the show started. Lune Rouge diverted the Clarke-Padillas' attention with a fantastic set of mixed swing and jump blues that capitalized on Ruby's big, gorgeous voice. When people weren't cheering, they were up and dancing, and Kyle quickly understood he was surrounded by fervent swing dance nerds, Luka's family among them. This fact set his toes tapping and made the smile he exchanged with Luka genuine.

After the band paused for a break, Kyle found himself alone at the table with Regina. Luka's sister had wide, dark eyes like their mother, and she was very beautiful, but Kyle felt like a bug under a microscope when she turned her focus his way.

"This probably isn't what you expected to be doing tonight," she said, her voice mild.

Kyle shrugged. Okay...not a bad opener.

"I like swing," he said. "My dad was a fan, and this all reminds me of him."

"My father listened to this kind of music, too. He liked anything he could dance to, but swing was his favorite." The faraway look on Regina's face told Kyle she wasn't speaking about Tomas.

"I haven't been to a show in a while," Kyle said. He grimaced under Regina's interested glance. "I'm a bit of a workaholic. I'm focused on changing that though."

Regina hummed. "How did you get into bartending anyway? I've never known anyone who mixes drinks for a living."

That sounds right, Kyle thought to himself. He'd expected a career-driven person like Regina to wonder what Luka—a man who saved people's lives—found interesting in a hipster dude-bro who stood behind a bar all night long. There was history behind Kyle's career choice however. And from what Luka had described of his childhood, Regina had more in common with Kyle than she might suspect.

"My brother needed financial assistance during his last year of college," Kyle said. "I was the only person around to pitch in and help, so I pulled out of an MFA program and went back to my hometown to work. I had an office job during the day and a friend got me a job slinging drinks at a tavern nights and weekends. I discovered pretty quickly that I could make a ton in tips, and over time, things fell into place."

An expression of understanding passed over Regina's face. She got it, at least to a degree. She and Kyle had been close to the same age when they'd lost their fathers, and both had given up parts of their young adulthood to help take care of family. Regina didn't need to know the rest. That Kyle's mother had refused to help her sons or that she'd told Kyle to leave her house soon after he'd arrived back in town. That Oliver himself had worked as a barista on top of studying. And definitely not that Kyle spent most of the first several years in the workforce homeless and living out of a duffel bag.

Onstage, the band readied themselves for another set, and the crowd cheered Ruby's return to the microphone. Regina and Kyle joined in the applause.

"Did your brother get his degree?" Regina asked over the racket.

"Yes. Oliver graduated on time and with honors. He keeps saying he'll pay me back, but the guy is a teacher, so I'm not holding my breath." Regina's lips twitched upward and Kyle picked up his margarita.

"As far as the MFA program I left…well, I guess fine arts just wasn't the direction I was supposed to go. Which is okay. Tending bar has been good to me, and if Oliver needs financial help again, I'm in a position where I can give it to him."

Wade dropped into the chair beside Regina as the music started up. Tomas and Marcus also took their seats, and Kyle spied Luka and Lydia still chatting at the bar.

"Okay, what is going on with the heavy conversation over here?" Wade asked.

Regina raised a brow at her husband. "We're talking, honey. What would you have us do, interpretive dance?"

"Great idea!" Wade beamed. "How about you interpret some of my moves next?"

He stood and held out a hand, and though Regina made a big show of accepting it, she was laughing. Tomas also appeared pleased as they made their way to the floor.

"See?" He knocked his shoulder against Marcus'. "You should have brought a date. Women like a man who can dance, son."

Marcus tipped his head back and laughed. "I don't know anyone around my age who dances to this stuff, Pop. I mean, we do because you and Mom made us a bunch of special-ass snowflakes."

"You know me." Kyle held up a hand. "I can dance to this stuff."

Marcus raised his brows. "You saying you're a special-ass snowflake, too?"

"Well, I don't know about special, Marcus, but my skin's the right shade of snowflake pale."

Laughter met Kyle's words, but his good humor faded under Lydia's scrutiny. She'd finally returned to the table, and her expression as she sat beside Tomas was far more serious than Kyle wanted to deal with.

Kyle stood before he became truly aware he'd moved, and he flashed a quick smile. "Excuse me — I need to see a man about a dance."

He caught Luka just heading for the table with drinks for them both and steered him back to the bar. Luka's snort of laughter did wonders to ease the tight feeling in Kyle's gut.

"What's going on?" Luka set the glasses down. "Did you want something other than a margarita?"

"Yep. I want to dance with you." Kyle picked up his margarita and took a healthy sip while Luka's eyes grew a little wider.

"Who says I know how to dance?"

"Your brother," Kyle replied promptly. "Regina, too, though I may have made an inference based on a couple of things she said."

"Oh, they're all a pain in the ass." Luka ran a hand over his head with a laugh. "Okay, you got me — my dad taught me when I was just a kid and Tomas picked up the torch once he was in our lives." He licked his lips. "I've never danced swing with a man before though, and I usually lead — "

"Yeah, yeah. We both know you're a big, bad toppy top." Kyle rolled his eyes and his heart squeezed at Luka's gleeful expression. "But I've told you before, Clarke — I'm flexible, and I like to do what feels good in the moment. So how about you lead and just let me know if you want to switch it up?"

Eyes gleaming, Luka held out a hand. "Okay, McKee. Let's see what you've got."

* * * *

"How tired are you?" Luka asked late that night.

They were in Kyle's apartment again, standing almost nude beside the bed while Luka peeled Kyle's sweater away from his body. They'd caused a stir with their dancing at the cabaret. Swing crowds could get wild, but it wasn't typical to see men of Luka's size dance, and especially with a same-sex partner. Luka danced well, too, his body movements clean and confident and his footwork sure. Despite his claims that he'd never danced with a man, he'd adapted to Kyle's height and lean, muscled build, and his smile when he realized Kyle could dance, too, lit up the whole floor.

"Not tired at all," Kyle said. He waited until Luka had pulled the sweater over his head before he looped his arms around Luka's neck. "Well, my head isn't, at any rate. My feet could use a rest."

Luka chuckled. "I'll bet. You're a hell of a dancer." He ran his hands over Kyle's ribs.

"I'm rusty. But I liked being out there with you."

"How'd you learn to follow as well as lead?"

"My dad taught Ollie and me both parts," Kyle said. "Told us it'd make us better dancers because we'd know how our partners felt."

He wrinkled his nose. That was truthful enough without having to go into the fact that his father had been the only parent willing to teach Kyle and Oliver anything once they'd hit school age.

"I hope we didn't embarrass your family too much," Kyle said. "I didn't consider what it would be like for them watching you partner with a man in time to change course. You need to go to Riverdale for dinner tomorrow, by the way."

"Hey, no talking about family dinner while we're naked." Luka pushed Kyle backward onto the bed and crawled on top of him. "Besides, they loved that you danced with me. Ruby is all about making a scene, and I know you heard her wolf whistle." He smothered Kyle's laughter with a kiss.

"Pop and Marcus were impressed too," he said after they'd come back up for air. "I think we've got Wade worried he needs to step up his moves a bit. Hell, we even got a smile out of Regina."

The group had broken up not long after Ruby's last set finished, Tomas and Lydia leaving first, followed shortly afterward by Regina and Wade. Marcus, Luka and Kyle had shared a final drink with Ruby, and there had been lots of talk of Thanksgiving plans at the house in Riverdale. Plans that didn't include Kyle and, indeed, should not have. Thanksgiving was for families and Kyle wasn't part of the Clarke-Padilla's. It made his heart wobble a little acknowledging that though.

Kyle ran a hand over Luka's hair. "Thank you for taking me to meet them," he whispered. "I had a good time."

He tried to mean those words. And he hated the part of him that wanted some of what Luka had. Luka deserved his big, joyful family and Kyle had enjoyed seeing them together. Watching love light Luka up from the inside out. As for Lydia and Regina...well. The least said the better.

Luka was watching Kyle though, his gaze moving over Kyle's face as if searching for something. He cupped Kyle's jaw in one hand at last, his touch soothing, and when he kissed Kyle again, it was so sweet Kyle sank into it like a stone in water.

They kissed and caressed one another in silence for a long time, connecting through touch. Kyle lost himself in Luka, reveling in his smooth skin and hard planes of muscle and the heat of his mouth. His breath caught as Luka skimmed a palm over Kyle's belly, then dipped lower to circle the base of the erection that lay rigid against his abdomen.

"Luka."

"I know," Luka murmured.

Luka wrapped his fingers around Kyle's shaft. He kissed along Kyle's jaw and pumped him, and he uttered a low rumble as he nuzzled Kyle's Adam's apple with his lips.

Kyle reached toward the nightstand, and Luka rolled off enough to give him room to move. He also bared his teeth against the skin of Kyle's shoulder and uttered a dark chuckle at his breathless curse. Kyle sighed when his fingers closed over the lube and condoms, and his hands shook as he passed them to Luka.

Luka pushed himself up onto his knees, his mouth swollen from kissing. He wet his fingers and took himself in hand, a hiss leaving his lips. Kyle spread his knees wide. Luka covered Kyle's body with his again and wrapped his free arm around Kyle's shoulders. He lined Kyle's cock up alongside his own.

"Wanna come just like this," Luka whispered.

Kyle shivered. "Fuck."

Luka closed his eyes. He took Kyle's mouth in a searing kiss, his touch on Kyle's cock perfect. Kyle's chest tightened so much he could barely breathe. He ran his hands over the muscles of Luka's back and ass, driven by a need to touch every inch of Luka he could reach. Desire coiled inside him at Luka's sharp inhale.

They writhed together, twisting hard and slow to get the friction they craved. Kyle's head spun, his senses filled with Luka's scent and heat and sounds of pleasure. A sweet, familiar ache pooled in his groin.

"Jesus," Luka ground out. He pressed his forehead hard against Kyle's temple. "Kyle, you... Fuck. Gonna come."

Kyle tightened his grip and thrust his tongue into Luka's mouth, then held him as Luka came apart at the seams. Luka's body went rigid and a hot slick of cum spread over Kyle's cock. Kyle gasped.

He peaked with a broken cry, the orgasm sweeping through him. It left him wrung out and dazed, unable to speak beyond a grunt when Luka let their spent cocks fall away.

Luka wrapped Kyle up in his arms. They lay quiet but for their racing breaths, their legs entwined. Kyle tried to rouse himself when Luka stirred, but the most he could manage was to slit his eyes open and watch Luka roll up and sit on the edge of the bed.

I want this every night.

Kyle closed his eyes again. Could he have it, every night with Luka, here in Chelsea or uptown in the Sugar Hill apartment Kyle had never seen? Would Luka even want such a thing, knowing Kyle would never fit in with the family he loved so dearly?

Kyle didn't know. He didn't want an answer either, at least not right now when he was warm and sated with Luka close by. So, he said nothing while Luka whispered to him about getting a cloth to clean them up and pressed a kiss to Kyle's shoulder.

* * * *

Kyle set his gym bag and yoga mat down on the floor and sat beside Malcolm at the gym's juice bar. Yoga had stretched his joints and muscles, but the relaxation he'd been searching for had eluded him, no matter how deeply he'd breathed or tried to center himself.

"My turn to buy," Malcolm said. He tipped his head toward the menu on the wall. "What are you drinking?"

"Thanks. I'll have the Pineapple Kiwi Kalm with protein," Kyle replied. He chuckled at Malcolm's grimace. "I've never met anyone who hates kiwi the way you do."

"All those seeds, ugh. There're so many nicer things to eat. Mango, for instance." Malcolm turned to the barista. "A Green Light with cayenne and a Pineapple Kiwi Kalm with the protein powder shot, please." He cast an appraising eye over Kyle. "Are you working tonight?"

"Yep. Masen's on at eight, so I'll be done around midnight. I don't suppose you'd be up for some gaming?"

Malcolm laughed and handed the barista some money. "Mmm, no. I've got at least three meetings tomorrow. I'll never make it if I stay up and let you turn my brain into Fallout mush." Earlier in the month, Malcolm had holed up with Kyle and Cam for an entire weekend and they'd played the game's new release. By Monday, Malcolm had been so sleep deprived he'd called into work sick and passed out in Kyle's bed for a solid eight hours.

Kyle blew a raspberry at his friend. "Another time, then."

"What about Luka?" Malcolm asked. "He doesn't play?"

"Nope," Kyle said. "He claims he's willing to learn, but he's working the next few nights anyway. I'll just have to play alone until one of you has time."

"Poor guy." Malcolm frowned. "You okay, babe? You look kind of stressed for someone who just spent ninety minutes breathing through his third eye."

"I'm okay. Can't seem to get out of my own head the last few days, that's all. I hoped class would help, but no luck."

"What's wrong?"

"Luka introduced me to his family," Kyle said. "I went in knowing his mom and sister don't approve of me — Luka and I have talked about it a bunch of times. I thought I had a handle on it. But sitting there with them...that was a lot fucking harder than I anticipated. Especially with Luka's mom."

"You know it's not about you, right?" Malcolm said. "They don't even know you."

The barista set down their smoothies and Kyle took hold of the plastic cup. He pumped his straw into the bright yellow-green concoction a few times.

"That's what Luka's been saying. That his mom and his sister don't know me, and once they do, they'll change their minds. But what if he's wrong?" Kyle blew out a long breath. "It's not as if they disapprove of my job or my politics or something I can change. I *can't* change the things they don't like about me. I'm...I'm always going to be white, just like I'm always going to be gay."

Malcolm reached over and laid a hand over his and Kyle's throat ached. He'd never spoken about those parts of himself as negatives before and it fucking hurt doing so now. Coming face to face with his privilege sucked.

"If Luka's family never comes around to being okay with me, how will that make him feel in the long-term?" Kyle mused. "Because one night out with them made me feel like shit, and the idea of putting up with that into the future... I don't know, Mal. It's daunting as hell."

Malcolm scooted his stool closer and moved his hand to Kyle's shoulder. He sat silent awhile, his grip strong while they sipped their smoothies. "Have you told

Luka how you're feeling about everything?" he finally asked.

"No. He's got enough on his plate." Kyle shrugged at Malcolm's quiet tsking noise. "He knows they don't like his boyfriend—I'm not going to add to that by whining about my goddamned feelings."

"You're doing a bang-up job whining to me," Malcolm replied. His dry tone dragged a laugh out of Kyle, and that put a smile on Malcolm's face. "That's better. I think Luka would want to know it bothers you though. Seeing as you two are boyfriends now."

"Yeah, I suppose." Kyle ignored the burn in his cheeks.

"Well, good for you, man." Malcolm squeezed Kyle's shoulder again and dropped his hand, but he stayed close.

"I don't want to be that guy, harping on Luka to fix things with me and his family," Kyle said. "He's working on changing his mom's and his sister's opinions, and I can't ask for more. I don't want to, honestly."

"So, you pretend it doesn't bother you at all?" Malcolm tsked again. "Denial is bad for you, dude."

"I'm not in denial," Kyle insisted. "I'm just…holding my tongue. Luka and I have only been dating a couple of months, and we're still figuring things out. Taking it day by day and focusing on stuff that feels good. Things we know we can control."

"Like what?"

"Hooking up with Jesse and Cam, for one."

Malcolm slapped a hand over his eyes. "You guys are fucking bananas."

Kyle bit back a laugh. "Hey, I know you think open relationships are weird and mildly offensive, but—"

"I never said that." Malcolm dropped his hand. He looked Kyle in the eye, his expression earnest. "I don't understand them, true, but I'm not offended. I promise, Kyle."

"Okay." Kyle'd been mostly teasing, but he appreciated Malcolm caring enough to clarify his comment. "I believe you."

"I think you're bananas to use the word 'control' with 'Jesse' though. Because that man is a whole big bag of unpredictable. Even with Cam around. Hell, maybe more so with Cam around."

"Nah. Jes has mellowed a lot this year. Emotionally, I mean. If you spent as much time around him as I do, you'd see it, too."

Malcolm nodded. "Fair enough. You really think hooking up all three of your boyfriends is a good idea?"

"Well, Jes and Cam aren't my boyfriends, so sure." Kyle shrugged. "Luka and I talked about it and we both think it'd be hot. We'll try it out and see how it goes. If it turns out we're wrong, there's no expectation for a repeat by anyone."

"Got it." Malcolm paused and licked his lips. "It doesn't get confusing mixing in sex with feelings and stuff?"

Interesting. Kyle was always candid with Malcolm about the men he dated, but they rarely talked about actual sex. They didn't discuss Malcolm's romantic life at all either, never mind Malcolm having sex. Kyle didn't know if Malcolm had or even wanted any of that in his life.

"No," Kyle replied. "For me, feelings and sex can be mutually exclusive. I'm close with Jes and Cam, but not in the same way as I am with Luka."

"You like him, huh?" Malcolm gave Kyle a small smile.

It's way more than like, Kyle thought. No way was he ready to talk about that though.

"Yeah, I do," he said instead. "I think getting him with Jes and Cam will be fun. I don't need to feel emotionally close to people I sleep with to have a good time, but it makes things a lot more enjoyable. That's why I like fooling around with Jesse and Cam. And why what I do with them is very different from what I do with Luka. That's just how I'm wired, by the way — doesn't mean other people would feel the same way if they were placed in the same situation."

Malcolm hummed. His eyes lost focus, as if he were looking inward, and Kyle thought maybe he'd say more on the topic of feelings and sex. But then Malcolm blinked, and the moment passed. He tilted his head at the door instead and pushed back his stool.

"I've got time to game right now if you do," he said.

"Heck, yes." Kyle leaned down to grab his stuff from the floor. "I don't have to be uptown until four-thirty, so you're all mine until then."

Malcolm chuckled. "Oh, hell. If I get nothing done today, it'll be all your fault."

Kyle winked. "Things usually are, babe — you should know that by now."

Chapter Ten

"I take it Matías had his way with you earlier?" Kyle asked as they stepped into a building on 29th Street that housed Jesse and Cam's loft. He waved at the concierge at the desk and kept walking. "It's subtle, but I can tell."

Luka chuckled. "He did. I couldn't argue his point that there is no time more appropriate to wear makeup than for an orgy. Or is this a foursome? I'm not sure I have the terminology down."

Kyle appeared to consider the question while they waited for the elevator. "I'd go with foursome. More than that would be an orgy."

"Well, I hope the makeup isn't over the top then. I wasn't sure of the etiquette."

Kyle grinned. "Whatever it is, I think you look incredible."

Matías had applied concealer on Luka's face, as well as mascara and lip gloss, and spritzed everything with setting spray. '*You don't want it all to rub off in the middle of things,*' he'd said, and Luka couldn't argue with that logic either.

"Thanks," Luka replied. "Hopefully, Jesse and Cam like it too."

"I don't think you have anything to worry about there," Kyle said as they stepped off the elevator. "They're both very enthusiastic about this."

"It's all I've been able to think about all day," Luka admitted. That was both good and bad. He'd looked forward to it but having time to think had also made him anxious. Luka'd never made plans to have group sex. Any threesomes he'd had with women in the past had been spur-of-the-moment endings to wild nights out, fueled by lust and booze. Tonight was different. Very different.

They reached Jesse and Cam's door. "Are you ready for this?" Kyle squeezed his shoulder.

"I think so."

"If you change your mind, we can stop at any point." Kyle's voice and words were reassuring, and Luka didn't have a single doubt he meant them.

"I know." Luka's tone sounded calm and sure. He was sure, at least, about trusting Kyle. The rest remained to be seen. But how would he know unless he tried?

"Whatever happens tonight, you're my priority, Luka." Kyle rapped his knuckles on the door. "Remember that."

Those words made Luka turn and reach for Kyle. He pressed their lips together, needing Kyle to know how much he appreciated the way Kyle cared. How Kyle's words lit him on fire from the inside out in the best of ways. Dimly, he heard the door open.

"Well, I see you two are getting started already." Jesse's tone sounded light and teasing, and Luka smiled against Kyle's lips. He pulled back to see both Jesse and Cam standing in the open doorway.

Luka's cheeks heated and he was grateful his darker skin would hide it, though the tips of his ears sometimes turned red enough for people to notice. But why should he feel embarrassed? Before the night was over, they were all going to see a hell of a lot more of each other.

"Come in," Jesse coaxed.

Once everyone was inside the apartment, he closed the door and leaned in to Luka, grazing his lips across Luka's cheek and greeting him with a hug. His beard was a soft, teasing prickle against Luka's skin, so different from Kyle's coarser stubble. Jesse drew back and gently pushed Luka toward Cam, who greeted him in a similar way, his lips lingering on Luka's cheek.

Luka glanced over at Jesse and Kyle. They were kissing. Not deeply, but far more than a peck on the cheek. A strange swooping filled Luka's stomach. Was it jealousy? *No. Not that.* He didn't feel threatened by seeing Jesse and Kyle together, but he was reminded of their history. A history Luka didn't share.

They drew back and Kyle immediately sought out Luka, as if checking in with him. *You okay?* his gaze seemed to say.

Luka tried to convey a yes with his eyes, and Kyle nodded, seeming satisfied.

"Let's go into the living room," Jesse said after he'd taken their coats. "I figured we'd have a bite to eat before we get things rolling."

Luka licked dry lips. "Sounds good."

Jesse and Kyle fell into step. "Hey, I hate to talk shop tonight, but I have a quick question for you about an idea I had for Under," Jesse murmured.

"Sure, let's get it out of the way," Kyle said.

Cam pressed a hand to Luka's back, his palm warm and reassuring. "How are you feeling?" His open gaze prompted the honesty.

"Nervous," Luka said.

"I've been there." Cam nodded toward Jesse and Kyle, who had their heads tilted toward one another as they spoke. "Feeling intimidated by their relationship."

"It's just…there's so much history there."

"I know." Cam gave him a smile. "But it's nothing to worry about. I promise. Jesse and I are rock-solid, and I can see you and Kyle are good for each other."

Luka felt strangely flattered by the observation. "Yeah?"

"Yeah. We don't play with couples who are using this to fix a shaky relationship. We made that mistake once. Never again."

That was reassuring.

Jesse and Kyle disappeared to the left into the kitchen, still talking. Luka glanced around. It came as no surprise that the loft was sleek and stylish, with softly gleaming wood floors. Windows ran along two walls of the long and narrow layout, and minimalistic furniture in steely grays and warm wood tones was arranged throughout the rooms. Luka glanced out of one the windows at the bright skyline, which offered a great view of the top of the Flatiron building, an iconic triangular-shaped skyscraper at the intersection of Fifth Avenue and Broadway.

"Beautiful," he murmured.

"Mine was better." Cam's tone was dry. "Mind you, that's the only thing I miss about living in Brooklyn."

"Much better commute now, I'm sure," Luka said. He wandered back to where Cam stood.

"God, yes." Cam nodded. "I feel like I have more hours in my day."

"Between Kyle's place, the firehouse and my apartment, I'm running all over the damn place these days."

"Worth it though?"

"Worth it."

"Are you two talking about commuting?" Jesse asked in a teasing tone. He carried a platter of food and Kyle followed behind with drinks.

"You and Kyle were talking about work," Luka pointed out.

"True." Jesse glanced back at Kyle. "You okay to table the work for the rest of the night, babe?"

"Absolutely," Kyle said.

"Excellent." Jesse set a cheese and fruit platter on the coffee table where they could all reach it. "Please. Have a seat." He sat and Cam settled down beside him. "Help yourself to anything you'd like."

Luka wondered if the double meaning had been intentional.

He took a seat on the other side of the expansive sectional and Kyle passed out drinks. Kyle sat on Luka's right at last, close enough so their hips and thighs touched. Luka sipped his cocktail and enjoyed the mellow warmth that flowed through him.

"How do you like it?" Kyle asked.

It took a second for Luka to understand Kyle meant the drink. "Oh, it's very good. What clever name have you come up with for it?"

"The Manhattan Foursome." Kyle's eyes gleamed with amusement.

Luka clinked his glass against Kyle's. "Here's to enjoying more of that before the night is over."

"Hear, hear!" Jesse said with a grin.

"What's in it?" Cam asked.

"It's a twist on a Manhattan, with a touch of maple syrup and spices. I ran across a recipe for one with vanilla but that didn't seem very appropriate for tonight."

They all laughed.

"I do love the way you think, babe," Jesse said. "Here's to a very un-vanilla night."

Conversation segued into mundane topics like a new restaurant that had opened around the corner and a show Jesse and Cam had seen recently. The alcohol calmed Luka's nerves and the friendly camaraderie put him at ease. He laughed a lot and enjoyed the food and company. He didn't mind at all when Cam—who sat on his left—brushed his fingers against Luka's as they both reached for a bite to eat.

The conversation turned subtly flirtatious and Luka watched Jesse stroke Cam's thigh. Luka's stomach tightened when Cam leaned into his partner for a kiss.

"Aren't they incredible to watch?" Kyle murmured in his ear. Luka shivered at the warmth against his skin.

"Yes." Kyle pressed his lips against Luka's neck, kissing his way down to the juncture of his shoulder. He slid a hand along Luka's abs, slowly teasing as he worked toward his groin. Luka pulled away, just long enough to set his nearly empty glass down.

Kyle gently bit down on Luka's earlobe, and Luka let out a needy sound. Jesse broke away from Cam and looked over at Luka and Kyle.

"What do you say we take this to the other room?"

Without any further discussion, they all stood, abandoning the meal. Luka followed the other three past the kitchen and down the hall to the bedroom, which was large and minimally furnished. Unsurprisingly, the dominant feature was an enormous bed that left plenty of room for whatever four people wanted to do.

An armless, upholstered chair also faced the bed, perfect for someone who wanted to watch.

Luka paused near it and Jesse did too. He ran a hand up and down Luka's arm. "Kyle said you wanted to start by just watching. Is that right?"

"Yeah. For now," Luka said.

"Well then." Jesse ran his hands over Luka's chest, leaving heat in their wake. Not until Luka's calves bumped against the edge of the chair did he realize Jesse had been guiding him backward. Jesse gripped Luka's shoulders until Luka dropped into the chair.

"Make yourself comfortable while we get started. And, please, feel free to join in any time you want."

"Will do." Luka's voice sounded a shade husky.

They'd done next to nothing and already his cock had grown thick. Sexual tension charged the air, leaving him dizzy, and Luka was mesmerized by the look in Kyle's eyes from across the room. *Hunger.* Kyle loved this. Frankly, so did Luka.

"I have one question." Jesse braced his hands on the chair back and leaned in, staring into Luka's eyes. "Are you good with me kissing you? Because you have the most incredible mouth and I've been wondering how you would taste."

Rather than answer verbally — Luka didn't know that he could at this point — he grasped the back of Jesse's head and drew him in for a kiss.

Luka's nerves sang. Knowing he was kissing a man while their boyfriends watched was strange, but exciting, too. Jesse teased at the seam of Luka's mouth with his tongue and, once Luka opened, dipped inside. Luka let go of the thread of worry and relaxed into the kiss. Jesse explored Luka's mouth with an unhurried thoroughness that made Luka's stomach clench with anticipation of what might follow.

Jesse drew back and ran the pad of his thumb across Luka's lower lip. "Mmm. Every bit as good as I hoped."

He left Luka still reeling when he turned and walked toward Cam. With a small, private smile just for Luka, Kyle turned to Cam and Jesse, too.

Luka watched Kyle kiss Cam, his fascination and arousal growing by the second. Then Kyle and Jesse kissed, the need between them palpable, and their sure touches speaking of the times they'd done this in the past. Kyle unbuttoned Jesse's shirt while Cam tugged Kyle's belt loose from his pants. All three kissed and caressed each other as they undressed, and when they were nude, Luka's cock throbbed at the sight they made. They were all so beautiful in such different ways.

Abruptly, Luka felt overdressed. Fingers shaking, he unbuttoned his shirt and shrugged out of it. His cock ached and while he wanted to touch himself, another part of him wanted to hold off and draw out the feeling.

He stifled a gasp as Kyle dropped to his knees in front of Jesse and took Jesse's cock in his mouth. Jesse reached out to stroke Kyle face. Kyle glanced at Luka, just a brief look out of the corner of his eye, but it warmed Luka. Even amid all this, Kyle thought to check in with him.

Luka rubbed his palm across his throbbing cock. He unzipped his pants, pulling himself out to lie hard and thick along his thigh. He wanted Kyle to know he was enjoying the show. Cam walked past Kyle and stood behind Jesse, his appreciative gaze trailing across Luka's body.

Cam kissed Jesse's shoulder, then reached around to stroke his chest and abs. Luka could hear the wet sounds of Kyle's mouth on Jesse's dick and Jesse's soft, answering moans.

Cam whispered in Jesse's ear. Jesse shifted, placing one knee on the bed without displacing Kyle. Cam kneeled on the bed behind Jesse, then grasped Jesse's ass cheeks in his hands, parting them.

Fuck, that's hot. Lust made Luka dizzy as he watched Kyle and Cam work together, one sucking Jesse's cock and the other rimming him. Luka wondered how Jesse could take all that sensation. He felt overwhelmed just watching. To be on the receiving end would be mind-blowing.

Luka couldn't wait another second to take his dick in his hand. Pre-cum slicked its head and Luka spread it around with his thumb, hissing at the touch on the sensitive area.

Jesse's abs tensed and relaxed, his whole body shuddering before he stilled Kyle and Cam with a hand to each of their heads. "You're going to have to stop unless you want me to be done right now." A sheen of sweat covered his forehead and shoulders and his voice sounded a little hoarse.

Cam and Kyle pulled back and stood. Kyle and Jesse kissed for a few minutes, hands roaming each other's bodies. Luka felt a twinge then. Not of jealousy, but a desire to touch Kyle himself.

Luka held himself back. He'd watched his share of gay porn over the years, but seeing it unfold live in front of him was hugely arousing. More so than he'd ever imagined.

Kyle gripped Jesse's hips. "It's been a long while since I fucked you, babe. You up for it?" His voice held a needy note.

"Yes. Cam did such a great job getting me ready it seems a shame to waste his hard work."

Jesse turned and grabbed Cam, pulling him in for a searing kiss. "You good with Kyle fucking me?" he asked when he pulled back.

"I'd love to watch that." Cam's voice was husky. He glanced at Kyle. "Just promise to give it to him good."

"Happily."

Once again, Kyle looked over to check in with Luka, who nodded. He wondered if Kyle would like to fuck him occasionally. Luka would have to ask him at some point. Luka also wondered if he'd have been so comfortable watching Jesse or Cam fuck Kyle. Probably. Luka thought so. Kyle fucking Jesse though? That Luka wanted to see.

Jesse and Kyle settled on the bed, perpendicular to Luka's chair. Cam brought lube and condoms, and Jesse stroked Cam's dick as Kyle dribbled lube on his fingers. Kyle worked one into Jesse's ass while Cam and Jesse kissed, pausing only for the occasional gasp that escaped Jesse's mouth, presumably when Kyle hit a good spot.

"Mmm, God," Jesse groaned.

"Ready for me?" Kyle asked.

"Just fuck me," Jesse said with a growl. "I want to feel it."

Kyle reached for a condom. Watching him roll it on was arousing, too, and Luka wondered how much more he could take before he joined them.

Kyle made Jesse gasp, and Luka's stomach tightened as Kyle pushed into Jesse.

"Fuck," Kyle said, voice rough. "You feel good, Jes."

He grasped Jesse's hips, his strokes slow and measured at first. Luka stroked his cock in time with Kyle's rhythm until it was almost as though Luka was fucking Jesse, too.

Cam caught Luka's eye. "Fuck. I love watching them."

Silent, Luka nodded and kept slowly stroking. Cam licked his lips, and Luka sped up a bit, putting on a show of his own. Cam stood then and moved toward him, a question in his eyes. Luka crooked a finger at him in response, and when he opened his thighs wider, he was hampered by his jeans.

"Need some help getting out of those clothes?" Cam asked.

"Please."

Cam stripped Luka quickly, and Luka settled back in the chair, holding his dick up and out in offering to Cam. With a naughty half-grin, Cam sank to his knees and wrapped his hand around Luka. He followed with his mouth and Luka lost himself in that warm heat. Gently, he grasped the back of Cam's neck, urging him on.

Even so, Luka was torn between watching Cam work him over and Kyle plunge his cock in and out of Jesse.

Mine, Luka thought with an appreciative sigh. Kyle was his. No matter who Kyle fucked. No matter who sucked Luka's dick. Luka could feel the connection to Kyle tugging at him, even when they weren't touching.

Luka grasped the back of Cam's ginger head, stilling his movements. Cam glanced up, clearly concerned, and Luka smiled to reassure him. "Let's move this to the bed."

Luka stood and gave Cam a hand up before they walked over to the bed. The mattress dipped as Luka knelt beside Jesse's hip and Kyle's gaze flared hot. He reached for Luka and drew him in for a sizzling kiss.

The air smelled of sex and clean sweat, masculine and full of heat. Blindly, Luka reached out, stroking down the length of Jesse's back to where he and Kyle were joined. Jesse moaned when Luka teased Jesse's rim. Luka gently grasped Kyle's dick at the base and squeezed a little, making Kyle groan.

"It's so hot watching you fuck him," Luka murmured against his mouth.

"Yeah?" Kyle asked as he drew back. "You like that?"

"You promised me live-action porn," Luka teased. "But this is so much better."

"I loved the glimpse I got of Cam sucking you." Kyle reached down, stroking Luka's cock with a deft, sure rhythm.

Kyle moved his hips again, slowly fucking Jesse, eyelids heavy and his face slack with pleasure. Luka glanced over and found Cam on his back while Jesse sucked his cock. *Christ.* It was total sensory overload and Luka could hardly stand it. He wanted to bury his dick in someone until he came.

"What if I told you I want to fuck someone?" Luka asked Kyle, his voice gruff.

Jesse lifted his head. "If you're looking for a volunteer..."

Kyle slapped his hip lightly. "I'm not enough, huh?"

"Fuck that." Jesse shivered. "I'm the only one who hasn't gotten a chance to enjoy your man yet though. I thought tonight was about sharing."

Kyle turned his focus on Luka. "You want to?"

"You don't have to ask me twice," Luka said. He'd worried this would be awkward or uncomfortable, but he found it surprisingly easy. Everything with Kyle was easy. Jesse and Cam made it fun, too, and because they were all so open and relaxed about everything, they put Luka at ease.

Luka licked his lips as Kyle withdrew from Jesse. He grabbed a condom for Luka and made the ordinary action of rolling it onto Luka scorching hot with his gentle teasing. In the background, Luka could hear the wet sounds of Jesse sucking Cam's dick and Cam's soft noises of pleasure. Luka gritted his teeth to hold it together. The sights, sounds and sensations around him threatened to do him in.

At last, Kyle drew back, and Luka placed a hand on Jessie's hip. "You ready for me?"

Jesse pulled off Cam. "Yes."

His hand shaking, Luka grasped his dick. Gratitude surged through him when Kyle wrapped his fingers around Luka's, too, and together they guided Luka's cock forward. Luka didn't waste any time, pushing into Jesse with slow, steady pressure until he was buried deep.

Jesse sighed. "Oh, fuck. That's good."

For a few minutes, Kyle stayed pressed against Luka. Luka set up a steady pace, and Kyle roamed his hands over Luka's body, tweaking Luka's nipples and reaching from behind to gently tug at Luka's balls. Luka threw his head back and his eyes rolled back in his head at the combined sensation.

"Kyle."

Jesse felt different than Kyle, of course. That was exciting, but knowing Kyle was there with Luka, feeling him as they both enjoyed themselves, sent a flood of pleasure through Luka.

Kyle whispered in his ear, "You keep going. I'm gonna fuck Cam."

Luka let out a low moan. He couldn't wait to see that.

Kyle held out a hand to Cam and helped him up, then he lay next to Jesse while Cam crawled over Kyle. Kyle and Cam kissed messily, both clearly too turned on for much finesse, and Luka almost closed his eyes at their hungry sounds. After a minute, Kyle pulled back and reached for another condom.

"Are you ready to ride me, Cam?" Kyle asked.

Cam pushed back onto his knees and nodded, his jaw slightly ajar. "Yeah, babe."

He straddled Kyle and Luka watched as Cam sank down. Kyle's face drew tight with concentration before smoothing out. The muscles of Cam's thighs tightened and relaxed as he rose up and down over Kyle, Kyle's hands on his hips. Cam moved with an eager, athletic grace that Luka found beautiful. And Luka didn't feel the slightest hint of jealousy.

Luka closed his eyes, afraid he'd come before he was ready. He focused on Jesse's sounds and movements, speeding up when Jesse grunted, and reached down and under to grasp Jesse's cock and stroke him. Luka opened his eyes and found Jesse had lowered his head until his cheek rested on his hands, his head turned toward Kyle and Cam.

Kyle pressed his leg against Luka's and the contact and heat from his body anchored Luka further.

Still rocking over Kyle, Cam reached out too, and ran a hand across Luka's back and ass. Cam leaned over, nipping at Luka's neck with his teeth. He teased his fingers between Luka's cheeks and when he rubbed across Luka's rim, Luka groaned.

"You okay with this?" Cam asked quietly.

Mute, Luka nodded. He was so good. With all of it.

Luka heard the squelch of lube, then Cam's cool, deft finger explored his ass and pushed inside. It was hard to concentrate and keep the rhythm going while being pulled in two directions. His balls ached and he fought back the rising urge to fuck as hard as he could until he was spent. Luka needed to come. He didn't feel ready to stop, however.

Kyle shifted and turned his head so he could kiss Jesse. Luka imagined he could feel the energy grow between all four of them.

All of them connected.

A tremor shook Jesse's body, and Luka noticed he'd let go of Jesse's cock. He reached under Jesse's body again and found Jesse's hand already wrapped around his own cock. Luka encircled it with his, helping Jesse along. A few short strokes later, Jesse came with a gasp, his ass clenching around Luka. His cum shot onto the sheets below and Luka's own balls drew up tight.

Lights sparkled on the edge of Luka's vision as Kyle broke away from Jesse. Kyle met Luka's gaze and something passed between them, a deeper energy than anything Luka had with Jesse or Cam. *A spark maybe.* It caught and tindered inside Luka, heating him from the center out.

I love him, Luka thought, shocked by the sudden and intense urge to say the words aloud. He couldn't deny it. Sure, he was balls-deep in Jesse, but all he could see was Kyle. Blindly, Luka reached out and grasped Kyle's hand. The physical connection sent him soaring, and in just a few more short strokes, Luka came with a roar.

Cam removed his finger and turned back to Kyle. He sped up, riding Kyle harder, and their groans filled the air as Luka withdrew from Jesse. A few moments later, Kyle cried out, digging his fingers into Cam's hips. Cam jerked his cock hard and threw his head back, shuddering as he painted Kyle's chest and abs.

Luka fell forward on the bed next to Kyle, head spinning, and Jesse sprawled on his stomach on Luka's left. Jesse leaned in and kissed Luka. It felt warm, friendly, like a 'thank you,' and Luka smiled against Jesse's lips. Kyle snuggled closer, dozy and seeking touch as he often did after orgasm. Luka wrapped an arm around him, and Kyle pressed his lips to Luka's shoulder.

Cam stripped the condoms from Kyle and Luka before disposing of them in the trash beside the bed. He disappeared into the bathroom and returned with damp cloths.

"You guys are fucking beautiful," Cam said, looking down at them as they cleaned up. He settled on Jesse's far side so Luka and Jesse were now in the middle of the foursome.

"Mmmhmm. So glad you decided to join us, Luka," Jesse slurred as he and Cam twined their bodies together.

Luka chuckled. "The feeling is mutual." He pulled Kyle closer and moved his hands over Kyle's skin, the familiarity of the body under his fingers settling his swirling thoughts. That had been incredible. Everything he'd hoped for and more.

But love? Of all the times and places, the lightning bolt strikes in the middle of a foursome?

Even with the haze of orgasm fading, Luka didn't feel the emotion any less strongly. While tonight had been a weird time for the feeling to crop up, that didn't make it any less valid. Still, it wouldn't hurt to sit with it a while and be sure.

Luka stirred again when Jesse sat up. "I have a massive shower. Who wants to join me?"

The enormous, black-tiled shower indeed had plenty of room for four people. "Did you tell your contractor you wanted a shower large enough to accommodate Roman orgies?" Luka asked. He leaned into Kyle, who was soaping Luka's back.

"Nah, it was like this when I bought the place," Jesse said. He ran his hands across Cam's abs. "But it was a major selling point."

Luka shifted so he stood in front of one of the wall-mounted shower jets and soaked up the feeling of the powerful jets massaging his skin. "I can see why."

"Please tell me you've done a firefighter calendar, Luka." Jesse licked his lips and eyed Luka up and down. "Preferably one where you're wet. Because you are fucking stunning."

Luka grinned. "I haven't. I've been asked to model for a couple and thought about doing one for charity. I've never gotten around to it though."

"You should," Cam said. "I'd be happy to support a good cause."

Kyle snorted. "They're not wrong, you know."

"How about you just take a few private pictures of me instead?" Luka turned and pulled Kyle against him.

Kyle dropped a kiss against the hollow of Luka's throat. "Let me know if you need any help with that."

"Make that us," Jesse said. "I am more than willing to open my loft to the gorgeous men of the FDNY."

"They'll need to be oiled up, too," Cam said in a thoughtful tone.

Luka laughed. Then Kyle wrapped a hand around Luka's cock, and he could hardly think at all.

* * * *

Later that night, when they were lying naked in Kyle's bed after more lazy kissing and groping in his much smaller shower, Kyle gathered Luka close.

"I hope you enjoyed yourself as much as I did tonight."

"I did." Luka had no reservations whatsoever about what they'd done. "I had a great time."

"It was amazing." Kyle's grip tightened. "I loved it. But it reaffirmed one thing for me."

Luka's heart beat a little faster as he looked Kyle in the eye. "What's that?"

"You're my priority. If you're up for it, I'm willing to hook up with Jes and Cam again, but as an occasional thing. I don't need it on a regular basis."

"Yeah?" Luka found Kyle's words oddly touching. "Me too. I'm up for doing it again. But this is what I want. This here with you."

Luka dipped his head and captured Kyle's lips in a heated and heartfelt kiss.

It felt too soon to voice the words ringing between his ears. But they were there now. They'd stay put until the time was right.

Chapter Eleven

November's private party at Under took place a week before Thanksgiving and Kyle expected the turnout to be lower than usual. With the full brunt of the holiday season upon them, obligations to family and friends always made it harder to gather until after the new year. So, he was genuinely delighted when the core group of speakeasy friends turned up anyway.

Jesse and his brother, Eric, were talking with Cameron, Jarrod and Gale in one of the seating areas, while Will and David chatted with Carter, Malcolm and Astrid at the far end of the bar. Carter's sister, Audrey, and her husband, Max, were talking to Riley's friends, Natalie and Colin, and Riley sat on the other side of the bar from Kyle, watching him mix.

"We'll see you next Thursday, right?" Riley asked. His bright blue eyes followed Kyle's hand movements. "Or will you be schmoozing around the Bronx with Mr. Hottie firefighter?"

"No Bronx schmoozing, so you're stuck with me." Kyle muddled thyme in a shaker. He and Luka had already decided they'd spend the holiday apart and meet up the day after. "My brother's going to be around, too, if you don't mind my bringing him. I know it's twice the McKee you asked for, but—"

"The more the merrier, babe, you know that. We're always glad to see Oliver." Riley gave Kyle a broad smile. "I feel like he's been around a lot more this fall. Or is that just my imagination?"

"It's not your imagination. He's been sort of...clingy since the fire." Kyle added bourbon to his mix. "Clingy for Oliver anyway. Meaning we talk every week instead of once a month, and he's already been down to visit twice since September. It's weird but nice."

Riley watched Kyle add maple syrup and fresh lemon juice to the shaker before he spoke again. "Maybe your brush with death scared him." He chuckled at Kyle's eye roll. "You don't agree?"

"It could be," Kyle allowed. "But the whole 'you almost died' thing sounds so dramatic."

"It's true though."

"No." Kyle stirred the shaker's contents. "I was in trouble, and yes, something dire *could* have happened. But it didn't because the fire department got there in time and pulled Charita and me out. End of story."

Riley shrugged. "For you, maybe. Oliver may feel differently."

"Maybe." Kyle split the drinks he'd mixed between two glasses filled with ice. "I don't mind that he's around more. It's unusual seeing Ollie more than once in a blue moon, but I like it."

"Well, he's welcome. You know that," Riley said. He nodded at Carter, who settled onto the seat beside him. "Car invited a few friends from work to dinner, too, and we'll see Malcolm earlier in the day."

Carter nodded. "There's plenty of room for Luka if he doesn't already have plans."

Kyle set the glasses, now garnished with lemon peel, in front of his friends. "Thyme Will Tell. That's the name of the drink, by the way, not me being cryptic." He smiled at his friends' chuckling. "Luka has dinner plans with his family but thank you. It means a lot to me that you'd welcome him, too."

"Who are you welcoming?" David slid onto the seat on Carter's right and eyed the fresh cocktail. "What's that?" He let out a soft 'ooh' when Carter slid the glass David's way.

Will leaned against the bar to David's left and turned a knowing look on Kyle. "I assume we're talking about Kyle's firefighter. Things still going well between you and Luka?"

Kyle smirked. "Very well, thanks. Carter and Riley were just inviting him for Thanksgiving. Luka's already got plans, but it's the thought that counts."

"Agreed," David said. He tasted Carter's drink and beamed. "This is delicious. You sure you want to give it up?"

"Yeah," Carter replied. "It's time I switched away from booze for the night."

David nodded and met Kyle's gaze. "One of these for Will and a mocktail for Carter the next time you're mixing, if you'd be so kind."

"Coming up." Kyle tossed several sprigs of thyme in the shaker.

"Luka's coming tonight, right?" Will asked. "And bringing some of his comrades along?"

David's laughter made Kyle raise his eyebrows. "Er...yes? Luka was on 'til six but he's working a couple of hours' overtime to cover for someone who had a school thing for their kids. He'll be here after he clocks out, but I can't speak for the number of people he'll bring or their relative hotness. Dare I ask where this is coming from?"

"Will has developed a sudden interest in firefighters and paramedics," David said. He shot a gleeful look at Will, who narrowed his eyes in response. "He's been binge watching every show about firefighters and EMS he can find, and every one of them is filled with the most gorgeous guys you've ever seen."

"I'm sad to say very few of them play for our team," Will threw in, his tone droll. His lips twitched at the others' laughter. "I'm hoping that changes soon, but for now, I'll enjoy the eye candy."

Kyle's cheeks ached from smiling so hard. "How did you develop this sudden interest, William?"

"Hmm, I think it was the evening you brought a bunch of attractive men skilled in the art of fire suppression into this bar, Kyle, and I enjoyed meeting them very much." Will joined in laughing. "Frankly, that was the first time I understood why you're so attracted to men in uniform, and I think only one of the squad that night was even wearing one."

"Aha! And you guys mock me all the time." Kyle's phone buzzed in his pocket, but with his hands full, a couple of minutes passed before he could check it. Disappointment settled over him like a cloud when he finally had the chance, followed by something darker.

Call came in – I'll be late.

Be safe, Kyle wrote back.

Unfortunately, he didn't know when Luka would see the message. Luka and the other firefighters switched their phones to silent when they responded to calls, and they didn't have time to focus on anything but the job anyway. Not that Kyle wanted Luka distracted either.

Kyle wasn't stupid. He knew how Luka made his living and the risks involved. Kyle had seen it up close and personal the day of the fire at Burger Barn. Luka and his comrades answered calls like that every day.

This felt different to Kyle however. Knowing Luka was on a call and that he might not reach out again for a while...ugh. The waiting—no, the uncertainty of the waiting—troubled Kyle. It could be hours before Luka got back to the station house. Or ended up in a hospital if the call went wrong. Who knew if anyone would even think to reach out to Kyle, given he wasn't a family member?

Nerves knotted Kyle's gut. Damn it.

"Hey, Kyle, you got a sec?"

Kyle turned to face Malcolm, who sat beside Carter. "Sure. What's up?"

Malcolm frowned at him. "Everything okay?"

"Yes, of course." Kyle slipped his phone back in his pocket. "Luka's running late, that's all. What do you need?"

The question lingered in Malcolm's gaze, but he gestured at Carter with one hand. "Car and I had a couple of things we wanted to run by you. Some stuff we're doing for a project actually."

Kyle smiled. "Is this about work?" He always enjoyed hearing about the Corporate Equality Campaign and that talk would make for a perfect distraction until Luka showed up.

"No." Carter pressed his hands flat on the bar. "It's about something else entirely."

"Okay." Kyle rubbed his hands together. "What have you got?"

* * * *

Kyle's ability to find distraction in anything evaporated over the course of the evening. He'd heard nothing from Luka. He'd made the mistake of checking the FDNY's Twitter account where he'd seen an all-hands alert for Manhattan in the area of Broadway and 125th Street. Then he'd made an even bigger mistake by reading tweets from bystanders to the fire, which had started in an apartment on the sixteenth floor of a building and spread to multiple dwellings.

By eleven-thirty, his focus shot, Kyle retreated to Under's office where Jesse found him pacing around while he tried to figure out what the fuck to do.

Jesse crossed the room at once, hands out and on Kyle's shoulders. "Whoa, Kyle. What's wrong?"

"I don't know. Maybe nothing." Kyle licked his lips. "Luka went out on a call and I haven't heard from him. I can't stop thinking that something could be wrong. Yes, I know how stupid that sounds. He's a first responder, for fuck's sake — it's his job to be there when stuff is going wrong."

"It's not stupid." Jesse rubbed Kyle's arms. "Has he ever gone dark like this before?"

Kyle shook his head. "It's not that. He usually tells me about a call after it's over and he's back at the station. Tonight, he let me know on his way out because he knew he'd be late getting here — "

"And you can't stop thinking about it," Jesse finished. His obvious concern made the knot in Kyle's stomach twist tighter. "Fuck, I'm sorry, babe. What do you want to do?"

"I have no idea. I thought I'd head over to the station...maybe someone there could give me some info." Kyle grunted. "I sound like a needy little brat and I hate it."

Jesse pulled Kyle into a hug. "Stop. You are the polar opposite of needy. You're just scared, and I get it. Want me to run over there with you? Or you could grab one of the other guys—"

"No. I don't want anyone watching me freak out. It's embarrassing enough that you're seeing it." Kyle swallowed at Jesse's sigh.

Jesse pulled back and showed Kyle a melancholy kind of expression. He'd been quiet about Kyle's decision to go mostly exclusive with Luka. Jesse had been completely supportive, though, and had also kept his word about staying better connected with everyone. He looked concerned now, and Kyle both hated and loved his friend for that.

"You're a big idiot for trying to hide it from us," Jesse said. "You don't always have to be the one holding everyone together."

That was kind of a problem for Kyle. There weren't many people in his life whom he loved. He supported and cared for them without hesitation but didn't know how to turn that off, even when he was the one who needed to be held up.

Kyle summoned up what he suspected was a lopsided smile. "You sure you don't mind closing up?"

"Not at all. You want to sneak out the back?" Jesse turned Kyle loose and walked with him to the closet.

Kyle grumbled. He pulled his black wool coat from the hanger and shoved his arms into the sleeves. "Yeah. I feel bad cutting out without saying anything though. I won't see some of them until after the holiday."

"I'll explain what happened. You can just call everyone tomorrow," Jesse reasoned. "I'm making a big-ass lunch for Carter and Riley's kids on Sunday incidentally, so come on over after your yoga class and bring anyone you want." He pulled a gray knit cap out of the pocket of his own coat and thrust it at Kyle. "Do you have gloves?"

Kyle stared for a moment before he accepted the hat. "I...yes. Who are you right now?"

"Your friend, jackass. I don't want you to freeze while you're out there. Or get mugged, ugh."

"Jes, it's fifty degrees out!"

"It's also been raining for hours." Jesse huffed at Kyle's spluttering laughter. "Go on, get out of here before I change my mind and walk you over there myself."

* * * *

The rain had tapered off by the time Kyle made it outside. He walked two blocks north then turned right onto 113th Street, thankful for Jesse's hat, which warded off a chill in the damp air. He forced himself to stop at a late-night deli for a cup of hot tea and swallowed some of it down before he arrived at the three-story brick and brownstone building that housed Engine Company 47.

Kyle saw the truck's empty bay through the frosted glass windows set in the big, bright red door. Still unsure what to do, he decided to wait a while before he made a nuisance of himself. He crossed the street and camped out under the awning of a residential building opposite the firehouse so he could stay dry and still see the doors.

The restaurants and bars on Amsterdam Avenue made for a decent amount of foot traffic, even as the clock on Kyle's phone ticked past midnight. Five minutes passed, then ten, and quickly closed in on twenty. Kyle attracted the odd glance from passersby, of course, but an unpleasant jolt went through him when he realized his skin color had a lot to do with no one giving him a hard time.

Guilt made Kyle's skin crawl. In all likelihood, someone would have already called the cops if someone like Luka had been standing in Kyle's place, wearing the same clothes and checking his phone, with no obvious sign of having business to do in the neighborhood.

Another ten minutes passed before the familiar rumble of a fire truck echoed against the taller buildings that flanked the firehouse. Engine 47 rolled up, its lights flashing, and Kyle tossed his long-cold tea into a trash receptacle by the door. He watched, lips pressed tight, as two firefighters exited the vehicle. One moved to the firehouse doors while the other came around the truck, and Kyle's heart jerked when he recognized the second figure as Luka.

He's fine, Kyle told himself. His eyes actually watered with relief, but he became aware he'd moved only after he almost stepped off the sidewalk and into the street. *Luka's fine and standing right in front of you, big as life.*

Luka was also staring at Kyle, his eyes wide.

"Kyle! Don't go anywhere!" he called over the beep of Engine 47's back-up alarm and Kyle returned to the building where he'd been loitering, glad for its unyielding presence behind him.

Luka held up one hand to stop an oncoming car, and the fire truck backed into the station. The moment the door began rolling again, Luka waved at the others and made his way over to Kyle. He limped slightly, and the smoke lingering on his turnout gear filled Kyle's nose. There were sooty smudges on Luka's face, but his hands were warm on Kyle's.

"What are you doing here?" Luka's voice sounded rough from smoke or fatigue, and his gaze moved over Kyle, as if checking him for injuries. "Everything okay?"

Had Kyle been less freaked out, he'd have kicked his own ass. "I'm fine," he said instead, his voice much quieter than he'd meant it to be. "I was… I worried. I didn't hear from you, so I came over here to check you made it back. I sound like an idiot. Are *you* okay?"

Luka grimaced. "Damn, I'm sorry. Of course, I'm okay. Strained my hamstring hauling more weight than I should have up some stairs, but otherwise, all good. There was a kitchen fire in an apartment on Broadway, and it took us a lot longer than expected to evacuate the residents and get everything under control."

"Yeah, I saw the tweets." Kyle swallowed at the way Luka's face fell.

"Kyle, you shouldn't look at those. That shit will just stress you out."

"Yeah, I get that." Kyle barked out a tight laugh and wrapped his arms around himself. He gave Luka a sheepish grimace. "Sorry."

"Don't be. I'm the one who screwed things up for you with your friends." Luka shook off Kyle's protest. He set his hands on Kyle's shoulders and squeezed. "I know you were looking forward to hanging with them, so give me a half hour to get cleaned up and changed, and we can head back for last call."

Kyle shook his head. His frame of mind was all wrong for Under. Besides, Luka had already been on duty for over fifteen hours.

"Forget it." He smiled to soften his words. "I'm wiped and I can't imagine how you're feeling right now. If…if you want to be with me tonight, I'll get us a Lyft back to my place. Or one for you if you'd rather go home and get some sleep. I totally get that, too."

"Going home to sleep sounds fantastic," Luka said, "especially if you're gonna be there. Luis said he'd run me home in his truck, so how about you come back to Sugar Hill with me?"

"Sure." Kyle blew out a long breath. His insides felt like a deflated balloon. "You want me to wait out here for you?"

Luka frowned. "Absolutely not. Come on and I'll introduce you to anyone you haven't met already."

The next hour passed in a haze for Kyle. He met the other firefighters on duty, then sat with another cup of tea in the kitchen while Luka washed off the smoke and grime and changed into his civvies. Kyle dashed off a quick message to Jesse to let him know Luka was okay, but only after he and Luka had climbed into Luis' Chevy Silverado did Kyle understand how much energy the evening had drained from him. Kyle hadn't done a damned thing other than quietly lose his shit either — how Luka and Luis could function at all baffled him.

Not that it mattered. Soon enough, he and Luka were climbing the stairs to Luka's apartment. Luka dropped his bag on a bench and wrapped Kyle up in a tight hug as soon as the door closed behind them.

Kyle buried his face in Luka's neck and breathed in the scent of soap, skin, and the grooming cream Luka used on his hair. "What do you need?" Kyle asked him.

"You. Sleep. A pizza twice the size of my head." A chuckle rumbled through Luka's chest.

Kyle laughed softly. "In any particular order?"

"Naw. You and sleep will do just fine for now." Luka yawned, then pulled back enough to study Kyle's face. His eyes were dull and rimmed in red. "We can order food if you're hungry though. Are you okay?"

"I'm good. Or... getting there," he said after Luka frowned. "You sure your roommate won't mind I'm here?"

"Yep. This is my chance to show Matías you're a real, live man and not a figment of my imagination."

"He thinks you made me up?"

"He's said as much." Luka turned Kyle loose but kept an arm slung over his shoulders. "He's just jealous 'cause I haven't brought him by the speakeasy yet."

"That's on you, darlin.'" Kyle tugged at Luka and got him moving. "C'mon, let's get you to bed."

Together, they ambled down the hall and past Matías' closed door to the bathroom where they stripped down to their boxers. Kyle brushed his teeth with a toothbrush out of the box while Luka brought their things to his room and turned down the bed. He'd wrapped his hair in a cap and crawled onto the mattress by the time Kyle sat beside him. Luka's eyes were sleepy, and his lips curved in a lazy smile when he spied a small brown glass bottle in Kyle's hand. He rubbed a palm over Kyle's thigh.

"What's that?"

Kyle laid a hand on Luka's belly. "It's oil. Roll over onto your stomach for me."

Luka's eyes opened a little wider. "O-o-kay? Is this where your secret kinky side comes out at last?" His brow furrowed in a way that tugged at Kyle's heart.

"Kinkier than a foursome? Not tonight. I want you wide awake for that." He chuckled at the gleam in Luka's gaze. "I thought I'd rub your back and legs and help you get to sleep."

"Mmm, I won't need any help sleeping tonight." Luka laughed. "No way in hell I'm turning down a back rub though."

He rolled onto his stomach and pillowed his forehead on his hands while Kyle slicked his palms with oil. Kyle set the bottle on the nightstand and rose up on to his knees.

"Where'd you find massage oil?" The tail end of Luka's question dissolved into a low groan as Kyle grasped his trapezius and kneaded the tight muscles that connected Luka's shoulders to his neck. "Uhh, my God."

"I found it in the bathroom." Kyle replied. "I don't think it's massage oil. But the label says it's good for skin and it smells nice, like almonds and citrus."

"Damn. That's Matías'. Dunno what it's for...probably cost me an assload of money to replace it."

Kyle snickered. "You want me to stop?"

"Fuck, no. I'll love you forever if you keep going."

Luka's joking words—and Kyle had no doubt that was what they were—stripped Kyle bare and filled him up, all at the same time. He leaned over and dropped a kiss on Luka's shoulder, working the muscles in his upper back the whole time.

"Feel okay?" he asked.

"Very okay," Luka replied, his words slurred and sleepy.

"Good."

Kyle shifted backward and moved his hands along Luka's spine. He rubbed slow circles into the skin, soothing knots of tension, the motions turning Luka into a languid heap. Luka uttered a soft moan when Kyle dug in to the muscles at the base of his spine. Kyle increased the pressure, pushing slow, deep strokes from Luka's glutes up and over the small of his back while Luka hissed and swore.

"All right, Luka?"

"Yeah. Aches like a bitch. Feels good, too."

"Okay." Kyle shifted again so he could turn his attention to Luka's sore leg. "You tell me if I hurt you," he said, his voice low.

Luka turned his cheek to lie on the pillow and tucked his hands under it, too. "You won't," he murmured, so quietly Kyle nearly missed it.

Kyle massaged the hamstring with gentle motions, taking his time before he moved on to Luka's long calf muscle. Luka didn't make another peep, not even when Kyle switched to the other leg. His breaths were slow and even by the time Kyle stopped and sat back on his heels.

The last traces of Kyle's worry drained away as he watched Luka slumber, replaced by a deep warmth that worked its way around Kyle's heart and into his bones. Kyle blew out a long breath. He felt this way around Luka all the time now, both grounded and turned inside out in the very best way.

Kyle had tried minimizing his feelings and even ignoring them, but it was no use. They were…consuming. They smoothed over his rough edges and lifted him high and they buoyed him whenever he felt down. Kyle had experienced similar kinds of emotions in the past with Carter and Jesse, but they had been whispers compared to the storm inside him now.

Compared to the way he loved Luka.

Kyle loved Luka with an intensity that humbled and frightened him. Nothing about his feelings could be controlled or even managed, and he had no idea what to do except hang on for dear life. Kyle was done trying to deny the words, too, though he didn't dare say them out loud, even to himself. Not yet.

* * * *

Sunlight brightened the shades on Luka's windows when Kyle woke later that morning. Luka was still out, lying on his side and facing Kyle, his features relaxed and one heavy, muscled arm slung over Kyle's waist. Kyle drifted for a while, too comfortable to remove himself from the snug warmth of Luka's bed, until the pressure in his bladder won out.

Kyle rose, moving carefully to avoid waking Luka, and picked his clothes up from the chair where Luka had laid them. He made his way to the bathroom where he relieved himself and did a quick job of dressing and cleaning up, then went in search of the kitchen, taking in his surroundings for the first time.

The apartment was neat and serviceable, with white walls and trim. It had a comfortable bachelor-domain kind of vibe, with low-key stylish IKEA furniture and lots of neutral grays and blues. A few framed movie posters hung on the walls, along with candid photographs of Luka's family and other faces Kyle didn't recognize. They gave the place a welcoming feel, though the squat wire cage against one wall seemed somewhat out of place. And was that a teeny hammock hanging from the top most bars?

A sudden motion close to the floor caught Kyle's attention. He wheeled around, his eyes going wide as a furry little something scurried across the floor in his direction. It looked like a tube with a head and feet, for crying out loud.

"*Ay no, bicho,*" a low voice said, and just as suddenly, a man stood in front of Kyle, dressed in a plain white T-shirt and black joggers. He bent and scooped up what Kyle now recognized as a ferret with a glossy dark brown coat and white markings on its face. The man held the animal close to his chest.

This must be the roommate, Kyle thought. *Or roommates, to be more accurate.*

"We've talked about this," the man said in a gently scolding tone. "No scaring overnight guests until I've had a chance to scare them myself." The ferret made a chirping sound.

"Matías, right?" Kyle asked.

"That's right," Matías replied with a smile. He stood a bit shorter than Kyle, his skin at least as fair and his hair almost as dark. His sweetly handsome face was bare of makeup, but the mischief in his hazel-green eyes made Kyle chuckle. "You must be the bartender. You're just as yummy as Luka described."

"I'm Kyle, yes. And this is Robbie?" He nodded at the ferret and it chirped again.

"The one and only."

"Okay to pet?"

"Hell, yes — he's a total whore."

Kyle rubbed Robbie's head and was rewarded with a satisfied cluck.

Matías tilted his head in the direction of the kitchen. "Want some coffee?"

"I'd love it."

Matías turned around and Kyle fell into step beside him. "Luka's still sleeping?" he asked. "That's weird. It's past nine and he doesn't usually crash this late."

"They got a call around seven-thirty last night and it went later than expected. The truck didn't make it back to the station until after midnight."

"Ugh, that boy. I told him he needs to stop covering for everyone in the house, but he never listens to me." Matías made a tsking sound that Robbie almost echoed. "There're mugs over the sink and K-cups under the brewer if you don't mind helping yourself. I was about to feed this beast when he heard you moving around and went to investigate."

"Sure. You want a cup, too?"

"Yes, please." Matías went to the counter where a carton of eggs sat beside a small ceramic bowl. The ferret's chirps increased. "I put dry pellets in Robbie's cage, but I feed him raw several times a week, too. What brings you to this neck of the woods?"

"Luka was supposed to meet me at the bar." Kyle set a mug under the coffeemaker's spout and programmed it to brew. "By the time he and his squad were done, it was too late to head back downtown, so we just came here."

Matías broke an egg one-handed into the bowl and set the shell in it, too. He aimed a look at Kyle. "You freaked, huh?" His tone was all statement—he'd guessed at Kyle's unspoken words.

"A little." Kyle fixed his stare on the coffeemaker, then grunted. "Okay, a lot."

"I get it."

Matías' knowing tone caught Kyle's attention. "I wait up when Luka's late getting back from a shift," he said. He set the bowl and Robbie down on the floor, and they watched the ferret go to town on his breakfast. "When I'm here anyway, and he hasn't told me he's got plans to go downtown for a booty call."

Kyle snorted with laughter. "Got it." The more he considered Matías' words, the less he wanted to laugh though. Matías and Luka had been roommates for a while now, and if Matías still worried about Luka's wellbeing...well. The coffeemaker sputtered. "It doesn't get any easier?"

"Nope. It gets...not easier, but more like a new kind of normal, I guess." Matías went to the refrigerator for creamer. "I stopped checking social media sites because that just made it worse."

Kyle set the cup of coffee on the counter. "I looked around Twitter last night. Luka says I'll just drive myself up a wall doing that."

"He's not wrong. Twitter is both the best and worst thing. You get info fast but it's super raw and there's no context. My advice—if you want it—is not to look beyond the stuff the FDNY puts out," Matías said. He doctored his coffee with the creamer and sugar from a small canister while Kyle set up another mug. "They'll give you enough info to know what's going on and it's always rational."

Kyle wrinkled his nose. "I don't know about rational. FDNY alert tweets go out in all caps. It's like reading someone shouting at the top of their lungs."

Matías snickered and lifted his mug. "Okay, I'll give you that. I guess it's a lot more intense, you being his boyfriend and not just a roommate."

"Probably." Kyle leaned a hip against the counter. "Maybe I could talk to Ruby."

"She'll give you shit for debauching her baby brother first." Matías laughed at the way Kyle covered his face with one hand. "You know she's all play though. And for what it's worth, that's a solid idea. Ask Ruby about coping mechanisms because I'm guessing she developed a lot of them."

Kyle nodded and turned his attention on his coffee. He needed to talk about this with someone who understood how he was feeling—he knew that now. Simply admitting he'd been stressed to Matías felt good. Kyle would find a way to pull Ruby aside the next time he and Luka met up with her and see what she had to add. Maybe she wouldn't think Kyle a neurotic mess for asking.

"Do you ever put any gloss on those lips of yours or are you too butch for that?"

Kyle blinked. It took a second to shift gears and consider Matías' question. "I'm more of a Chapstick kind of guy," he said.

Matías grunted. "Oh, God. You buy everything over the counter, don't you?"

"Mostly." Kyle smiled. "Has nothing to do with being butch or femme though. I'm kind of picky when it comes to spending money on non-essentials."

"Honey, good skincare is totally essential," Matías said. He set his mug down and stepped closer. Taking hold of Kyle's chin with one hand, Matías tilted Kyle's face back and forth, the movements gentle despite his frown. "For someone like you especially, what with all of this whiteness happening. Please tell me you use moisturizer and sunscreen at least?"

"I use a two-in-one kind of thing," Kyle replied.

"Did you buy it in a drugstore?"

"Well, yes—"

Matías made a raucous noise like a game buzzer. "Not good enough, Kyle!" He sniffed, his disgust plain, and dropped his hand from Kyle's chin. "You need to keep the sun and smog off your face, even if you're not the makeup type."

"I like some eyeliner occasionally," Kyle said. He swallowed down a laugh at the spark in Matías' eyes. "But that's it. I work with my hands all night, man. I can't be worried about whether or not my face is still matte or dewy or whatever the fuck."

Matías laughed and the merry sound made Kyle join right in.

"You're cute," Matías said. "And I'll change your mind about skin care by the time you leave this apartment. Mark my words." He hazarded a glance at Robbie, who'd finished a good portion of the egg and had turned his attention on the eggshell. "Luka says you know your way around a kitchen, so how about you help me throw some breakfast together while the beast is still distracted?"

In short order, Kyle and Matías put together a big spread of pancakes and a tomato-egg scramble, and they were nearly finished when Luka walked in wearing a faded T-shirt with his boxers. He was still limping but appeared much better rested and bright-eyed. He took in Kyle and Matías working together with a big grin, and just looking at him made Kyle's heart jump around.

Luka inhaled deeply. "Smells fantastic in here."

"Figures you'd show up just when all the hard work is done." Matías aimed a glare at him. "Glad you took a second to style your hair at least. Are you okay? Kyle said you hurt yourself being a big he-man last night."

"I told him you pulled a muscle," Kyle said, his tone as mild as he could manage. He turned back to the griddle he'd been working with and used the spatula to move pancakes onto a serving dish.

"I'm fine, as you can see." Luka stepped up to the stove and slipped an arm around Kyle. "My leg's sore but it's nothing ibuprofen and a couple of days off won't fix. Need any help?" he asked.

"Nope. The cooking is finished." Kyle turned the burner off. He glanced up at Luka and frowned at the concern in his expression. "What?"

"Things got kind of heavy last night. Then I fell asleep on you, and when I woke up you weren't there. I thought at first maybe you'd left." Luka licked his lips. "I saw your phone on the dresser and your shoes and figured you'd just wandered off."

Kyle swallowed over the ache in his throat. "Sorry. I woke up and heeded the call of coffee. I'm still getting okay with last night," he said more softly. "I talked with Matías. I might talk to Ruby, too."

"Okay." Luka rubbed Kyle's shoulder. "You can talk to me if you want, you know."

"I'm not sure I should," Kyle murmured. "But thank you for saying that."

Luka sighed, but his smile made the corners of his eyes crinkle. He kissed Kyle, sweet and chaste, and Kyle's knees went all mushy.

"Dudes, stop slobbering over each other and get your asses over here." Matías carried the platter of eggs and sausage links to the table. "I'm about to starve to death and I don't want Robbie eating my corpse face."

Luka groaned and Kyle laughed against his lips.

"He's so gross." Luka squeezed Kyle again before he turned away. "Let me just make some coffee."

They gorged on food and chatted about their weekend plans while Robbie prowled around the apartment, stopping in the kitchen at regular intervals to wind around their ankles and nip at their toes under the table. Naturally, talk turned to the upcoming holiday and the various kinds of cooking each of them would be doing.

"All anyone ever expects from me is booze," Kyle said. "I'm staying over with Carter and Riley though, and they've always been into breakfast. Maybe I'll make this scramble." He considered the eggs that remained on his plate. "I know you used fresh tomatoes, but have you ever cooked this with canned?" he asked Matías.

"Sure," Matías replied. "Don't always have fresh on hand, and there's usually a couple of cans in the pantry. Salsa works too and tastes bomb. You just have to drain it a bit."

"What about canned beans or corn?" Kyle asked. "Like if you wanted to stretch it out for a couple of people or maybe have it for dinner instead?"

"Ooh, like a funky huevos rancheros." Matías nodded. "I approve. Rice would be good, too, though maybe nicer on the side. I've never done any of that but you're making it sound damned good."

Luka chuckled, his expression bemused. "Where are you going with this?"

"Oh, well, I do some volunteer work at a shelter for LGBTQ youth. Carter, Riley, Malcolm and Will, too."

Kyle shrugged. "Carter and Malcolm asked me to help out with a project for the shelter, and it involves food."

Luka furrowed his brow. "Like donating money?"

"No, though we do that as well. See, a lot of the kids in the shelter are young enough they've never lived on their own. When they end up alone, it's sudden and overwhelming, so the shelter staff do their best to teach them some life skills and help them function independently."

"Things parents would normally teach their kids," Luka said in a quiet voice.

Kyle nodded. Of course, Luka got it. "Carter and Malcolm had an idea to put together some practical resources the kids can use after they leave the shelter," he said. "Information like how to buy and cook food on a budget." Kyle waved at his plate. "A meal with eggs like this is filling and nutritious and can cost just a couple of dollars to make. Plus, it tastes really fucking good, so bonus points."

Matías' eyes lit up. "I love this idea. I just thought of at least six other things that might work for you, too. Are you guys writing a cookbook?"

"Oh, no, nothing like that," Kyle said. "Malcolm found a couple of existing cookbooks written expressly for people on tight budgets, and we're adding to those, so there's some variety, you know? We're making buying guides, too, because one thing no one ever tells you is how to buy cheap food that's better for you than frozen pizza and ramen. Both things I enjoy eating, by the way."

"I have some great instant ramen recipes," Luka said, "and I swear, there are fresh vegetables involved."

The genuine, eager pleasure in his and Matías' faces warmed Kyle's insides. "Excellent. We're all going over to the shelter early on Thanksgiving Day to help prepare dinner for everyone and to talk with the staff about the buying and food guides. I'll add anything you guys suggest if you're into it."

"I am totally in." Matías stood and headed for the kitchen door before Kyle could even blink. "We need paper so we can write stuff down!"

"No, bring your tablet so we can look up the ingredients and calculate cost," Luka called after him. "What's cheap to you might not be cheap to the masses! Besides, your handwriting is garbage!"

The muffled swearing that followed in reply made Kyle laugh until Luka planted a kiss on him. Luka gave him a devilish grin when they came back up for air.

"Much as I enjoy hanging out with Matías, I can't wait until he leaves so I can return the favor and give you a back rub."

Kyle hummed. "I like the sound of that. Fair warning though — he said he wants to try out some new product on my face before he goes to work. Which means I might mess up your sheets."

"I'm counting on that regardless." Luka waggled his eyebrows like a cartoon villain. "But what kind of product are we talking about?"

"I'm not sure." Kyle rested his forehead against Luka's. "There was talk of moisturizer, decent lip balm and eyeliner, at the very least."

Luka leaned back and away from Kyle. "Eyeliner?" He uttered a growly laugh that made Kyle's cock twitch. "You'll both be lucky if I let him leave before I start peeling your clothes off."

Chapter Twelve

The scent of roast turkey hit Luka when he opened the kitchen door to the house in Riverdale, followed by a wave of heat and noise.

"Marcus, will you check the appetizers and see if anything needs to be refilled?" Lydia called out over a babble of voices.

"Sure, just give me a minute," Marcus answered from the other room. "We're seconds from kickoff."

Luka smiled at the controlled chaos and stepped inside. Regina was cutting the ends off beans while Ruby sliced carrots, and both were chattering about something.

"I made it," Luka said, shutting the door behind him.

Lydia faced him and her face lit up as usual. "Hey, baby."

Several others called out greetings, including Tomas, who was helping one of Daniela's sons, Elias, stir something on the stove. He waved rather than leave Elias alone.

"You look tired." Lydia brushed her fingertips across Luka's face, and he leaned in to kiss her cheek.

He'd worked the night before and slept as late as possible but had still gotten up earlier than he would have liked. No way would Luka miss dinner unless he had to though. He'd worked plenty of holiday shifts over the years and gotten lucky this year, and that was one thing to be thankful for.

"I'll be fine with more coffee in me," he said and shrugged out of his coat, draping it over a nearby chair.

"I just put a fresh pot on," Lydia said. "Help yourself."

"I'll grab it as soon as I say hi to everyone. Unless you need my help?"

"No, we've got it under control."

"Oh, here's the butter you asked for," Luka said, handing the package to her. He set the bottles of wine he'd bought on the counter, too.

"Thank you. I don't know how we went through so much so quickly!" Lydia sounded miffed. "Just wait, I'll find some tucked behind the mixer or in the vegetable drawer tomorrow. There's too much going on to tell."

Luka chuckled. Controlled chaos indeed.

"Is Kyle spending Thanksgiving with his family?" Lydia sounded casual, though Luka knew the topic was anything but. Clearly, his mother wanted to try being pleasant about Kyle.

"No. Kyle's father died when he was in college and his mother isn't around for him," Luka explained.

Sympathy flickered across Lydia's face. "I'm sorry to hear that. Is it because he's gay?"

"Doesn't sound like it." Luka chose his words carefully. "From what I know, Kyle's mother didn't want to have kids. She's...not interested in Kyle or his brother."

"Oh." Lydia's voice was soft. "I can't imagine that's been easy for him."

"He doesn't talk about it much. Kyle is close to his brother. Oliver lives out of state, but they get together whenever they can. I met him the last time he came to town."

"Well, I'm glad Kyle has some family."

"He does. They're just not his biological relatives." Luka leaned against the counter. "The guys from the speakeasy are his family now. A lot of them lost their own when they came out or for various other reasons. So, they're one another's family now."

Lydia nodded. "I'm glad Kyle has people, then."

"They're good people, too. They're spending the day volunteering at the LGBTQ youth shelter, in fact."

"I'm guessing it's not for a photo op either."

"It's not," Luka said. "I think they all do as much to avoid the spotlight as possible, except when Senator Mori needs to be in it for his career." Luka bumped one of the wine bottles with his elbow and he straightened. "Is there room for the white in the refrigerator?"

"No, but there's a bucket of ice in the dining room on the sideboard."

"I'll take care of that now then."

Luka plucked two bottles and headed out of the kitchen but stopped to give Tomas a one-armed hug and kiss Elias on top of his head. "Hey there, Eli. Whatever you're cooking smells good!"

"We're cooking plantains for *tostones*, Uncle Luka!" Eli said with a big grin. "Pop is showing me how."

"Yum. I can't wait to try them."

"I made empanadas yesterday," Tomas told Luka.

"Mmm. I hoped you would."

Luka also stopped to peck his sisters' cheeks.

"Glad you finally showed your face," Ruby said.

"You're just happy that, for once, you're not the last one to arrive," he said.

"I'll take my victories where I can."

"Is Wade working?" he asked Regina.

She frowned. "Yes. He drew the short straw this year."

"I was afraid of that. We seem to be on opposite years."

Regina shrugged. "Hazard of the job, right?"

"At least Mom's not working on Thanksgiving anymore." When Lydia had been a floor nurse, they'd had to work around her schedule, sometimes celebrating on Friday, sometimes eating early or late when she needed to sleep.

"Uh-huh," Regina muttered. "Guess who was up at six to put the turkey into the oven back then?"

"Oh, right. We had the dry, overcooked birds on those years."

Regina swatted at him, but Luka dodged her and disappeared into the dining room with an, "I love you, Queenie!"

Once he'd put the wine in the ice bucket and carried his coat to the spare bedroom, Luka went back to the kitchen for coffee and searched out the rest of his family. He found Marcus on the couch with a couple of friends, probably guys from out of state who couldn't make it home for the holidays. They barely looked up from the football game on TV, but Marcus stood and gave Luka a hug.

"Hey, glad you could be here this year."

"Me too." Luka dropped his voice. "Don't forget, Mom asked you to top off the appetizers."

"Shit." Marcus' eyes got big. "I almost did forget. Thanks, man."

Luka patted him on the shoulder. "Just looking out for you, brother."

A pretty young woman with box braids and deep brown skin stood from her seat. "Good to see you again, Luka."

"Hey, Stella." Luka smiled at Ruby's close friend. "You too. Glad you could make it today."

"My parents are in California with my grandparents, but I couldn't take the time off work to go, too. Ruby was nice enough to invite me here."

"We do have a habit of picking up strays." He gestured to Marcus' friends and Stella laughed.

"I can think of worse things to be called." She reached out and touched his shoulder. "I can think of better, too."

Luka chuckled. He knew for a fact Stella and Ruby had checked out Under last week and that she damn well knew he and Kyle were dating. But she'd always been a flirt.

Daniela waved at Luka but couldn't move with a sleeping toddler in her arms. Luka took the seat beside her and kissed her cheek. "Hey, gorgeous. You look tired."

"Luka, it is never okay to tell a woman she looks tired!" Daniela scolded, but she winked and Luka could tell she wasn't serious. "I could say the same to you."

"Long shift last night," he said. "You?"

She squinted at him. "I've been up for about a week, baking like it's going out of style. We were open this morning from six until noon so people could pick up their orders."

Luka had made the mistake of going to Sugar Street before a holiday once and there had been a line out of the door that wrapped halfway around the block.

"Loved the blackberry pie you sent for dinner a while back," he said.

She beamed. "You are going to love the blackberry custard pie I brought today then. I've been experimenting with ginger and nutmeg to bring it into fall."

"Sounds amazing." Luka's mouth watered. "Knowing you, there's even more."

"Oh, I might have brought a few more things. Sweet potato pie and pecan, Dutch apple, chocolate chiffon. You missed the pumpkin sweet rolls I brought earlier, but I might have stashed a few away for you and your man. Oh, and there's guava cake!"

"You'll have to roll me out of here after dinner then. No way I can resist your baking," Luka teased. "And that reminds me, I need to bring Kyle to the bakery sometime."

Daniela smiled. "Ruby said he's hot as fuck."

"I second that," Stella said with a wink.

Luka chuckled. "I'm pretty partial to him."

Less than an hour later, everyone sat in the dining room. An extender had been added to the table as well as some folding tables to further increase its length, and everything was decorated for the holiday. Tomas said the blessing and carved the turkey, and they passed around more food than any of them could hope to eat in a week. Luka was determined to do his best, however, and piled chorizo and cornbread dressing on his plate next to turkey and collard greens, mashed potatoes with giblet gravy and an empanada.

"How are things going with Kyle, Luka?" Ruby asked from a few seats down. "He was so sweet when Stella and I scoped his speakeasy out last week. Very welcoming to both of us."

Luka tried and failed to hide a smile. Subtlety had never been Ruby's forte, but he appreciated the support. "Kyle's great. He's volunteering at a LGBTQ youth shelter today with some of the guys who hang at Under."

Stella whistled. "Your boyfriend's friends are rich, handsome and socially conscious? Damn."

"They're great guys," Luka agreed. "Matías and I helped Kyle come up with some recipes and tips for buying and cooking meals on a budget. They're for kids living on their own for the first time who might not have had parents to teach them those skills."

"Ooh. Let me know if you need any more suggestions," Stella said. "I can come up with a few."

"That would be great."

Lydia cleared her throat. "Does anyone else need anything? More turkey? Some wine?"

Ruby shot their mother a look from the other end of the table, and Luka responded with a look of his own, telling his sister with his eyes to cool it. Luka and his mom had already talked about Kyle's work at the shelter. And provoking a fight at Thanksgiving dinner was no way to win her over.

The rest of dinner passed without incident, and Luka relaxed into the easy vibe. He wondered what it would have been like to have Kyle there. His sister and mother had been polite to Kyle when they'd met him, if not welcoming. What would it take for them to see how important Kyle had become to Luka? How good he and Kyle were together? Because Kyle was another thing Luka felt grateful for this year. And he hoped Kyle would be around for future Thanksgivings.

After the meal, Luka felt ready to get horizontal on the couch and not move for a week, but he pushed back from the table and picked up a stack of plates.

"Mom, Pop, you did so much work. I'll get the dishes," he said. "Marcus, you want to help?"

The long-suffering look Marcus gave him made it very clear he didn't want to help at all, but he stood and took another stack of plates without complaining. Everyone helped carry things into the kitchen, and Luka rolled up the sleeves of his button-down shirt to get started on things that couldn't go in the dishwasher.

"How are things going with you?" Luka asked Marcus as he swirled soapy water in the gravy boat.

"They're going. I'm trying to get ready for finals." Marcus dried the turkey platter. "I feel like studying's all I do these days."

"It'll be worth it," Luka said. "I'm thinking about going back to school."

"Fire science, I assume?"

"Yeah, I think so. I want a backup plan for the future."

"Got it. That's smart." Marcus elbowed him. "Let me know if you need any tips for studying."

"I will. And hey, if I haven't said this already, thanks for being so cool to Kyle."

Marcus scoffed. "He's great, man. It's not like it's a hardship. I want to stop by that bar of his and we talked about grabbing lunch sometime. After I'm done with exams because I don't have time for anything else."

"That means a lot to me that you're making the effort."

"I can see how much you like him." Marcus dropped his voice. "Besides, I figure I can make up for Mom and Regina giving him the cold shoulder."

Luka hummed. "Tell me about it."

"Does it bug Kyle? I mean, it would bother me if I stood in his shoes."

"He doesn't talk about it much," Luka admitted. "But I've wondered about that."

After the dishes were dried, Luka went in search of his phone, which he'd left in his coat. When he pushed open the door of the spare bedroom, he found Regina in there with May, Daniela's littlest. May was sound asleep, and Regina pressed a finger to her lips. Regina pulled a blanket over the child and smoothed down May's hair, a wistful expression crossing her face.

Luka pocketed his phone and waited for his sister in the hallway. "You okay?" he asked when she'd shut the door behind her.

"It's hard sometimes," Regina said. "Do you have a minute?"

"Of course."

Regina gestured for him to follow her into the room that had once been Luka's bedroom and now housed Tomas' office. Luka pulled the door closed after them because he had a feeling this wouldn't be an easy discussion.

Regina settled on the window seat and crossed her legs while Luka sat in the desk chair nearby.

"Wade and I got some bad news from the fertility doc earlier this week." Regina clasped her hands on her knee. "We've exhausted our options and are no closer to getting pregnant than when we started."

"Oh, damn." Luka said, frowning.

"I haven't told anyone but it's looking like we need to accept the fact that it's not meant to be." She tilted her head back and took a deep breath, as if she was trying not to cry.

Luka's heart ached for his sister. He hated seeing her hurt so much and know he could do little to help. "I'm sorry, Regina."

She nodded. "My age is part of it. You know I love what I do, but now there are some days I'd go back and make different choices. Not wait so long. Focus less on my career. But I wanted to be in a better place.

"I saw how things were for Mom after Dad died," Regina said. "She worked all those hours to help care for us. And Wade. I love him so much, but he has the same kind of job Dad had. I knew there was no guarantee Wade would be around to help me raise our children, and I wanted to be able to support them myself if it came to that. The city pays out death benefits but..." She shook her head, as if she couldn't continue

"I had no idea that's part of why you pushed yourself so hard," Luka said. "You know we all would help out if anything happened."

"I know." Regina wiped her eyes. "But I had to be sure I could handle it myself, and now ... Now I wonder what was the point? We may never have children at all."

"I wish I could say something to make it easier for you," he said.

"We're looking into adoption. I know it's not a bad choice, but I feel like a failure."

"You're not a failure," Luka reassured his sister. "You'll be a wonderful mother, however it happens."

Luka wanted to have kids someday, but because he'd dated both men and women, he'd never had any concrete plans about how it would happen. Would Kyle want that?

Regina shook her head as if to clear away the earlier conversation. "How are things with you?"

"Work's been hectic so I'm glad I got today off. I'm sure the station is elbow-deep in grease fires."

Regina chuckled. "I remember that story you told me about the guy who lit his porch on fire making deep-fried turkey."

"There's at least one Thanksgiving turkey fire a year," Luka replied, "but I remember the one you're talking about. The neighbor spotted the fire and called it in before rushing over to help."

"Right! The neighbor who'd been in the tub and ran down wearing a towel and nothing else."

"Yeah. That so-called Good Samaritan lost his towel mid-conversation with Lane." Luka shuddered at the memory. "Ugh."

Regina frowned. "I heard about the apartment fire last week. Mom said you pulled a muscle?"

"Nothing major. It was just uncomfortable for a day or two. Kyle helped me work it out." He wanted to curse at the expression that crossed Regina's face. Damn it, he shouldn't have brought up Kyle. But what the hell, why did he have to walk on eggshells all the time?

"It seems like Marcus and Ruby are getting chummy with him," Regina said, sitting back. "What's this about Ruby going to his bar?"

"Kyle gave her an open invitation a while ago," Luka replied, "and she and Stella took him up on it."

"I notice Kyle hasn't extended the same invitation to me." There was a trace of hurt in Regina's voice.

Whoa. Does Regina feel left out? What's that about? Luka reminded himself to take a deep breath before he blew up at his sister.

"In fact, he has," Luka said as gently as he could manage. "Kyle has told me anyone in the family is welcome any time. But, honestly, why should he? You made it clear you don't think much of me dating men. You weren't rude to Kyle, but you didn't go out of your way to make him feel welcome when we went to hear Ruby sing either."

Surprise crossed Regina's face. "I'll admit I didn't think much of the idea when you first mentioned him. But after watching you two together at the club, I could tell how happy he makes you."

Luka stared at her. "You didn't do a good job of making your change of heart clear to either of us."

"I'm sorry." She sighed. "It's true. I went into that night thinking nothing he could do would change my mind. But then I saw how hard Kyle tried when he was clearly uncomfortable. He did that for you, and it made me feel differently. Watching the two of you dance…" She shook her head. "I can't remember the last time I've seen you so happy with anyone, Luka. As your older sister, I like to think I know what's best for you, and for a long time, I thought it had to be a woman. Why choose to make your life harder than it has to be? Dating a man is harder, right?"

"Only in the way other people treat us."

"But it isn't a choice, is it?" Regina said. She sounded thoughtful, as if she'd never considered that fact before.

"Choosing means closing myself off to people out there who could make me happy."

"Like Kyle?"

"Yes, like Kyle."

"You're in love with him, aren't you?"

"Yeah, I am."

She reached out and squeezed his hand. "Then I'm sorry I didn't do more to welcome him. Can you forgive me?"

"Of course." Luka stood and pulled Regina to her feet, crushing her against him in a bear hug. "Thank you for admitting you were wrong," he murmured against her hair. "I know it can't have been easy."

"Your happiness is worth more than my pride," she muttered, her voice muffled by his shoulder.

Luka's eyes pricked with tears. "Think you can help bring Mom around?"

Regina drew back and smoothed down her dress. "I can try."

"That would mean a lot to me."

"Okay." Regina offered Luka a fleeting smile. "Should we see if they've left any pie for us?"

"Sounds good." Luka moved toward the door, but Regina caught his elbow.

"Would you and Kyle have dinner with Wade and me sometime in the next few weeks? Whenever we can make all of our schedules mesh."

"I'd like that," Luka said, his heart feeling light. "I'd like that a lot. I'll talk to Kyle about that soon."

The rest of the evening passed pleasantly for all of them. They ate pie—the family had waited to dig in until he and Regina emerged—and watched football and played board games. Only one thing was missing as far as Luka was concerned. *Kyle.*

As usual, saying goodbye took a long time, but Luka left the house with a bag of leftovers and a promise to call Regina when he and Kyle had some dates that worked for them.

He texted Kyle as he walked to the train station.

How was your day?

Good. Makes me sad to see kids with no families – reminds me of losing my dad. Really glad we could give them a sense of belonging. How was dinner?

Better than expected. I'll call you. Hands are full of leftovers.

Luka's phone rang a moment later.

"Better than expected, huh?" Kyle asked.

"Yeah. Regina and I had a good conversation. She's invited us to dinner with her and Wade." His words were met with a brief silence.

"That would be nice." Kyle sounded surprised but pleased. And there, proof that he'd been bothered by Luka's family's behavior.

"I also have cake and pumpkin sweet rolls from Daniela. With her famous cream cheese icing."

Kyle let out a low hum. "That sounds amazing."

"Wait until you taste them. I don't know though. I had no idea I'd have to compete against food to make sounds like that come out of your mouth."

Kyle laughed. "It sounds like your family is coming around," he said more seriously. "That's good."

"They are," Luka agreed. "And yeah, it's a big relief."

"Next, I just have to win over your mom."

Luka ached for Kyle. "I hate to put a damper on your good mood, but she's going to be the hardest nut to crack."

"Good thing you're worth fighting for."

A lump rose in Luka's throat. He was so close to telling Kyle he loved him but saying it over the phone was nearly as bad as in the middle of a foursome. Worse, maybe. At least at Jesse and Cam's, Luka would have been able to reach out and touch Kyle.

"You're staying at Riley and Carter's tonight, right?" Luka asked instead. "We kinda left things open-ended, depending on when stuff wrapped up for both of us."

"Yes, I'm there now."

"And they're cool with me coming over?"

"Definitely. Ollie's here, too."

"I'll head that way then."

"I'd like that," Kyle said. His voice was warm. "It's getting harder and harder to fall asleep without you in bed with me."

"Same here," Luka said. "I'll be there as fast as I can."

"I'll wait up."

Chapter Thirteen

"How many of your friends own second homes?" Luka's eyes were on the road when Kyle glanced his way.

They'd borrowed Ruby's car again for this early December weekend on Long Island with the speakeasy guys and were moments from entering the Queens Midtown Tunnel. Luka looked relaxed behind the wheel in a hoodie and jeans, and Kyle mentally crossed his fingers that the light traffic they'd encountered so far this Friday afternoon would hold.

"Very few," he said. "Jesse's brother and sister-in-law bought a farmhouse in Vermont a few years ago, and Carter and Riley have the place in Southampton, but that's it. Well, Will and David sort of co-own a pool at Will's sister's house. However that works. Why do you ask?"

"Just curious. My buddy Lars and his wife own part of a timeshare in Virginia Beach, but they do that with three other couples. They also rent it out when the owners aren't using it." Luka pushed his sunglasses up onto his head as they approached the tunnel's entrance. "It's not like they have an extra house just sitting there empty and waiting for them to pay it a visit," he said.

Kyle scoffed. "Dude, it's a building, not a puppy— you're such a romantic." Luka's laughter filled the car. Kyle pulled off his own sunglasses and peered at him through the tunnel's gloom. "Jesse's too much in love with New York to want a getaway house, and he and Cam are more into traveling for vacation anyway. David and Will are happy in Freeport, so I don't see them wanting another home."

"And you and Malcolm?"

"He and I are regular guys, Luka." Kyle chuckled. "So is David when you get down to it—he just happens to have a high-profile job and a rich boyfriend."

"You don't collect a 'regular guy' kind of paycheck," Luka said, his tone reasonable.

"Not anymore, no, but it's not Murtagh-level money-making either, and nothing like Carter's and Riley's wealth," Kyle replied. "Besides, I don't need anything bigger than the place I already have." He smiled at Luka's exaggerated throat clearing. "You got something to say about my apartment, Clarke?"

"Nope." Luka used a hand to mime zipping his lips closed, then spoke anyway. "Okay, I do wonder why you're still in such a small place. Don't get me wrong— your apartment is great, but a second bedroom might be nice."

"I'll give you that," Kyle replied. "It'd be nice to stash my brother and his stuff somewhere other than my couch when he's in town."

He'd never hesitate welcoming Oliver or any friend who needed a bed, even though the lack of privacy sometimes left a lot to be desired. But Kyle was attached to his apartment, probably more so than typical.

He licked his lips. "Pretty sure you've noticed I'm a creature of habit," he said. He gestured to his plaid flannel and jeans. "I bought these clothes right after I moved into the Chelsea apartment, and I've owned my boots even longer. It took me a while to save up enough money to rent anything back then, but I was glad to find it, even though I shared it with two other guys at the time. The shoebox is in a great building, and my landlady cuts her tenants a good deal on rent."

Luka nodded. "When did you start living alone?"

"Around the time I met Carter. I had to stretch making ends meet, but some creative budgeting helped." Kyle glanced at him. "After Jes and I decided to open the speakeasy, I thought about moving uptown, but it seemed too risky. Moving and then having to do it again if Under closed and I got a job somewhere else? No, thanks."

"Makes sense." Luka squinted at the approaching tunnel exit. "Am I in the right lane?"

"For now, yep. Once we're aboveground, keep left for the Expressway."

Luka nodded. "Got it. Okay, you thought about moving then decided against it. What about now? Under's clearly a success."

"Eh, I don't know." Kyle smiled at Luka's sidelong glance. "Creature of habit, remember?"

Plus, I like knowing where I'll lay my head for more than a few days at a time, too.

Kyle shook off the thought. No need to get heavy on a sunny Friday afternoon. "A big apartment with lots of rooms means way more cleaning. Look at Carter and Riley," he said over Luka's laughter. "They've got a three-story house in Murray Hill, and they both work full time — they had to hire a housekeeper to help them out once a week. No way would I choose to clean all those rooms."

"You are bananas," Luka replied, his tone fond. He guided the car out of the tunnel and slid his shades back on. "Do you think Carter and Riley should downsize?"

"Mmm, no — I don't see that happening. They have Sadie and Dylan part-time, so they actually do need more room." Kyle squinted against the change in light. "And Riley was given the beach house before he and Carter got together. Ri loves that house. I think he'd live there year-round if he could."

"It's that nice?"

"It's great, but he'd love the place even if it were a shack. Not that the Porter-Wrights would own something junky. The house used to belong to Ri's parents," Kyle said. "He spent a lot of time there growing up, and they gave it to him as a gift."

Luka whistled. "Some gift. What was the occasion?"

"His engagement."

"The engagement to the now ex-wife? Hoo boy."

"Yup." Kyle turned his eyes back on the road but reached out so his knuckles rested against Luka's hip. "After he took it over, he and his wife would bring Carter and Kate and other friends out for vacation weeks and that kind of thing."

"That sounds so weird considering their lives now."

"Right? Carter's ex is nice, but it's impossible for me to picture him with anyone but Ri."

"What about Riley's ex?" Luka asked.

"I've never met her in person," Kyle replied. "From what I hear, she's a world-class ice queen with a resting bitchface that could turn you to salt."

Luka cackled. "Damn. But they were all split up when you met them, right?"

"Yes. When I met Carter, he and Kate were either already divorced or about to be — otherwise, I wouldn't have dated him at all." Kyle sniffed. "Car introduced me to Riley a few months later, but Riley and Will were dating at the time."

"Oh, man, that's right!" Luka snapped his fingers. "Didn't Ri say he and Carter used to fool around before their divorces, too?"

"Yep, but there were more than just the two of them involved."

"We're so gossipy."

Kyle laughed. "We really are! Calling a stop on the gossip, starting now."

"Just as well." Luka smirked. "I need a scorecard to keep track of the dramas at this rate."

Kyle scoffed. "There's no drama. Or, there's rarely drama. Malcolm keeps a spreadsheet with all the hook-ups and pairings if you're interested in getting the juicy details, by the way."

Luka burst out laughing. "He does not!"

"He does — Malcolm knows all the tea. Ask him about it when we get there."

Kyle and Luka continued chatting as the car traveled the Long Island Expressway, trading news and, yes, a little gossip about their friends and family. A quiet happiness filtered over Kyle when he considered how those circles had begun to overlap.

Despite the differences in paychecks and family fortunes, Luka fit in with Kyle's friends, the same way Malcolm and Will had, and David and Cam after them. The speakeasy guys liked and respected Luka, and so did Oliver, despite the miles separating him from New York.

Kyle's connections with the Clarke-Padillas were still forming, but he'd gained traction through Marcus and Ruby. Ruby'd infiltrated the speakeasy, and Kyle had enjoyed watching her and a friend flirting with Jesse, Cam and Astrid.

Regina and Wade had extended an olive branch to Kyle, too. They'd welcomed him into their home and to their table, and Kyle recognized Regina's genuine efforts to get to know him. Did bemusement sometimes cross her face when her gaze swept over Kyle and Luka? Yes. She might question Kyle's rightness for her brother—as an older sibling, Kyle understood her impulse—but she was trying. She'd even pulled Kyle into the kitchen after dinner for a chat.

'I know it's not easy meeting this family and being tossed into the middle of everything.'

Regina had arranged apple and raspberry turnovers from Sugar Street on a platter while they'd waited for coffee to brew. Kyle had seen the resemblance between her and Luka around their eyes despite Regina's being a deep, warm brown.

'It's fine,' Kyle had replied. *'Every family's dynamic is different.'*

'True. Wade told me it took a while before he felt like he belonged however,' she'd said, *'and I'm glad you're willing to put yourself through it. I think you're good for Luka.'*

'Thank you for saying that.' Kyle's face had gone hot. *'Luka's good for me, too.'*

Regina had smiled. *'Lord, your cheeks are red. Luka's going to think I upset you.'*

'No worries — he's used to it by now. There's no in between for me, so when I'm not paper-white, I'm pink.'

The coffeemaker had gurgled and Kyle had accepted the platter of sweets from Regina, but he hadn't spoken again until she'd met his gaze.

'I meant that – Luka's good for me, too,' he'd said. He hadn't missed the pleasure in Regina's eyes.

'I'm glad.' She'd set the carafe on another tray holding empty cups and tipped her head in the direction of the dining room. *'We should get back before they think we decided not to share.'*

Kyle flipped the car radio on and turned his attention to the passing landscape. He hoped he'd get a chance to talk like that with Luka's mother too sometime, but he wouldn't hold his breath. A dark part of Kyle thought Lydia Padilla would never crack. On paper, Kyle didn't have much to offer anyone. Outside of Oliver, he had no family. And despite his success with Under, Kyle didn't consider himself very far removed from living out of a big green sea bag and sleeping on strangers' couches.

Somehow, though, Kyle made Luka happy despite Lydia's disapproval. Kyle planned on doing a hell of a lot of work to make sure Luka didn't regret sticking with him.

Like moving closer to Harlem so he's not forced to drag his ass all over Manhattan just to see you?

Kyle worried his bottom lip with his teeth as the thought settled in. He'd overheard Luka's and Cam's good-natured complaints about the commute into Midtown from both south and north. Kyle and Luka had started spending more time in Sugar Hill since then, particularly because doing so shaved good time off Kyle's commute to and from work, too. They tried to be considerate of Matías however. Kyle's work hours could be disruptive and while Matías hadn't complained, neither Kyle nor Luka wanted him feeling uncomfortable in his own place.

So maybe...maybe now Kyle could make a move. Chelsea had been his home for years, but who said he couldn't make a new home closer to Morningside Heights? A bigger place would mean room for Oliver during his visits, as well as space for Luka's things, if a time came when he'd need it.

"I can hear you thinking over there, McKee."

Kyle blinked and the world came back into focus around him. He turned his gaze on Luka. "Hmm?"

Luka's expression softened. "Wow, hey. We're coming up on the turn off to 111, and I asked if you wanted to stop anywhere first."

"Sorry." Kyle sat up straighter in his seat. "We'll be in Southampton Village in about twenty minutes. There's a market and bakery there. Ri asked me to pick up a bagel spread for tomorrow's breakfast and I need fruit, too."

"I assume to go with the boozy wonderland you've got stashed in that big brown bag?"

"Um, duh."

Luka laughed. "Cool, just tell me where to stop when I get close." He turned his attention back to the road and dropped a hand to rest over Kyle's on the seat. "You okay? I don't know where you went a minute ago, but you look a little shell-shocked."

Kyle flipped his hand and captured Luka's fingers with his own. "I'm good. Just got stuck in my head for a minute."

He smiled. Kyle didn't want to have a heart-to-heart in the car, but he had the rest of the weekend to find the right opportunity to broach the topic of moving.

Ninety minutes later, Kyle stood at the island in the spacious kitchen of the beach house, mixing drinks while Riley gave Luka a tour of the property. Music from one of Cam's playlists filled the air with sultry beats, and Carter stood on Kyle's right making salad.

"What time does Jes get in?" Kyle asked Cam.

Cam stood at the counter behind Kyle, arranging cheese and fruit on a wide plate. "Around six," he replied over his shoulder. He'd dressed head to toe in black and with his ginger hair, Kyle thought he looked like the lovechild of a ninja and a leprechaun. "Unless something happens with his flight, that is. He's aggravated the trip kept him out of town because he got a recipe for Japanese curry from his friend Isaac and wanted to make it for dinner tonight."

"I've had that curry and it's totally delicious," Carter said. He appeared extra tall and lean in his cable-knit sweater and dark jeans. "David was happy to switch nights though. He and Will are on their way now, and he has plans for beef stew with Guinness."

Cam hummed. "Damn, that sounds great. You know how Jes can be when he gets an idea into that big head of his though."

"A complete pain in the ass until he executes, yes," Kyle said over his friends' laughter. A gleam of light from Carter's salad bowl caught his eye and he watched his friend's motions, spying a slim rose gold band on his right hand.

"Jes said he's taking a chopper from the city to Easthampton," Cam said then, and Kyle almost dropped the jigger of gin he'd been pouring over ice.

"What?" Kyle tipped his head back and laughed hard. "That man is turning into a total diva!"

"What do you mean 'turning'?" Cam asked. "Jesse is a born diva and proud to show it every chance he gets."

"Very true."

Kyle added sloe gin and apricot liqueur to his mix and followed with fresh lemon juice. He'd covered the shaker with a bar glass when Luka, Riley and Malcolm strode in. Kyle only had eyes for Luka, however, whose face was alight with curiosity and delight. He came to stand on Kyle's other side, while Riley and Malcolm sat together across the island.

"You were right on both counts," Luka said to Kyle. "The house is beautiful and Riley loves it even more than you love your apartment."

Kyle winked at Riley, who beamed.

"I've known this house almost my whole life, so you can't compare the two." Riley's eyes reflected the faded blue of the old chambray shirt he favored during these beach house weekends. "I don't see Kyle staying in the shoebox forever, by the way, no matter what he says on the topic now."

"Oh, Lord," Kyle muttered and rattled the shaker. Odd the way Riley's words echoed his own earlier thoughts. All his friends had an opinion on his teeny one-bedroom, ranging from amused acceptance to blatant disdain. Kyle wondered what kind of uproar he'd cause voicing his ideas about a move. He caught Luka's eye, who smiled.

Luka's voice slipped under the others' talk. "What's that face for?"

Kyle rose up on his toes and stole a kiss. "Tell you later," he said and busied himself filling six of the cocktail glasses he'd taken from the bar cart in the living room. He topped each drink with a splash of champagne, then topped them with curls of lemon peel. He set the first in front of Luka.

"Great color," Luka said. "Smells fantastic, too. Is this one of the apricot things you put up before Thanksgiving?"

Kyle nodded. "Good nose, Lieutenant. That's the apricot liqueur, but I brought the brandy, too." Kyle handed glasses round to the others. "This is a Lita Grey," he said. "Named for one of Chaplin's wives. I can mix Charlie Chaplin Cocktails with the brandy, too, but they're a bit sticky for my taste."

Malcolm hummed around a sip. "No need, as far as I'm concerned," he declared and fingered the zipper on his hoodie. "These are delicious. Which is funny because I don't even like apricots."

"That's how these weekends often play out," Cam said to Luka with a chuckle. "Kyle makes potions we've never tried, oops, we love them, and oh hell, what day is it?"

"Jesus Christ, it's not even dinnertime — what the hell have you guys been up to this afternoon?"

A dog barked, sharp and excited, and Will appeared in the kitchen door, cloth grocery bags in both hands. His brown hair was windblown, but he looked somehow stylish in his designer sweater and jeans, and he gave them all a broad smile. David followed just behind with more bags and Mabel, their Inu-Husky mix, who wagged her tail madly.

"I see a shaker and a bunch of Kyle's unmarked bottles," David said, "so clearly you've all been up to business as usual." He grinned at Carter, who'd come around the island with Riley to greet them. "Hope you don't mind that we let ourselves in," he said. "Is your cat here somewhere?"

"Of course, we don't mind." Riley exchanged a quick kiss with Will, then David. "Where's the rest of your stuff?" he asked.

"By the door," Will replied. He handed off half the sacks to Riley and they moved them to the counter. Riley then made a beeline toward the front of the house.

"Miss Zebra is in our room," Carter said to David.

Jesse had found Miss Zebra one weekend in Brooklyn during his and Cam's early dating days and given the cat to Carter and Riley's children. The kitty got along well with Leo, the kids' Australian Shepard, who was older and mellow. Miss Zebra was not a fan of Mabel however. So, while Mabel adored every hair on Miss Zebra's gray and white head, thus far, her love remained unrequited. Carter and Riley made special efforts to maintain peace between the animals by keeping Miss Zebra on the second floor and Mabel on the first.

"We bought a pet gate for the stairs, so don't worry about Mabel getting up there when your back is turned," Carter said. He lifted the groceries out of David's hand.

David's face fell. "You didn't buy a gate just for Mabel?" He hugged Carter, then Malcolm, who stepped up next. Mabel whined and bounced on her paws until Malcolm knelt to greet her.

"We did not," Carter replied. He carried the sacks to the counter. "We wanted one anyway for when the kids bring Leo with them. Sometimes, Riley just needs a break from our collection of wild animals, human and otherwise."

"I heard that!" Riley called from somewhere outside of the kitchen.

"I swear, he has bionic hearing," Will muttered. "It's a wonder he sleeps at all when everyone's here." He reached up and hugged Carter. "Hey, big guy — thanks for having us."

Greetings and laughter filled the kitchen for the next few minutes, along with lots of fawning over Mabel, who made a point of checking in with everyone.

"She's really well behaved," Kyle said to Luka, who, he'd noticed, had been slower at squatting down than everyone else. "David and Will keep a close eye on her if you're not into dogs."

"Oh, I don't mind." Luka smiled when Mabel approached him. He stayed still, his hands loose on his thighs. "The animals I encounter when I'm working are usually scared and that can translate to aggression," he explained. "I've learned to let them come to me if I can, but that's not always possible on scene."

Mabel sniffed Luka's hands, then stepped right up into his space, her tail wagging harder and her tongue hanging out of her smiling mouth. She uttered a groaning grumble when Luka rubbed her shoulders.

"She's a love bug," David said to Luka. His navy sweater stretched tight across his broad chest when he crossed his arms. "I can see she definitely loves you."

Luka scrubbed Mabel's ruff with his fingers. "Ye-e-a-h, Mabel." He watched Kyle hand off the cocktail he'd just poured for himself to Will. "What are you doing?"

Kyle raised his eyebrows. "Oh, um. Force of habit, I guess. I always serve myself last."

"Mmm, you work too hard." Luka petted Mabel a final time and stood. "You're supposed to be taking time off though, so why don't you take a break?"

"What? Like go sit down?" Kyle laughed when Luka held up his hands.

"Don't go too far. I need you to tell me what to do!" He pointed at the stools on the other side of the island. "You can sit that bubble butt of yours down right there though, and let me mix you a drink for a change."

* * * *

Later that evening, following Jesse's chopper ride and a long, fantastic dinner, Kyle mixed up Black Russians, and Luka set out the tartlets he'd brought from his cousin's bakery.

"Good Lord, these are good," Will got out around a mouthful of lemon curd. He sat at the foot of the table, David on his left and Malcolm on his right. "Are there more for tomorrow?"

"Sadly, no," Luka replied. "But Malcolm said something about making cookies tomorrow?"

"Is that a euphemism for having sex?" Jesse asked. He looked travel weary in his long-sleeved black T-shirt and faded jeans, but he smirked at Malcolm over the laughter that rang out.

Malcolm scoffed. "No, you pervert. I plan to make actual chocolate chip cookies. Chocolate chunk, to be more specific, and maybe caramel chip."

"Oh, yes." Kyle rubbed his hands together and looked past Luka to Malcolm. "Your cookies are amazing, dude."

"I can attest to that," Carter chimed in from his place beside Riley at the head of the table. "He brings them to work sometimes and they are profanity delicious."

"Thank you." Malcolm smiled. "Everyone is welcome to help me, by the way. Especially you, Kyle. Because by help I mean supply me with drinks to keep me cheerful while I'm up to my elbows in dough and chocolate."

"I'll help." Luka raised his hand. "I never say no when chocolate is involved."

Jesse waved too. "Ha-a-a-y. Same. I hope you brought straws," he said to Kyle, "so I can drink without having to handle glassware with greasy hands."

Carter slid his eyes Riley's way. "I fear for the safety of your kitchen."

Riley raised a brow. "I think you mean our kitchen," he said, his words teasing but his voice gentle.

"You still do most of the cooking," Carter said with a shrug.

"And you still do most of the cleaning," Riley replied. "This place has been as much yours as mine for a long time now."

He covered Carter's hand where it lay on the table with his own and another glint caught Kyle's eye, just as had happened in the kitchen earlier that afternoon. Kyle's stomach did a funny flip this time, though, because he saw a slim rose gold band on Riley's right hand, too. A ring that matched Carter's, right down to the cluster of thin grooves carved into the surface of the ring.

"Kyle?"

Kyle forced himself to look away from his friends' hands and met Carter's gaze across the table. Carter's heavy eyebrows were knitted, and concern mixed with puzzlement in his expression.

"What's up, babe?" he asked. "You look kind of weird right now."

"Um." Kyle blinked, aware of Luka's hand coming to rest on his shoulder. He shifted his focus to Riley, who beamed at him. Riley gave Kyle a tiny nod. Kyle's throat went tight.

"I thought maybe you and Ri had something to tell us, Car," he prompted, his voice rough. "Something to do with those rings you're both wearing?"

The room went quiet, and Carter's cheeks flushed deep red. He gave Kyle a shy, absolutely beautiful smile, then glanced around the table at the others.

"I asked Ri to marry me last night." Carter turned his focus on Riley, whose blue eyes were shining as bright as Kyle had ever seen. "And he said yes."

The strains of Troye Sivan's delicate synth pop filled the silence that continued, and no one moved for a long moment. Then Luka's grip tightened on Kyle's shoulder and Kyle covered it with his own. He sought out Jesse's gaze across the table and chuckled at his huge grin.

"Holy shit!" Kyle and Jesse said at the same time.

They were on their feet and swarming toward their friends an instant later while the room echoed with a chorus of congratulations. Kyle pulled Riley out of his chair and Jesse hauled Carter up and the four of them pulled each other into a big group hug. Will and Malcolm joined the huddle a beat later, and though Cam, David and Luka hung back, waiting their turn for hugs and handshakes, all three were laughing and contributing to the chaos. Everyone spoke at once, and Mabel raced around the table, excited by the humans' behavior.

"I'm so happy for you guys," Kyle told Carter over the din. Carter didn't reply, but Kyle saw he was simply overwhelmed. Carter pressed his forehead to Kyle's temple instead and curled a hand around the nape of Kyle's neck. Kyle pressed a kiss to Carter's cheek and held on to everyone a little tighter, his heart warm and full.

* * * *

"This is a hell of a start to a weekend," Luka said as he and Kyle climbed the stairs to the second floor. They'd bade the others good night after Carter and Riley had gone to bed and Jesse had pulled out Cards Against Humanity. Even now, raucous laughter echoed up from the living area. Luka chuckled, too. "Not sure anything can beat that dinner and a proposal."

"Both were outstanding," Kyle said. "We didn't even get the actual proposal! That's very Carter and Riley though. They like to keep that kind of thing to themselves until they're ready to share."

Luka nodded. "I get it. They pop up in the gossip columns quite a bit."

"Well, there's more to it than that," Kyle said. "Getting to where they are today was hard on them and their families for a long time." He stopped in front of the door and turned to Luka. "When I met Carter, he was still getting over the split with his wife and coming to terms with his sexuality. He struggled with all of it. He and Riley were barely friends at that point and he'd given up hoping they could ever have a relationship.

"Riley didn't have it easy either. He tried to make things work with Will and put his friendship with Carter back together but doing both at the same time didn't pan out. It sounds like his father made his work life hell." He sighed. "Carter and Riley lost their families and all because they didn't fit into a straight-guy mold. Carter was terrified his ex would bar him from seeing his kids, or that his parents would figure out some way to cut him out of Sadie's and Dylan's lives.

"Seeing them together tonight, knowing they made it despite everything that happened ...I don't know." Kyle smiled and shook his head. "I just think it's an amazing thing."

Luka caught him off guard with a heated kiss. "I love the way your mind works," he said when they'd surfaced again. He backed Kyle up against the door, both breathless. "And I love the way you care about everybody." The gleam in his eyes sent a jolt of need straight through Kyle.

God, Kyle wanted this man so much. Every day, every night and any damn place for as long as Luka wanted him too. Fuck, Kyle hoped Luka wanted him around forever because that was where Kyle saw this thing between them going, if only he played his cards right.

Luka cocked his head. "What's going on in that head of yours, McKee?" he asked with a gentle frown. "You've looked like that a couple of times today, like you're keeping secrets."

"I've been thinking that I love you." Kyle's voice sounded far steadier than he felt inside. He watched Luka's expression freeze, and for just a second, Kyle wished the words back. He didn't really want to unsay them, though, because he meant them. They were words Kyle didn't want to hide from Luka any more. They felt good. Right.

"Maybe this seems fast. I know we haven't been dating for very long." Kyle glanced at the darkened hallway around them and snickered. "This is probably the most unromantic place in the world to tell you, too, but I mean it. I love you, Luka. I've never been happier to know someone as I am to know you."

Luka's blank expression morphed into a blinding grin. "I love you, too," he said, his tone rich with emotion. He brought his hands up to frame Kyle's face. "And I don't care where we tell each other, Kyle, because I plan on telling you every place we go."

Kyle thought his heart would burst. He wound his arms around Luka's neck and kissed him hard, aware that the door behind him had opened only after the solid mass at his back disappeared. But before he lost his balance, Luka hauled him up and off his feet. Kyle gasped at the shift in momentum and his whole body seemed to catch fire.

"You're so strong," he murmured against Luka's lips. Kyle wrapped his legs around Luka's waist, and Luka walked forward several steps so the door clicked shut behind them. "Can't remember the last time I dated a guy who could literally pick me up or wanted to." Kyle ran his hands over Luka's hair and groaned as Luka palmed his ass. His cock twitched between their bodies.

Luka smirked. "Doesn't seem to bother you."

"It doesn't." Kyle closed his eyes and drew Luka closer. "Maybe it should, but I'm always too fucking turned on to care."

Luka chuckled. He took several more steps and Kyle unwound himself so Luka could set him down beside the bed. They undressed each other, hands roaming as their clothes fell away. Kyle's skin prickled and heat pulsed deep in his groin. He skimmed his palm over Luka's torso and dipped his hand lower.

Luka drew in a sharp breath. "Want you," he whispered. "Need to touch you."

Kyle stepped away and turned the bedding down. Luka watched him the whole time, his gaze intense. He held a hand out after Kyle had finished, but Kyle shook his head.

"Need the stuff," Kyle murmured. "Don't start without me." He went to the attached bath for the lube and condoms in his kit.

Luka had stretched out on the bed when Kyle returned, and Kyle paused simply to admire the beautiful body waiting for him. Luka's cock lay rigid against his abdomen, and there was a wild cast in his gaze. But he held his hand out once more and he dragged Kyle down beside him when their fingers met.

Kyle kissed along Luka's chest, licking and nuzzling the skin, and teased Luka's nipples with his tongue. Luka murmured curses, his hands on Kyle's shoulders and neck, guiding Kyle with touch. Slowly, Kyle worked his way down Luka's torso and pelvis, and Luka murmured an endearment when Kyle nuzzled Luka's cock.

"Love the way you taste," Kyle said, his voice low. "Need the lube, darlin'."

He pressed his lips against the base of Luka's cock and Luka moaned. Luka rocked his hips up, his hand trembling as he handed the bottle of lube down to Kyle.

Kyle pushed up onto his knees. He wet his fingers, and though his cock jutted stiff against his body, he ignored it and focused on the man laid out before him.

Kyle spread Luka's legs and settled down between them, hissing at the sensation of the sheets against his erection. He wrapped a hand around Luka's dick, then leaned in and swiped his tongue over Luka's balls. Luka's whole body jerked.

"Oh, fuck."

Kyle closed his eyes. He rested his cheek on Luka's groin and his skin prickled at the sensation of Luka's fingers sliding through Kyle's hair, rubbing his scalp, tugging here and there and keeping things interesting. Kyle mouthed the base of Luka's shaft while he pumped, and he took care to caress Luka's cockhead on each pass. Soon, Luka was panting and Kyle felt desperate to be touched himself. Reaching down, he wrapped his other hand around himself and fucked his fist, keeping his movements slow in a bid for control.

"Kyle."

The plea in Luka's voice caught Kyle's attention. He opened his eyes and the hunger he read in Luka's face made his balls tighten. Fuck, he was going to lose it before they even got started.

Quickly, Kyle let go of himself, though it almost hurt to do so. Shifting his weight and position, he opened his lips over Luka's cock and took him down in one long, slow slide. Luka wound his fingers tighter in Kyle's hair and the sting of that possessive touch made Kyle's cock jerk.

Oh, God.

Kyle swallowed. Luka swore and pumped his hips, using Kyle's mouth. Kyle moaned long and low, a sweet ache pooling deep inside him. He didn't care anymore where or how he came. He just wanted this man. But then Luka pushed at Kyle shoulders with both hands until Kyle pulled off.

"Need you," Luka murmured, his grip on Kyle tight enough to leave bruises.

"Okay, Luka," Kyle replied, his voice rough and reverent. He lifted his knee and straddled Luka, his own body pulsing with need, and the sweat on their bodies mingled. Luka ran his hands over Kyle's thighs, raising goosebumps over the skin, and Kyle spread a hand over Luka's belly. "Gonna ride you."

Luka bit his lip. "Yeah. Want that. Want you on my cock."

Kyle reached back and fingered himself, a low grunt rumbling through him. The flood of sensation made his head spin, as did Luka's needy sound. Luka moved his hands over Kyle, touching him everywhere until Kyle's whole body shook. Kyle was panting by the time he forced himself to stop, and he felt grateful for Luka's steadying touch on his waist.

"I've got you." Luka's voice was strained thin.

He guided Kyle up and onto his cock. Kyle sank down slowly, his breath catching as Luka filled him up. He gasped when Luka wrapped him in his arms.

Kyle's throat went tight. He loved being like this with Luka, watching his face, kissing until he could barely breathe. Kyle set his hands on Luka's shoulders and breathed through the ache in his body. He started rocking, each movement purposeful so the strokes were long and deep, and the pain transformed into pleasure. He was close, had been for so long, and every sensation running through him pushed him higher.

Wonder filtered through Luka's gaze. "Beautiful," he murmured.

Kyle was too far gone to reply. Luka hauled him closer, and his body surrounded Kyle's cock with the heat and pressure he craved. Kyle's breath stuttered. He stopped breathing entirely when Luka dropped one hand and fingered Kyle's rim. It was all Kyle could do not to scream.

Luka thrust up, his movements rough and perfect, and Kyle soared. His mouth fell open and he curled forward, his cock pulsing untouched between Luka and himself. Luka's eyes went wide.

"Holy shit," he whispered, voice awed as he stared at Kyle.

Trembling and slack-limbed, Kyle held on as best he could, coasting on the high and the knowledge Luka wouldn't let him fall. Luka fucked Kyle hard, thrusts swift, and came with his face pressed into Kyle's throat.

They huddled together, their breaths slowing as they came back to earth, and Kyle started drifting. He peeled his eyes open when Luka stirred, but Luka's hold tightened around him as Kyle shifted his weight, too. Luka laid Kyle down and shushed his sleepy protest.

"Just lie with me a minute longer," Luka coaxed.

"Mmm, Luka. I love you, but we're both a mess," Kyle murmured.

Luka made an agreeable noise. "Yeah, I know. You're already half asleep though. How about you stay here, and I'll clean us up in a minute?"

Kyle smiled. "You don't wanna take a shower?"

"I'd rather sleep right now," Luka said. "I need to recharge so I can fuck you awake in the morning."

Kyle chuckled. "Oh, well played."

He closed his eyes, though, because Luka whispered, "I love you back, you know." Those words followed Kyle down into sleep, and he knew Luka would be there when he woke up.

Chapter Fourteen

"That was a lot of fun, but I'm pretty sure you knew as much as the tour guide," Luka said as they left the Widow Jane Distillery in Brooklyn. He smiled. "Based on the things you kept muttering under your breath anyway."

Kyle's cheeks turned pink. "I'm a booze nerd, I guess. Besides, it was the guy's first day. I'm sure he'll know more than me by the end of the week."

Luka's grin changed into something softer. "You try to see the best in people, don't you?"

"Yeah, I suppose I do."

Luka captured Kyle's elbow, slowing him to a stop. "It's one of the things I love about you." Luka glanced around, but they'd lingered for a while after most of the tour had left and the street was deserted. He leaned in and stole a quick kiss.

The 'I-love-yous' they'd exchanged had been unexpected but perfect. After seeing so many happy couples and hearing Carter and Riley's announcement, the mood had been just right. If Kyle hadn't said it in that moment, Luka probably would have. He didn't mind being beaten to the punch however.

Kyle reached out and touched Luka's face before he stepped back. His expression made Luka want to pull him in for another kiss, but they started walking again instead, heading for the subway on Van Brunt Street. It was too cold to linger outside.

"You said there are more distilleries in the area?" Luka asked.

"Yeah. At least a dozen, and maybe a dozen and a half by now," Kyle said.

"Are most of them here in Brooklyn?" They turned a corner and out of nowhere an icy blast of wind hit them. It snuck down Luka's collar, making him shiver. He wrapped his scarf tighter around his neck. Kyle tucked his hand into his coat pockets and hunched his shoulders.

"The vast majority are, yes. There's at least one up near Yonkers, and more upstate if we ever want to take a long weekend now that Christmas is behind us. There are several near Saratoga Springs and the Finger Lakes area."

"Sure, that would be fun," Luka said. "Let me look at my work schedule and figure out when I can put in for some time off. Probably not until after the holidays though."

"That sounds perfect." Kyle nudged Luka with his elbow. "Anything you'd like to do when we take that vacation? I appreciate you nerding out with me about booze, but there must be something you'd like to do."

Luka considered the idea. "There's a firefighting museum up in Hudson I've thought about checking out. It's supposed to be interesting, and they have a bunch of cool antique engines and equipment."

"We can do that!" Kyle agreed. "Let's look online and see what else is going on in that area."

"Maybe something active? If we're going in January or February, we could go cross-country skiing or snowshoeing."

"That sounds fun."

Luka slowed to a stop again. "God, you make me happy, Kyle."

"You make me happy, too," Kyle said softly.

He faced Luka, and Luka pressed another kiss to Kyle's lips, intending it to be brief, but Kyle responded with more enthusiasm than Luka had expected. Luka let himself be drawn in, tasting the faint flavor of liquor on Kyle's tongue. A car honking nearby reminded Luka where they were however, and as much as Luka wanted to continue, they were a long way from either of their places. Reluctantly, he lifted his head.

"Mmm. Too bad we have a long ride back to Manhattan," Luka said. "I don't want to wait to get my hands on you."

Kyle slid a hand under Luka's jacket. "The feeling is mutual. But it's too damn cold to be standing around like this. Let's get going. The sooner we leave Brooklyn, the sooner we get back to my place."

Luka shot him a quick grin and leaned in for another, longer kiss. Just one more until they were back in Chelsea.

"Get the hell out of here, you dick suckers!"

The shouted words pulled them apart. Luka spun to look behind him and tensed when he saw three guys moving toward them. *Oh, fuck.* They were big guys. Similar in size to him and Kyle.

One wearing a red jacket sneered. "You heard me, queers. Get the fuck out of here and go back to where you belong."

Kyle bristled beside Luka.

"Yeah, to Harlem," a bald guy jeered. "Stick to your own kind."

Seething, Luka battled to keep his temper in check. "Look, we're not bothering anyone here and — "

"You're sure as fuck bothering me." That guy wore a baseball cap and his voice was quieter than the others. Colder.

"We're going, all right?" Kyle said. "Let's get out of here, Luka." He pulled on Luka's arm.

"Fuckin' cowards." The red jacket guy sneered.

"What'd you expect from a couple of queers?" muttered the bald one.

Luka's pride told him to stay and stand his ground. To fight. But the larger, smarter part of his brain urged him to leave. There were three against him and Kyle and the odds were not in their favor.

Luka held up his hands. "We're going, just leave us alone."

Trying to keep one eye on them, Luka half-turned to leave, but before he could take a step, pain exploded in his cheek. Luka staggered back a step, and when he touched his face, his fingers came away wet with the blood that dripped from his nose.

He staggered to his feet as the guy in the baseball cap went after Kyle. The bald guy lunged at Luka, and they grappled, each trying to knock the other down.

Luka had the advantage of size, but the bald guy was strong and fast. The guy in the red jacket turned the tables against Luka even further when he stepped in and pulled at Luka's arms. Luka grunted as the bald guy landed a punch to his ribs, and a blow to Luka's chin made his head swim.

"Don't touch him!" Kyle shouted.

Luka looked over in time to see Kyle pull away from the baseball cap guy and lunge at the two men surrounding Luka. But the guy in the baseball hat caught Kyle by the collar. He yanked Kyle back around and laid him out with a punch Luka swore he could feel, too. Kyle hit the ground hard.

Luka cried out in fear when Kyle didn't move. Everything became a blur as all three men descended on him, and though Luka tried to fight them off, there were just too many of them. He soon lost his balance and fell to the ground.

"Faggots!" one of his attackers snarled. "You'll get what you deserve."

Fear gripped Luka more tightly as he caught another glimpse of Kyle, who still lay motionless on the ground. And all along, the insults and slurs kept coming. The hate in the men surrounding him was palpable.

What if we don't survive this?

"Kyle!" Luka reached out, but a hard kick to his side sent searing pain through him.

He curled into a ball, trying to protect his head and vital organs. Another vicious kick to his midsection made Luka gag.

Get to your feet, he told himself. *Get to your feet. Get out of here. Get help.*

"What the fuck are you doing? Get away from them!" a man's voice yelled in the distance.

Then another voice, a woman this time. "I've called the cops. They're on their way!" she shouted.

A staggering relief swept over Luka.

With one final kick and a "stay in Harlem where you belong!" the men who'd attacked Luka and Kyle disappeared, their feet pounding the pavement as they ran off.

Luka struggled up onto one elbow and squinted at Kyle, who hadn't moved. Luka started crawling toward Kyle, his body buzzing with a mix of fear and pain.

"Stay still! Don't move," the woman's voice called. She sounded closer.

"Kyle?" Luka croaked, reaching for him. Kyle was still too far away to touch. "Kyle, answer me!"

"Hey, take it easy," the woman urged. She was right beside Luka now. He reached for Kyle again, but a wave of nausea made him double over, and he lay back down on the sidewalk. "You could hurt yourself worse," she said.

"Kyle?" Luka called again. "I need to know. Is he okay?"

The woman disappeared for a second, then came back. "His eyes are open now. There are ambulances and police on the way. Just rest, okay? You're both gonna be fine."

Luka heard the distant screaming of sirens. There were more people now, a man beside Kyle, and more voices. Luka rolled onto his side and saw Kyle's eyelids moving in slow blinks. Kyle's face was covered in blood, but he was staring at Luka, and when Luka reached out again, this time Kyle met him halfway. Kyle's expression twisted when their fingers brushed.

"I'm okay, Luka," he said, voice gritty.

Luka's racing heart slowed a little. He kept his gaze trained on Kyle for as long as he could until the EMTs arrived and began checking them over. Luka did his best to respond to their questions, and he heard Kyle doing the same with another team of EMTs. Both were bundled onto stretchers, then loaded into separate ambulances. It was torture not having Kyle in sight anymore, but Luka knew he couldn't get around protocol.

His head started to clear as they drove, and the shakes started halfway to the hospital.

"Shhh, you're okay," the female EMT said. She'd told Luka her name was Jen. "You're safe, I promise."

"I know," Luka said, his voice unsteady. "I'm a firefighter."

Jen gave him a reassuring smile. "Then you know it's just the adrenaline wearing off."

"Yep. Still sucks though." He managed a strained laugh. Jen squeezed his hand. "And I'm worried about Kyle."

"The guy you were with?"

"Yeah, my boyfriend. If something happened to him…" Luka's throat closed and panic swept over him again. His breathing grew short and shallow.

"Hey, easy there, big guy." Jen strapped an oxygen mask over Luka's nose and mouth before he could argue. "Take slow, deep breaths for me, okay?"

Luka focused on her voice rather than the anxiety clawing under his skin, and his ragged breaths evened out and grew deeper.

"There we go," Jen said, her tone soothing. "You'll need to get checked out, and I know they're going to want to run tests on you both, but it could have been a lot worse."

Luka pushed the mask off, ignoring her frown. "This was bad enough."

A look of sympathy crossed Jen's face. "I know. The police will want to talk to you."

"Good," Luka said grimly. "I hope to God they find the bastards who did this to us."

* * * *

The next few hours passed in an Emergency Department blur as Luka was poked, prodded and tested. Being away from Kyle chafed at him, and he finally sweet-talked a nurse into giving him an update, which indicated that Kyle was in much the same boat as Luka.

Eventually, Luka was wheeled into an observation room where he'd be monitored for signs of concussion. Luka closed his eyes. Despite the pain medication he'd been given, his head throbbed and his ribs ached. X-rays had shown they weren't broken, but they still hurt like a bitch. He was bone-weary, but his brain whirled with thoughts of the attack, and not being able to see and reassure Kyle was driving him up the wall. Luka just wanted his own bed and Kyle sleeping beside him, and even if he got some peace for a few hours in the ED, he doubted he'd settle enough to truly rest.

He'd fallen into a half-doze when he heard a knock and a familiar voice.

"Luka? Are you okay, baby?" Lydia made a beeline for his bed. "I've been so worried. When the hospital called —"

"I'm okay, Mom."

"Do you have a concussion?" She took his chin in her hand and tilted his head back and forth so she could examine his face.

"Minor. I got punched in the jaw, so my head got rattled a bit and I saw stars. But I never hit my head on the pavement or lost consciousness. I promise."

"They're keeping you overnight for observation, I hope." Her lips thinned.

"Yes. I won't argue about it." In truth, he felt physically sore and exhausted in every possible way. He didn't have the energy to argue about wanting to go home, much less the energy to make it happen.

Lydia went silent, and Luka looked down, aware his mom still grasped his wrist and that she was staring at the clock. "Are you taking my pulse right now?" he asked, amused.

"Hush. Let me concentrate."

Luka dutifully remained silent until she sat back.

"Well, your pulse is fine."

"I know that. I can see it on the monitor." Luka gestured toward the machine beside the bed.

"Oh, they're nowhere near as accurate as a well-trained nurse and you know it."

True or not, Luka's mother had said that enough times that he knew not to argue with her about it.

"I'm surprised Regina and Marcus and everyone else aren't here, too," Luka said with a sigh. He wanted to see his family, but he wanted to see Kyle more.

"I convinced them to stay home, but they'll stop by your place when you get discharged, I'm sure." Lydia gently patted his shoulder. "How's Kyle?"

A lump rose in Luka's throat. "All right, I think. His face is more beat up than mine. And it sounds like they want a head CT because he lost consciousness. It scared me shitless seeing him like that and with blood on his face, Mom. But he was awake and talking by the time EMS got there, and it sounds like he's doing okay."

He looked up at Lydia. "He tried to protect me, you know? Two of the guys who jumped us were all over me, but somehow Kyle got loose and went after them.

He bought us enough time for someone else to arrive and scare them off."

Lydia pressed her hand to her heart, her expression anguished. "I'm so grateful you're both okay. And to Kyle for trying to protect you."

A soft knock sounded on the door.

"Mr. Clarke?"

A man and a woman stood in the doorway, both neatly dressed and with an official air about them.

Detectives, Luka assumed. "That's me."

The woman stepped into the room and held up a badge. "I'm Detective Bowen and this is my partner, Detective Schwartz. We're with the Hate Crime Task Force in the Special Victims Division. We'd like to talk to you about what happened tonight."

Luka sat up with a grunt and winced when the dull ache in his side turned sharp. "Sure."

"Let's start with your full name," Detective Schwartz said.

"Luka Clarke. I'm a lieutenant with the FDNY." He gestured to his mother. "My mother, Lydia Padilla."

"Nice to meet you, ma'am. You're welcome to stay, if you like."

Lydia glanced at Luka. "Unless you want me to, Luka, I'll grab some tea in the cafeteria."

"No, you go," Luka said, relieved. Better his mother not stay. She was a strong woman, but he didn't want her hearing the gory details.

Lydia kissed his forehead. "I'll be back."

"Thanks, Mom."

After she'd left, Luka focused on the detectives. "What do you need from me? You should know my brother-in-law is on the job, too. Wade Owens. He's with the 28th precinct."

The detectives exchanged a glance and Bowen made a note on her pad. "Thank you for your candor, Lieutenant. As far as tonight, just tell us what happened. Start at the beginning and go slowly."

"My boyfriend and I had just left the Widow Jane Distillery," Luka said, his voice catching as he began to recount the night's events. It was draining, trying to remember details, and he struggled to describe the attackers. Luka told the detectives what he remembered but knew it wasn't much.

"I've never experienced anything like this," he said when he'd finished. "Sure, I've dealt with racism before, but this? On top of the gay bashing?" He swallowed hard. "Never dealt with that level of hate before. We were in Brooklyn, for fuck's sake. And we're both big guys. I can't believe they came after us. It doesn't make any sense."

Detective Schwartz nodded, his expression sympathetic. "We've seen a bit of an uptick in cases of this type lately."

"What are the odds of catching these guys?" Luka asked.

"There were a few witnesses," Detective Bowen said. "And we're checking the surveillance cameras in the area."

"How likely is it you'll find them?" Luka asked.

Schwartz frowned. "We'll do what we can."

"I know that," Luka said. Despite the historic rivalry between the NYPD and the FDNY, he knew the detectives had his back. Hell, he'd get preferential treatment because he was a firefighter and had a brother-in-law on the force. That idea bothered Luka sometimes, but right now, he wouldn't argue.

"I also know you guys are overworked," he continued. "You've got a ton of cases and this sort of thing is hard to prove, right?"

"It can be difficult to prove, yes. We can't promise that we'll find and arrest these guys. Or that they'll be prosecuted if we do find them. But don't give up hope yet." Schwartz looked him in the eye. "I promise you we'll do everything in our power."

"Thank you," Luka said. After a few more questions, they gave him their business cards and left, just in time for Lydia to come back.

"You look ready to drop," she said.

"I feel like I've been run over by a truck," Luka admitted. "Not sure I can sleep though."

"Is there anything I can get you?" she asked.

"No, I don't think—"

"Hey," a familiar voice said from the doorway. Luka looked up to see Kyle in a wheelchair in the doorway. One of the transport people stood behind him, but Luka focused on the bandage on Kyle's face. It covered a good portion of Kyle's lower right jaw.

"Kyle!" Luka threw back the blanket and struggled out of the bed.

Lydia tutted. "Luka, you really—" She subsided when he threw her a look. "Let me help you at least," she said.

The transport guy pushed Kyle's wheelchair into the room, and Lydia guided Luka over.

"I've been so worried about you." Luka bent down and pressed his forehead against Kyle's.

"Hey, I'm okay," Kyle said hoarsely. His fingers trembled when he reached up to touch Luka's face.

"It's just seeing you unconscious like that...and the blood...I thought I'd lost you," Luka admitted with a shudder. "I don't know what I'd do if that happened."

"I promise you're not going to lose me," Kyle assured him. "I'm banged up, needed a few sutures, but I'm fine. You're okay?"

"I'm fine. Hated being helpless to protect you."

"Me, too." Kyle's voice sounded thick and his words somewhat slurred, probably from the anesthetic he'd been given for the sutures. He was so pale, his normally fair complexion was almost gray, and there was a far-off kind of expression in his dark eyes. "Made them stop on the way back from radiology so I could see for myself you were okay."

"I'm glad you did." Careful to avoid the bandages, Luka pressed a brief kiss to Kyle's lips and settled back on his haunches, ignoring his own discomfort as he took Kyle's hand. "Did you talk to the detectives?"

"No. You?"

"They just finished up here. They're probably waiting for you now."

"Yeah, okay."

Kyle didn't let go of Luka's hand though, and Luka didn't argue. He ached all over but didn't want to look away from Kyle. Seeing and touching him reassured Luka that Kyle would be all right despite the bandages.

"Mr. McKee, we need to get you back," someone said, their tone brisk. "You need monitoring, and Mr. Clarke should be in bed."

Luka glanced up at the nurse who'd appeared in the doorway and saw his mother behind her. Lydia must have stepped out to give them some privacy, but Luka had been so focused on Kyle he hadn't even noticed. Luka got to his feet and leaned down to kiss Kyle again.

Kyle gripped the back of Luka's neck. "I love you," he whispered.

"I love you, too," Luka said.

He straightened, grateful when his mother stepped forward and took his elbow, and the nurse wheeled Kyle out.

"I talked to the head nurse on duty," Lydia said quietly as she guided Luka back to the bed. "She'll try to get you and Kyle into the same room. If everything goes well, you'll both be released tomorrow, but that way you won't have to be apart tonight."

"Thank you." Luka didn't have the words to express the gratitude he felt toward his mother right then.

"I heard what you said about Kyle protecting you, baby." Lydia squeezed Luka's hand. "I saw the way you looked at each other, too. Kyle's not running despite what happened tonight, and that's what I want for you, baby. I was wrong about him, and I'm sorry."

Chapter Fifteen

"You don't belong here, cocksucker."

"Fuck. You're queer and you go for the dark meat, too? God, you're disgusting."

"Does that moolie fuck you hard?"

"Kyle? Kyle, answer me!"

Kyle woke with a start, Luka's shout echoing in his ears. A harsh grunt tore out of him, and he flailed at the memory of fists flashing toward his face. Fuck, he hurt.

"Hey, Kyle—take it easy," a low voice said, soothing and warm in a way that made his throat constrict.

Kyle tensed anyway despite the pain in his torso and head. And his face, fuck. Kyle felt like he'd been slapped with a hammer. He blinked and stopped struggling as Lydia Padilla came into focus, however, and forced himself to stop moving. She'd perched herself in the guest chair by his hospital bed, and Kyle still hadn't decided if he'd fully woken when she put a hand on his shoulder.

"All that jerking around could tear your sutures. No one wants that," Lydia said. "Just settle down and take some deep breaths."

"Luka's okay?" Kyle's words came out mashed and mumbling over the numbness in his lower lip and the bandages covering his chin and part of his right jaw. Lydia didn't answer right away, and he swallowed, then clasped his hands together in his lap to keep them from shaking. "Miz Padilla? Is Luka okay?"

Lydia squeezed Kyle's shoulder. She looked both incredibly tired and ready to do battle. "Luka is fine. I left him sleeping and came to check on you but found you asleep too. I didn't want to wake you."

"Oh." Kyle kept right on talking over her frown. "I'm good. You don't need to stay, ma'am. Luka'll worry if he wakes up alone."

"He'll be fine," Lydia replied. "Wade drove over as soon as he finished his shift at the precinct, and he's with Luka now. So how about you stop worrying about everyone else for a minute and worry about yourself instead?"

Kyle bit back a grumble. He didn't want to focus on himself just then, but he was too wrung out for arguing. Especially since Lydia appeared ready to force him into chilling out.

He concentrated on the deep breaths she'd prescribed. They made his bruised ribs and abdominal muscles ache but also eased the tension knotting his stomach. Oddly, he found he didn't mind being the focus of Lydia's attention just then. If she'd come in to bitch him out for getting Luka into a jam, she was being nice about it. Of course, Kyle had a concussion and that might have something to do with her attitude. He still felt muzzy, but things had gotten better in the last couple of hours. The world had been jumbled inside of his head earlier, and he'd puked several times when he'd tried to move.

Ugh.

Lydia stood. She picked up a plastic cup and spoon from the bedside table and held them out. "No water yet, I'm afraid, but you're allowed some ice chips. Can you manage?"

Kyle eyed the cup and only then noticed the fine tremor in her hand. Despite Lydia's ultra-calm demeanor, she had to be freaked out, Kyle realized. No wonder, considering what her son had been through.

"Yes, ma'am," he said. Lydia handed everything over and Kyle got a couple of chips down. He sighed at how goddamned good they tasted after all the other crap that had been in his mouth since he'd left the distillery and he only dropped a couple. Between Lydia and himself, they got him cleaned up.

"The attending came by while you were sleeping," Lydia said. She'd seated herself again, her gaze sharp and watchful. "The results from your CT scan should be back soon. If everything's clean, the nurses have agreed to move you into Luka's room until you're both released."

A giddy flutter went through Kyle. Knowing Luka was safe helped, but being able to see him would be so much better. Kyle would take sharing one of the observation rooms regardless of his state of consciousness.

"Thank you for doing that."

"You're welcome. Short of sedating you both, I figure it's the only way any of us will be able to relax for longer than ten minutes at a time." Lydia's expression softened at Kyle's soft chuff of laughter, but her brow creased as she stared at the lower part of his face.

Kyle couldn't blame her. The glimpse he'd caught of himself in the mirror of the men's room after his trip to radiology had turned his stomach. He was a mess — swollen, bruised and bloodstained.

"Are you in a lot of pain?" she asked.

Everything hurt — even his toes for fuck's sake — so Kyle decided to be honest. "Some. Might be the worst headache I've ever had. One of the guys had a lot of rings on. He hit hard. The chin isn't so bad though. They pumped it full of anesthetic after they stopped the bleeding. Or, that's what the doc said anyway. It's kind of a blur right now."

He raised his fingers to the bandages on his face and touched them very gently. "Twelve sutures, a few on the inside. The wound missed the nerves, so no paralysis they think. I'm not really a beard guy, but it'll be nice to take a break from shaving." If Kyle's voice hadn't wavered on the last word, he might have sounded like he meant it.

Lydia pressed her lips together in a hard line. "Kyle —"

"I'm so sorry about what happened, ma'am," he said in a rush. "The last thing I'd ever want is for Luka to get dragged into a mess like this."

"Oh, Kyle — I'm sorry, too." Tears sheened her eyes. "I'll never understand what makes people do such terrible things to one another. But it's not your fault Luka was hurt tonight. Neither of you is to blame." She blew a breath out her nose when Kyle said nothing. "You don't blame Luka for what happened tonight, do you?"

"No, ma'am." Rocks filled Kyle's throat. "I'd never blame him."

"Of course not. This isn't the first time someone's gone after him because of his race, and it won't be the last."

"They came after us because we were together though. Because we're queer, and because I'm white and Luka's—"

"Because of who you are." Lydia covered Kyle's hand with hers. "I know. That's what makes it so painful, isn't it? You and Luka were just being yourselves and living your best lives, as Ruby would say. For some reason, there are people in this world who won't accept that."

Guilt made Kyle's eyes burn. "I should have been more careful. I—I know better than to be so open like that in a strange neighborhood."

"Don't you do that." Somehow, Lydia's scolding was the gentlest Kyle had ever received. "What happened today could have happened anywhere. It does happen anywhere. Knowing your neighborhood is important, but those men...they would have made trouble for you in Chelsea or the East Village. They'd have come after you if you and Luka had played straight. I think you know that deep down." She rubbed Kyle's shoulder with her hand. "They were bent on hate and violence, no matter what you and Luka did or didn't do."

"I do know. I just wish I'd been faster." Kyle shook his head and groaned at the way the ache behind his eyes ricocheted and sharpened.

Fucking ow.

"I should have stopped them." Kyle closed his eyes when his stomach roiled. *Please, God,* he didn't want to vomit in front of Luka's mom.

"This is not your fault, Kyle. You can't blame yourself." Lydia clucked her tongue. "And you are never going to get out of here at this rate. Is this propensity for stubbornness a white-boy thing or a you thing? Because I am not impressed."

"Me thing." Kyle huffed out a breath when Lydia set a plastic emesis basin against his fingers. Her teasing helped take his mind off his lurching stomach. Unfortunately, his mouth kept right on going. "Maybe it's a family thing. Lord knows, my brother is five times the stubborn ass I am."

"Well, I'm just as guilty of being willful when I want to be," Lydia replied. "I'm sure Luka's told you the behavior runs through our family."

"Luka's never said anything like that about you."

"You're lying." Kyle heard amusement in her voice. "I won't hold it against you though." Lydia kept hold of his hand, and if she noticed the sweat beading on his face, she didn't mention it.

Eventually, Kyle opened his eyes and met her gaze. "Sorry. My head feels like it's stuffed with old newspapers."

Lydia smiled. "That's oddly specific."

"Concussions will do that to a guy, I guess."

She laughed and gave his hand a squeeze. "I'm beginning to understand why my children enjoy your company." Her expression sobered. "I want to thank you, Kyle, for what you did for Luka."

"I didn't—"

"You did. You took on two men to keep them from going after my boy," Lydia said over him. "They could have hurt Luka worse, even killed him. They could have killed *you*."

Kyle's chest tightened. Lydia was right. He'd glimpsed awful things in the faces of the men who'd attacked them, heard the menace in the slurs they'd flung. Something destructive and hateful had colored the air around them, and the way they'd looked at Luka had frightened Kyle far more than their clenched fists. A bone-deep chill went through him.

"Lots of men wouldn't have done it in your place," Lydia said. She let go of Kyle's hand and busied herself pulling an extra blanket over his shoulders, probably because he'd started shivering and couldn't stop. "Luka's not in worse shape because of you. Did you know that?"

Kyle shook his head again, slowly this time to keep from hurting himself. "I don't understand."

"Luka said you distracted the men hurting him long enough to allow other people to step in and help." She dropped into her seat again. "So, thank you. For stepping up for Luka, even though it meant getting hurt yourself."

"I love him," Kyle murmured. He hadn't expected to bare his soul in front of Luka's mother today, and typically he'd be blushing like a fool. He felt okay about it now though. Talking to Lydia like this was good. Really good.

"I know you do. I could see it in the way you looked at each other out there," she said. "What you did when those men came after you, what you're doing now...that's what I want for my son, Kyle. Someone strong. A partner who won't run when things get hard like they did tonight."

Something like this will happen again, Kyle thought. *Maybe not tomorrow, or next week, or even next year.* But moments like the ones they'd endured today were out there, lurking. While not all of them would be violent, each would be painful. Kyle and Luka would encounter people who decided everything about them was wrong and needed correcting. Maybe even decided he and Luka deserved to be hurt.

Kyle swallowed hard. "I'm not going anywhere," he said.

"I can see that." Lydia gave him a jagged smile, but her eyes stayed dry. "It's not often I'm happy to be wrong about anything, but I'm glad I was wrong about the kind of man you are. You're good for Luka. I can't tell you how sorry I am that it took a night like this for me to see it."

"It's okay."

Kyle could have said more to assure Lydia he meant those words. He wanted to leave behind the misunderstandings she'd formed about him, and he glimpsed doubt in her expression. His doctor chose that moment to make an appearance however, tablet in hand.

"How are we doing, Kyle?" Dr. Murray used the hand sanitizer by the door before she crossed the small room to his bed.

"I'm okay," he said. "My head hurts, but it's better than before."

"How's his scan?" Lydia asked. Concern marked her face, Kyle noticed, just like it had everyone else's when they'd talked about the X-rays that had been taken of the insides of his skull.

"Scan looks good." Dr. Murray flicked her gaze over the tablet. "No detectable skull fractures or bleeding, and no clots, either."

Okay, that explained everyone's concern.

Dr. Murray met Kyle's gaze again. "No more vomiting, right? And you're feeling less dizzy?"

"Yes, to both."

"Good. We're going to keep you here to make sure that trend continues. If it does, I don't see why you can't go home in the morning." The doctor eyed the blanket on Kyle's shoulders and lowered the tablet. "Outside of the obvious injuries, how do you feel?"

Kyle licked his lips. He didn't know how to articulate what he'd been feeling. He'd had a great day with Luka, but they'd been jumped, and Kyle had woken up on the sidewalk, his memory jumbled and with a face full of blood. He had no idea how to process any of it.

"I feel fucked-up," he murmured and grimaced. "Sorry. I didn't mean to say that out loud."

Sympathy softened Lydia's face. "It's okay. I imagine you're feeling off-balance."

Off-balance. Yes. That was what Kyle had been feeling, like the earth beneath him was uneven and full of holes he couldn't even see.

"I don't know. It's like this is happening to someone else, even though I know it's not. Like…like I'm not here, even though I know I am." He paused, aware just how out of it he sounded. Jesus, Kyle was scared. His voice came out thick when he spoke again. "That sounds bad, huh?"

"Not at all." Dr. Murray patted his shoulder gently. "Generalized anxiety is common in victims of violent crime, Kyle, and your head injury isn't helping. I'm going to refer you to a colleague of mine. He specializes in counseling people who have been through experiences like yours."

"Counseling?" Kyle blinked. The comment threw whatever composure he had left right out the window and, to his horror, his eyes filled. "Um. I live in Manhattan."

"Yes, I know. Dr. Okafor's office is in Tribeca." Dr. Murray nodded. "You and your boyfriend went through something traumatic tonight, and you may find it hard to move forward without talking about it. If you want to do that with someone outside of your friends and family, I'd like you to consider speaking with Dr. Okafor. Okay?"

"Okay."

The word slipped out of Kyle's mouth without his thinking about it, and once it had, he tuned out a little. He wiped his eyes, aware of Dr. Murray checking his vitals and of her speaking in soft tones with Lydia, but not until she said Kyle would be moved into Luka's room did his focus snap back into place. Despite the fatigue sliding over him, slow and thick as molasses, Kyle managed a small, genuine smile.

"Thanks, Doc."

Dr. Murray squeezed his shoulder again. "Hang in there, Kyle. You're going to be okay."

After she'd gone, he glanced at Lydia, who still watched him like a hawk. "You don't need to stay, ma'am. They'll be moving me down the hall soon."

Lydia nodded. "Were the desk staff able to get in touch with your family?"

"They called my brother." Kyle said. "Ollie's taking the train down from Boston. He should be here in a couple of hours."

"What about your mom?" Lydia asked. "Luka told me your dad passed on a while back but that she still lives in your hometown."

"Oh… Yes, ma'am, my mother still lives in Swanton. Ollie and I haven't seen her for some years now though." Kyle ran a hand over his hair and fought back another wave of emotion. The idea of someone calling

Joanna McKee and telling her Kyle was hurt… His skin crawled to even think of her response. "She's not close to us the way you and Tomas are with your kids. I don't know her phone number now anyway."

"I see."

Lydia drew her eyebrows together, and Kyle knew she didn't see at all. A familiar hot shame flashed over him. No one truly understood the disregard his mother showed her children, and that included Kyle and Oliver. They'd never known anything different, though, and chose not to dwell on it unless they had to.

"There's no one else you want to call?" Lydia's expression was kind, as if she'd guessed at Kyle's feelings. She stood. "What about your friends from the bar?"

"Mmm, no, thank you." Kyle blinked heavy lids. "I don't want to drag anyone else away from their weekend."

"Too late."

Kyle's drowsiness fell away at those words spoken in a dear, familiar voice. The next thing he knew, Jesse stood by the bed with Carter, Malcolm and Will, all four of them eating up the space with their wide shoulders.

"Hey," Kyle said, his voice almost a whisper. He knew he must look dumbfounded, but Lydia chuckled.

"Looks like your friends don't pay much attention to that stubborn streak of yours either." She shook the hand Jesse held out and he flashed his megawatt smile.

"Mrs. Padilla, hello. I'm Jesse Murtagh."

"How are you guys here?" Kyle asked after the hubbub of introductions began to die down.

"Oliver called," Carter said, his expression more somber. "Said you and Luka got into a jam tonight, so we figured we'd come out and check on you."

"I had a meeting with my editor and Ri and Car are putting me up for the night, so I tagged along," Will said. He didn't bother hiding his frown. "We stopped by Luka's room on our way in," he added and shifted his focus to Lydia. "He's awake and looking for you both."

"Oh, Lord. He probably thinks we've been gossiping about him this whole time." Lydia patted Kyle's foot through the blanket. "I'll go back and tell him you're being moved soon."

Kyle swallowed. "Thank you."

Silence fell over the room after Lydia slipped out, and Kyle fixed his eyes on his lap. He'd never felt so exposed around his friends, like every inch of him had been put on display. The bandage on his face...there might as well have been a spotlight aimed directly on it. He was still trying to figure out what to say when Carter seated himself on the mattress and Jesse plunked Kyle's green duffel onto the foot of the bed. Just looking at it made Kyle's eyes smart once more.

"What's that for?" he asked.

"We brought you a change of clothes 'cause you might not get a chance to go home for a bit," Jesse replied. "Oliver asked us to pick up some stuff on our way over, and we packed extra for him, in case he didn't have time to run home for his things. He said the nurses put your stuff in a bag, by the way, and according to them, your shirt and coat looked like a crime scene."

Kyle frowned. "He did not." He'd bet his clothes were indeed wrecked though. Kyle had a vague recollection of the nurses cutting off his scarf then and his breath hitched. Luka had given Kyle the soft gray infinity loop scarf for Christmas and he'd loved it.

"Okay, true." Jesse smirked. "The nurses told Ollie you had stitches in your face though, and he figured you'd need a change for the trip home. Not even you are cute enough to pull off a hospital gown in December."

Carter ran his knuckles along Kyle's upper arm, and the touch raised goosebumps along Kyle's skin. "Doin' okay, babe?"

"Nope." Kyle tried to clear the boulder out of his throat, and oh, fuck, his eyes were wet again. "I wanna get out of here."

"Hmm, I can't imagine why," Jesse said, his tone light. "Luka's mom seems a lot more fun than I expected though. Did you two make nice with each other?"

"Yeah. She apologized for giving me a hard time. Got me into Luka's room tonight, too." Kyle swiped at his eyes and moved his shoulders up and down. "My doc said I can probably leave in the morning."

"That's good," Malcolm said. "Luka thought they'd be ready to release him in a couple of hours, but it's pretty clear he's not leaving until you do."

Carter reached up and smoothed Kyle's hair back from his forehead. "Ollie's been messaging. He's worried because he can't reach you or Luka. I told him we'd find you."

Hell.

"The nurses had my phone. I was too out of it to dial. I'm not sure where it is now." Kyle sniffled.

"We'll find it. You can use mine for now." Carter pulled his phone from his pocket and handed it to Kyle, but Kyle just stared at it until Carter spoke again, his voice very gentle. "You need to call Ollie, Kyle."

"I dunno if I can," Kyle whispered.

"The poor guy's stuck on a train and about to climb the walls," Malcolm said. He'd stepped closer to the bed and stood between Jesse and Carter. "I feel bad for his seatmate."

Kyle choked on a laugh. A hiccup escaped him when one of the guys handed him a tissue, and he rubbed his eyes hard. "Oh. I almost lost it telling the cops what happened. Talking to Ollie...not sure I can handle that."

"We'll stay with you," Jesse said. He curled his fingers around Kyle's wrist and guided the hand away from his face. He stayed silent until Kyle met his gaze. "Call him. I know you want to."

Kyle hauled in a deep breath. His eyes were watering freely now, and his friends' faces were somber. They were all touching him somehow though, anchoring him in a way he hadn't known he'd needed. Kyle knew they'd stay for as long as he needed them.

"Don't tell Luka about this, okay?" Kyle waved at his face. His breath hitched when Carter drew his eyebrows together. Carter hated lying, even by omission, and asking him to do so was a big deal. He simply rubbed Kyle's arm again.

"Why don't you want Luka to know?"

"He'll blame himself. He already does, and it's not his fault." Kyle's voice broke on the last word.

Jesse sighed. "It's not your fault either, buttercup. Luka's mom already told you that, right?"

Kyle wiped his nose, then frowned. "Um...yeah. You weren't here for that though."

Malcolm shared a grin with their friends. "We kind of were," he said. "We stood in the hallway and eavesdropped without shame."

A strangled laugh bubbled out of Kyle, along with a fresh wave of tears. It was okay, though, even if the tears made him even more of a mess. "I really hate you guys."

"Yeah, we know." Jesse poked Kyle in the shoulder with his finger. "Now call your brother. We need to get you cleaned up before the nurses move you into Luka's room."

Chapter Sixteen

"Hey."

Matías tapped Luka's thigh with his toes. They'd been hanging out on the couch all evening, watching TV. Well, Luka had been at a loss as to how to focus on the show — one he normally enjoyed — and Matías had been staring at him out of the corner of his eye the whole time.

"What are you and Kyle doing tomorrow night?" Matías asked.

"Hmm?" Luka met his roommate's gaze.

"New Year's Eve," Matías said. "What are you and your boyfriend up to? I'm going to a party at Bethany and Diego's house and you guys are invited if you don't already have stuff at the speakeasy planned. Is Kyle working?"

Luka shook his head. "No. Jesse forbade him from coming in for at least a week. Kyle didn't argue, so I can tell he's still not feeling great. We're staying in."

"That'll be good."

"Neither of us has been in the mood to go out." Truthfully, Luka's nerves skittered every time he left the house and he spent a lot more time looking over his shoulder than he ever had before. He assumed that feeling would fade eventually, but it was unpleasant, to say the least.

"How are you doing?"

"Me?" Luka shrugged. "I'm cleared for duty, but the chief suggested I take a few more days off. I'll probably be glad to get back to work on Monday, but for now, I'm fine relaxing. I knew Kyle wouldn't fight the idea of staying home if I did, too."

"I'm surprised you guys have been apart at all after what happened."

"Kyle's brother has been visiting. I'm giving them some time."

Oliver had been a mess when he'd arrived at the hospital in Brooklyn and Kyle only just holding it together. Giving them space had been the least Luka could do. Besides, Luka had needed time with his family, too.

After Luka had been discharged, he'd gone home, and the Clarke-Padillas had descended on his apartment en mass. He'd been hugged and fussed over by the entire clan, which left him both overwhelmed and grateful. He'd had a long, private talk with Wade, too, about what would likely happen with the investigation. Wade was confident that the detectives assigned to Luka and Kyle's case were good people with the drive to do everything they could, and that gave Luka a bit of comfort.

The family had also filled Luka's and Matías' kitchen with food. Tomas had cooked Luka's favorite dishes, and Daniela had brought over half of the bakery. Luka felt very full and much loved, but now he really wanted this peaceful evening in with Matías and Robbie, who was currently snoozing between the couch armrest and Luka's thigh.

What Luka didn't know was how to tell Matías that he felt almost relieved Kyle wasn't there with them, too. Even thinking that made Luka feel like a shitty boyfriend. But seeing the bandage on Kyle's chin and knowing he was taking medication for his headaches made guilt churn in Luka's stomach.

Kyle had convinced Oliver to go out for New Year's Eve in Manhattan however, which meant Luka and Kyle would be alone the next night. Unfortunately, Luka had no idea how to tell his boyfriend that his guilt over what happened made it almost impossible for Luka to stand being in the same room together.

* * * *

"I don't know about you, but I'm fine with this becoming our New Year's Eve tradition from now on," Kyle said, his voice lazy.

They'd put a decent dent in the food the Clarke-Padillas had brought and were halfway through a superhero movie.

"Yeah, it's nice." Luka draped an arm across Kyle's stomach. Kyle sat between Luka's thighs and he had his back pressed to Luka's chest. "I think you'd miss slinging drinks behind the stick in your bar though. I'm surprised it's not driving you up the wall tonight."

"Normally, it would, but I'm enjoying taking it easy this year. After everything we've dealt with, I mean."

Luka didn't know how to respond so he just pressed a kiss to Kyle's head. He wanted things between them to be easy, like they used to be.

Thankfully, Kyle continued speaking. "You're right. Next year, I'm sure I'll be thrilled to be at Under, but maybe this could be our New Year's Day tradition."

A hollow feeling settled in the pit of Luka's stomach. A week ago, he would have been glad to be making plans for a year from now with Kyle. But now, Kyle's words just brought Luka worry. What if he and Kyle didn't make it until next year? Luka had a dangerous and unpredictable job. If the assault had proved anything, it was that happiness came without guarantees. A string of events had led Luka and Kyle to be in the wrong place at the wrong time — who could say it wouldn't happen again? Or that the outcome wouldn't be even worse if it did?

The empty feeling settled deeper into Luka, as if it had taken root and had no intention of going anywhere.

Movies and even a brief nap on Kyle's part had kept them occupied for the last few hours, but with five minutes to go until midnight, Luka switched to the television. The celebration in Times Square was being broadcast of course, and he shook his head at the massive throngs of people gathered to celebrate. Luka was glad they were both far from Midtown. In addition to the usual FDNY presence in the Times Square area, there were always additional firefighters and paramedics on hand during the New Year's Eve celebration.

The NYPD had a heavy presence, too, of course, especially with the possibility of terrorist threats. But the fire departments had an equally large role to play to keep the massive crowds safe. Luka had worked

New Year's Eve in Times Square several times, and while nothing major had ever happened, it was still a grueling shift.

Working New Year's Eve out of his own firehouse was bad enough. Drunk drivers, idiots with fireworks and Christmas tree fires kept them hopping. He wasn't sorry to be staying in this year.

"Chances are I'll be working either New Year's Eve or New Year's Day most years," Luka said to Kyle.

"Hmm?" Kyle craned his neck to look at Luka, who tried not to wince at the white bandage on his chin. "Oh, sure, that makes sense. I'm glad we get to ring in the New Year together this year. Even if the reasons are shitty."

Luka heard the crowds on the television counting down. "Five-four-three-two—"

Kyle shifted and pressed his lips to Luka's as they hit one. Luka kissed him back, but he was hyperaware of Kyle's injury and that he might hurt him if he kissed him too deeply.

Kyle pulled back, a tiny frown furrowing the space between his eyebrows. But all he said was, "Happy New Year."

"Happy New Year," Luka echoed, wishing he could muster up more enthusiasm this year.

"What do you say we finish this celebration in bed?" Kyle stroked Luka's thigh.

"You sure you're feeling up to it?" Luka asked, concerned. There were dark circles under Kyle's eyes, and the bruising on his face had turned a sickly yellow-green shade.

"Yes." Kyle's tone was firm. "I'm sure. We haven't had sex since…" He winced, like he couldn't quite bring himself to say the words "the attack" aloud.

"I know," Luka said quietly.

He was glad Kyle had made the overture though. Luka's head was a jumbled mess, and he hoped some time in bed together would fix that. Luka didn't like feeling so distant from him.

But later, as he turned Kyle onto his side and slid inside of him, he felt as far from Kyle as he'd ever been.

* * * *

"I feel like I've hardly seen you," Kyle said as Luka shrugged out of his bulky winter coat.

"Yeah, I know. I'm sorry."

Luka glanced again at the scar tissue bisecting Kyle's chin, then away. The external sutures had come out five days after they were put in, but Kyle's skin was still red and puffy despite the oil he carefully rubbed on it several times a day. To Luka, the scar stood out like a beacon against the dark beard Kyle had been growing because his face was too tender for shaving. While Luka liked the beard, he hated the reason for it.

"Work's been tough," Luka said now.

He had been working a lot of hours since resuming duty, but Kyle didn't know that was because Luka had volunteered for extra shifts to avoid being around Kyle. And while Luka hoped Kyle didn't notice, the guilt inside Luka threatened to choke him.

"Glad to be back at the speakeasy?" Luka asked. He bent down and unlaced his boots.

"You have no idea. Even with Jesse driving me up the wall. He's hovering like a mother hen."

Luka laughed. "I can just picture it."

"He's not letting me do anything." Kyle sounded exasperated.

"He'll settle down. You've had two really serious things happen to you in less than six months, after all."

"Two? Oh, the fire at Burger Barn. Yeah, I hadn't thought about that."

"Your friends love you and want you to be safe," Luka said.

"I know." Kyle leaned against the wall near the door. "I'm just saying I might strangle him if he doesn't calm down soon."

"That's fair." Luka tucked his wet boots out of the way next to Kyle's.

A timer beeped and Kyle straightened. "I picked up a chicken pot pie at the market the other day. The store makes them onsite and they looked great. I'm in the mood for comfort food, I guess."

"Sounds great," Luka said. "Need any help?"

"Nope." Kyle went around the corner to the kitchen, still talking as he moved. "I'm just putting it in the oven now. We'll eat in about an hour, if that's okay with you."

"Sure." Luka walked into the compact living space. As he sprawled on the couch, his knee bumped a pile of papers stacked on the table and they tumbled to the floor. Luka automatically reached for them, and though he tried not to read, words leapt out as he straightened the pages.

Dr. Okafor. Counseling. Tribeca. Anxiety.

Luka glanced up at Kyle, but he stood at the stove and had his back turned. Luka looked back down, scanning the documents more thoroughly. It appeared to be paperwork from a therapy practice. And it looked like

Kyle was a patient there, seeking treatment for feelings of anxiety.

Feeling terrible for having snooped, Luka finished gathering the paperwork and set it back on the coffee table, and by the time Kyle turned around, Luka was playing on his phone as though nothing had happened.

"All set—I put a pan of vegetables in to roast, too. I figured we'd watch a movie until everything's ready."

Luka tried to smile at him. "Sounds good."

Kyle sighed as he took a seat next to Luka. "Sorry I'm so boring right now. We're usually a lot more active than this. I've just been in hibernation mode. It's cold and snowy and I just want to sit on the couch and do nothing."

"Hey, it's okay," Luka said. He understood the impulse, but now he wondered if there was more behind Kyle's comment. Luka's thoughts flickered back to the therapy paperwork. How much was Kyle struggling with that he wasn't letting on?

An uneasy expression crossed Kyle's face then. He gathered up the paperwork from the table and stood. "Shit, I'm sorry. I'll get all of my stuff out of your way."

He carried everything to the file box he kept on the bookshelf nearby, and Luka frowned as Kyle tucked it away with quick, sharp movements. Kyle was a tidy person but not obsessively so, and the small pile hadn't been in Luka's way at all. What was going on here?

All evening, through the movie and dinner, Luka waited for Kyle to mention that he was seeing a therapist. But he hadn't said a word and seemed to fall asleep almost as soon as his head had hit the pillow. Luka lay beside him, staring up at the ceiling and wondering what came next for them.

Physically, they'd survived the attack. But it seemed to be driving a wedge between them that he had no idea how to repair.

* * * *

Luka tossed his tablet on the couch beside him with a heavy sigh. Sometimes, the wealth of knowledge on the internet was more of a curse than a blessing. He'd spent the past few hours digging through the NYPD's crime statistics for the past few years. They'd just released the data for 2015 a few days before, and the more he read, the harder his stomach churned. The sheer number of crimes staggered him, and the percentage of crimes that went unsolved was even more disturbing.

He'd followed that reading with news articles about gay bashings and race-related hate crimes, and now his head swirled with frightening statistics and images of incidents that had ended far worse than the one he and Kyle had endured.

Was this what their future held? A lifetime of fear and checking over their shoulders to look forward to? Even though Luka hated thinking it, he'd started to understand why his mother had pushed him toward dating people of color and Regina had pushed him toward women. His life still wouldn't be easy — living as a black man in a white man's world never was — but at least he wouldn't have to endure additional strikes against him and whomever he was with.

Luka's heart ached as he thought of Kyle. He loved Kyle so much. But what if being together endangered him? What if they went out some night and were attacked again? People said lightning didn't strike twice in the same place, but that wasn't true at all. Luka couldn't deny that gay and interracial couples were lightning rods for hatred and bigotry. As a lightning rod, being struck at some point was an inevitable outcome, wasn't it?

Luka didn't want to lose Kyle. But what if losing him meant Kyle would be protected from harm?

Maybe letting Kyle go is the best way to keep him safe.

That toxic thought bounced around Luka's head like a ping-pong ball every time he looked at Kyle's face. A beautiful, kind and good man had done nothing but love Luka, and now he was permanently scarred. Because of Luka.

How could he ask Kyle to sign on to a future filled with fear?

"I thought you were making chili for dinner?" Matías' tone was light, but Luka saw a crease in his brow. Luka blinked at his roommate and wondered how long he'd been staring at the floor stressing about his future. "Isn't Kyle coming over tonight?"

Luka glanced at the clock on the entertainment center and winced. "Shit. Yeah, I should have started that half an hour ago. I got caught up reading on my tablet."

Matías gave Luka a searching glance. "Are you sure you're okay? You keep saying you are, but you've seemed off lately. I feel like you aren't being honest with me."

Luka stood. "I'm fine. I promise. Just a bit distracted."

"You know I'm here if you need to talk."

"I know. Thanks." Luka brushed by him toward the kitchen. "Going out tonight?"

"Can't you tell?" Matías twirled. He was dressed to the nines, complete with skin-tight pleather leggings and a face full of makeup.

Fear gripped Luka, but he forced a smile onto his face. "You look great. Be careful out there though, okay?"

Kyle and Luka were substantially larger than Matías and more masculine in appearance. More butch, as Matías liked to tease. If three guys hadn't hesitated to go after the two of them, what might happen to Matías as he walked alone to and from the subway station late at night?

"I will. I've got my pepper spray." Matías patted the bag he carried. "I'll be fine. Don't wait up for me tonight, Dad."

Luka couldn't manage a lighthearted reply to Matías' breezy tone. "I worry," he said instead.

"I know you do." Matías leaned in and pressed a kiss to Luka's cheek. "I appreciate it and I promise I'll be careful. What happened to you is rare. It's a dangerous world out there, but not everyone has it in for us."

Matías' words continued to ring in Luka's ears long after his roommate had left.

Maybe not everyone, but enough people had it in for them. Enough that Luka couldn't stop his fear every time he thought about the people he loved and what could happen to them if they were in the wrong place at the wrong time. His siblings. His mother. His stepfather. His roommate. His friends. People of color. LGBTQ people.

Luka's worries gnawed at him as he chopped onion and sautéed beef. He knew the chili recipe by heart, so his mind was free to wander as he dumped beans and tomatoes into the pan and seasoned the mix with chili powder and cumin. He almost wished he'd chosen a more complicated recipe so he could focus on something other than the thoughts in his head. The more Luka thought, the more hopeless he felt.

He set the chili to simmer, then cleared the counter and was about to start on the dishes soaking in hot, soapy water when a knock sounded on the door. Luka dried his hands as he walked toward the door, and when he opened it, he could hardly see the figure on the other side through their thick winter coat.

"Kyle?"

"Fucking hell, it's cold out there!" Kyle said as he stepped into Luka's apartment. His words were muffled by the scarf wrapped around his face. He unwound it and pulled off his stocking cap. "Feels nice in here though. And it smells great."

Luka closed the door behind him. "I just put chili on. I meant to start it earlier, but I got distracted."

"That's fine. I need to thaw first anyway." Kyle peeled off his coat and stepped out of his boots. His cheeks were pink from the wind, and though the dark beard now covered the scar, Luka saw a hint of it below the dark hairs.

Luka averted his gaze, unable to stand the painful reminder. "Want some coffee?"

"Please." Kyle snagged his belt loop. "But I'd like a kiss first."

Luka turned back and pressed his lips against Kyle's. Kyle's nose felt cold against his cheek, and Luka was careful not to bump their chins together. For the first time since they met, his heart wasn't fully in it.

When Kyle drew back, he kept his hand on the back of Luka's neck, holding him in place. Worry lurked in his eyes and Luka wanted to look away. "Are you okay? You seem...not yourself."

"Just tired. I had a long shift last night." The thoughts whirling through Luka's head were still too disorganized for him to share.

"Okay." Kyle let go. "If you're sure."

"Why don't you pick out a movie to watch while you warm up?" Luka suggested. "I'll finish up the dishes and brew some coffee for us both. I'll be there in a few."

Luka was grateful for the distraction of the movie and put in another one as he and Kyle settled down to dinner. Staring at the screen was easier than looking Kyle in the eye, but truly focusing on what he was watching was another thing entirely. Kyle had told him the film's name but damned if Luka could remember it or the movie's plot.

The chili had turned out pretty good given the short cooking time, but Luka's portion went mostly uneaten. He poked at it, hoping his appetite would magically return, and before long, Kyle set his half-empty bowl on the coffee table, too.

"Luka, are you sure everything's okay?" Kyle asked.

"Yeah, I'm fine," Luka lied. He stroked a hand over Robbie's soft fur. The ferret had been spending a lot of time with Luka lately, as if he could sense Luka's unspoken distress. His warm little body and soft chirping noises were soothing in their own way, but they did nothing to shake Luka's uneasiness.

Kyle paused the movie and shifted toward Luka but waited until Luka met his gaze before he spoke again. "You're not fine."

"I had a long shift, that's all," Luka said again. He hated lying, but what else could he say to Kyle right now? "Christmas tree fire. I wish people wouldn't let the damn things get dried out and crispy, then leave the lights on when they go out."

"Forget the Christmas tree. I'm worried about you." Kyle frowned. "You've been tired and down. Are you sure you weren't injured worse than anyone realized?

Maybe you hit your head but didn't notice at the time. Have you thought about going to see the doctor again?"

"I've been fully cleared." Luka shook his head, aware he'd started to bristle but unable to stop the reaction. "If the FDNY is content with my fitness for duty, then I am too. I feel fine other than being tired. Maybe it's just the lack of sunlight. It's been so overcast and cold. It makes me want to sleep a lot."

Robbie squirmed and Luka realized his grip on the ferret's small body had tightened. Not enough to hurt him, but enough to wake him. Luka lifted his hand and the animal gave him a disgruntled look before jumping down and scampering toward the bedrooms.

"Don't bullshit me, Luka!" Kyle sounded frustrated. "I can see you're struggling. I know we went through something traumatic, but I feel like you won't even talk to me about it."

"Like you haven't talked to me about your therapy sessions?" Luka bit out.

Kyle stared at him, open-mouthed. "How—how did you find out?"

"You left the damn paperwork on your coffee table when I was at your place last week," Luka said, his annoyance now full and hot. "I saw it because I accidentally knocked it on the floor. I didn't say anything because I hoped maybe you would tell me about it. But you obviously weren't going to."

Kyle sat back and rubbed at his forehead. Although they were getting better, Luka knew he'd had periodic headaches since the attack and might for some time. Just one more reminder of the danger Luka posed to Kyle's life.

"I'm sorry," Kyle muttered. "I should have talked to you about it. I just didn't know how."

"Why did you decide to go in the first place?"

"I...I need to talk to someone about what happened."

Hurt flared in Luka's chest. "Why can't you talk to me about it?"

"I don't want to worry you! You've been treating me differently since that night, Luka, and I'm worried I'll make it worse. You won't even look at me anymore." The pain in Kyle's voice was clear. "Is it the scar? Is that what's bothering you?"

"Of course, it's bothering me!" Luka said.

"Oh." Kyle's expression turned flat and closed off. "I didn't realize it would matter so much to you."

"How could it not?" Luka stared at Kyle. His heart ached every time he saw the reminder that it was his fault Kyle had been injured. "You say you didn't want to worry me, but how could you not tell me about going to therapy?"

"I wanted to deal with how I was feeling without impacting you. Or our relationship. But apparently, it has anyway."

Luka swallowed hard. "Is the therapy helping?"

Kyle looked away. "I thought so. Now I'm...I don't know anymore. I need some time to think about everything."

Time to think.

So, Kyle didn't want to be around Luka right now either. Maybe that was for the best. It would be better for them both if they had time apart to think about what came next. Time and distance might help. Luka had been trying to distance himself from Kyle in the past few weeks anyway, so he could do this.

"Time to think would be good," he said softly. "Actually, I think I need that, too."

Kyle's throat worked. "Do you…want me to go?"

Luka laughed awkwardly. Why were his thoughts spinning like this? He couldn't even think straight, and now Kyle's face had gone a sickly shade of pale. "I'm not kicking you out or anything."

"That's not what I asked, Luka."

"Yeah, maybe that would be for the best." Luka knew he sounded stiff, but how did he tell the man he loved to leave? Not because he wanted Kyle gone but because it was best for them both?

Luka couldn't change who he was. He glanced down at his hands. He'd never been ashamed of being biracial. Guilt washed over him now for wondering how things would have happened differently on that Brooklyn street had he and Kyle been the same race. If Luka had been different—had looked different—would it have happened? Maybe it wouldn't have made a difference, but what if it had? Kyle had been injured because of his relationship with Luka. Nearly killed. Maybe Kyle really was better off with someone more like himself.

Kyle would be safer.

Maybe they both would.

Kyle's expression was grave as he stood and crossed in front of Luka. Luka scrambled to his feet, and Kyle paused in front of him. Oh, God, the hurt in his eyes nearly killed Luka, but this was for the best. It had to be. Nothing made sense at all, but if he could just protect Kyle from getting hurt again, that was all that mattered.

Kyle didn't say anything more and neither did Luka. He watched Kyle bundle up again with stiff, jerky movements.

"Be safe," hovered on the tip of Luka's tongue as Kyle stepped out of his apartment but the words weren't a magic talisman. They wouldn't protect Kyle from the dangers of the world. Nothing could.

Chapter Seventeen

Kyle's phone buzzed on the nightstand and he went still, black button-down shirt in hand. He watched the screen light up with an incoming message, and the mix of hope and dread that filtered through him weighed heavy on his heart. After the notification faded, he forced himself to set down the shirt and move toward the phone. He tapped the screen and his insides tightened further at Luka's words.

Hey. Just checking in.

Kyle stared at the little speech bubble for a long time.

Working the next few nights, he replied at last. *What's up?*

The usual – work, eat, sleep, repeat. Broke in a new pub in 2 Bridges w Luis and Stefan. Decent drinks, pretty fun.

"Great," Kyle murmured. "Glad one of us is having some." Because what could he say to a guy who'd bypassed the bar Kyle owned in favor of a pub so far downtown it was practically in Brooklyn?

Kyle sat down on the mattress, the task of getting dressed forgotten. He sent a thumbs-up to Luka, then set the phone face down on the nightstand and wondered again how the fuck his life had turned so completely upside down in such a short time. Kyle hadn't felt this lost in years.

He'd been numb after Luka's oh-so-polite dismissal. The trip back home that night had passed in a blur, Kyle functioning on autopilot through over a dozen subway stops. He'd only truly come back to himself after he'd reached the stairs to his building. He'd gone inside and gotten drunk, a thing he almost never did alone, though it seemed like a fine idea after getting kicked to the curb. He'd needed to shut up the voices in his head, too—voices that had squeezed his heart and threatened to steal his breath. That had told Kyle he wasn't worth anything—never had been—and only pure, dumb luck had kept Luka from figuring that out on day one.

That drunktastic strategy had worked only as long as it took the booze to work its way out of Kyle's system, and all he'd been left with by morning was a hellacious headache and a sour gut. He'd skipped yoga in favor of more sleep, then headed for the bar in the late afternoon where he'd worked until close and stayed locked in the bar all night working to refine Under's latest menu. Kyle had headed home after the city started to wake so he could start the cycle all over again, minus the bourbon drinking that solved nothing.

No matter how many days passed, nothing about his conversation with Luka made any more sense or felt less awful. Luka had started messaging again, too — a development that only increased Kyle's mental turmoil. He tried to view the messages as a sign Luka wanted to work things out, but outside of asking how Kyle was feeling, the words in the speech bubbles were so bland and impersonal they could have been sent by a stranger. Worse, they were worded in such a way that Kyle felt in his gut he'd become an afterthought for Luka, more a task to be checked off than a real person who needed contact.

What did you expect? You've got a two-inch scar on your face, and Luka can't bear to look at you.

Kyle's stomach hurt. He didn't know what to expect, from Luka or even himself, and he just wanted to bury his head in his arms and hide.

Not an option, he told himself exactly as he imagined his therapist would if Kyle had said the words out loud during a session. But even Kyle's internal voice sounded strained and weak, as though it belonged to someone else.

A sudden knock sounded at the door, the sound ripping through the buzz in his head like a gunshot, and he bit back a yelp, his whole body jolting.

"Kyle?" Jesse's voice echoed through the silence in the apartment along with another knock. "It's Jes and Cam. Okay if I use my keys, babe?"

Kyle reached for the discarded shirt with unsteady hands and dragged it on, then got to his feet. Jesse had taken to knocking and asking permission to enter in recent weeks rather than letting himself in as he'd always done in the past. Carter, Riley and Malcolm were doing the same, a change Kyle suspected had everything to do with the fact he was as jumpy as an over-caffeinated Chihuahua.

Fuck, being on edge all the goddamned time was exhausting.

He walked out of the bedroom, working at the buttons of his shirt as he moved. "C'mon in, guys," he called.

The deadbolts on the door clicked and slid open one after another, and the door swung open to reveal Jesse and Cam, both loaded down with bags.

"Hey, gorgeous," Jesse said with a smile nowhere near typical levels of Murtagh-brightness. He and Cam stepped inside. "We were hoping we'd catch you."

"You didn't answer when we called," Cam added, "and we thought maybe you'd gone out to do errands."

"Shit, I'm sorry. I didn't hear my phone." Kyle frowned. He'd zoned out after messaging with Luka. Had he turned his phone off?

"No worries." Jesse closed the door and locked it, his grin wider, though his gaze stayed sharp. "We come bearing food and grooming products."

"Okay, and what the heck does that mean?" Kyle asked.

"I figured we'd throw dinner together, and I'd show you how to take better care of the growth on your face."

Kyle's stomach dropped lower than his feet. "Why?"

"Well, as hot as you are, you still need some grooming," Jesse said. He and Cam set the bags down and crossed the room toward him. "Your beard is starting to wear you, babe, instead of the other way around, if you know what I mean."

That's the whole point, Kyle thought in a rush. *If people are looking at the beard, that means they're not looking at my —*

He fought off a flinch as Jesse laid his warm palm against Kyle's right cheek.

"Cam makes a hell of a roasted chicken," Jesse said, his voice low and sweet. "I also brought a big-ass bag of the best beard products money can buy. We're talking Murtagh tested and approved, so you know they're good."

"I hope you don't mind that we're crashing your Thursday night," Cam threw in with a soft smile. He stepped up to Kyle's left. "We brought enough food for at least four if you're expecting anyone for dinner."

Kyle huffed out a weak laugh. He wasn't on shift for another five hours, but he'd planned to stop in at the reopened Burger Barn to say hi to Maya and Nestor, then spend the afternoon at Under, researching recipes and filling out paperwork so he could ignore the shambles of his personal life. He recognized the gleam in his friends' eyes however. Neither Jesse nor Cam would leave before they were good and ready, and arguing with them would just make them dig their heels in harder.

"I'm not expecting anyone," Kyle said, "but let me change my shirt if we're gonna cook."

He let out a soft 'oof' when Jesse pulled him into a hug, and Cam was on them a second later, long arms dragging Kyle and Jesse in tighter.

"First, you have to greet us properly, you fucking heathen," Jesse murmured. "So rude." The petulance in his tone brought a real smile to Kyle's face.

The three spent the next hour jockeying for position in Kyle's tiny kitchen. They chatted about a low-key celebration of Kyle's birthday during Under's private party the following week and a much noisier affair planned for Southampton a few days after that, and Kyle assured his friends he'd be okay with both. He didn't really feel like any kind of party, and he'd have to explain away Luka's absences, but Kyle would work it out. He'd always been good at telling half-truths when the occasion called for them.

Despite his earlier dark mood, Kyle felt looser and more buoyant than he had in weeks. Jesse and Cam had brought several bottles of very good wine as well as two large chickens, and once the birds and an enormous pan of root vegetables were roasting in the oven, Jesse inclined his head in the direction of Kyle's bathroom.

"Okay, you. Time to get your beard on. Bring your wine and try not to get any hair in it."

Kyle worried his bottom lip between his teeth. "I'm...I don't want to trim much," he said, "and nothing sharp near the scar."

"Does it still hurt?" A furrow worked its way between Cam's eyebrows.

"It doesn't hurt so much as zing. I know that's not the right word, but I don't know how else to describe it."

"It's sensitive," Jesse guessed.

"It can be," Kyle replied. "I'm working on desensitizing it, but the thought of something catching there..." A shudder worked its way along his spine.

Jesse rubbed Kyle's shoulder "I get you. Why don't I show you what I brought, and you can decide if anything could pose a problem?"

And that was how Kyle ended up perched on a barstool in his bathroom while his friend walked him through caring for the facial hair he'd grown in the wake of the injury to his face. He was overdue for a clean-up in general, Kyle saw now. On top of not shaving, he'd put off getting his haircut, too, and the longer, bone-straight locks and beard shone shaggy and almost blue-black against his pale skin.

Jesse raked the hair off Kyle's forehead with a fond smile. "If you grow a man bun, I'm going to punch you so hard."

"Promises, promises," Kyle muttered.

"Kinky. Okay, first, you moisturize." Jesse held up a small brown bottle with a dropper. "Your beard's full, so I say go oil instead of balm." Taking Kyle's hand, he squeezed four drops onto the palm.

Kyle rubbed his hands together and breathed in vanilla and bourbon. "Oh, wow."

Jesse chuckled. "I had a feeling you'd like that." He oiled up his own palms and led Kyle through the motions of moisturizing his beard and skin.

"This feels nice," Kyle said, mostly to himself.

"Right? Now, I know you're leery about sharp edges," Jesse said, "but you need to comb the hairs out so you can see where it needs trimming." He held up a flat brush in one hand and a wide-toothed comb in the other, both fashioned out of warm-toned wood. "These are designed to be super smooth. Start with the brush and work your way up to the comb with time."

Kyle nodded and swallowed down the itchy feeling skittering under his skin. "Okay."

With some guidance, he used the boar-bristle brush and a pair of shears to groom his beard to a length slightly greater than Jesse's more tailored style. Satisfaction thrummed in Kyle's chest as he uncovered the shape of his face. He'd never gone longer than a week without shaving before, and though he didn't look at himself in the mirror much these days, the lush beard felt both comforting and strange. Kyle looked better with some clean-up. He felt better, too, and that was a nice change.

"You know, I prefer you with stubble, but this wolfman thing is a good look on you," Jesse murmured, his eyes on Kyle in the mirror. "Not that I'm surprised."

The open admiration in his gaze warmed Kyle's insides. Maybe he didn't look so bad with the scar under wraps.

Jesse caught his eye. "You're really carrying a hipster-fuckface vibe right now though, and it'll be way over the top if you wear those stupid suspenders of yours."

Kyle smiled. "Think it'd be too much if I rocked a bowtie, too?"

"I'd probably hump your leg," Cam said from the doorway. He grinned bright as Kyle's and Jesse's laughter echoed around them. Kyle noticed the camera in Cam's hands then, and his shoulders tensed up all over again. Before he could protest, Jesse handed him a compact electric trimmer.

"Use this to clean up any hairs on your cheeks and neck. You could change the lines on your face, too, but I wouldn't—the shape you've got going works." Jesse stepped behind Kyle and pressed against his back, reaching around Kyle's body and guiding his movements.

Despite the task at hand, Kyle's brain wanted to focus on the camera that told him Cam was capturing images and probably had been all along.

"What's with the camera?" he asked, though he didn't dare look away from his reflection.

"Are you kidding?" Cam asked, a smile evident in his voice. "I've got two beautiful men engaged in exaggerated grooming behavior right in front of me—do you expect me not to record this for posterity?"

"That's Cam's way of saying he needs fresh images for his spank bank."

Jesse's dry tone pulled another laugh out of Kyle, but luckily, Jesse had turned off the trimmer in time to prevent any damage from being done.

It feels good to laugh, Kyle thought.

The timer in the kitchen sounded, and Jesse stepped back around Kyle while Cam slipped out to see to his chickens.

"I wasn't lying," Jesse said. He set the trimmer down and turned so he could rest his ass against the sink. "It's been a while since you played with Cam and me, and we miss you. Cam says you haven't been around for gaming either."

The words tugged at the frayed edges of Kyle's heart. "I know. I miss you, too. I just need to get my head back together some more. Especially now that..." Kyle bit his lip.

Jesse shifted forward until he stood between Kyle's knees and slipped his arms around Kyle's neck. "Especially now what?"

Now that Luka doesn't want me.

Kyle closed his eyes. Saying those words out loud — admitting Luka was all but gone from his life — made it too real. And damn, they hurt.

"It's nothing," he murmured instead. He wound his arms around Jesse's hips and pressed his forehead against the tight torso in front of him. "Thanks for this, Jes."

"Of course," Jesse said. "You want to talk about it, babe?"

"Not really."

"Okay." Jesse stayed quiet for a beat, then pressed a kiss against Kyle's hair. "Anything you need, you call."

* * * *

"You look well, Kyle," Dr. Okafor observed. He and Kyle settled into a pair of oversized chairs upholstered in pale blue wool.

"It's the beard." Kyle ran his fingers over his jaw. "Some friends staged an intervention a few days ago and helped me get it under control."

Dr. Okafor raised his brows, his interest clear. "Ah. I hoped to hear you'd gotten more than a few hours' sleep, but I daresay it was time well spent. You look refreshed."

"It was nice hanging out with them." Kyle licked his lips. "Nice doing something for myself for a change, I suppose. I had dinner with some other friends yesterday, too. Outside of work, I haven't been going out as much."

"Any particular reason why?"

Kyle leveled a look at his therapist. "You already know the subway makes me nervous sometimes."

"I do. We've discussed that you could always call for a car. Is there more to it than that?"

"Yes." Kyle frowned. "I've been feeling…disconnected from myself since the night I got jumped. At first, I thought it was the concussion, but now I think maybe it was a reaction to what happened. Coming here and talking to you helped me see that."

Talking to Dr. Okafor had helped Kyle see a whole host of things about himself, many of them unrelated to the bashing.

"Anxiety after a traumatic experience is very common, and those feelings can manifest in all sorts of ways." Dr. Okafor tilted his head. "Your sleep problems, for example, and lack of appetite."

"Right." Kyle nodded. "Overall, I haven't been taking the best care of myself."

"Why do you think you're neglecting your own needs?"

"They don't always seem important." Kyle tapped his scar with his fingertips, so his nerve endings zinged. "After the bashing, my first impulse was to take care of my boyfriend. Make sure he was okay and not blaming himself for what happened."

"Did you blame yourself instead?"

"For a hot minute, yes. But I don't anymore."

"What about your boyfriend?" Dr. Okafor asked. "Does he blame himself for what happened that night?"

Kyle rubbed his lips together for a beat. "I think so, yes, even though he's never said as much. He...we've been spending time apart. Actually, he asked me to leave his apartment the last time we got together." Kyle forced a wry smile. These appointments were keeping him honest since Luka's angry words. "I haven't seen him since. I haven't told anyone else about what happened yet."

"I can imagine it hurts to be apart."

"It hurts me. It certainly gave me an excuse to slack on the self-care." Kyle turned his eyes to the window and stared unseeing at City Hall Park spread out before him four stories below. "Being away from me is better for Luka, though."

"What makes you say that?"

"He acted like he couldn't stand being around me. Couldn't stand seeing me. My face in particular. He — "

He looked relieved when he asked me to go that night.

Kyle swallowed against his tight throat. "I asked Luka if the scar bothered him and he said yes. Now, I'm not stupid. I know it looks bad. But I thought…" Kyle shook his head. "I thought we'd both get used to it."

"Is that why you grew the beard?"

"No. I couldn't shave while the sutures were in, and now, I'm just afraid to. I don't want to make the scar worse while it's so fresh."

"Okay, and what about a month from now?" Dr. Okafor asked. "Or three months from now, or six?"

Kyle's cheeks went hot. "I'm not sure. I'd like to say I'll be okay with shaving it off, but the truth is, I don't know. I know Luka wouldn't be. When he looks at me now, all he sees is my scar. He can't see past it to me."

Dr. Okafor said nothing for a moment. "What do you see when you look at yourself, Kyle?"

Something broken.

Kyle shrugged off the thought. "I'm not sure about that either," he said. "I haven't wanted to look at myself much, literally or figuratively. So, it seems I can't see past the scar either."

"Have you considered scar revision?"

"Yes." Kyle hauled in a deep breath. "I know from talking to my doctor that there'll always be a mark there though. So what's the point?"

Dr. Okafor hummed. "The revision could improve the look of the scar, so it bothers you less."

"On the outside, maybe. But I'll still know it's there." Kyle shook his head. "That probably sounds stupid."

"It doesn't." Dr. Okafor frowned. "Why do you say that?"

"Some days, I feel mostly okay, but other days…they're dark. I don't always recognize myself, if that makes sense."

He shifted his gaze back to meet the doctor's and pressed a hand on his heart. "I don't look good or feel good, but I'm still in here somewhere, right?"

Dr. Okafor leaned forward in his chair, his dark eyes kind. "You are most definitely still in there, Kyle. I know you don't feel your best, but the fact you're asking yourself that question tells me you're getting back to being you. That includes coming to terms with the way your face has changed.

"Scars are proof of life," he said, smooth voice even gentler than usual to Kyle's ears. "Signs that we survive and heal. That is what you're doing, even on your darkest days."

Lines from a poem Kyle had always liked popped into his head.

come celebrate
with me that everyday
something has tried to kill me
and has failed

He gave a slow nod. Okay, maybe something didn't try to kill him every day—that was a bit over the top despite the things he'd experienced in the last six months. Dr. Okafor had a point though.

Kyle would turn thirty in a couple of weeks. He'd survived a fire and the bashing and come out battered but alive. He wouldn't change a single thing about his part in making sure Luka had survived the attack either, not even the mark on his face or losing Luka in the process.

Which meant Kyle needed to get okay with that scar so he could keep moving forward.

* * * *

Kyle was headed back uptown after his appointment when his phone buzzed in his pocket. He fumbled it when he saw Detective Bowen's number on the screen and connected the call with a murmured curse. He hadn't heard from anyone at Special Victims Division for a couple of weeks and was relieved that his voice sounded steadier than he felt.

"Hi, this is Kyle."

"Mr. McKee, it's Detective Bowen at Special Victims. Have you got some time to come out to the station this afternoon? We've taken a person of interest into custody who we believe may have been involved in the attack against you and Lieutenant Clarke."

Kyle blinked. "Um. Yes. I'm…I'm downtown now, and I'll get on the first ferry I can."

An hour and a half later, Bowen ushered Kyle into a small, nondescript room containing a table around which were arranged four chairs. Large windows covering one wall were the room's only distinctive features.

"We'll get started in a few minutes, Kyle."

Detective Schwarz, who'd followed behind Kyle and Bowen, closed the door. "You know how a police line-up works, right? From TV shows?" He aimed a crooked smile at Kyle. "Another officer will come in and act as administrator. He's going to give you instructions, and you'll sign a form stating you understand what's happening today. Then the suspects will be led in" — he nodded at the windows — "and you'll look them over, see if you can make an ID."

"This is a good time to remind you that you could be called back again," Bowen added.

"That's fine," Kyle replied. "I work nights and I can come in if you need me to." He glanced at the windows. "The glass is mirrored on the other side?"

Schwarz nodded. "Yes. The suspects can't see into this room."

The door opened again and what seemed like a crowd of people trooped in, including two uniformed officers and several people in suits. Kyle shook hands with an attorney from the DA's Hate Crimes Unit and a defense lawyer, as well as an investigator and another detective from SVU. They all faded into the background when the lights in the room beyond the windows switched on, illuminating a white wall decorated with height lines, just like Kyle had seen in countless TV shows and movies.

Holy shit. This is really happening.

One of the uniformed officers turned to Kyle.

"I'm Officer Riddick, Mr. McKee." He focused on a sheaf of papers in his hand and read aloud. "You'll be presented with a series of individuals. A person who is involved in the crime may or may not be among them. You'll be shown all of the individuals, and you can take your time looking at them."

Kyle waited, a frown on his face while Riddick continued, and he signed off on a form just as Schwarz had described. Riddick issued a command through a microphone in the wall, and six men filed in to the room beyond the windows, all fair-skinned and wearing baseball caps. Each man looked to be around Kyle's own height, and most were broad shouldered and muscular. Every one of them looked annoyed with life. Awareness buzzed through Kyle's body.

'You go for the dark meat, huh?'

One of the men had growled those words at Kyle that night. A man in a baseball cap who'd looked at Kyle and Luka with disgust, lips curled in a sneer when he and Kyle had grappled with each other.

Riddick gestured Kyle forward. "If you'd step up, Mr. McKee, we can get started."

Kyle moved, his eyes on the figures beyond the window. One by one, they were called up and he searched their features, looking for something—anything—that sparked recognition. The hairs on the back of his neck stood up as number four stepped forward.

'Does that moolie fuck you hard?'

Kyle swallowed. He scanned the man in front of him head to toe, taking in his plain black cap, black T-shirt and dark jeans. He was handsome, with strong, elegant features, but his eyes were cold and dead and his mouth hard. Familiar. Kyle's gaze stopped at the big, meaty hands holding the placard identifying the man as suspect four and his guts wound tight. Thick silver rings adorned every finger, including a huge Iron Cross on the man's right hand.

A chill ran through Kyle. He knew those rings. He'd told the cops about them when he'd answered their questions. They'd made every punch thrown during the beating hurt that much more. That Iron Cross had likely ripped Kyle's face open. And the eyes glittering like blue ice on the other side of the glass...yeah, Kyle knew them. They dragged him out of sleep in the darkest part of every night.

'Jesus, man. You let an ape fuck you? What the fuck is wrong with you?'

"Four," Kyle ground out, his voice rough. He sensed a burst of quiet activity in the room around him. "It's number four." He stared, unmoving, as suspect four was instructed to move back into place.

"You're confident that number four is the perpetrator, sir?" Riddick asked.

"Yes."

"Can you tell me why you picked number four?"

"His rings," Kyle said. "I recognize his rings — especially the Iron Cross. And his eyes." He swallowed down a wave of nausea and forced himself to face Riddick. "He held me back while the others went after my boyfriend. He...he used slurs and knocked me down."

Kyle signed the form again, his hands shaking slightly, and not until the line-up room had emptied out again did he feel like he could draw a deep breath. By then, the top of his head was tingling, and Detective Schwarz guided him into one the chairs at the table while the crowd in the room dispersed.

"You did great, Kyle," Schwarz said. He took the chair opposite. "Just sit here and get your bearings for a second."

"Here." Bowen set a small carton in front of Kyle and popped it open. "Drink some of this, nice and slow."

"What is it?" Kyle's ears rang faintly.

"Orange juice," Bowen said. "You look pale, and we want to raise your blood sugar before you go moving around."

Kyle picked up the carton and sipped without tasting. "Okay," he muttered, too dazed to feel embarrassed that he needed someone to keep an eye on him. "That was surreal."

"It's intense," Bowen said. "We had a guy pass out cold last week, and that was before the suspects were even brought in."

Kyle let out a rusty chuckle and that lightened the air around him like magic. He recovered his wits over the next fifteen minutes and felt more himself again by the time he exited the station. A familiar voice calling his name froze Kyle in his tracks though, and oh, he'd missed hearing it.

He forced himself to turn around, and there stood Luka, right there on the sidewalk in front of Kyle, tall and beautiful in his overcoat, his blue eyes bright. Kyle's heart twisted so hard it hurt.

"Hey," he managed and watched the corners of Luka's mouth twitch up, though his expression was far too serious.

"I saw you come in to the station," Luka said. "I was with someone from the DA's office though, so I waited." His forehead puckered. "You okay?"

"Sure."

Kyle wanted to roll his eyes at the obvious fib. He looked less than spectacular these days and knew it. There were circles under his eyes, and he could have used an extra meal or two. But who cared when he could have been crushing Luka in a hug instead of making polite conversation? Kyle didn't move though.

"I had to view a line-up and that was weird," he said instead. "I'd tell you about it, but I'm not supposed to. Actually, I don't want to talk about it for a million different reasons." Kyle made a face, but Luka nodded, his expression sympathetic. "I'm sorry."

"No, I get it."

"It wasn't what I expected, I guess," Kyle said. "Not that I knew what to expect in the first place."

This time, a real smile crossed Luka's face. "Yeah, I understand. I have Wade around to answer questions, and I'm still lost when it comes to this stuff."

"Is Wade here?"

"No, he's on duty. I called him on my way down here though, and he coached me as best he could."

We could have coached each other, Kyle thought. A bitter wave swept through him. *We could have come here together. We should have come together and had each other's backs through the whole thing, but Luka turned to Wade instead of me.*

Not that Kyle had done any better. He hadn't even known Luka would be here. He'd pulled Luka's number up on his phone more than once during the ferry ride to Brooklyn, intent on asking him to meet Kyle. He'd stopped himself from calling each time because he didn't want to hear Luka say no. Even now, Kyle jammed his hands in his pockets to keep himself from reaching out.

"That's good," he murmured.

Emotion flashed across Luka's face too fast for Kyle to read. Apprehension, maybe? Regret? "You headed back?" he asked.

Kyle nodded. "I took the ferry. I was in Tribeca when I got the call, figured I might as well take the scenic route."

"Right." Luka pressed his lips together in a grim line. No doubt he knew what Kyle had been doing downtown, but still, he didn't ask. "I'm, uh, headed back that way, if you want company. I'll buy you a cup of shitty coffee or a beer if you want one."

"I'm working tonight, but I never turn down shitty coffee," Kyle said, and there, some of the tightness in Luka's face disappeared and Kyle counted that as a win.

Neither said much during the walk to the docks, but Kyle didn't mind. He'd never needed his time with

Luka to be filled with chatter, and just being around him now was nice. A boat had docked as they arrived so Luka quickly bought a ticket and they boarded, heading inside just as the ferry departed for its next stop.

"So, the beard," Luka said. They'd bought their coffees at the concession and sat at a table by the window, the hum of other passengers' voices rising and falling around them. "I never imagined you wearing one, but it works."

"You're not the first person to say this." Kyle ran his knuckles against his cheek. "I think I wigged Carter's kids out when they got a look me this weekend though."

"Yeah?"

"I had dinner there on Saturday," Kyle said. "Dylan actually accused me of wearing a fake beard and insisted on pulling on it before he'd accept it was real."

"Ouch." Luka laughed.

"He thinks it makes me look like a 'movie villain.'" Kyle made air quotes with his fingers. "They got over it though—you know how kids are. Sadie even offered to help me dye it different colors. She thinks blue would work for me."

Luka's eyes crinkled with his smile. "She said that?"

"Oh, yeah. Hell, I may take her up on it. It's not like I plan to keep the beard forever, so I may as well have some fun with it." Kyle's stomach tumbled at the way Luka's expression faltered.

"You're going to shave it off?"

Kyle blinked. "Well, yeah. At some point."

The light went out of Luka's eyes. "I figured you'd want to keep it, all things considered."

"Considering my face, you mean." Kyle tried not to let his hurt show but knew he'd done a poor job when Luka's expression fell.

"Oh, shit, I'm sorry. I shouldn't have said that."

"No, I get it." Kyle turned his eyes away from Luka, who just saw too goddamned much. "You were being honest. I've always liked that about you.

"I'm trying to do that, too, actually, and stop keeping things from the people in my life." He stared, unseeing, out of the window as the ferry slipped into the dock at DUMBO. "I do it a lot, it turns out. Mostly because I don't want to worry or hurt people I care about. Unfortunately, that backfired with you."

Kyle met Luka's eyes again. "I'm sorry I didn't tell you about Dr. Okafor. I know I should have."

"Kyle—" Luka paused in whatever he'd been about to say and frowned. "Has it helped? I mean, I still don't really know why you decided to go in the first place."

"Right." Kyle nodded. "Because I didn't tell you anything. I've been having trouble coping. I'm nervous all the time. Anxious. Some days, I feel like I shouldn't leave my apartment, most of all when I'm alone. Going out to your place is hard. Hell, going to work takes a fuckton of energy."

"Why didn't you say anything?"

"I don't know. I didn't want to be a burden. You seemed to bounce back okay, and I didn't want to get in the way of that." Kyle blew out a long breath at Luka's pained expression. "I thought it'd be easier for both of us to move on if I acted like nothing was different."

"Oh, Kyle."

"The problem was that everything is different." Kyle drained the last of his coffee and crushed the cup in his fist. "I feel off-balance a lot. I have bad dreams. I stay at the bar sometimes instead of going home at night."

Luka's mouth fell open slightly. "You stay at the... But why? You can come to Sugar Hill anytime. Why don't you?"

"I didn't know how to tell you I was freaked out about riding the subway after hours and a Lyft wasn't much better." Kyle laughed — a hard, ugly sound. "I've lived in this city for years and never been afraid, Luka. And...I don't know. I wasn't sure you'd want me at your place."

"I'd never turn you away, Kyle. Never." The hurt in Luka's eyes humbled Kyle.

"I think you mean that," he said, his voice soft. "But not turning me away isn't the same as wanting me." Kyle ran his fingers over his beard. "I guess I didn't want to take any chances."

He rushed on when Luka opened his mouth to speak. "The therapy is helping. I'm talking to Carter, too. He's been dealing with anxiety for a long time and he gets it. I haven't stayed at Under overnight for almost two weeks now, and I'm starting to feel less like I'm falling apart." He bit his lip. "I should have talked to someone like Dr. Okafor a long time ago."

Luka frowned. "You mean about what happened to you in the Burger Barn fire?"

"No." Naturally, Luka's mind went back to that trauma. Kyle didn't blame him for jumping to that conclusion because, again, he'd chosen not to share much about his past. "About what happened with my mother. The way she treated Ollie and me, the way my dad sat back and let her act like we were nothing. Like we *are* nothing. My mother is where my, um... Where my, uh, abandonment issues started."

Fire licked up under Kyle's shirt collar. He couldn't even say it without stammering. He dropped his gaze to the table and clenched his jaw when Luka laid one hand over his on the table. Neither spoke until after the ferry had pulled back out and started for Manhattan.

"She tolerated us when we were growing up because of my dad," Kyle said at last. "After he died, she didn't need to do that any longer. I told you that I needed to go back to Vermont to work and help Ollie. Well, I had nowhere to stay." He inhaled deeply. "I was twenty-one. Dad was gone, I'd dropped out of my MFA program to go to work, and my mother told me I couldn't stay in her house because she didn't want me there. Because I didn't belong there."

"Jesus." The rawness in Luka's voice beat Kyle's heart all to hell. He made himself meet Luka's gaze, and the pain he saw there ran through him. "What did you do?"

"I left. It's not like I could change her mind about me—I'd learned that by the time I entered kindergarten. I stayed with friends. I slept in my car when I needed to and worked until I saved up enough to rent a room. And as soon as Ollie's school was done, I watched him graduate then sold the car and left for New York."

Kyle turned his hand up and wound his fingers with Luka's. His breath hitched when Luka squeezed back. He'd missed that touch so much.

"That was the last time I let my mother close enough to hurt me. But it turns out, the way she treated me has me all messed up."

"You are not messed up," Luka bit out. His eyes flashed with fire and sorrow. "You're one of the strongest people I've ever met."

"Yeah, well. I'm messed up. I have problems with rejection." Another laugh worked its way out of Kyle, this time choked with the tears he refused to spill. "That's why I had a hard time when Jes stopped coming around last year. And why it hurt me when your mom acted like I didn't exist." He shook his head at the way Luka's eyes went wide.

"I hid the way I felt about it, so don't you blame yourself." He rubbed the bridge of his nose with his free hand. "And you. Man, I was so blindsided when you asked me to leave that night, Luka. You laughed about it. I never saw that coming. Not from you."

"Fuck. I'm sorry. God, I really am." Luka pressed his lips together, and Kyle could read his struggle to stay calm. "I had no idea what you were going through, Kyle. But I needed the time. I still do."

Kyle drew in a big breath. "I know. I'd almost rather you get it over with and end it though."

"I don't want that."

"Don't you?"

"No." Luka's headshake was almost violent. "I'm just not sure where we go from here."

"Yeah. I don't know either." Kyle sighed. "Can we, I don't know, start over? Come to the bar on Thursday for the monthly party," he urged. "We can talk and hang out with everyone and just be."

"I'd love to, but I'm on duty."

Luka's sad expression told Kyle everything he needed to know. They couldn't come back from this if Luka didn't want to. And right now, he didn't. It still fucking hurt Kyle to force himself to go on.

"Right. I get that. I'm out though, okay?" His eyes burned at the way Luka shook his head, the movement almost imperceptible.

"What does that mean?"

"It means this isn't all about you." Kyle squeezed Luka's fingers. "I'll...if you need me, I'll be there for you. But I can't do this back and forth where you say you want me and pull away at the same time. It *hurts*. It gets in my head, Luka, and breaks my heart and I'm—"

Scarred. Ruined. Nothing.

Kyle swallowed hard. "I can't deal with it. And I need you to stop messaging me for a while."

"What?" The concern in Luka's expression sharpened. "Why?"

"Because I know you're only doing it to be nice. But I don't need a buddy or a bodyguard. I need a partner. Someone who's okay with my flaws, no matter how big they are."

Pain crossed Luka's face when Kyle pulled his hand free and stood. "Where are you going?"

"Outside. I want a head-start for the subway when we dock because I need to get my head together on the ride uptown and I can't do that with you." Kyle tried to clear the gravel in his throat. "I've missed you, Clarke. Take care of yourself, okay?"

He managed a smile before he turned for the door, but every step away from Luka just hurt more. Kyle stepped out into the freezing January wind and kept moving until he reached a spot close to the ferry's egress points where he huddled up against a wall.

Fuck.

Walking away was the right thing to do. Kyle knew it despite the pain he'd caused them both. They each needed time to heal. Kyle more than anyone, it seemed. Maybe he and Luka could find a way to be friends again—stranger things had happened. Kyle knew better than to count on it, though. Instead, he willed himself to ignore the sting in his eyes and focused on the city in front of him instead of looking back the way he'd come.

Chapter Eighteen

"You...don't seem okay."

Ruby frowned at Luka across the table. His sister had badgered him into meeting for lunch at a Cuban restaurant on his day off. Now that they were partway through the meal, he'd begun to regret he'd agreed.

"What's going on?" she asked.

"Why does everyone keep asking that?" Luka asked irritably.

"Well, maybe we know what we're talking about." Ruby pushed her hair off her face and the bright bangles on her arm clinked.

"I'm fine."

"You're full of shit and you know it."

"I'm tired is what I am." Luka fidgeted with his tiny cup of Café Cubano. "This time of year is shitty. The last of the Christmas tree fires and a bunch of suicides. It's not fun. Especially on top of the nearly two feet of snow we got last week. All I've been doing is digging people out."

"Okay, but you've never been in this kind of post-holiday slump before. And what's this about Kyle not coming to my show next Saturday?"

Luka gave her a quizzical look. "I'm not sure what you mean."

"I texted him about it weeks ago. He said he was coming and now, all of a sudden, he isn't. Something obviously happened."

"He does have a job."

"Yeah, a job that I know for a fact is flexible if he has enough notice. Based on the way you've been acting and his cancellation, I'm pretty sure work isn't the problem. So, tell me what's up." Ruby leaned forward and frowned, a furrow creasing the soft skin on her forehead.

Luka's resolve crumbled. Ruby looked and sounded so much like their mother just then. If Luka didn't spill to Ruby now, she'd send in the big guns, and Luka really didn't want to face Regina or Lydia now.

He cleared his throat. "Kyle and I are…a mess."

Ruby nodded. "That's understandable. You both went through a horrific thing." She rested her hand on top of his.

"It's more than that," Luka admitted. "Things got weird a few weeks ago. We had a fight."

"That does happen in relationships."

"Sure. But Kyle and I haven't fought until now." Luka looked down. "And he said he wanted time to think."

When Ruby didn't reply, Luka gave her a searching look. She remained silent and nibbled at her lip before she leaned in. "There's something I need to tell you."

"Okay?" That didn't sound promising at all.

"Mom and I went to Under the other night."

Luka gave her a baffled look. "So? You're always welcome there, unless… Did Kyle have a problem with it? If he's taking our fight out on you and Mom…"

"What? No. No, of course not. He was very gracious. Something just seemed off with him though, so I cornered him when things were slow." Ruby pursed her lips. "He said he'd been having a hard time coping since the bashing, which didn't surprise me. It took him a while to admit it, but he also said you've been freezing him out since."

"I've been freezing him out?" Luka's laugh sounded hollow. "Kyle started seeing a therapist and hid it from me. He told me he wanted some space. He didn't even call me when it came time to do the police line-up! He made a positive ID and one of the suspects has been arrested. We should have been celebrating together, and yet…"

Ruby frowned. "It sounds like you're not communicating well at all."

"Yeah. But I don't know what to say to him anymore." Luka sighed heavily. "I don't know what to do about any of it. I think maybe Kyle's better off without me. Maybe it's just…better this way."

"Seriously? What the fuck are you talking about, Luka? I get it that you guys have been dealing with some serious shit, but you should be holding on to him tighter not pushing him away. Gah! What is wrong with you?"

"This isn't all on me, you know? Kyle's been acting distant, too."

"So, you close the distance. You fight, you figure out what needs to be fixed, then you move forward." Ruby sounded exasperated. "You don't just give up."

"I don't know if there's any fixing this."

"Why wouldn't there be?"

"Because the problem isn't the two of us. The problem is the world out there."

A puzzled look crossed his sister's face. "What do you mean?"

"I mean the problem isn't only between Kyle and me. It's that being with me is endangering him further. Look what happened to us! What if it happens again? What if it's worse the next time?" Luka felt ill at the thought.

"Yeah, it could happen again. It could happen whether you're together or apart."

"But if Kyle is dating some white boy from Chelsea, it's a lot less fucking likely."

Ruby scoffed. "He could get bashed by someone who hates gay people. What the hell do you think happened back there in Brooklyn? Those guys weren't after you only because you're a mixed-race couple. You could date a white woman, and somebody might take issue with that. People who hate will find an excuse to spread it no matter what. Are you really telling me you're going to let them win?"

She leaned in and stared Luka in the eye. He flinched, struggling to meet his sister's gaze. She saw too much.

"I can't look at Kyle without seeing that scar," Luka confessed. "It makes me feel guilty about what happened. And after I told him that, he shut down on me."

Ruby narrowed her eyes at him. "What did you say exactly? Before he shut down, I mean."

"That the scar bothered me. That I can't stop thinking about it every time I look at him."

Ruby let out an aggravated-sounding huff as she lightly swatted his hand. "You dumb shit! No wonder he shut down. He probably thinks you're rejecting him because of the way he looks with the scar! I'm sure he's self-conscious about it already."

Luka's eyes widened. He'd never considered that possibility. "Fuck!"

Ruby tilted her head and gave him a knowing look. "Am I right?"

"You might be," he grudgingly admitted.

"Have things been okay in the bedroom department since the attack?" Luka gave Ruby a confused look. "Does Kyle know you still find him attractive or were you pushing him away there, too?"

"It had been a while," Luka replied.

At first, neither of them had felt up to having sex. They'd spent a quiet night in for New Year's Eve because they'd lacked energy for socializing. They'd had sex that night and it had been slow and easy. Physically, they'd been close, but Luka hadn't been able to quell his panic or fear.

So, he'd pulled away to gather his thoughts. He'd hoped to talk to Kyle more about his problems getting past the attack but then he'd discovered Kyle's therapy appointments. They'd fought not long after and then...well, he hadn't seen Kyle at all until they'd run into each other in Brooklyn. The conversation had been stilted and awkward, but Kyle had spilled a ton of information, too, before he'd said he was out. Out of what, Luka didn't know for sure. The one thing he did know was that Kyle didn't want Luka messaging him anymore.

Luka's life had been empty without Kyle. He'd spent those weeks feeling the same way he did when his chief called on him and the crew to fall back during a fire because it was too dangerous for them to continue.

Luka would watch buildings burning to the ground, unable to do anything but stand by, helpless. The same thing happening to his relationship with Kyle, but Kyle had ordered Luka to fall back, and Luka was trying to respect that. What had that time apart gotten either of them, though? Luka still didn't know what the hell he was doing or how to keep Kyle safe. He still worried way too much that the people in his life would be hurt.

The distance Luka had thought he'd needed had given him some perspective however. He knew he still wanted Kyle desperately in every way he could get him. But he could feel Kyle slipping away. Luka knew that was on him. He'd pushed Kyle away out of fear. Because as frightened as he was of losing Kyle, Luka felt even more terrified of being the reason Kyle got hurt.

Again.

But, hell, Luka had hurt Kyle himself with his words and his actions. The way Kyle had looked at Luka on that ferry, like his heart had been in pieces...

Luka's head spun. He hadn't known the full extent of Kyle's problems with his mother or about his abandonment issues. Luka had been afraid for Kyle since the incident, but had Kyle misinterpreted that fear as rejection?

Kyle's words on the ferry echoed in his brain. *'I need a partner. Someone who's okay with my flaws, no matter how big they are.'*

Had Kyle meant his scar? That he believed Luka didn't want Kyle anymore because of a mark on his face?

"Fuck," Luka said again, more quietly as the enormity of what he'd done settled over him. "When Kyle and I talked the other day, he said he wanted out.

I didn't understand what he meant. He said he needed me to stop messaging him for a while. I thought he just needed space," Luka said, "but if you're right about what he's been thinking, maybe he meant something more permanent. Did he...did he break up with me?"

Ruby gave him a sympathetic look. "I don't know. I think you need to talk to him."

Luka nodded, deep in thought.

"Can I get you anything else? Dessert perhaps?" the waiter asked, startling Luka with his appearance. "We have an excellent flan and *arroz con leche* available today."

Luka shook his head. "No, thank you."

Dessert wasn't what he needed right now. No, Luka needed time to figure out what to do next.

* * * *

Luka rubbed at a spot on Engine 47's chrome bumper that was already clean and shiny, lost in his thoughts. He'd considered his sister's words more than once since their conversation. A part of him had wanted to run to Kyle's place right then and set things right. Tell Kyle he was flat-out wrong if he thought Luka was disgusted by a scar.

Luka swallowed past the thickness in his throat at the idea Kyle would ever doubt that Luka found him attractive. Kyle was handsome, scar or no scar. But Luka hadn't been in a relationship with him just for Kyle's good looks. Kyle's quiet humor, his kindness, who he was as a human being — those were things Luka loved most about him. The happiness he brought into Luka's life. The way he made Luka feel.

And what had Luka done? Brought stress into Kyle's life in the form of Luka's meddling family. Sure, Regina and his mom were on Team Kyle now, but it had been a difficult road for Kyle. He'd put himself in uncomfortable situations and worked hard to win all of Luka's family over and not once complained.

Luka had repaid Kyle how? He'd put Kyle in danger. Made Kyle feel rejected. Made him doubt that Luka's feelings were more than skin-deep. And broken open old wounds from Kyle's troubled upbringing.

Kyle's scar was not the problem. Luka's guilt was.

Luka hadn't run to Kyle because Kyle had asked for space. What kind of a jerk would Luka be if he ignored that request? He didn't want to be the asshole who disrespected Kyle's boundaries.

Kyle was right, too. Luka had been saying he wanted Kyle but pulling away at the same time. That wasn't fair. Before Luka did anything, he needed to get his own head on straight and be sure he could handle the possible repercussions to their relationship.

Kyle had clearly been working on himself in the form of seeing a therapist. Maybe Luka needed to do the same. Talking to Ruby had helped purge some of Luka's awful feelings. He could reach out to a departmental therapist for more. Or, hell, talk to his stepfather. Tomas had been Luka's sounding board for years. Maybe he could help Luka put things in perspective now. After all, he was in an interracial relationship himself—he had to know some of Luka's worries.

The intercom crackled to life. "Engine 47. Rescue squad. Bakery fire at the corner of Manhattan Avenue and 116th Street."

Luka threw the soapy sponge into the bucket and strode to the locker room to put on his gear. Minutes later, the truck pulled out of the station house, sirens screaming.

For now, Luka had to put all his focus on the job.

* * * *

Several days later, Luka pushed open the doors to Tomas' accounting firm. He waved at Camila—the office receptionist—who was on the phone. She waved and pointed toward the back of the space.

"Go in," she mouthed.

Luka nodded and headed for Tomas' office where he found the door open. Tomas looked up with a smile after Luka rapped gently on the doorframe.

"Hey, Pop."

"Hey, son." Tomas got out of his chair and walked around the desk to greet Luka. "Perfect timing. I just finished up with a client."

"Good. I worried I might be too early."

Tomas hugged him tightly. "I was surprised when you called."

"I know this is a stressful time of year for you." Mid-January through the end of April was always Tomas' busiest season, and Luka knew his stepfather wouldn't take a break for just anyone.

"I'll always make time for you."

"Either that or the lunch I picked up," Luka teased.

"I'll admit it's a toss-up." Tomas grinned. "But, please come on in. Close the door and have a seat, and we'll catch up over food. You said you needed to talk?"

With the door shut, Luka and Tomas unpacked the bag of food from the deli and spread it out on the desk, which was tidy beyond Tomas' computer set-up, some pens and a framed photograph of the entire Clarke-Padilla family. Seeing it made Luka's chest warm.

"I do need to talk," he said once they'd both sat down. "I've been having a hard time."

"Because of the attack?"

"More because it's impacting my relationship with Kyle."

"Oh, I see." Tomas frowned. "What's going on?"

Luka licked his lips. "Have you ever been afraid that someone would go after you and Mom because of your race?"

"The thought has crossed my mind," Tomas said. "But I haven't been in a situation where it's happened, or I've felt like it was imminent. Everything has been much more subtle than that. Certain looks and comments, that sort of thing. It's rarely overt. And nothing like what you and Kyle experienced."

Luka had expected as much. "I know what happened to us isn't that common. I've always known I'm more likely to get mugged for my wallet than be the victim of a hate crime, but I thought…I don't know. I thought it could never happen to me, I guess. I figured I'm a big enough guy to intimidate anyone if I wanted to. Feeling so helpless, not being able to protect Kyle… That was the worst part."

Tomas offered Luka a sad smile. "You're a protector, Luka. You always have been. Your father died protecting people, and while your mother's job isn't as dangerous, her focus is her patients. If something happened in the hospital, she would die protecting them. Protecting people is in your blood and your bones, and I can't imagine how frightening it must have been to feel you couldn't do what every instinct in you was screaming to do."

Luka dipped his head and mulled over Tomas' words. His feelings from the night of the attack rushed back. "It was awful," he said hoarsely. "I don't ever want to feel like that again."

"Did something happen between you and Kyle? Because you seem really down."

"Kyle and I are having trouble. We've been drifting further and further apart…" Luka closed his eyes for a moment as emotions threatened to overwhelm him. "And I don't know if I should let it happen or fight for him. I want to be with Kyle, but I'm afraid being with me puts him at a greater risk."

"I understand that, but whether you're together or apart, you can't protect Kyle from everything. And you're far more likely to manage it if you're with him."

"I know that," Luka admitted. "Intellectually, I do. But I'm scared shitless of choosing to put myself in that position again."

"That's what life is, Luka. That's what relationships are. Choosing to risk being hurt. Otherwise, what's the point? You're not moving forward, you're not taking risks, you're just stagnant. And that's no life at all."

The words settled deep in Luka's brain, and he knew he'd have to think about them more after he left. "What if this relationship is riskier than others?"

"What if it offers you more? What if the reward is worth the risk?"

"I don't know."

"I can't answer that for you," Tomas said. "What I do know is that you love Kyle. That much is clear. The family is happy about that. He's a good man. He's good for you. I know this situation has you both rattled, but

I don't believe it has to tear you apart. Unless you choose to let it."

They ate in silence and Luka took time to think about his stepfather's words. "What if I did something that hurt Kyle?" he said at last.

"Was it deliberate?"

Luka scowled. "Of course not."

"Then why do you look like you think he won't forgive you? Have you spoken with Kyle about it?"

"No. I didn't realize it until after he'd already asked me to give him some space."

Tomas sighed. "That's tricky then. But perhaps he'll be open to talking if you tell him that you need to apologize. Just don't do it until you're sure you want to be with him."

"Okay. You're more right about that than you know." Luka's grimace made Tomas frown.

"I wish I had more concrete advice to give you, Luka."

"No, that's okay," Luka said as he gathered up the trash from their lunch. "This has helped a lot. It's given me plenty to think about."

"I'm glad. It was nice to see you today, even with all the serious talk."

Luka cracked a smile. "Nice to see you too, Pop. I'll try to make it home for dinner on Sunday."

"That would be nice."

"Love you."

They stood and Tomas came around the desk to fold Luka into another hug. "I love you too, son. I hope you're able to work out everything with Kyle."

* * * *

Luka spent the next few days really thinking about what to do. Ruby and Tomas had made excellent points. The more Luka thought about the way he'd been acting, the more ashamed he grew. He'd fucked up. He'd pushed away the person he loved when Kyle had needed him the most. Now all Luka could hope was that he hadn't done irreparable damage.

He thought long and hard about what to say to Kyle. He wanted to find the words to fix what he'd broken. But in the end, he realized there were no perfect words. All he could give Kyle was his honesty.

Kyle had asked Luka not to message, so Luka called instead. He didn't know if that was better or worse than texting, or if Kyle would welcome either, and he wasn't surprised when the call went to voicemail. Luka hadn't expected anything else, but it still hurt.

"Kyle?" Luka's voice cracked a little. "You asked me not to message you, and I want to respect that. I know you need some space, and the last thing I want is to make what you're struggling with more difficult. But I've been talking to people and thinking about what happened, and Ruby said something that made me question some of the conversations you and I have had lately. I think I wasn't clear about your scar and I want to fix that."

Luka breathed deep. "When you feel ready, please call me so we can talk. No matter what we decide, I don't want to leave things the way they are now."

For two days, there was nothing but silence. The guys at the station teased Luka about checking his phone obsessively, and Luka jumped at every notification that made the damned thing buzz. But still no word from Kyle.

On the second night, Luka fell asleep with the phone clutched in his hand and Robbie curled around them both. Disappointment swept over Luka in a crushing wave when he woke the next morning and found only junk email notifications and tags from friends on social media.

He brought up the folder of pictures he'd saved of him and Kyle and thumbed through them. A lump rose in Luka's throat. Why had he let his fear get between him and the man he loved? At the time, it had all made sense, but now it seemed only absurd. Luka loved Kyle. Yes, he feared what their future could hold, but Tomas was right. That future was nothing without Kyle in it.

With a sigh, Luka rolled out of bed, but he took his phone with him, just in case. He'd stepped out of the shower and was drying off when his phone buzzed on the bathroom vanity.

Hastily, he wrapped a towel around his hips and reached for it, and when 'Kyle' flashed across the screen, Luka's heart took off, pounding like he'd just run drills. He sat on the edge of the bathtub before he answered it.

"Kyle?"

"Oh, hey, Luka." Kyle's voice sounded strained and far more subdued than Luka was used to. "I got your message."

"Good."

"I needed time to think about it."

"I understand." Luka's heart ached at how stilted their conversations had become. They'd been so easy before. Almost effortless. Not that he was afraid of hard work. Luka would do whatever it took as long as he and Kyle wanted the same thing.

"Do you have some time in the next few days where we could talk?" Kyle asked.

"Today, if that works for you."

"Oh." Kyle sounded surprised. "Yeah, I could do that. You're not on duty?"

"I'm scheduled to go in later today, but I'm sure I can find someone to pick up my shift. I don't do it often so if I tell them it's important, someone will fill in."

"Are—are you sure? Tomorrow's fine if that's better for you."

"I don't want this hanging over us any longer than it has to," Luka said firmly. "Tell me where and when, and I'll be there." If need be, he'd call in sick. He'd never played hooky from his job, but he would now if he had to.

Kyle stayed silent a moment. "Why don't you get back to me once you get someone to cover for you and we'll figure it out then?"

"Okay," Luka agreed. "Talk to you later?"

"Later."

* * * *

That afternoon, Luka buzzed Kyle's bell. Thankfully, he'd found coverage for his shift without a problem, but his stomach was tied in knots. This had to go well. Luka couldn't imagine any other outcome.

Kyle buzzed Luka in, and when he opened the door, Luka smiled. Kyle looked good. His beard and hair were neatly trimmed and the circles that had been around his eyes the last time Luka had seen him had faded. Kyle's answering smile still seemed a little forced though.

They made small talk while Luka removed his coat, talking about the case the district attorney had been building against the man in the baseball cap, as well as the two other men he'd implicated.

"Can I get you anything?" Kyle asked after they'd taken seats on the couch.

Luka shook his head. "I'm fine. I'd rather just clear up what I think is some really bad miscommunication we had."

"Okay." Kyle clasped his hands together between his knees. "I'm listening."

"I talked to Ruby the other day and she mentioned a conversation you two had at Under."

Kyle's expression fell. "I shouldn't have said anything to her. I was hurting and —"

"No, I'm glad you did. It made me realize I'd fucked up."

"Fucked up how?"

"I have never been disgusted by your scar or how you look." Luka's voice wavered. "And if I gave you that impression, I'm sorry."

"Really? Because every time you looked at me, you'd look away again. I was sure you were repelled by me." Kyle swallowed. "By the way I look now."

Luka's heart ached. "I never meant for you to think that, Kyle. After the attack, I couldn't look at your face because I felt so guilty. I hated not being able to protect you that night, and the scar was a constant reminder of my failure. The way I feel about you…it's not just about the way you look. I like *you*. You've brought so much to my life, just by being you. You're beautiful inside and out."

Kyle closed his eyes. "I got so in my head about all of this. Like I said, it brought up shit with my mother and—"

"I know." Luka reached out for Kyle's hand, and a weight lifted off his shoulders when Kyle opened his eyes again and twined his fingers around Luka's. "I'm sorry about that. I should have made sure you knew where my head was."

"You said you were feeling guilty? Why? What happened wasn't your fault any more than it was mine."

"I kept thinking that if I were different, you never would have been in this position."

"Different?" A furrow appeared on Kyle's brow. "Different how?"

"If I weren't black—"

"No! Luka, that thought never crossed my mind. I don't want you to be anyone but who you are."

"I don't want to be either," Luka said. He ached at the distress he read in Kyle's face. "I've never hated myself or my ethnicity before, but all I could think was that race was to blame."

"No one is to blame but those assholes." Kyle squeezed Luka's fingers and the touch made Luka's heart leap. Maybe he hadn't damaged their relationship beyond repair.

"I know. I talked to Tomas, which helped. He helped put things in perspective for me." Luka hauled in a deep breath and exhaled. "I don't really believe it. I guess it was just easier to focus on that than admitting I had no control over the situation. There was nothing I could have done to prevent it, and I don't like feeling helpless."

Kyle nodded. "I understand. Especially with your job. You're used to saving people from catastrophe. Being a victim must have been hard."

"It was. I need to deal with that, too. Talking to Tomas helped, but I'm thinking about seeing the departmental counselors. Just to be sure I've dealt with all this shit."

"That could be good for you, Luka. Therapy has helped me." Kyle sat back and Luka reluctantly let go of his hand.

"I'm glad." Luka licked his lips. "And if I haven't said it already, I want you to know how sorry I am about everything. I've been so terrified of losing you that I pushed you away and I regret that so much." He breathed in deeply again. "I know it won't happen overnight, but do you think that there's any way you can forgive me? I want so much to get back what we had together, and I know we need to move forward together."

Kyle didn't say anything. The moments ticked by, one after the other, every second agonizing. Luka's pulse pounded in his ears as he waited to hear Kyle's answer.

"I'd like that," Kyle said. "I really would."

"Why does it feel like there's a 'but' there?" Luka asked, his voice tight.

"I guess because I'm scared." Kyle's eyes were too bright, and his laugh was strained. "I'm scared you'll reject me again. Or I'll get tangled up again and so afraid of being rejected that I'll convince myself you've pushed me away even when you haven't. I'm working on all of this with Dr. Okafor, but it takes time, and I'm just...afraid."

"I'm afraid too." Luka reached out and took both of Kyle's hands in his again. "Of losing you. Of hurting you. Of not being able to protect you. But in the end,

I'm more afraid of letting you slip away from me. I love you, Kyle. I'm scared too, but I'm not going anywhere. Not if you'll have me."

The press of Kyle's lips against his own set every nerve in Luka's body alight. It was a soft kiss, almost chaste. But the familiarity in the touch of Kyle's lips reassured Luka. The nerves that had been coursing through his body all morning quieted. That kiss was all the answer Luka needed.

Kyle shifted back and Luka followed until they were lying side by side.

"Missed this," Luka murmured.

"Me too."

Luka pressed his cheek against Kyle's. The soft prickle of his beard was unfamiliar, but nice, too. There were new things about Kyle for Luka to discover and he was eager to do so. But for now, he wanted to breathe Kyle in and hold him close. Kyle's heart thumped against Luka's chest, strong and steady. The heat of Kyle's body and his nearness were reassuring. Comforting.

For the first time since the attack, Luka felt as though he could breathe again.

Chapter Nineteen

Kyle's phone buzzed as he exited the subway station at Spring Street in SoHo, and he stepped back inside the doors so he could check the message in relative warmth.

Be done in 15-20, Luka wrote. *Meet you outside?*

I'll be there, Kyle replied.

He slipped his phone in his pocket and headed out, a strange mix of melancholy and gratitude twisting in his chest.

True to his word, Luka had sought help from the FDNY Counseling Services Unit. He was in the Manhattan outreach office now, in fact, and he wanted to buy Kyle dinner afterward. While glad Luka was taking care of himself, a quieter part of Kyle grieved, too. Luka saved people's lives nearly every day — Kyle had never met anyone so courageous. Knowing Luka still grappled with feelings of fear after the bashing stung. And that Kyle had been too busy picking up the pieces of his own drama to understand? That hurt his heart.

Not productive, Kyle reminded himself. Supporting each other was key in getting past their guilt over what had happened, and falling into another shame spiral wouldn't do either of them any good. Luka was trying and Kyle wanted to meet him halfway.

Or as close to halfway as possible, at least.

It had taken Kyle all these weeks to build himself back up, and he'd almost backslid after breaking things off with Luka. There were still parts of him that felt broken, but he was getting back to his "normal" — he could feel the change. He'd been sleeping better and started yoga practice again, and his appetite was improving every day. Knowing Luka was working on his own needs helped, too.

As he walked, Kyle tucked his chin deeper into the scarf he'd wound around his neck. The snow that had buried the city the week before had been cleared away and the weather had been mild since. However, temperatures were dropping now that the sun hung low in the sky and another chilly blast sent him searching for additional warmth. By the time Kyle approached the busy station house on Lafayette Street, he had a bright orange paper bag hanging over one arm and a steaming cup in each hand. Luka emerged a minute later, and just seeing him made Kyle's heart flip.

"Hey, Luka."

"Hey, yourself."

Luka's answering grin made Kyle feel ten feet tall. Kyle smiled back but didn't move otherwise because even here, in a gay-friendly neighborhood he knew well, he was very aware of the people on the sidewalks around them.

Luka stopped in front of Kyle and glanced at the cups in his hands. "What's this?"

"Spiced apple cider." Kyle handed one over. "I thought it'd be nice to have a warm drink while we walk."

Luka's expression softened. He popped the plastic lid on his to-go cup and sniffed. "Mmm, smells fantastic. Thank you. And the bag?"

"Also for you." Kyle moved his arm, so the bag rattled. "Although, I have a couple of items for me, too. There're croissants and pastries and you and Matías can fight over them at breakfast. I know your vacation started when you clocked out today." Luka's eager expression made him smirk. "They can't compete with the stuff your cousin makes, but—"

"Don't ever apologize for buying me baked goods, Kyle," Luka said. "Thank you, again." He frowned. "Wait, do you still want to have dinner?"

"Yes. What do you feel like eating?"

"Well, you're working tonight, right?" He waited for Kyle's nod, then glanced back the way Kyle had come. "Let's head back toward the station on Houston so we can ride uptown afterward. I know there's a tapas place that way, and a couple of bistros, so we should be able to find a place we can both agree on."

Fifteen minutes later, they were seated in the tapas restaurant with a pitcher of sangria and Kyle was savoring the flavors of cranberry, pomegranate and hibiscus-soaked strawberries. His happy hum brought a smile to Luka's face.

"The drink meets with your approval, I take it?"

"It's delicious. I like the substitution of tequila for brandy, but I don't know if this glassware is working for me." Kyle set the highball glass down with a chuckle. "Sorry. I'll stop now."

"I don't mind. You agreed to eat tapas even though they're not your favorite."

"I like tapas! I find all those teeny plates ridiculous, that's all. Anyway, you can listen to me geek out any old time. How did your appointment go?" Kyle paused. "Wait, am I allowed to ask you that? Like, with your department rules and everything?"

"Of course, yes." Luka folded his hands on the tabletop. "The appointment went well, I think. I got a referral to talk to a counselor next week and we'll go from there."

Luka fell silent and Kyle guessed he was trying to organize his thoughts. Talking about what they'd been through wasn't easy, even several weeks later.

"The person I spoke with was so angry about what happened to me. To us," Luka said at last. "I mean, she stayed professional and helpful and all that, but I saw how upset my words made her. It helps knowing I'm not overreacting, you know? That I'm still thrown by the whole thing. It's been a while since it happened and I guess I thought I'd be over it by now."

Kyle nodded. "I don't think you get over it so much as past it. That night in the ED, your mom told me it'd be normal to feel off-balance, and I got what she meant immediately. It was like everything I knew had shifted and I couldn't get back on track. Does that make sense?"

"Yeah, it does." Luka sipped his drink.

"The weirdest thing was feeling that way after we were sent home. That's why I made an appointment with Dr. Okafor in the first place. I knew something was wrong. I just couldn't figure out what." Kyle frowned again.

"You were smart about it." Luka blew a noisy breath out through his nose. "I got busy trying to act fine instead of looking at what was going on."

"I hid my problems, too, Luka. And you weren't fine."

"Not even close, though I fooled a lot of people. You said something to me about that on the ferry last week. That I seemed to bounce back okay and that was one reason you didn't want to admit you were having a hard time. That you didn't want to mess me up."

"I'm sorry. There were lots of reasons I didn't say anything about feeling off. In my defense, you seemed okay a lot of the time." Except for when Kyle had tried to get closer. However, Luka had explained that behavior, and Kyle was feeling better about what had happened. Mostly. Kyle tapped his scar with his fingertips. "Did the ED doc refer you to Dr. Okafor, too?"

"She might have. The referral went right in the trash as soon as she left the room though." The tips of Luka's ears turned red. "Wade was with me and you know he wasn't going to rat me out."

"Your mom was with me," Kyle said.

Luka grimaced. "Oh, man."

"She was great. Super calming, which helped because I was wrecked." Kyle inhaled deeply and dropped his gaze to his sangria. "She didn't make me feel bad about any of it, and I could tell she just wanted to help us both."

"My mom's been through a lot," Luka said. "What with my dad dying, then raising us kids on her own while trying to hold down a job—I don't know how she did it. I should talk to her more about what happened to us. I hate the idea of upsetting her though."

Kyle picked up his glass. "I feel like that about talking to Ollie. Most of my friends, too. Carter's the only one who doesn't get this look on his face like he can't handle hearing the words. Everyone says they're ready to listen if I want to talk, but it's hard to watch their reactions." He sipped while Luka's eyes got big.

"Right? Wade's the only person I know who doesn't get that look." Another sheepish expression crossed Luka's face. "All the more reason we should be talking to each other instead, huh?"

Kyle swallowed. He wanted to be there for Luka, but part of him shied away from it. It was all too easy to imagine a distant, cool look falling over Luka's face, the way it had so often in previous weeks. That expression haunted Kyle. Now that he understood the reasons behind it though, he thought he could get past it, given time and patience.

"Let's work on getting there," Kyle said, and when Luka laid a hand over his, he didn't feel the need to pull away.

They ate an excellent meal, dozens of miniature plates notwithstanding, and Kyle enjoyed himself thoroughly. They linked fingers on their way out of the restaurant and he only forced himself to let go of Luka once they hit the sidewalk and started for the subway station on Houston. For the first time in a long while, being around Luka felt easy despite Kyle's occasional flashes of insecurity.

"Do you still worry?" Luka asked him. "About being out here with me and what people might think or say? I know I do."

"Yes." Kyle cocked his head. "It's not like I didn't think about that before. I grew up queer in a small town and learned to be aware of my surroundings. I feel less stressed out than I did a couple of weeks ago though." They crossed 6th Avenue and Kyle let out a laugh. "Of course, I got stuck inside during the blizzard for a couple of days, and that definitely helped my stress. I can't remember the last time I had an excuse to do so much nothing!"

Luka laughed, too. "Where were you during the storm? Obviously, you didn't go to work."

"Were you working?"

"You know it," Luka said. "We got called out a few times in the middle of it, of course. I don't like to drive the rig in snow, but Luis loves it."

Kyle chuckled. "Figures. Under was open for a while on Saturday but only because Masen and Jeff both live in Morningside Heights. They covered on Sunday, too. I had that time planned off anyway. I was with the crew at Carter and Riley's where we camped out and ate all the food in the house."

"Sounds like a grown-up version of a slumber party."

"That was the vibe! It wasn't to plan, though. We were supposed to be in Southampton for the weekend, but after watching the forecast, we decided staying in the city would be a wiser choice." Luka held the station door for Kyle, and they stepped inside. Kyle scanned his MTA card and walked through the turnstiles. "Ollie came down, and Will and David were already in town for the party at Under, which made things even easier."

"I see. Was there a lot of debauchery?"

"A fair amount. Jesse, Will and my brother know a shocking number of drinking games, I'll say that much." They shared a laugh. "We also ended up on the balcony without our coats at one point because…I don't know why. It must have seemed like a good idea at the time."

Luka laughed harder, and Kyle waited until they had come to a stop on the platform before he went on. "We were celebrating my birthday."

Luka's expression fell. "Shit. That's why you asked me to come to Under last Thursday."

"No, that's not why." Kyle stepped closer. "I couldn't have cared less about my birthday. I asked you to come last Thursday because I wanted to spend time with you. I'm telling you now so you don't hear about it from one of the guys."

"Still, I missed it. Ugh, and you and I are the same age, which means you turned thirty." Luka grimaced. "I suck."

Kyle dropped a hand so his knuckles brushed against Luka's. "You do not. I told you I don't care about my birthday. I let the guys throw a mini-party because I knew they wouldn't shut up about it if I didn't."

Luka sighed. "How much shit am I in with the crew?"

"You're not. I told them we were taking time apart because I needed it." Kyle wet his lips with his tongue. "Ollie knows we've been having problems. He encouraged me to reach out to you. He knows it wasn't just on you."

"Mmm, okay." Luka looked at Kyle askance. "Why didn't you tell me it was your birthday?"

Kyle shrugged. "Birthdays were never a big deal in my family so I don't think about mine much. It's just a day."

"It wouldn't be just a day with my family," Luka said. "It's not with your crew either."

"Those guys will take any excuse to gather. We've been known to throw down over the start of Daylight Saving Time."

Luka barked out a laugh. "You're all so weird."

"Out and proud." Kyle smirked. "You know, I don't know your birthdate either."

"It's September 16th."

"Got it." Kyle slipped his hands in his coat pockets. "Technically, my birthday hasn't happened yet, by the way. We did it last weekend because Carter and Riley didn't have the kids and that was a better time for them."

A gleam lit Luka's eye. "I see. So when is Kyle McKee's actual birthdate?"

"Tomorrow. January thirtieth." The delight in Luka's face made Kyle feel light.

"I haven't missed it."

"Nope. And you have" —Kyle checked his watch— "twenty-four hours to redeem yourself with a cheesy greeting card."

"I can handle that. In fact, I can do better. How about you come to my place for dinner tomorrow? I'll pick up dessert from Sugar Street and cook up some steaks."

"I like the way you think. Can it be the cake with the guava?" Kyle had fallen in love with the Sugar Street confection, a buttery yellow sponge sweetened with guava juice and topped with cream cheese frosting, and he felt no qualms asking for it now.

"I don't see why not. I'll ask Daniela on the ride uptown. Hey, what's your middle name?"

"Umm, why?"

"Call it research." Luka waggled his eyebrows and the sheer silliness made Kyle snort. "You know, so I don't get caught off guard again."

"I see. My middle name is Daegan. It means 'black-haired' in Gaelic."

The heat in Luka's eyes distracted Kyle so he hardly heard the low, echoing roar of the arriving train.

"That's kind of perfect." Luka raised his voice over the noise. "Now I can ask Daniela to write your full name on the cake instead of 'HAPPY BIRTHDAY, OLD MAN MCKEE.'"

Kyle tipped his head back and really laughed. "Don't you dare. My birthday may be before yours, Clarke, but know that any abuse you heap on me now you'll get back double."

"Okay, okay. Such a tough guy!"

Luka held on to Kyle's elbow as they boarded the train, and even though he let go almost immediately, the touch warmed Kyle through and through.

* * * *

Kyle's good feelings about where he and Luka stood increased over the next twenty-four hours. Did he still harbor some misgivings? Yes. He and Luka had work to do. Kyle had work to do on himself. He wanted to do it though. Wanted to get past his doubts and put himself back together because seeing Luka over the past several days had been wonderful. He wanted more of those times and was incredibly happy to understand Luka wanted that, too.

Butterflies bounced around Kyle's stomach when he arrived at the Sugar Hill apartment just after six, but the gleam in Matías' eyes when he answered the door soothed some of those nerves.

"Thank God, you're here," Matías said. "Luka's been making me bananas all afternoon. He cleaned where it was already clean, Kyle, and no one needs that in their life!"

"Yikes, sorry. I'm not late, am I? Luka told me to come after five." Kyle set his bag on the bench by the door and started to remove his coat, but he went still when Matías drew him into a hug.

"No, you're not late. Who cares if you are anyway? We missed your face around here! Where have you been?"

Kyle hugged Matías back, surprised by the lump in his throat. "Eh, around. You know how it is." He smiled at the tugging sensation by his left ankle, a sign Robbie had arrived to say hello, too.

Matías drew back and peered at Kyle. Matías was dressed for a night out, all long fluttering false lashes and pouty crimson lips, and his black clothes were tailored so close they appeared almost painted onto his lean form. But for all his sharp glamour, Matías' pretty eyes held genuine warmth.

"You look good, white boy. You could use some sun, but that's probably always the case, hm? I can tell you've been taking better care of your skin, too, so you're welcome for the advice."

He raised a hand and stroked Kyle's cheek with the backs of his fingers. "I am all about a hairy face, you know." Matías looked very smug. "Especially when a man takes care of it the way you have been. Look at this sexy-ass growth!" He leaned in again and rubbed his cheek against Kyle's. "Ohh, and you smell good, too. I swear I could eat you!"

Kyle laughed and glanced down at Robbie, who was busy scaling his right leg. "Thank you, I think. You both sure know how to make a guy feel welcome."

Matías started to reply, but whatever he'd meant to say got lost in a yip because Luka emerged from the kitchen and swatted his roommate on the ass with a dishtowel.

"Down, boy," Luka ordered, his voice lowered in a playful growl that made Kyle's insides go all gooey.

"Oh, fine." Matías sniffed and turned Kyle loose. "No need to go all alpha male on me, baby. I know this one belongs to you. I suppose that's my cue to make myself scarce."

"Stay for dinner if you like," Luka said, his tone mild. "I told you already there's plenty for three."

"Girl, do I look like a third wheel to you?"

Their playful bickering washed over Kyle, and he took the opportunity to pry Robbie loose from his jeans. He stroked the ferret's sleek head a few times with his fingers while it chirped at him, and he held still as Robbie scrambled up his arm and onto his shoulder. Several moments passed before Kyle noticed the room had grown silent around him, and he looked up to find Luka and Matías watching him, amusement plain on their faces while Robbie curled his tail around Kyle's neck.

"Sorry," Kyle said. "What were you saying?"

"Nothing." Luka grinned so wide his eyes crinkled. "Looks like Robbie's a better host than his humans, though, because we haven't even asked you to take off your coat."

Matías scoffed. "You're the shitty host, *bicho*. I'm just the roommate who's on his way out." He held his hands out to Kyle. "You want me to take the beast?"

"No, I'm good." Kyle chuckled. "I guess I could use a hand with my coat though, and there's booze in my bag—"

"I've got it," Luka said, and he was there in Kyle's space, big and gorgeous, and holy hell, Kyle wanted to touch him.

Luka peeled Kyle's coat away while Matías carried the bag into the kitchen, and the next thing Kyle knew, Luka was guiding him into the living space while Robbie climbed atop Kyle's head.

"He's not going to pee on me, right?" Kyle asked over their laughter.

"No, he wouldn't do that." Matías came back out of the kitchen. "Clearly, Robbie missed you just as much as we did. Don't get too comfortable with him though, or Luka will be jealous. He thinks he's Robbie's favorite, and I haven't had the heart to tell him he's full of shit."

Luka gestured to himself. "I'm right here, you know."

"Psshh." Matías moved toward the closet and pulled out a black wool coat, then slid it on. He laid his hand on the doorknob and aimed a look Kyle's way. "I'd be real pleased if you saved me some cake, okay? It looks just as yummy as the box of goodies you sent home with your man last night."

"How was your breakfast?" Kyle asked once Matías had flounced out the door. "Did you have to arm-wrestle to get a share?"

"I'm not sure you could qualify what happened as wrestling because Matías just grabbed as much from the box as he could and ran back to his room." Luka stepped closer and took one of Kyle's hands in his own.

"He's right, though. We missed you. I missed you," he said, his voice going lower. "It's good seeing you here, Kyle. I'm glad we could do this tonight."

Kyle's heart seemed to swell. "I'm glad, too."

His breath stuttered as Luka leaned in closer, but the moment their lips met, Robbie was on the move, crawling from Kyle's head onto Luka's and Kyle couldn't help his laughter.

"Cockblocked by a goddamned ferret. How did this happen to me?" Luka chased after Robbie with one hand but slid the other around Kyle's waist. "Can I pour you a drink?"

"Sure." Kyle slipped his arm around Luka, too. "But why don't you let me pour since you've already got your hands full?"

They went into the kitchen where Luka deposited Robbie by his bowl with some snacks, and Kyle unpacked the supplies he'd brought. He mixed up a round of Manhattans and poured them in some lowball glasses he found in the cabinet, and they chatted while Luka finished prepping their dinner of steak with kale and a white bean mash.

"This all looks good," Kyle said once Luka had shut Robbie in his cage and they'd settled at the table. "If I didn't know better, I'd say you were trying to impress me."

"Would that be so bad?"

"No. You don't have to try though. I'm where I want to be tonight."

"Good. I figured I'd have better luck making dinner here than in your shoebox."

"Oh, Lord." Kyle snorted. "I've made some very good meals in that little kitchen, I'll have you know. Some of them were for you!"

"True. I still prefer to cook in a bigger space." Luka held up his glass. "Happy Not Belated Birthday."

Kyle tapped their drinks together. "Thank you."

The ghosts of Kyle's tension relaxed bit by bit over the course of the meal. He hadn't lied when he'd said he was where he wanted to be. There was a sweet, almost first-date air in their interactions now, very much like he and Luka were getting to know each other again. That felt right in Kyle's mind, and he knew they wouldn't be sitting there together if Luka hadn't wanted it. Kyle's head was on straight at last, and now he just needed to convince his heart of the same thing.

"You're not working tonight, are you?" Luka asked.

"Nope. Gave myself the night off. Jes told Jim and the bartenders to keep me out if I show up anyway, unless I'm there with the intention to hang out and not get behind the bar."

Luka cocked his head. "Do you want to do that? We could grab something at Under and check out the crowd, or go to another bar, if you'd like."

"No, I'm fine staying put. Besides, I have dessert and bourbon here and that makes me happy." Kyle forked up another bite of the cake. "You know I love my bar, but it's a nice change of pace hanging outside of that space, too."

Luka hummed. "In hindsight, we should have done this at your place instead of making you take the train all the way up here on your night off."

"I don't mind the ride. If I've got a book to read or a show to watch on my phone, I don't even notice it much." Kyle shrugged. "I use the time to decompress after work, too."

"I get that," Luka replied. "Though, I'm more likely to take a nap on my way home than read."

"You work a lot harder than I do," Kyle said in sympathy. He turned his attention to his drink. "This conversation is making me think about my habits though, and how I'll have to rethink them if I leave Chelsea."

"What does that mean?" A frown marred Luka's forehead when Kyle met his gaze. "You're thinking about moving?"

"Yeah. I have been for a while now."

Luka's frown deepened, but he settled a hand over Kyle's where it rested on the table. "Where to? You're staying in New York, right?"

"Oh, shit, yes." Kyle flipped his hand and wrapped his fingers around Luka's. "I'm staying in New York." He almost laughed at Luka's near glare. "I'm sorry."

"Way to freak a guy out, man."

"I didn't think about how that would sound without context. I've been thinking about moving uptown, closer to Under." *Closer to you.* Kyle squeezed Luka's fingers. "I'd like to find a place in Morningside Heights, if I can, but Manhattanville would work, too."

"That's great. Not to be selfish, but I'll take a shorter train ride to see you any day. Hell, I could ride my bike on a nice day and see you in under half an hour!" Luka chuckled when Kyle laughed, but his expression turned thoughtful almost immediately.

"Are you going to miss Chelsea? You've always seemed attached to that neighborhood, and I don't care what you say—you love your shoebox."

Kyle laughed again. "Yeah, I do."

"And you'll miss it?"

"Sure." Kyle brought his other hand to his chin and ran his fingers over the beard. "My landlady, Mrs. Bell, is great. She used to let me pay in trade back in the day when I sometimes ran short on rent. Like, I'd help her out doing repairs or clean her house and use the labor for actual money." He turned a crooked smile Luka's way. "I've counted on the shoebox to be there, every day, no matter what was going on in the rest of my life. Even when I had roommates. It's home. I'm sure that sounds silly."

"It doesn't." There was no pity in Luka's face, only understanding. "Are you sure you're ready to give it up?"

"I'm sure. I talked about it with Dr. Okafor. Told him I'd been thinking about it even before we got jumped in Brooklyn. I'm…well, I'm thinking about buying it and renting it out."

"What?"

"Mrs. Bell's son is moving to California and he wants her to move with him. She said she'd cut me a good deal on the place if I wanted it."

Luka shook his head. "That's amazing. But it doesn't make sense you'd leave it behind, right? Why buy it if you're not going to live in it?"

"Well, like I said, I'd like to be closer to the bar. So I'm still working on that part." Kyle wasn't worried about it. "I'll figure it out, one way or another. And Ollie's made up his mind to move down here from Boston, so the shoebox will house another McKee, at least for a while. Eventually, I'd like to rent it to people who need an affordable place, like I did when I first moved in. It feels right to move on. Find a new place to call home."

Luka nodded. He said nothing, his gaze on Kyle's fingers as Kyle moved them over his chin. "Does it hurt?" he asked.

Kyle went still. "What?"

"You touch the scar sometimes," Luka said. He raised his hand to his own face and motioned with his fingers, tapping roughly the same area where Kyle had been injured. "I wondered if it hurt you or —"

"Oh!" Kyle chuckled and dropped his hand in his lap. Fire licked its way across his cheeks, but the tenderness in Luka's eyes kept him from pulling away. "No, it doesn't hurt. The nerve endings were hypersensitive for a while and the tapping helped desensitize them. The scar zings sometimes, but the tapping is more habit than anything else now."

Luka nodded. Moving slowly, he reached for Kyle, his touch light as his fingers came to rest on Kyle's face, lingering over the scar hidden by his beard. "Okay to touch?"

Kyle forced himself to breathe. "Yes," he whispered.

He tensed as Luka leaned in, but Luka kept his motions easy. He caressed Kyle's jaw then kissed him, his lips soft against Kyle's. He drew back just far enough to press another kiss to the corner of Kyle's mouth, then lower onto his chin. Luka moved again, his lips lingering over the scar for a long, long moment that made Kyle's insides tremble. He continued in the next breath, dropping kisses onto the apple of Kyle's cheek, against his closed eye and his temple before he cupped the back of Kyle's head in his hand. Luka met Kyle's lips again and kissed him deep and slow.

Kyle's breath hitched. He wound his arms around Luka and sank into him, heat radiating from his belly and out through his body. Both of them were panting lightly by the time they came back up for air, and Kyle pressed his forehead to Luka's, eyes closed and his heart thudding in his throat.

Luka held him close, his breath warm against Kyle's face.

"Feels so good to touch you again." Luka's voice was rough. "I missed you so much, Kyle."

"Missed you, too."

"We can stop here if you want, but I'm kind of hoping you won't say you want to."

Kyle huffed out a laugh. "I don't want to stop. I haven't been with anyone since that last time with you, though, and…" He opened his eyes when Luka drew back.

"We'll go as slow as you need to," Luka said.

The understanding in his eyes was like a balm on Kyle's heart. Luka got it. He wouldn't walk away, no matter what happened next. Kyle could trust him. And knowing that put Kyle's fears to rest at last. He didn't hesitate when Luka urged him to his feet.

Neither spoke as they moved through the apartment. Once by Luka's bed, they fell on each other, the awkwardness of the last several weeks melting away. Kyle felt only eager as Luka undressed him, and his skin prickled with anticipation as they stretched out together on the mattress. He shivered when Luka ran his hands over Kyle's thighs.

Ducking his head, Kyle caught Luka's lips with his own, fire racing through him as Luka hauled him close. He slipped his fingers through Luka's tight coils of hair and shuddered when Luka slotted their groins together.

Luka broke away, his gaze intense. "I want to make you feel good. Can I do that?"

"Yes. I want that, too." Kyle smiled at the warmth in Luka's face.

Luka leaned over him toward the nightstand and his muscles flexed under Kyle's touch. He paused as Kyle started to roll onto his stomach, however, and set a firm hand on his shoulder.

"Stay," he said, his tone sweet and coaxing, as if he thought Kyle might refuse. "I want to see you. Watch your face while we do this."

Kyle could only nod. He lay back against the pillow again, heart hammering while Luka found lube and a condom.

Luka slicked his fingers, then spread Kyle's thighs wide. He took his time opening Kyle up, one arm wrapped around Kyle's shoulders the whole time, holding him close, and he swallowed Kyle's groans with kisses that made Kyle dizzy with lust.

"Mmm, Luka."

"I know, baby."

Luka twisted his fingers and the movement sent sparks of pleasure shooting through Kyle. Kyle gasped. His body buzzed and his gut twisted with need. It was all too much but not quite enough, and the world around him fell away. He floated, his own mutters rough in his own ears, almost too undone to return Luka's kisses. Luka pressed his cock, hot and hard, against Kyle's thigh, and though Luka trembled with need, his focus never wavered.

"You're beautiful," Luka murmured. The expression on his face was so bright and open and adoring Kyle's heart clenched tight. "Love you so much, Kyle."

"Oh, God." Kyle's voice shook. He pulled at Luka's shoulder, urging him to move. "Come here, please."

Luka pulled his fingers free and soothed Kyle's whine with a kiss. He shifted, covering Kyle's body with his own, and when he slid home, Kyle's throat went tight.

Home.

That was what being with Luka meant. He grounded Kyle and made him sure in ways Kyle hadn't known in years, if ever. Made him feel safe. Known. Loved.

Kyle closed his eyes against the sting of tears. He moved to press his face into Luka's neck, but Luka stopped him, his fingers light along Kyle's jaw. His gaze held compassion and love when Kyle opened his eyes, mixed with the smallest measure of concern.

"No more hiding," Luka said, his voice gentle, just as Kyle had known it would be.

"No more," Kyle agreed. He framed Luka's face with his hands and poured all the emotions tangled up inside him into a kiss that made Luka moan.

Luka surged against Kyle. The ache in Kyle's groin expanded as he and Luka moved, and he shivered when Luka reached between them to take him in hand. A few strokes were all it took to send Kyle flying, his pleasure so intense it robbed him of his breath, but not once did he look away from Luka's eyes.

An age seemed to pass before he came back down, but Kyle had wits enough about him to hold Luka tight while he chased his own peak. Luka dropped his forehead against Kyle's and found his rhythm again. Kyle watched him, taking in the deep flush of color on Luka's neck and chest and the almost desperate cast in his eyes, and—just as Luka had done to Kyle only a minute before—raised a hand and cupped Luka's cheek.

"Love you," Kyle whispered, his soft words filling the space between them.

Luka's chest heaved. He let loose a sob, his eyes wide and locked with Kyle's as he came. His movements stuttered, gradually slowing, until he sagged, and Kyle wrapped him up in a hug.

They curled up together, exchanging kisses, and the broken pieces inside Kyle started knitting themselves together again.

Chapter Twenty

March 2016

Luka finished wiping down the white quartz countertop and turned so he faced Kyle. "What's next?"

"I think we're ready," Kyle said. He surveyed the appetizers spread out on the kitchen cart that served as an island and the neatly laid dining table, but his tone sounded more questioning than sure, so Luka wrapped his arms around Kyle. He dragged Kyle back so they were pressed together full-length, but his concern deepened when Kyle stayed tense.

"Are you nervous about having my family over?" Luka asked. If that was the case, he'd be surprised. Kyle had been the one to suggest inviting the Clarke-Padillas over for a housewarming of sorts.

"I'm nervous, but not because it's your family," Kyle said. "I've just never hosted this many people before. Not in an apartment anyway."

"My family wouldn't have fit in the shoebox," Luka countered as he looked around Kyle's new — and very spacious — apartment. It had two bedrooms and was more than twice the size of his previous place.

"That's putting it mildly." Kyle laughed and his body finally relaxed against Luka's.

Kyle had left most of his furniture behind for Oliver and bought new things that were a better fit for his new place. It had taken him a little while to truly settle in, but Kyle seemed very happy there. And he and Luka both spent a lot less time on the train.

The bigger-than-a-shoebox apartment was located on the edge of the Manhattanville and Morningside Heights neighborhoods. Luka had gone with Kyle to check out several areas, but they'd agreed the apartment on West 123rd Street near Morningside Park felt right to them both. Manhattanville's population was primarily Latino followed by African-American, while Morningside Heights was predominantly white, and both Kyle and Luka felt safe and welcome on the border of the two. Luka had helped Kyle pick out the furnishings, too, and the place had become as much his as Kyle's.

The apartment search had done more than find Kyle a place to live though. It had continued bringing Luka and Kyle close together again and helped mend the remaining cracks from the attack and their struggles after.

Luka wasn't officially living on West 123rd — he still had some time left on his lease in Sugar Hill — but he'd spent at least as much time there as he did at the place with Matías in the past several weeks. And he was damned okay with that.

Luka's thoughts returned to the party they were about to host. "So, if we're all ready, is there anything I can do to help you relax before everyone gets here?"

Kyle shifted in his arms until he faced Luka. He pressed close, backing Luka up until he gently bumped the cabinets. And the once more clean-shaven planes of his face moved into a smile. "Kiss me?"

"That I can definitely do." Luka captured Kyle's mouth with his and tasted blackberry and thyme, ghosts of the cocktails Kyle had mixed up earlier. Luka hummed in pleasure.

The kisses turned into full on making out, and when Kyle fitted their hips more tightly together, Luka didn't mind the edge of the counter digging into his low back. He just wanted more Kyle. A few minutes later, the buzz of the intercom interrupted them and made them groan in unison.

Kyle pulled back, his cheeks flushed, and his mouth turned down in a slight frown. "Why did we invite people over again?"

"Because you wanted to introduce my family to Ollie," Luka said with a laugh.

"Right. That." Kyle shot him a pointed look. "Terrible idea."

Luka rested his palms on the counter behind him and watched Kyle straighten his clothes on his walk to the door. Damn that man was fine.

Kyle had kept his beard for nearly six weeks following his reconciliation with Luka. He'd taken good care of it and made sure it was always neat and glossy, but Luka had sensed that, deep down, it had never truly suited Kyle. Luka had even caught Kyle frowning at himself in the bathroom mirror, dark eyes focused on the part of his chin they both knew bore the hidden scar. So Luka hadn't been surprised when Kyle had made an appointment at a high-end barbershop in Chelsea and invited Luka to meet him outside. Kyle had emerged fresh faced and rosy-cheeked, the mark on his chin, now silvery-white, laid bare for the world to see. Kyle had held his head high and met Luka's gaze with steady, clear eyes as he smiled. And Luka had practically hauled Kyle off his feet trying to get him back to the shoebox so he could kiss his boyfriend into a stupor.

Kyle pressed the intercom button now and shot Luka a smile as Oliver's voice crackled through the speaker.

"Hey, let me in."

Kyle removed his finger from the panel. "Speak of the devil and he shall appear."

Oliver had just stepped inside the door when the doorbell sounded again, and with quick succession, Regina and Wade, Lydia and Tomas and finally Marcus arrived. Matías had been invited as well, but unfortunately, he'd been scheduled to work. The room grew louder with cheerful greetings and conversation as Kyle welcomed people in and Luka hung up their coats.

Luka warmed at seeing his family fill Kyle's apartment, and particularly his mother hugging his boyfriend.

"Thank you for inviting us," she said, her voice and smile warm.

"You've made me feel so welcome at your Sunday dinners," Kyle said. "It was my turn to treat you."

Luka had been enjoying those dinners more than ever. He loved seeing Kyle sit down to dinner at the Clarke-Padilla home. Despite the rocky start for Kyle with Luka's family, they'd done their best to make him feel welcome since, and it made Luka happy to watch their easy conversation and camaraderie.

"Hey, baby." Lydia kissed Luka's cheek. "You're looking well and happy."

"I am," he said with a smile in Kyle's direction. "I definitely am."

Kyle slung an arm around his brother and raised his voice. "Before I forget, I'd like to introduce you to my brother, Oliver. After years of my pestering him, he's decided to move to Manhattan. I may live to regret this someday, but for now, I'm very happy to see him more often."

Oliver scoffed. "Be honest. You just wanted someone to take over the shoebox so you could move closer to your hot fireman."

Luka grinned. He could handle being called that.

"Oliver may be on to something," Kyle admitted with a laugh. "Oh! But I feel like I've been a bad host, making you all stand in the entrance. I'm not used to having all this space. Please, come in." Kyle waved Luka's family into the apartment. "Grab a bite to eat, have a drink and make yourselves comfortable."

Kyle and Luka had decided to go for small bites and some prepared pitchers of drinks to help people mingle, as opposed to a sit-down dinner. Kyle was more than ready to mix cocktails, too, however.

"I brought empanadas," Tomas said as he walked toward the kitchen. "Mind if I borrow the oven for a few minutes? I want to heat them up a little."

"Go right ahead." Luka rubbed his hands together in anticipation. "Thank you, Pop."

Tomas scoffed. "Did you think I'd let you down?"

"No, but tax season just wrapped up and I wouldn't have blamed you if you didn't have time."

"The new people we hired have taken a lot of the load off."

"This is the most I've ever seen my husband from January to April in years," Lydia said, the delight in her voice clear. "It's a nice change!"

"I'm enjoying it, too." Tomas leaned in to kiss her. The sight made Luka smile. He liked seeing a couple who had been together for such a long time so happy together. He glanced over at Kyle, who was talking with Regina, Wade and Marcus. For the first time, Luka was with someone he could picture spending his life with, too.

His mother's gaze followed his and she smiled at him as though she'd guessed his thoughts.

Tomas had just laid the reheated empanadas on a platter when the intercom buzzed again.

"That's got to be Ruby," Regina said with a laugh. "That woman...I swear, we should just tell her everything starts a half hour before it does to get her there on time!"

"She's too smart for that. She'd be onto us in a minute and then she'd just show up even later out of spite."

Regina hummed. "Honestly, you're probably right."

They fell quiet as Kyle pressed the intercom again. "Identify yourself!" he teased.

"I come bearing desserts!" an unexpected but familiar voice to Luka called back. "Please let me in!"

"Daniela!" Luka strode to Kyle's side. "Do you need help?"

She laughed. "I didn't bring that many. Just buzz me in, please."

When Daniela knocked on the apartment door, Luka took the boxes from her hands and gave her a one-armed hug. "You are always welcome, desserts or not."

Daniela grinned. "I'm not sure I believe it, but that's nice to hear!"

"I'm so glad you could come! It's been a while since I've seen you."

"I can't stay for long, but I've heard so much about Kyle from everyone that I just had to meet him for myself."

Kyle held his hand out to Daniela with a big smile. "It's nice to officially meet you. I've been enjoying your pastries and cakes so much I feel like I already know you."

She beamed. "You liked the guava cake for your birthday then?"

Kyle hummed. "It's so good. I think it may be my favorite flavor. I've been trying to figure out a guava cocktail that would echo the cake but it's a work in progress."

"Maybe we can discuss ideas sometime! You'll be pleased to hear I brought a cupcake version of the guava cake today, by the way."

The way Kyle's face lit up made Luka chuckle under his breath. If Kyle had a bad day in the future, Luka now knew exactly how to cheer him.

"Please, come on in," Kyle said, "I'll introduce you to my brother and you can have a bite to eat."

"Where are James and the kids?" Luka asked her.

"Oh, Julian and Eli have baseball practice," she said. "I told James I'd bring May with me, but his mom volunteered to watch her."

Everyone congregated around the food table, laughing and talking, but Luka paused so he could check in with Kyle.

"How are you doing?" He slid an arm around Kyle's waist and pressed a kiss to his temple. Regina gave them a small smile that warmed Luka through.

"I'm good." Kyle nodded toward Oliver and Marcus who were deep in conversation. "Glad everyone seems to be having a good time."

Luka just shrugged. "I knew they would."

Once they'd gotten over all the hurdles, Luka had been sure his family would be just as supportive of Luka and Kyle's relationship as they'd been of Regina and Wade and Daniela and James. That was who they were—loving, loyal and true.

Kyle looked at Luka, his eyes so filled with love Luka's breath caught. "It feels good to be a part of a family like this," he said.

"You are part of it," Luka said. "And this is just the beginning."

Luka leaned in to kiss Kyle, but the buzz of the intercom interrupted them again. "This is getting to be a bad habit," he muttered against Kyle's mouth. "And if that's not Ruby, then she ain't comin'."

Ruby made her dramatic entrance, breathlessly explaining that she'd gotten stuck on a stopped train, and thrust a bottle of wine at Kyle and Luka.

"I'm sorry I didn't have time for anything more personal, but I hope you like this!"

"We're just glad you could come," Kyle said. He pressed a kiss to her cheek. "Come in."

"Thanks." She hugged Kyle, then did the same to Luka before moving on to the rest of the family. As she strode across the room, Luka heard her say, "Oh, good, I got here before you left, Daniela. I want to talk to you about something!"

Oliver walked over with wide eyes. "That's Ruby?" he whistled low. "Damn, hotness does run in the family."

Luka raised an eyebrow but stayed quiet when Kyle uttered a pained-sounding noise.

"Nope. Please, no. We just got Luka's mom and sister on board with me, Ollie. Don't go there, for my sake." Kyle clasped his hands together as if in prayer.

"Don't go where?" Oliver grinned at his brother, then shot Luka a wink. "I'm just stating facts. And relax, I'm not planning on hitting on her. Much."

"It's a good thing I love him," Kyle muttered under his breath. "A damn good thing."

Luka laughed and pulled Kyle close. "Hey, with everyone here, I want to make my announcement."

Kyle's expression brightened. "Go for it."

"Hey, everyone!" Luka cleared his throat and raised his voice. "Now that I have you all in one place, I want to tell you about what's coming up next for me. I just got accepted at the Fire Science Institute, and in the fall, I'll be taking some classes. It's time I think about a career after active duty. That way when I'm ready to transition to something else, everything will be in place."

"Oh, that's wonderful!" Lydia beamed. "I am so pleased to hear that, baby. I'm proud of you and what you do, but I will be thrilled the day you move to a desk job."

Luka chuckled and hugged her. "I know you will. And I'm happy where I am now — I'm just ready to start thinking about the future." His gaze landed on Kyle's face.

He'd told Kyle about his acceptance first, of course, and he knew Kyle was relieved about a possible change in career for Luka. Kyle would never ask that Luka give up what he loved, but Luka knew everyone in his life would rest easier once Luka's job was less dangerous, including Kyle.

Anything could happen to them at either point — the attack in Brooklyn had shown them that. The scar on Kyle's chin, faded now to a thin white line, was a reminder all its own, too, but if Luka stopped courting disaster daily, the odds of things going bad would be lowered. And Luka was determined not to miss out on a future with Kyle.

* * * *

"Hello, hello!" Jesse greeted Luka as he stepped into Under. Before Luka could blink, Jesse swept him into a hug and kissed him — a bit more than chastely — on the mouth. "Good to see you, Lieutenant," he said when he drew back.

"Good to see you, too," Luka said, and he smiled when Cam stepped up to kiss him, too. Luka might never get used to how open Jesse and Cam were with their affections, but he certainly wouldn't complain either. He liked having a great group of friends with whom he and Kyle could occasionally hook up, too.

The rest of the crew was there, and he greeted Riley, Carter, Malcolm, Will and David, plus Astrid and a friend of hers Luka had never met before. Oliver waved at him from across the room where he was chatting with Jarrod, Gale and Matías, but Kyle was nowhere to be seen.

"Your boyfriend's in the office," Will said with a smile. "He disappeared just a few minutes ago."

Jesse nodded. "The door's unlocked. Just try not to make too much of a mess of that couch. And don't forget," he said with a smirk. "There's a camera in there and I have access to all the footage."

Luka laughed and thanked Jesse and did indeed find Kyle in the office when he poked his head inside. Kyle gave Luka a big smile.

"Hey there, darlin'. You're early."

"Yeah, I made good time and caught the earlier train."

Kyle came around the desk. "I'm glad you did. I don't mind a few extra minutes with you before I start slinging drinks." He grabbed Luka and hauled him in before planting a hard, eager kiss on his mouth.

"Jesse said we weren't allowed to make a mess of the couch," Luka said, a little breathless once they'd surfaced again.

"Oh, did he?" Kyle smirked. He dropped his hands to Luka's back pockets and dipped his hands inside. "That almost sounds like a challenge to me."

"Don't tempt me," Luka muttered. Kyle's body felt so good against his and desire rose hot and fast within him. "Or I will fuck you over the back of that couch without giving a shit how much of a mess we make, regardless of the camera."

"Mmm." Kyle shuddered against him. "Talk about tempting."

Luka kissed him some more, then pulled back. "I'll behave for now. But if you can cut out early tonight…"

Kyle grinned. "I can do that. Masen's here 'til close and I know he won't mind."

Luka and Kyle went back out into the bar a few minutes later, and Kyle headed behind the bar to mix Luka a drink. Luka took it to one of the couches where he sat beside Carter, content to listen while everyone else talked.

"How was the housewarming?" Carter asked during a lull in conversation.

"It was great. Almost my whole family made it, and they managed not to scare Oliver."

"That's good to hear." Carter smiled back at him. "Ollie's tough just like his brother, so it'd take a lot to really freak him out."

"I'm surprised you haven't moved in with Kyle," Riley said from Carter's other side. "I mean, now that he's got the new place and all."

Luka shrugged. "We're not far off from that. When my lease is up, we'll talk about it. It hasn't been that long anyway. Kyle and I have only been together around seven months."

"That's true," Carter said. "I guess it seems longer."

"Maybe now that you and Riley are off to tie the knot, you're just in a hurry to pair everyone else off?" Luka teased.

Riley laughed. "Don't listen to Carter. It took us fifteen years to admit we had feelings for each other. We have no place telling anyone what the ideal timing for a relationship is."

"Have you set a date for the wedding?"

"Not yet." Riley took Carter's hand. "We know we'd like to do it in Southampton at the beach house, but we haven't settled on exactly when."

Luka looked at Malcolm, who was sitting across from him. "Looks like you're the last relationship holdout around here, buddy."

"Looks like it," Malcolm replied, his tone dry as dust, then glanced down at his phone.

"Mal, please tell me you're not still working," Carter said. "It's okay to turn yourself off once in a while."

Malcolm glanced up long enough to offer him a half-smile. "I'm terrible at it, and so are you. But I just want to check a couple of emails I got on my way up here. I promise I'll stop after that."

"Carter shouldn't give anyone grief about being a workaholic either," Riley joked.

"Hey!" Carter held up a hand. "I'm in recovery now. Mostly."

Malcolm's curse cut through the good-natured teasing.

"It's a good thing I did check my email," he said. "We have a problem, Carter."

Carter leaned forward. "What kind of problem?"

"A big one." Malcolm's expression turned grim. "The caterer we had lined up for the upcoming fundraising event just pulled out."

"Shit." Carter set his glass down. "That is big. Finding a replacement on this short notice will be tough."

"I can recommend some good caterers, but they're out on Long Island," David said with a frown.

"What about the guy we took the couples cooking class with?" Riley suggested.

"While you were still dating me," Will teased. "Don't forget that part!"

Everyone laughed.

"You mean Stuart?" Carter asked. His expression turned thoughtful.

"Yes," Riley said. "He gave you remedial cooking classes when you barely knew how to boil water, remember?"

Carter nodded. "Definitely worth checking. He was a sous chef under Marisol King at her restaurant last I knew, but he still does the classes, and I'm pretty sure I remember him saying King's does some catering."

"The food at King's was excellent the time we went," Riley said.

"That's good enough for me," Malcolm said, "if you're on board, Carter."

"Yeah, see what you can do," Carter said. "We should explore every avenue we've got."

"King's is the name of the restaurant?" Malcolm asked.

"Yes," Carter supplied. "Reade Street in Tribeca."

Malcolm's fingers flew across his phone's screen. "Got it. I'll give them a call. Who should I approach first? The head chef? Or this Stuart guy?"

"Stuart Morgan," Carter supplied. "And, yeah, start with him. Ri and I know him enough you can lean on that angle, I think."

"If you meet him, try not to drool too much," Riley said. "The man is hot. If you like sleeves of tattoos, that is. I don't know if that's your type."

"Does Malcolm have a type?" Jesse joked as he slid into an empty seat, but he winked when Malcolm sent a narrow look his way. "Just teasing, babe. Why haven't you guys introduced me to this hot tattooed chef anyway?"

"Because I don't think he's looking to be anyone's *very personal* chef," Riley joked.

Jesse retorted with something Luka didn't catch, and the group erupted with laughter.

Kyle took a seat next to Luka and handed him a fresh drink. Luka thanked him quietly, then wrapped an arm around him. Contentment hummed through him as he sat listening to the laughter and happy banter fly around the room. His life was in a good place now.

He loved his career and the possible changes on the horizon. He was in a relationship with a man who made him very happy and got along well with his family. Luka had a great group of new friends in addition to the people at Station 47, too.

Luka turned to Kyle. "If life can get better than this, I don't know how," he said quietly.

Kyle's answering smile was blinding in its brilliance. "I feel the same way."

Luka captured Kyle's mouth in a quick, heated kiss that he quickly got lost in. Dimly, he heard teasing from their friends and a wolf whistle that sounded suspiciously like Matías. It all faded away as he got lost in Kyle's heat. Luka knew fire, and it was there, carefully banked under the surface. When they went home that night to the apartment on West 123rd Street—and it was very quickly beginning to feel like home to Luka—he'd stoke the flames until they burned bright and hot.

Want to see more from these authors? Here's a taster for you to enjoy!

Calm
K. Evan Coles and Brigham Vaughn

Excerpt

Riley Porter-Wright whistled as he let himself into his West Village apartment on a warm Thursday night in April. He'd left work with a spring in his step. He had a date with Will Martin—his boyfriend—that night, and a three-day weekend ahead of him.

As senior vice president and head of the e-pub division of his family's publishing house, Riley had been delighted to share the year's first quarter data for his division at the board meeting that afternoon. The numbers had been high enough to impress even Jonathon Porter-Wright, the CEO of the company and Riley's father. He was a demanding man under the best of circumstances and the flicker of pleased surprise that had crossed his face during Riley's presentation had been gratifying.

Although completely estranged from his parents since his coming out and divorce the previous fall, Riley still had to deal with his father at work. He was no longer concerned with living up to his father's expectations, but Riley felt perversely pleased that the better he performed, the more of an ass his father appeared to be. There was a certain measure of satisfaction in proving to his father that being an openly bisexual man hadn't done a thing to affect his career. If anything, finally feeling content with his life had *improved* Riley's performance.

He'd left the office immediately after the board meeting and hurried home. He hastily dressed in a tux, then checked his watch to be sure he wasn't late as he dashed out of the door. Why the Metropolitan opera held premieres on a weeknight, he didn't know, but thankfully, Will didn't have any classes to teach at NYU that evening.

Riley texted Will on the way to his building. He came out to meet Riley after the town car pulled up. The driver held the door while Will slid inside and gave Riley a brief, warm kiss. "Hey, good to see you."

"You, too." They'd both been busy in the past few weeks and hadn't been able to spend much time together. Riley smiled at him, struck again by Will's high cheekbones and classic good looks. Riley hadn't seen him in a tuxedo before, but he wore it well. "How was your day?"

"Mmm, faculty meeting this afternoon and most of my students seem to have spring fever, so I'm glad it's over," Will replied with an easy grin, his blue eyes brightening. "Getting better now, though. Yours?"

"Great, actually, and I'm looking forward to tonight."

They kept the discussion light while the car crossed Manhattan, but Riley's anxiety rose as they neared the Kennedy Center. He straightened his bow tie for the umpteenth time. Will set a hand on his thigh, the touch warm and heavy.

"Are you sure you want to do this tonight?" Will asked softly. "You seem jittery."

"Of course." Riley gave Will a reassuring smile. "I'll admit I'm...anxious about how it will go, but I refuse to let anyone keep me from living my life. I love opera and I want to share that with you."

That night was the gala premier of *Giulio Cesare* and Riley had spent the better part of a week debating if he should invite Will to be his date. Riley had done little socializing with anyone from his past since his abrupt coming-out the previous November and subsequent divorce from his now ex-wife Alex. The possibility of seeing his parents was nerve-racking. Even worse was the thought of seeing his former best friend, Carter, and Carter's wife, Kate. Carter had been shocked by Riley's coming out and Riley's confession that he loved Carter had driven a wedge between them. Riley hadn't had any contact with Kate and, other than a brief and awkward run-in during the holidays at Serendipity when Carter had been out with the kids, Riley hadn't seen Carter, either.

Will knew enough about his past that he wouldn't be caught off-guard if an awkward situation arose, but that didn't make it any easier. The thought of Will and Carter in the same room caused his anxiety to rise.

In the three months Riley and Will had been seeing each other, Will had more than lived up to Riley's first impression of him. Not only gorgeous, he was thoughtful and well-read. Patient, too, while Riley shook off the hang-ups from his past and struggled to figure out the new path he was on. In fact, he'd been more than patient.

Although they'd been intimate in every other way, Riley hadn't reached a point where he was ready to let Will penetrate him or vice versa. Will assured Riley he shouldn't feel rushed and reminded him some men never wanted anal sex, but, still, it bothered Riley.

They'd decided not to see other people, but sometimes Riley held Will at arm's length when he should have been pulling him closer. Taking him to the opera tonight was one way to include Will in another part of his life. He genuinely cared for Will and thought maybe, in time, he could fall for him.

Riley could hardly say he was *over* Carter, but thoughts of Carter had grown less and less frequent. As time passed, the acute pain of losing him had faded to a dull ache. Time certainly did heal wounds, but, unfortunately, it did nothing to lessen the feeling that something important was missing from his life.

"I'm glad you invited me," Will said, bringing him back to the moment.

Riley smiled warmly at him. "I'm glad you were willing to come. I don't think my ex-wife will be there — she really only bothered with the events here to network — but I can't promise anything. Let's just hope we can make it through the night without any drama."

"If there is, we'll either ignore it or cut out early." Will shrugged and slid his hand a little higher. He leaned in to whisper in Riley's ear. "No matter what happens, the night can end in my bed with your dick in my mouth and you coming so hard you see stars."

"Promises, promises," Riley teased, his voice more breathless than he intended. He closed his eyes for a brief moment as Will feathered kisses against his jaw, then glanced at the driver in front of him. He was grateful for the man's discretion and that he hadn't once glanced at them in the rearview mirror. Although finally at ease with showing affection with Will in public, Riley didn't want to make the driver uncomfortable.

Will pulled back when the car slowed to a stop and Riley looked up in surprise, realizing they were already in front of the Lincoln Center. He stepped onto the sidewalk and waited for Will to follow, nodding at a few people mingling outside the entrance whom he recognized. He couldn't resist a peek at the fountain, half-expecting to see Carter standing beside it. But the familiar silhouette was nowhere in sight, so he turned back to Will.

"Still nervous?" Will asked quietly as they walked through the lobby, with its endless red-carpeted floors and the mid-century Sputnik-style chandeliers that had been a gift from the Austrian government.

"A little," Riley replied. "Mostly trying not to think too much about your comment in the car. I'm afraid these pants don't hide much." He grinned wryly wry and Will laughed.

"Sorry."

"As long as you follow through, I have no complaints." Riley's grin faded when they stepped into the cocktail reception. He glanced around anxiously. To his relief, the only familiar faces in sight were distant acquaintances and he and his date were able to get a drink and mingle. People stared, of course—he'd expected that—and there were a few who gave him and Will a suspiciously wide berth, but frankly, it went better than he'd anticipated.

Riley had just begun to relax when he spotted his parents. His good mood immediately plummeted, replaced by an increasing tightness in his chest. "That's my parents ahead," he murmured. "Brace yourself."

The woman standing next to his mother noticed him. "Oh, look, Geneva, it's *Riley*." Her tone held a nasty note, as if she merely wanted to make a jab at his mother. Riley didn't know Helena Finch well but enough to remember she was someone who should be aware of the current situation. Perhaps she disliked his mother, or maybe she just wanted to catch a bit of the gossip. He smiled thinly when he approached them, hoping for Will's sake that the typical Porter-Wright way of handling difficult situations would hold out tonight. Ignoring the situation and acting politely in front of company sounded good to him.

"Will, this is Jonathon and Geneva Porter-Wright." He nodded to his parents. "Jonathon, Geneva, this is William Martin." He didn't see any point in elaborating on Will's part in his life. "Will's a law professor at NYU."

His mother nodded frostily and his father put out his hand. The gesture seemed hesitant and begrudging.

"Nice to meet you both." Will's tone came across as polite, but there was little of his usual warmth.

"Likewise." His father didn't try to hide his disdain.

A rotund gentleman who looked as if he might pop the buttons on his jacket at any moment held out his hand to Will. "Marcus Finch. I went to NYU law myself back in the day."

Riley glanced at his mother, but she wouldn't meet his eye. Outwardly, she appeared cool and composed, but Riley would bet agitation churned under the surface.

Helena gave Riley a knowing smile. "And Will is here *with* you? How *interesting*." Her voice dripped with innuendo.

"We've been seeing each other for a while." Riley kept his tone polite but cool. "On top of being a law professor, Will is a writer. We have a great deal in common."

Will made small talk with Marcus while Riley remained silent.

"It appears they're seating for dinner," Geneva said after a few minutes, her voice brittle. "Come, Jonathon, we should find our seats. Nice seeing you, Marcus and Helena. Riley. Mr. Martin." She disappeared before they could reply and Riley made polite excuses to the Finches. He and Will found their table, grateful to end the encounter. His parents would make sure their paths didn't cross again that evening.

Riley didn't relax until dinner had concluded and Will followed him to his box for the beginning of act one. He took a seat next to Will, relieved that dinner had been calm and uneventful.

"I'm glad you came with me tonight," Riley told him with a smile. Will briefly touched Riley's knee.

"I am, too."

The final knot of worry in Riley's chest dissipated and he got comfortable, eager to see the production. Unfortunately, the good mood only lasted until intermission.

Riley and Will were enjoying the champagne and dessert when a blonde in an ice-blue dress crossed his field of vision. Riley tensed at the sight of Kate Hamilton. He glanced around, trying to be casual as he searched for Carter, but found him nowhere in sight. Riley frowned. The crowd was thick, but Carter stood tall enough to be seen in any group. Perhaps he was in the restroom or had stepped outside to take a call. Kate headed toward him, although she hadn't made eye contact yet.

Riley set down his champagne glass, his hands suddenly nerveless and clumsy when Kate spotted him. Her eyes went wide and she came to an abrupt stop. "Riley."

"How are you, Kate?"

"I'm fine." Her smile seemed automatic, forced. Riley paused, really looking at Kate. She appeared to have lost weight and her normally bright eyes and smile were dimmer than usual. Although beautifully made up as always, something was off.

"Will, I'd like to introduce you to Kate Hamilton, a good friend of mine. Kate, this is Will Martin, law professor, writer and my date this evening."

The corners of Kate's mouth briefly tightened before she smiled at Will and held out her hand. "It's nice to meet you, Will."

"Likewise." Will, in turn, appeared relaxed and comfortable. Clearly, whatever was obvious to Riley wasn't to someone who had never met Kate before.

"Are you as big of a fan of opera as Riley is?" Kate asked.

Will grinned. "I'm not sure anyone's as big of a fan as Riley, but I do enjoy it." Will brushed his fingertips across Riley's back. "I'm glad he wanted to share it with me."

"Oh, I've been known to give Riley a run for his money," Kate said lightly.

A little more warmth appeared in her eyes, but she still seemed off and Riley turned to Will, laying a hand on his arm.

"Would you get me another glass of champagne? I'd like a moment to talk to Kate, if you don't mind."

"Of course," Will reassured him.

"Thank you. I'll try not to be long." Riley squeezed Will's arm.

"Take your time. I'll be over by the bar when you're done." He nodded at Kate. "Very nice to meet you, Kate."

"You, too."

Will left with a smile and Riley felt grateful for his understanding. He turned back to Kate, growing serious. "Are you sure everything's okay? You don't seem..." He wasn't sure how to finish. Kate seemed unhappy, stressed. "Is it that Carter's around and you're worried about us running into each other?"

She shook her head. "No. Carter's…Carter's not here with me."

Kate's fingers trembled as she smoothed them over her pale blue dress and, although it took him a moment, Riley finally registered what was wrong with the picture. A faint stripe of lighter skin adorned the third finger of her left hand instead of the glittering diamond ring Riley had carried in the breast pocket of his tux the morning of Carter's wedding. He wanted to ask her about it but realized there were too many people around. "Can we talk? Privately?"

She nodded, the motion tense and jerky. Riley steered them toward a secluded alcove, reminded of the night he and Carter had discussed finding a woman to join them. It seemed like it had been a lifetime ago, rather than just over a year. "What's going on, Kate? I know you well enough to know you're not okay."

She let out a shaky breath. "Riley, a lot has happened since we last saw each other."

He bit back a disbelieving laugh. "I'm well-aware."

Her expression softened. "I know. You've been dealing with…well, more than any man should. I'm sorry to hear about your parents. They're completely out of line."

"It wasn't unexpected."

"That doesn't mean it doesn't hurt."

"And what about you? Is something going on with you and Carter? I noticed you aren't wearing your ring."

She glanced down at her left hand with a wistful glance. "Carter and I are separated. We're in the process of filing for divorce."

Riley blinked at her. "You *what?* Christ, what happened, Kate?"

The sad smile was trained on him, her tone gentle, but the words barbed. "You came out."

Blanching, Riley tried to make sense of what she'd said. "I don't understand."

Her gaze remained unflinching, but her voice became so quiet he could barely hear it. "Carter told me the truth, Riley. The girls in college, the escort...your feelings for him."

The news hit him like a ton of bricks. "I'm so fucking sorry, Kate." His voice grew raw. "We never meant to—"

"I know. But it hurts deeply to know my husband and a man I considered a good friend betrayed me that way." Kate's voice shook. Riley saw the strain on her face as she struggled to keep it together. She looked away and he gave her a moment to compose herself before she continued. "How long, Riley?"

"What do you mean?"

"How long have you loved him?"

"Since college," he admitted. "Probably since the moment I met him."

She shook her head and dropped her voice to a whisper. "The whole time. Long before Carter and I met."

Riley swallowed, his throat suddenly tight.

"How could you let him marry me?" she continued. "How could you stand beside him at the altar and hand him the ring when you loved him?"

"Because I truly believed it was the right thing to do. I couldn't tell him how I felt—I could hardly even admit it to myself. He loved you—he really did—and I thought if he married you, the feelings I had for him wouldn't matter. Asking Carter to divorce you to be with me last November was out of line. I shouldn't have done it, but I couldn't cope with hiding my feelings for him anymore. I thought he needed to know the truth. I've never loved anyone the way I love Carter, but I understand he doesn't feel the same way about me. I know that now." His voice sounded strained, even to him. "I wish it hadn't taken the end of both our marriages and our friendship to prove that, though."

"Me, too." She stared him straight in the eye. "You know, he's been a wreck since then, Riley. And when he ran into you before New Year's, he became so depressed. He barely slept or ate—he just…wasn't himself. He couldn't live with the lies anymore and it all fell apart after that."

"It kills me to know I hurt both of you." He looked down, unable to meet her gaze. "I've come to terms with the fact I've lost Carter. I'm moving on now. Figuring out my life."

"And Will?"

"We're seeing each other. I care about him, but we're—we're taking things slow. He doesn't know the exact details, but he knows there's someone else I still have feelings for."

"As long as you're being honest with him."

"I am." Riley shoved his hands in his pockets. "I won't live a lie like that again. I never should have done it in the first place."

"I think the worst part is, I didn't know I was," Kate said softly, tears shimmering in her eyes. "I think somewhere deep down, I knew there was something between you and Carter, but I truly didn't want to believe it. I wanted to believe the happy marriage and family were real."

"Carter loves you and the kids. I know he does," he whispered, his voice raw. "There are so many things I wish I'd done differently. Hurting you and the kids…I hope you know how much I regret it. Although I hoped Carter would want to be with me, I don't think I ever believed he'd leave you. I *know* he didn't want to tear apart your marriage or your family."

"We can't always predict the outcome of these things." She laid a hand on his forearm, her smile wistful. "Besides, you coming out may have precipitated this, but it became inevitable. Once Carter stopped being honest with me, this was bound to happen. I am so, so angry at both of you, but I am trying to understand it. I can't imagine what keeping your feelings a secret must have been like. Maybe once the hurt passes, I'll be able to forgive you."

He nodded, his heart aching. "It's more than I deserve."

Before she could reply, the lights dimmed briefly, indicating intermission had ended. She offered him a small, sympathetic smile. "I need to head back to my seat, but, Riley, I'm glad we talked."

"So am I. Take care of yourself, Kate."

"You, too."

He stood staring after Kate until someone gently touched his upper back. He turned to see Will staring at him with a worried frown.

"Are you all right?" Will asked.

Riley shook his head to clear it. "Yeah. We should get back to our seats, though."

Will nodded and fell into step beside him, his gaze worried. Riley couldn't blame him. The conversation with Kate had completely thrown him and he knew he was acting oddly. He needed some time to process it.

Throughout the second half of the performance, Riley felt grateful for Will's silent presence. He hadn't asked Riley to explain, had merely sat beside him and laid a comforting hand on his knee. Riley didn't know what to think of the conversation with Kate. Despite having wanted Carter to end his marriage, the news that Kate and Carter were no longer together felt like an unexpected blow. It would be difficult to come to terms with his partial responsibility for it. He'd never wanted to hurt Carter or Kate and his heart ached for Sadie and Dylan.

He instinctively wanted to reach out to Carter and see if he needed to talk, but Riley wondered if Carter would welcome it or not. Would he blame Riley for the end of his marriage? Was there any hope of repairing their friendship?

PUBLISHING

Sign up for our newsletter and find out about all our romance book releases, eBook sales and promotions, sneak peeks and FREE romance books!

About the Authors

K. Evan Coles is a mother and tech pirate by day and a writer by night. She is a dreamer who, with a little hard work and a lot of good coffee, coaxes words out of her head and onto paper.

K. lives in the northeast United States, where she complains bitterly about the winters, but truly loves the region and its diverse, tenacious and deceptively compassionate people. You'll usually find K. nerding out over books, movies and television with friends and family. She's especially proud to be raising her son as part of a new generation of unabashed geeks.

Brigham Vaughn is starting the adventure of a lifetime as a full-time writer. She devours books at an alarming rate and hasn't let her short arms and long torso stop her from doing yoga. She makes a killer key lime pie, hates green peppers and loves wine tasting tours. A collector of vintage Nancy Drew books and green glassware, she enjoys poking around in antique shops and refinishing thrift store furniture. An avid photographer, she dreams of traveling the world and she can't wait to discover everything else life has to offer her.

K. and Brigham love to hear from readers. You can find their contact information, website details and author profile page at https://www.pride-publishing.com